SWEET MEMORIES

"I've never seen anything so beautiful as you." Hugh turned to Molly with bold eyes, devouring her face. "There is no other beauty when you are near me. You are more beauty than my eyes can behold."

Astonished that mere words could have such effect, Molly felt transfigured from a marble statue to glorious being and faint with joy that he did find her beautiful. She closed her eyes to hold herself strong against the overpowering sensual pleasure of the golden sunlight, the lush awakening of the spring woods and the glory of such words and such a moment. It was already beyond anything she had dared dream.

Hugh, too, was overcome by emotions long held prisoner by the demands of his honor, but unlike Molly, he was not content with meaningful looks and tantalizing words. He pulled his hand from hers, and brought hers to his lips, then let her hand go and raised her face to his.

She could not help but meet his lips and revel in his kiss. The memory of that long ago night returned and now past and present, time and eternity joined and soared so that nothing mattered but that destiny had promised them to one another.

CAPTIVATING ROMANCE FROM ZEBRA

MIDNIGHT DESIRE (1573, $3.50)
by Linda Benjamin
Looking into the handsome gunslinger's blazing blue eyes, innocent Kate felt dizzy. His husky voice, so warm and inviting, sent a river of fire cascading through her flesh. But she knew she'd never willingly give her heart to the arrogant rogue!

PASSION'S GAMBLE (1477, $3.50)
by Linda Benjamin
Jade-eyed Jessica was too shocked to protest when the riverboat cardsharp offered *her* as the stakes in a poker game. Then she met the smouldering glance of his opponent as he stared at her satiny cheeks and the tantalizing fullness of her bodice—and she found herself hoping he would hold the winning hand!

FORBIDDEN FIRES (1295, $3.50)
by Bobbi Smith
When Ellyn Douglas rescued the handsome Union officer from the raging river, she had no choice but to surrender to the sensuous stranger as he pulled her against his hard muscular body. Forgetting they were enemies in a senseless war, they were destined to share a life of unbridled ecstasy and glorious love!

WANTON SPLENDOR (1461, $3.50)
by Bobbi Smith
Kathleen had every intention of keeping her distance from Christopher Fletcher. But in the midst of a devastating hurricane, she crept into his arms. As she felt the heat of his lean body pressed against hers, she wondered breathlessly what it would be like to kiss those cynical lips—to turn that cool arrogance to fiery passion!

Available wherever paperbacks are sold, or order direct from the Publisher. Send cover price plus 50¢ per copy for mailing and handling to Zebra Books, Dept. 1781, 475 Park Avenue South, New York, N.Y. 10016. DO NOT SEND CASH.

Passion's Gold

NANCY KOVATS

ZEBRA BOOKS
KENSINGTON PUBLISHING CORP.

ZEBRA BOOKS

are published by

Kensington Publishing Corp.
475 Park Avenue South
New York, NY 10016

First printing: February 1986

Printed in the United States of America

This book is dedicated to the late William Foster-Harris of the University of Oklahoma's Professional Writing Division of the School of Journalism, who made me believe I could write a novel, and to Jack Bickham of the same school, who showed me how.

Every man has reminiscences which he would not tell to everyone but only to his friends. He has other matters in his mind which he would not reveal even to his friends, but only to himself, and that in secret. But there are other things which a man is afraid to tell even to himself, and every man has a number of such things stored away in his mind. The more decent he is, the greater number of such things in his mind.

Dostoyevsky,
NOTES FROM THE UNDERGROUND

THE MYSTERIOUS BLACK HILLS
or
Shall Pa-ha-sa-pa be Invaded?

As spring approaches, there is but one question on the lips of the thousands of adventurers who have gathered throughout the winter in Nebraska and surrounding territories: Should we try for the Black Hills?

Ever since the first hardy trappers explored this mysterious island of pine-clad mountains in the midst of our great plains territory, rumors that gold sparkles in its clear mountain streams have filtered back to civilization. But a full-scale invasion and exploration of this region, so enticingly close, has been prevented by the cession of the Black Hills to the Sioux as part of the Laramie Treaty of 1868, and it has been government policy to remove by force any white man found trespassing. Yet this same government, two years ago, sent General George Armstrong Custer and over a thousand men of the Seventh Cavalry on a scientific expedition to map the region with the stated purpose of establishing a military outpost there.

The news that the Custer expedition found gold on French Creek electrified the nation and brought suspicion to many who questioned the government's true purpose in sending such an expedition into the Hills.

These suspicions seemed confirmed by the outfitting of a second expedition a year ago.

Ordinary citizens have not fared so well. Last spring a party from Sioux Falls was tracked down by the military and forcibly removed from the Hills, but not before they confirmed the presence of gold on French Creek.

Last summer General Crook continued to uphold official government policy when he escorted some 600 miners from the area. It is reported, however, that many wily miners eluded the military and wintered in the Hills, no doubt staking their claims in the choicest spots.

It should be pointed out that it has by no means been proved that a bonanza on our doorstep does exist. The geologist with Custer's expedition claims he saw no gold, though Custer himself supports the claim of his men that they did pan gold from the creek. Custer is also reported to have said the region is almost unsurpassed in its pristine beauty.

And so to those waiting for the snow to clear the prairies so they might risk their scalps seeking fortunes in the Black Hills, we say there are three questions to be answered: First, does gold exist in paying quantities? Second, will the government relent and offer its protection, or will the U.S. Military continue to remove trespassers by force? And third, but perhaps most important, is it right for the white man to invade Sioux lands?

To the last question, we point out the Sioux hold the Black Hills in great regard. They call it Pa-ha-sa-pa, which means "Hills That are Black," and consider these hills their sacred hunting ground. Others argue that since the red man neither plants nor tills these lands, it is the white man's destiny to tame this new territory.

One thing is certain — with the whole country still in the grip of a depression and many out of work, a beckoning bonanza of gold nuggets provides an almost irresistible lure. Those of the pioneer persuasion say there is no more fitting endeavor in this year of our nation's Centennial than for the hearty sons and daughters of Liberty to extend civilization by exploring and settling the Black Hills.

Whatever the right or wrong of the matter, this writer predicts the summer of 1876 will see the question of the Black Hills resolved at last.

Hugh Everett's first and last editorial for
THE CARPENTER SENTINEL,
Nebraska Territory's Leading Bi-Weekly Newspaper
April 13, 1876

Chapter One

Spring was near and promise should have been in the air. Instead, a cold wind swept soil from prairie and fields and shifted it to the crusted drifts of dirty snow banked along the road down which Jake Lewis drove his mules while the boy, Edwin, nestled close to him on the wagon seat. The road went west and led to the railroad which could take Jake to Sidney, Nebraska, the gateway to the Black Hills, but although half of Iowa's discouraged homesteaders in that spring of 1876 were dreaming of joining what was to be the last great American gold rush, it never occurred to Jake Lewis to do so.

He was not a man who dreamed of escape. He knew his homestead was a sorry place, but he figured if he kept at it, his luck was bound to change. He'd been lucky once and gotten Molly to wed when she was the prettiest girl in the county and he only her father's hired man. He'd never regretted paying the price on that luck, and he figured that sooner or later he'd be lucky again. So he kept his eyes on the road and his goal in mind. He was depositing Edwin at the Tuttle homestead and fetching Lizzie Tuttle to sit with Molly through her ordeal. He was a man with responsibilities.

He was also a man who lacked imagination and seldom wasted his energy in idle thought, but after arriving at the Tuttle homestead he had to wait for Lizzie to settle Edwin with her oldest daughter and gather her things, so he lit a pipe and found a moment to envy Sam Tuttle. Tuttle had a large and healthy family, a prospering homestead, and even a frame house with four glass windows — just the sort of house he'd promised Molly when he brought her West.

Tuttle came out with his wife and attempted to strike up a conversation while Lizzie settled herself on the wagon seat. Jake puffed his pipe and scratched his beard and nodded often enough to be polite. He had never found conversation easy with the Sam Tuttles of the world, and he didn't like finding himself, once again, in the position of being beholden to his neighbor. Just once, he'd like Tuttle to owe *him* a favor.

He finally judged he'd endured enough talk and made to turn his mules. Tuttle, still talking, took hold of the lead mule's bridle and turned the team for him. The gesture annoyed Jake. If there was one thing he understood, it was mules.

"Make sure it's a boy!" Tuttle fired a parting shot at him.

"Don't mind Sam," Lizzie said. "I guess it's in a man's nature to want sons, but I expect you and Molly would be satisfied with a girl this time."

Jake just nodded, and she went on filling in both sides of the conversation. "Just so it's healthy. I know how you feel. That was real sad last time, but those things can't be helped. You didn't need to go to the

12

expense of having Dr. Morgan. I've birthed ten of my own and Lord knows how many for other people. But I expect after last time you'd feel better having a doctor. Though I don't know what one could do that I couldn't with a baby that never lived like that." She patted his arm and talked on while Jake tried to think of a decent way to shut her up.

"How's Molly been feeling lately?"

Jake frowned, trying to picture Molly. Pretty, he saw her, but he couldn't say that. Big. Couldn't say that. He finally settled on *tired.*

"Land sakes, I imagine she's tired. That sod house would wear anybody out. You can't keep one clean."

"Thought I'd have her out of it before now," Jake grunted and clipped the mules with his reins to hurry them. "Can't seem to get the cash ahead."

"I know. I know. It's terrible, ain't it? Between the drought and the grasshoppers, why nobody's had a good year since you two moved out here."

Something in the way she said it made Jake know she was thinking, *Still, you've had worse luck than anybody. Some people just never get ahead.*

"And now with the whole country in a depression," she rattled on, "it almost makes a body wish the war was still on. I just don't know where it's going to end. Something's got to get this country moving again. Why, I think a man like you, a man with nothing to lose, would want to join the gold rush, head for the Black Hills!"

Jake felt like turning the wagon around and taking Lizzie home. What kind of lout did she think him? He might not be a great provider like Sam Tuttle, but he didn't abandon his family to follow crazy dreams. He

13

prided himself on having his feet solidly rooted in the earth. He didn't answer, and finally Lizzie grew tired of butting against his taciturnity, and they finished the trip in silence.

Lizzie Tuttle was right. The Lewis homestead had the look of a place haunted by failure, a failure made worse by the evidence someone had tried. There were curtains hung at a window which admitted no more than a memory of light, a foundation laid for a frame house never more than a promise, and the skeleton of a cottonwood tree which had survived long enough to make its loss loom larger. The dead tree and a broken fence stood guard over a patch of ground that looked to be the beginning of a cemetery, but even this seemed unfinished. And the wind endlessly shifted the soil against the sod house.

The doctor met them in the yard. Jake didn't have to see his face to know something was wrong. Doctors don't meet you outside in their shirt sleeves in a March cold snap with good news. Dr. Morgan was a large, mustached man who parted his dark hair straight down the middle. He had a bad eye and wore a little eyeglass on a ribbon pinned to his vest. When he was being professional, he put the glass to his eye, holding it in place with a lopsided squint. He wore it now.

Skirting the mules, Dr. Morgan came around to Jake's side of the wagon. His face was grave and careful, as composed as it could be and still keep the monocle in place. "It's over, Mr. Lewis. Your wife is fine, but the baby was born dead."

"Again?" Jake heard Lizzie gasp the word and wanted to put his hand over her mouth. "Again?" she exclaimed. "Just like last time! Isn't it awful! I delivered the poor little girl for her, Doctor, and I knowed there wasn't nothing I could do, and now here it is, the same thing again. It's like a curse."

Jake sat silent on the wagon seat. He closed his eyes for a moment, heard the doctor moving around the back of the wagon saying, "Come on, Mrs. Tuttle. Let me help you down. I know Mrs. Lewis will be glad to have you here. Come in and sit with her, and I'll get my coat and help Mr. Lewis with the mules."

So there's more, Jake thought. *He's got more to tell me.* Doctors don't help you with the mules unless they want to talk to you away from the women. He had only a moment to hold his grief to himself before the doctor was beside him in the wagon, putting on his coat as he talked. "Let's get the mules out of the wind and I'll talk to you."

Outside the lean-to, the monocle disappeared, and the doctor worked with him unhitching the mules from the wagon, but leaving them in harness so Jake could drive him back to town later. The doctor followed Jake's lead in slipping the bridle from his mule so as to replace it with a feed bag. Jake thought, *He's a good man if he can handle women and understand mules too.*

"I did everything I could, but the baby was already dead." The doctor put more grain in his feed bag than Jake would have allowed. "It was a boy this time." He said the last hurriedly as if he wanted to get the information out while they had the mules between them.

Jake put his head down against the warmth of the mule's neck. For a while the only sound was that of the animals' crunching their grain. It would have been a boy this time. His son.

15

"I know how you feel, Mr. Lewis. It's unfortunate, but we don't know why these things happen. Some would say it's the sins of the fathers, but I'm inclined to take a more scientific view. Something in the blood, perhaps." He'd put the monocle back in place, and, as he looked at Jake, one eye was big and accusing.

The doctor went on discussing his theories, but Jake had caught his meaning when he said *sins of the fathers*. He thinks it's something I've done, Jake thought. He tried to think of something terrible he'd done. Getting drunk was all he could think of, but it didn't seem that should count. A man was entitled once in a while when his luck ran sour. He wondered if it had to be sins of the *fathers*. He figured it did. Women's sins wouldn't count for much. Molly had sinned once, but that had been long ago and she had paid the price. Molly was good, so it had to be his fault, but he couldn't reason it out. He'd put it out of his mind.

"At least you have a fine boy there in Arnold," the doctor said, his monocle gone now.

"Edwin."

"Yes, of course, Edwin. How old is he now?"

Jake had to stop and think. "Almost six."

"A fine boy."

Jake accepted the compliment. He had so long thought of Edwin as his son that only in the loss of the male child did he remember. He did not dwell on it. At least he had one boy to help around the place.

"And your wife. A fine woman, your wife."

Jake thought he caught something in the doctor's tone. Where was all this talk leading? "You sure Molly's all right?"

The doctor walked around the mules, but instead of

heading for the house, he stayed in the shelter of the lean-to. "So far as I can tell. Of course we'll keep her in bed. Mrs. Tuttle can stay a few days?"

Jake sighed and nodded, still feeling there was more to come.

"There is one thing," the doctor busied himself with wiping his monocle with a none-too-clean linen handkerchief while he spoke.

"What's that?" Jake felt himself go hard inside.

"Well," the doctor hesitated. "This isn't easy to say to a man, but if she was my wife . . . well . . ."

Jake had never seen an educated man look so uncomfortable.

"I wouldn't try again," the doctor finally said.

"Try again?"

"Try to have children. What I mean is you shouldn't *try* to have any more children. For a while anyway." He put the monocle in place.

"No more children?"

"Yes," the big eye peered at him. "I think you should be content with the boy, Arnold — er — Edwin, for now. What I'm saying is, you shouldn't *try* any more."

"You mean we can't—"

"That is correct." Morgan's face was red. "You will just have to control yourself. That's what I'd do if it were my wife. I've already explained the situation to Mrs. Lewis. She seemed to think you'd be reasonable. You will, won't you?" The big eye in the monocle stared.

"What?"

"Be reasonable."

"Oh . . . yes . . . sure," Jake nodded.

He had always been a reasonable man.

17

Lizzie Tuttle had entered the sod house with a certain eagerness, for she felt that by sharing this latest tragedy with Molly Lewis she might have another opportunity to penetrate the mystery of the woman and her husband. They did not seem a couple made to each other, and Lizzie had speculated on how they came to be wed. She had pried openly, but, although Molly accepted her friendship, she did not confide her innermost thoughts in the usual way of women who are too much alone. There was something secret and sad about Molly. That she came from a good family was revealed by her speech and manners and the remnants of her china proudly displayed on a rough plank shelf. The dirt floor of her sod house was well swept and the walls were covered with layers of newspaper and whitewash and pictures — wifely attempts to make pretty with what she had. Her only son was kept so neat and had so diligently been taught his manners, his letters, and his prayers, that sometimes Edwin seemed more like a young prince than the son of a bearded old farmer like Jake Lewis.

Lizzie had often thought that Molly herself was more like a queen than a homesteader's wife. She had been beautiful and young when Jake first brought her to Iowa some six years before, and somehow, despite the plagues of grasshoppers and drought and the general misery of the times and climate, she had managed to retain her looks — not just her prettiness, her womanly and graceful figure, her cornsilk hair and cool blue eyes and well-shaped mouth, but her vitality, her quick laugh and blush and way of reaching out to ife. Now Lizzie wondered if Molly could survive this atest tragedy with her spirit intact.

Lizzie strode through the parlor-kitchen and pulled aside the curtain that separated it from the bedroom. Molly lay on the bed, covered by a faded quilt. Lizzie, seeing the way her arms still protectively cradled her belly, burst into tears.

When Molly saw her friend crying, her own tears began, and that was good, for since it had happened, she had been beyond tears. Lizzie's hug released more tears. *Mother*, Molly thought. *I want my mother*. Lizzie hugged harder as if she understood. And then Molly's face was being washed and her hair patted back, and Lizzie was talking about making soup while Molly lay back, comforted by the touch of the other woman's hands and the way she brought something of home to the dark little house.

Then she heard the outside door opening and closing and thought, *Jake's home. The doctor will have told him by now*. There were footsteps, and the doctor pulled aside the curtain. "Feeling better?" he asked. His monocle gleaming in the lamplight. Without waiting for her answer, he added brightly, "Here's your husband."

Jake stood in the doorway, silent and awkward, his hat in his hands. He was only thirty-six, fifteen years older than she, but he had looked middle aged ever since she had known him. He had never been handsome, and he had been clean shaved only on their wedding day, but sometimes there was a look of gentleness about his eyes that moved her, and today his whole face was so filled with suffering that she could hardly bear her guilt. She had tried so hard to love

19

him, and it always ended in failure. She closed her eyes and tried to control herself, but she could feel tears trickling down her temples.

"You got pain, Molly?" Jake stepped to the bed.

She shook her head.

"Sure?"

She nodded.

He patted her hand silently for a long time. Then he asked, "Will you be wanting some wood?"

She opened her eyes, trying to fathom his meaning. "Wood?"

"For a box." Jake shifted his weight awkwardly. "I thought I could get it when I take the doctor back to town."

"Box?" Then she understood. She said yes to stop him from saying the word, *coffin*. Was that all he could think to say, to talk about a coffin? Couldn't he hold her or say something to ease her pain?

"I'll get something real nice, Molly. I'll make it strong."

He's trying, she thought. There were some that wouldn't think of making a coffin for a baby that never lived. It was the only gift he'd ever give his son. Why should she want more from him? She forced herself to whisper her thanks and he kissed her on the forehead, gently, awkwardly, his beard scratching. "I'll get the wood when I take the doctor home. Lizzie will stay with you." She nodded but he didn't leave. "The doctor wants to examine you again," he finished lamely.

She must have winced at the word *examine*, for he added, "We got to get you well. That's all that's important now. Don't worry. I'm not going to . . . bother you anymore."

His words stuck in her mind throughout the doctor's brief and silent examination of her body. *I'm not going to bother you anymore.* When the men were gone, Molly lay listening to Lizzie puttering in the kitchen and was glad to be alone. So the doctor had told Jake. She could no longer try to be a wife to him. She had not minded doing her duty to Jake. She had tried to find joy in giving to him and, having only once tasted of passion, did not know there could be joy in taking. She had no expectations from Jake's embrace other than it should give him release and give her children to love. Now there would be not even this to give to Jake, and no baby to hold to her breast.

She touched her breasts. It seemed they were already fuller, and knowing she must have Lizzie bind them against the milk that would come unbidden and be wasted, she thought she could not endure the pain. She wished for Edwin, needing to hold him. But she knew her son was already growing up and taking on Jake's ways. She saw her future, even more lonely than her past, and pictured herself shut away in the sod house, safe from the heat of the summer and the cold of the winter, but always alone in the dark little house and not even a baby to hold life to her, and she was afraid.

She thought the fear must be another punishment. A punishment for once again thinking of Hugh. For even in labor with Jake's son, she had remembered the other time. Needing so desperately to escape the pain, she let her mind return to home and family, and that led to remembering a walk in a spring meadow. And after all the years passed since *he* had gone away and she had married Jake, she had escaped to the world that was sweet and secret and beautiful in the memory of *him*. Then as the next pain mounted her, she had tried to push away the memory, and when it would not go but only turned dark, she was afraid that in the anguish of childbirth she might forget and call his name.

Hugh.

She had pushed the memory away then, terrified for the child within her, the child that like the last one, had grown still in her womb. She had told herself it could not happen again, that this child would live, and she had promised God that if he would deliver her of a live and healthy child for Jake, she would never think again of Hugh. She would ask for no more, dream no more, but be content.

But the baby had been born dead, and she could not fathom what that meant. Why had she born a healthy son to another man while the babies of her lawful husband stilled within her?

She wanted so badly to be a good wife to Jake, for though plagued by bad luck and not given to saying and doing the tender things a woman foolishly yearns for, he was a good man. He had saved her from disgrace, treated Edwin as his own, and been as good as a father to her. He had never thrown it up to her either, never even spoken of it, though sometimes she almost wished he would, for when so much welled up inside her that needed sharing, Jake's silence was oppressive.

She had tried to love him, and in a way she did, but she had never succeeded in quelling the longing in her heart, the feeling that something was missing and needed to be searched for. She had never been able to forget her first love and moments made intimate not just by touch but by a sharing of the spirit she could not hope for with Jake.

She thought the remembering was wrong and that it was for cherishing that memory that she was punished, not for the act itself. That had been sweet and good, and she too young to realize the consequences of giving herself to a boy who knew no more than she the price of love. It was the *remembering* that must be wrong, the way she took out the memory and held it to her as if it were a real thing like a locket concealing a faded tintype of the beloved and kept in a secret place to be taken out for the pleasure and pain of it. It was her refusal to let go of the memory that she thought kept her from being a truer wife to Jake. She believed that if she could will it she would stop thinking of Hugh forever, except, of course, in those moments when Edwin smiled a certain way, and she knew it was his father's look about him.

Molly did not know it was the memory of love that sustained her through the cold and lonely winters on the homestead, and it was the never-quite-lost hope of recapturing it that enabled her to feel the promise of spring. She did not know, and would not have admitted it if she had, that life with a man like Jake can never be more than comfort and duty, can never be a love that sparkles and gleams even when lost, and that once having known this kind of love, a woman can never be satisfied with less.

She thought she would be happier without her longings and be a better wife. And she might have been. There are women who do not remember, or who have nothing to remember, and if they marry men who are good and steady, all is well. If they do not know the heights of passion, neither do they know the depths. But Molly Lewis was a woman with that unnameable yearning for something more. She belonged with a man who had a restless need of his own to strive and fight and build and love in a way that went beyond the ordinary.

But she was married to Jake and she didn't know, nor was ready to know, any of this. She thought only of going home, returning to Pennsylvania and being her father's daughter again. She looked at her work-worn hands on her faded bride's quilt and remembered the reason she had left and why she could not go home. Many a day she had kept herself going with the dream the homestead would flourish and they would go home with new clothes and a family so large and beautiful no one would remember why she had married Jake Lewis. But now she could dream that dream no more. She was barely past twenty, but it seemed her life was over. Her pain spilled over into more tears.

Lizzie, bustling in with steaming cups of tea in the china teacups, saw her tears and commanded her not to start up again. "We had ourselves a good cry and that's enough for now."

Molly accepted a cup of tea and held it carefully while she regained control. She did not want to break another cup, one of her last links with home.

"He don't have much to say, does he, that husband of yours?" Lizzie pulled the rocking chair close to the bed to drink her tea.

"No. But he's a good man."

"Oh, I know that," Lizzie rocked and sighed. "Anyone could see how hard he took it, but he sure don't have much to say."

"No, he's quiet." Realizing Lizzie had seen his awkwardness in comforting her, Molly felt protective of Jake.

"I guess men are all like that." Lizzie sighed. "Can't hardly get a word out of my Sam unless it's about crops and such. Nothing tender, and he's a real talker compared to Jake. I guess it's just not in a man's nature to want to talk with women."

"I knew one once who was different. He made me want to share all my secrets, and he told me his and—"

"And?"

Molly blushed and studied her teacup, knowing she had said too much. "Oh, nothing. He was just a schoolboy I once knew. It was a long time ago. I expect they all change, get to worrying about life and all and get too busy to . . . you know."

"I know. I know. It's a man's way, but you'd think once in a while, like with your loss and all, Jake could say something more, show he cares."

"He shows by doing. He works so hard here. He really tries."

"I expect he'll feel better driving into town and doing his chores. He'll take real good care of you now. 'Course he'll probably stop off at the saloon."

So Lizzie knew. "You can't blame him, can you? I mean a man has to have some release, losing—losing—his son."

"I know. Don't blame him a bit. Even Sam would today. It's just that you'd think he'd want to talk about it. Say something to you or share it with his neighbors. But not Jake. He won't ever say how he feels. Won't let it out. If he sees men he knows today, he'll talk about something else, politics or crops or going to the Black Hills. But he'd never confide in anyone. He'll leave it to Sam and me to spread the word about your loss. Why I tried to talk to him on the way over. Asked him about going to the Black Hills, but he shut me off. Wouldn't even answer me."

"You and Jake talked about going to the Black Hills?"

"I talked. Not him. No imagination, that man. You'd think he'd want to make a try for it. They say there's a fortune in gold in there for those that have the gumption to face the Sioux."

"You think Jake should go?"

"I didn't say that. Just said I'd think a man like Jake would *want* to go. It's not like he's got anything to lose, like Sam. Sam said he'd go, but he's got to get crops in this spring."

"So does Jake."

"Of course."

Then Molly said what she knew Lizzie was thinking. "It doesn't do much good to get crops in if it doesn't rain or if the grasshoppers come. Lizzie, if our luck doesn't change, if it hits us worse than anyone else again this year, I don't think I can go on."

"Now don't you worry. Jake'll make a go of this place yet," Lizzie said without much conviction in her voice. "The last few years have been bad for everyone."

"But not like it was for Jake and me," Molly picked at the edge of the quilt she'd made for her hope chest. "We just get further and further behind. Jake tries so hard and everything he does goes sour." She stared at the curtain which hid from her sight the room where the doctor had laid the little bundle containing the

26

baby until Jake could tend to the burying. She felt the tears coming again. This failure was hers, but it made it no less bitter.

"Don't talk that way, Molly. It's going to get better. Jake's going to make a fine farm here."

A fine farm, Molly thought and remembered that morning. Just before she started labor she had been restless and had made Jake walk with her. They stopped to examine the cottonwood tree and saw that despite all the water they'd hauled for it, the tree had finally winter-killed. It might come back from the roots, but there would be no shade again that summer. The tree was to shelter the grave of the child she had lost two years before. Jake had run a few strands of wire to protect the grave and the tree from livestock, but the fence was sagging. He'd marked the grave with a homemade wooden cross. You don't put up head-stones for babies that never lived, but the grave looked like something made by children to bury a dead bird. Jake must have seen it through her eyes because he said, "I thought I'd make a real fence this summer. We could plant flowers again."

"They won't grow," she said, already afraid for the new baby and tense from keeping that fear from Jake. She saw her remark had hurt him, but her fear spilled into anger. "We can't even have a real graveyard on the place."

"Christ, Molly, what can I do?"

"I'm sorry. I shouldn't have said it." But she had looked at the homestead, the flat, endless loneliness of it all, and had closed her eyes and thought, this isn't home and never will be. *Home is white houses and streets lined with trees and folks visiting back and forth and sitting on their porches after supper*. She wanted to do something desperate, to send Jake out into the gold fields, to risk his life even, anything to get them beyond that homestead, but it was at that moment she felt the first pain of labor and realized she could not care for a new baby and the homestead without Jake. Now, realizing there would be no baby, but only another pitiful little marker in the cemetery to symbolize their failure, she felt again a desperate urge to find a way out. She sensed that if she did not act now, she would simply dry up and turn inward within the walls of the sod house, never again touched by anything.

"We've got to get out, Lizzie. I can't take the place any longer. I'll go crazy. We've got to get out of here someway. I want to go home."

"Hush, girl," Lizzie pushed her down in the bed and tried to cover her up. "You're talking crazy. This is your home now, and you got to accept it."

"I can't. I just can't. I'll die."

"Nonsense. You won't die. No woman dies of it. You'll just grow up. Get practical and forget all the fairy tales and dreams."

"It's the same thing. I'll go crazy if I stay here, Lizzie. I've got to get home."

"I wish you *could* go back to your people for a visit. That would be what you need now after your loss. But Jake can't afford to send you. What about your family? They're comfortable, ain't they? Why not write and ask them for the train fare?"

"I'd never do that. That would be admitting—no, I can never go home unless . . . unless it's all right with Jake and me. We have to have the money to go on our own. So they see . . . so they see I've . . . made a go of things."

"There ain't no way Jake Lewis is going to come up with that kind of money. No way anybody could come up with that kind of money short of striking it rich in the gold fields."

"Then you think he should go! You think I really should send Jake to the Black Hills?"

"My God, woman, where did you get such a notion? Not cause I brought it up to him? I was only trying to find something he'd talk about. Nobody but a fool would try for the gold fields."

"Why not? You said that was the only way to make enough money. Everybody says there's piles of gold just waiting to be picked up."

"If the Sioux don't get you first. And if you've got rail fare to Sidney and cash to buy horses to get you to the Hills and supplies. Just suppose for a minute Jake was brave enough or fool enough to face the Sioux. How's he going to get the cash to get there, and how are you going to get a crop in here alone?"

"We could sell the homestead."

"Sell the homestead? The only security you have in this world?" Lizzie saw Molly's reaction to that and began to talk faster. "And what would you do while he was gone? Where would you live? And how would you feel all alone, not knowing what was happening and Jake off for months and maybe never coming back, and you not knowing if the Sioux got him or what?"

Molly was silent, and Lizzie gave a grunt of satisfaction and began to gather up the tea things. She had her back to her friend and was about to leave when Molly spoke again, her voice calm and controlled.

"I could go with him. Now that there's no baby, I

could go with him. Edwin and I."

Lizzie set down the tea things with a crash and, turning back to the bed, felt of Molly's forehead. "You must be getting the fever. That's crazy talk. The whole country is crawling with Indians. It's bad enough a bunch of fool men think they can go in there, but to take a woman and boy! Why, the only women going to a place like that would be camp followers! It's not the place for a woman like you."

"But I've heard women are going in, and, even if they're not, even if I were the first—"

"Molly, not even Jake Lewis would be fool enough to take you!"

The remark momentarily stunned Molly. She slumped back against the pillows and Lizzie, thinking she had done her duty, bustled off. But Molly was not defeated; she was angry. She was tired of people telling her Jake was foolish, that he didn't have luck or gumption. He was a brave and good man, and if it was right for them to go to the Black Hills, then he would find a way to take her and he would protect her.

But *was* it right? She tried to reason it out, but she was tired and confused. Her vision began to blur and as the kerosene lamp flickered, the sod walls of the house seemed to be closing in on her. She willed herself to think. She could not endure it here. There had to be a way out.

She had heard the Black Hills were beautiful. In the summer they would be cool and green, like the hills of home. It would be good for Jake to have an adventure. All men need adventure. It would make up to him for the fact she could no longer be his wife. Maybe his luck would change. If she could only get him to go, it would give him new hope.

She made up her mind. She would ask him in the morning. She would make him see the right of it.

She truly believed she was doing it for Jake and not to still the longing in her own heart.

Chapter Two

The whole country was talking of the Black Hills that spring, but the possibility of following the gold rush, should it develop in earnest, aroused particular interest among the men who plied their trade in the gaming rooms of the great riverboats of the Mississippi. On the river the talk was relaxed, idle, speculative. There was none of the tense, desperate search for opportunity and adventure that marked the yearnings of the men of the western territories. Among the frock-coated men who worked the river there was no need to prove one's manhood by conquering new territory, fighting the red men, or staking a claim. There was no need to be among the first. It was better, in fact, to watch and wait, to let others risk their scalps with the Sioux, bend their backs hacking out the wagon trails, and break their heart proving the worth of the gold fields.

There was time in that spring of 1876 for a frock-coated gentleman to stroll idly along the streets of a Mississippi port town. There was time to pick and choose from the enticements offered such gentlemen by the shops and restaurants and bawdy houses which serviced the river traffic.

Such a frock-coated gentleman could play gamblers' games with himself. He could glance idly into a shop window, and if he saw something he liked, he could take it or leave it, or set up a challenge and make a game of it—and call it *destiny*.

Sally O'Brien's Ready to Wear and Fine Dressmaking did not cater to the river-boat trade. The shop sat along a side street and from the outside was impressive in no way except for the fact that due to Mrs. O'Brien's persistent nagging the window was unusually clean and a fine assortment of men's handkerchiefs was there displayed.

A man who stopped to admire the handkerchiefs and happened to glance into the shop itself on a particular day in that spring of 1876 would have seen two women unpacking a shipping crate. One was old and fat and gray. The other was startlingly beautiful even in the brown serge skirt and high-necked white shirt of a shop girl. Her profile was fine, not with the classic lines of a cameo, but with the upturned nose and saucy pouting lips of a dance-hall girl. Her hair was raven black and escaped from its knot in enticing tendrils. One could not tell about her eyes from the shop window, but her body, as she bent over the shipping crate, was graceful and petite, yet excitingly round.

Such a man could have admired and walked on. He could have stored up the image and taken his need to a bawdyhouse. Or he could have stood a moment admiring the way his own reflection in the window was enhanced by the image of the woman within.

He could have taken out a coin, flipped it and

caught it on his sleeve, making a wager with himself. And then he could have strolled across the street to watch and wait.

"Oh, Ma, isn't this lovely?" Emma O'Brien exclaimed as she unpacked the bolt of green velvet. "Isn't this the loveliest piece of goods you ever saw?" she unfastened the bolt and pulled out a length of the fabric to touch to her cheek. "It's so soft and rich-feeling and look—" she held the fabric so the light caught its sheen, "the color! It's the color of emeralds."

"And how would you be knowing the color of emeralds?" As she reproved her daughter, Sally O'Brien's speech lilted in the Old Country way, though it was her husband who had been Irish.

"I saw some in the shop down the street. Emerald earbobs. They were the most beautiful things I ever saw. They would match my eyes."

"Emma! I've told you a hundred times not to be loitering around shop windows. A girl can get in trouble that way." Her mother dipped into the box Emma had been unpacking and began to lift out the heavy bolts of fabric. "They were probably paste anyway."

"Yes, Mama, I'm sorry." Emma sighed and lowered her sooty lashes, trying to look demure and succeeding, for she was a natural actress. Longingly she fingered the green velvet until she could no longer resist asking, "Ma, couldn't I have a piece of this? I could make me the most elegant gown. Please, Ma? I won't ever ask for anything else."

"Why, I never heard of such a thing! Did you look at the price of that stuff? That's the most expensive goods

34

we've ever had. Imported and all. I only hope we can get our price for it with times so hard."

"Maybe if we don't sell it, if there's a piece left over . . . maybe it will get a little faded and—"

"And nothing. Even if you needed a new dress, which you don't—your blue serge is still plenty good if you turn the cuffs—velvet is not for shop girls. You know that."

"But, Ma, it's so lovely. Couldn't I just this once—"

"I don't want to hear another word about it. You're a hard selfish girl to be thinking of taking money from my own pocket. Money I need to feed your little brother and sisters. Besides, I told you. Velvet is not for the likes of us." Sally O'Brien reached out and let her stubby fingers touch the material for just a moment. "This will go to some fine lady, or to some whore. Though whores are partial to red, and I don't cater to such anyway. Now forget it, girl, and give me a hand with this unpacking."

Emma sighed, and rolling up the bolt of green velvet, she put it on the shelf, a little apart from the rest. It was no use arguing. And she certainly didn't want to get her mother off on the subject of whores again. Sally O'Brien was daft on the subject, talking as if it were the camp followers and not the urge to help save the union of his adopted country that had sent Cornelius O'Brien off to war a decade before. He had left her with five children, Emma, the oldest, barely nine and the only one who could help in the store. He had never been heard from again. Sally O'Brien had run the little dry-goods store herself after that, setting up her sewing machine in the back and featuring fine dressmaking as well as high quality ready-to-wear as it became available after the war. At the same time, she had left Emma to manage her large brood of children in the rooms above the store, running upstairs every few minutes to check on things. But now the younger children were in school and Sally was feeling her age, so she had turned most of the shop work over to Emma, having taught her to sew a perfect seam by pinching her every time she daydreamed and stitched crookedly. Emma hated the shop. It was just far enough off the riverfront to have little custom with the river boat passengers. Their customers were all women and all dull. But at least by working in the shop Emma could make beautiful clothes and dream they were hers, for she loved fashion and read the pages of *Godey's Lady's Book* like some girls read the Bible. Her fantasies of a world beyond the shop were fed by *Godey's*, the beckoning whistles of the riverboats, and her memories of the theatre. Though she'd never dream of anything so wicked as being an actress, drama was central to her life. That was thanks to the lovable rogue of a father who had secretly taken Emma to the vaudeville shows for he saw no reason why his favorite daughter should not have a taste of excitement, despite the fact his wife regarded theatres as no better than bawdy houses. Sally O'Brien was not a mean woman; she was a realist who had learned that dreams and dreamers get a girl in trouble. She would have cringed to know Emma's fantasy of being a beguiling creature somehow *on stage* winning the attention of a most desirable man. She knew she had been harsh about the velvet. It would have matched her daughter's eyes. Still, she had to be practical.

"Don't be pouting, girl. If we end up with a piece of

that gabardine left, I'll let you make up a new collar and cuffs for the serge. I let you make that waist there last spring, didn't I?" She studied the white top Emma wore with her brown skirt. "Now that's suitable for a shop girl and right pretty the way you did it with the eyelet edging. We don't want you to look too poor to catch a husband."

"If you want me to find a husband, why don't you let me have something really pretty to wear?"

"Because you tend to be a bit flashy-looking as it is with all that black hair and green eyes. You got your father's good looks, curse that it was, and if I don't watch you, you'll attract some man who's no good. A nice, steady businessman, that's what you need. Not someone who's here today and gone tomorrow."

"Father was a nice, steady businessman, wasn't he?" Emma bit her lip as soon as she said it. She should have known better than to bring him up. She remembered her father as a handsome, laughing man whose black hair fell over his forehead and green eyes danced. She hated to hear her mother speak bitterly of him.

"That was different. He had the grand and glorious cause to run off to, though if you ask me, he only joined to get away from the responsibility of a family, for the war was no cause for an Irishman, and with half Missouri on the other side, he could as easy have stayed home. But some men got to have their adventures. Got to go and find trouble as if enough doesn't come to your door."

"Don't women?"

"What?"

"Need adventure. Don't women need to have excite-

37

ment and to dream and . . . to wonder?"

"Wonder! Oh, yes, think that way, girl, and you'll wonder. You'll find one that will leave you wondering night after night 'till he's finally gone for good. You listen to me, Emma. Life is hard enough. Don't look for trouble. And don't think about love and such foolishness. It's all a trap. No, you go to meeting and dress proper in your dark serge and learn to keep your mouth shut, and we'll find you a man who will make you a respectable living and never, ever leave you wondering. That's what you need, girl. Not green velvet."

Emma nodded seriously as if she believed it all and she bided her time, and the minute her mother left the shop for the afternoon, she made for the green velvet.

"Cranky old bag," she said to herself, listening to her mother's footsteps on the outside stairway and then moving across the floor overhead until the sounds told Emma her mother was making her cup of tea. Soon she'd be sprawled on the bed, sleeping the afternoon away while Emma worked. As if she would ever meet an interesting man at church. It was full of women, doddering old widowers who'd killed their first wife or two with child bearing, and beardless boys who blushed just to look at her. Besides, her mother rushed her away after the services so fast that even if she ever did see someone interesting, she'd never have a chance to get acquainted. Emma doubted if her mother intended to let her out of the shop, ever. She had learned the trade too well and her younger sister, Colleen, pretended to be a simpering idiot who couldn't add a column of figures or sew a simple French seam so she could stay in school and avoid Emma's fate of being trapped in the shop.

Emma picked up the bolt of green velvet and carried it to the mirror which stood at the dressmaking end of the shop. If she could just make a dress out of this elegant piece of goods, she thought, then she'd have a gown that would really show off her looks, and somehow she could find a way to escape spending the rest of her life in the dreadful little shop.

She picked up the kerosene lamp and set it on the bracket beside the mirror. She could at least see how she would look. Holding one end of the fabric, she let the bolt drop to the floor. She held the velvet up before her and studied herself in the mirror. Yes, the color was perfect. It brought out the green of her eyes.

Smiling, she unbuttoned the top of her waist and pulled it open. She would just tuck this velvet into the top of her chemise to see how it would look against her skin. How she would love to have a low-necked gown like this! What was the use of having skin that was white and smooth as silk and breasts that swelled over the top of your chemise if no one was ever going to see them? She reached up and pulled the pins from her hair, releasing it from its knot so that it tumbled around her shoulders in black waves. The lamplight sparked her eyes and danced around her naked throat. She caressed the velvet where it touched her skin. It was almost as soft as her breast.

The bell jingled as the shop door opened. They never had customers at that time of day. She turned, still holding the green velvet tucked into her bodice. She was aware of the nakedness of her neck and breast and her hair tumbling down around her shoulders.

It was a man.

The kind of man she'd seen strolling along the riverfront where the steamboats docked. The kind of man who made her mother walk faster and jerk at Emma's arm.

For a moment they stared at each other.

He spoke first. "That shade of green is perfect for you. It matches your eyes. All you need to set it off is a pair of emerald eardrops. I just saw some in a shop down the street."

She felt the color staining her white skin. Pulses deep within her began pounding. She turned back to the mirror as if embarrassed, and in the moment before she pulled the velvet from her chemise and began buttoning her waist, she saw herself as he had seen her. Beautiful and desirable. She also saw his face reflected in the mirror, and she knew he was enchanted.

He turned his back as she arranged her clothes. Obviously he was a gentleman.

"Pardon me, I didn't realize you were indisposed."

She was afraid he would leave. "I should have put out the closed sign," she said quickly. "We don't usually have customers after dinner."

"Then you are the proprietress of this shop?"

"It's my mother's shop. I just work here. The velvet is not for me. I was just seeing how it would look made up."

"But you should have it. It's made for you."

"It's really not suitable for a shop girl," she willed her voice to be steady. "Now what can I help you with, Mr. —?" She drew out the *Mister*, surprised at her own boldness. But she had to know his name. And whatever he had come for, she intended to give it to him, to

40

keep him there as long as she could. She had not seen a man this handsome since her father had gone to war.

He studied her before he answered. He had removed his broad-brimmed planter's hat as he came into the store, but now he swept it before him in a courtly gesture.

"My name is Austin Avery."

"Austin Avery. What an elegant name."

He smiled, showing the edge of a gold tooth. "It is a name well respected down the river. Or it was until the war, although it is a comfort to think that even we who lost everything in that dreadful holocaust kept our good names."

"You're a Southerner?" She hoped she could avoid revealing her father had fought on the other side. In Missouri, the war was still a touchy issue.

"Yes, from Louisiana. But come now, Madam, you know more about me than I of you. May I be so bold as to ask your name?"

It *was* bold, of course. She was surprised that a gentleman should be so bold, and she prayed her mother would not take a sudden urge to wake early and come downstairs. She really should turn the subject to business, but he was so handsome. God knows when she'd get another chance to flirt with such a man. She knew she had hesitated too long, but she hated to say her name was Emma O'Brien. Here he was a Southern gentleman and all, and Emma O'Brien sounded as common as wash water.

"My name is Em—" she began and then her eye caught the green velvet. "Emerald. My name is Emerald O'Brien."

"Emerald O'Brien! How perfectly it suits you! I

41

could not have thought of a better name myself!"

Now what does he mean by that? she wondered. But his face was impassive. Well, she'd not let him disconcert her. Making her voice cool, she said, "And what are you looking for, Mr. Avery?"

He looked straight into her eyes and what she saw there made her blush and look at her feet. And then, just when she would have rebuked him for his boldness, he turned the conversation deftly to talk of linen handkerchiefs and ruffled dress shirts. They did not carry the shirts, but they had a large enough stock of handkerchiefs to linger over. They discussed the merits of each until finally he selected the most expensive, those of India silk at a dollar each. She suspected they were what he had wanted all along. She suggested he have some shirts made, wanting to keep him there as long as possible, but he said he was just passing through on his way up river. She wondered frantically what she might do to detain him and then, after he had paid for the handkerchiefs and she was wrapping them, he peeled off a wad of greenbacks and tossed them on the counter.

"Would that be enough for a gown of that green material? Made up and ready to wear, I mean."

She stared at the bills, dumbfounded. What did he mean? "Why, yes," she stammered. "It's more than enough." *Of course, you fool*, she thought. *A man like that would have a wife or mistress*. She made her voice cool again. "Will you bring the lady in to chose a style? We have the latest copy of *Godey's Lady's Book* and I can copy whatever she—"

"That won't be necessary," he said. "Make it up to suit yourself. I'm sure you know the latest style."

"But," her throat was so dry she could hardly speak. "How will I know what size to make it?"

"Make it to fit yourself. I'll be back at the end of the week. Can you finish it by then?"

She said she could, knowing she'd have to sew day and night. Without further comment, he left. She stood there with her head spinning and her heart pounding. What did he mean? Did he have some other woman who was just her size or did he mean what she *thought* he meant? She had not dared to ask. If she were wrong, she'd have made a fool of herself. She stared for a moment at the green velvet while she tried to sort it out.

Then she picked up the bills and shoved them into the cash drawer. She reached under the counter and got out the latest copy of *Godey's*. She knew just the dress she would copy. It had a fashionable bustle back and a low neck to show off her breasts and a cunning little jacket for daytime. She would have to think of an excuse for her mother. A new customer with lots of cash. Maybe even an actress. A rush job.

She turned the pages rapidly, her heart hammering, knowing something momentous had begun. An adventure. A drama in which she, Emerald O'Brien, would star.

Chapter Three

In Carpenter, Nebraska in that spring of 1876 there were two main topics of speculation among the men who divided their hunkering-around time between the stove at Hornbringle's Hardware and the brass rail of the City Saloon. The first was the endless possibilities in, and ramifications of, joining the gold rush to the Black Hills. The second was whether or not there would be a fight between Phineas P. Crandall, editor of *The Carpenter Sentinel*, and the Everett boy. The men followed Crandall's lead in calling his new employee *boy* despite the fact Hugh Everett was obviously a man — and a man who looked like he could hold his own in a fight. But that was the fun of it — old man Crandall persisting in calling Hugh *boy* and expecting him to act humble and do all the dirty work around the *Sentinel* office when Crandall barely reached five feet in height even in his high-heeled, patent-leather, spat-covered shoes, and Hugh Everett was as tall and strong as a young oak and had the steely gaze and powerful grip of a frontiersman.

Most of the men figured it had to come to blows, though some argued that Everett seemed to be the idealistic type who felt he owed Crandall his loyalty for the editor's letting him take over his father's position while old John Everett coughed his lungs out at last, and his poor wife worried herself into the grave beside him. Hugh Everett, they argued, was an educated and civilized man, having been away from Carpenter reading law until his father's illness brought him home. He would control himself and never pick Crandall up by his embroidered silk lapels and give the pompous old goat the shaking he so richly deserved.

Further complicating the speculation was the question of Luther Everett. Everyone knew Mrs. Everett's last words to Hugh had been *take care of your brother*, and everyone knew sixteen-year-old Luther was going to cause problems. So by the time Luther's name came up, it was generally agreed that Hugh was locked in. Such a responsible young man would not dare give up an office job in a first-class establishment like the *Sentinel* with times so hard and so many out of work.

There were even those who argued that a young man who wanted to get ahead could do worse than to follow in the steps of Phineas P. Crandall. True, he was an arrogant bastard, an unscrupulous businessman, and personally obnoxious, but he was also, one had to admit, a true entrepreneur who was amassing both capital and power, and, moreover, was loyal to his advertisers. He had successfully promoted the Nebraska route to the Black Hills as being safer than the Wyoming route by playing up every skirmish with the Sioux in Wyoming territory, and thus keeping in Nebraska the profits from outfitting the gold seekers.

It was difficult to find fault with a man with such a keen editorial policy.

The men hunkering around the hardware store and saloon were not the only ones in Carpenter to speculate about Hugh Everett. The thoughts of most of the unmarried women and even some of the good wives of the city turned frequently to the need to comfort the young man in his bereavement with gifts of homemade bread and jam and even washing and ironing. The women said they would do the same for anyone who had suffered such a loss, but each knew in her secret heart she offered more than sympathy. And each knew her cause was hopeless. For although Hugh responded with smiles and a squeeze to the hand or even the waist, and he might have taken a woman who dared to offer herself without marriage, it was obvious he could not be led into marriage. He acknowledged a woman, but he seemed always to be looking beyond her, as if what was promised was not enough, but there was some other woman in his past or in his future who would offer something beyond even the dreams of the women of Carpenter, Nebraska.

Some women thought the distant look in Hugh's eyes was only the haunted gaze of a man who has suffered tragedy and that, in time, he would be ready to settle down. Others, older and wiser women, said young Everett had *that look* about him when he first came to Carpenter; that he had the wanderlust and was best left alone, being the kind of man who must roam and will bring grief to any woman who dares love him.

The truth was no one in Carpenter, Nebraska, understood Hugh Everett, least of all Hugh Everett himself.

Phineas P. Crandall had studied the young man ever since Hugh gave up his law studies to help his father by taking over his duties at the *Sentinel*. The editor had decided, almost immediately, that he wanted to keep Hugh working for him. He did not have the delicate hands of a natural typesetter as did Crandall, but he was intelligent and skillful and had been quick to master the layout of the print drawers and the mechanics of the lever-operated printing press. Most important, he was an articulate man who could write polished copy. With such a man running the office, Crandall would at last be able to devote his full time and attention to the various schemes he fancied would establish him as one of Nebraska's leading entrepreneurs.

First, however, Crandall decided, Hugh must be taught who was in charge. Though Hugh had never been anything but polite, there was something about him that Crandall found disturbing, even threatening. He sensed there was a fire inside Hugh, a sort of terrible power, that Crandall felt he had to get under control. He told himself that Hugh, like all men, had within him a beast, a beast that must be leashed for the boy's own good. He did not admit his true motive, which was that if he could make someone as strong, handsome, and virile as Hugh Everett seem small, then he, Phineas P. Crandall, would be a bigger man.

Crandall fancied that because of his respect for Hugh's grief over the illnesses and deaths of his parents, he had been easy on him. But on the day he read Hugh's Pa-ha-sa-pa editorial he decided the time had come for a showdown. He had not seen the editorial

47

until it was in print, having trusted Hugh to fill in a gap on the front page while he took a long lunch at Meyer's Saloon. Although he was pleased by parts of the editorial, other parts infuriated him. It seemed a good place to begin the boy's education.

Hugh was setting type for the next edition. He stood in his black apron and matching sleeve protectors before the California job case, a waist-high rack containing drawers of different-sized types. Crandall folded the newspaper so as to display the Black Hills article and slapped it down on the type drawer. "What is this Pa-ha-sa-pa garbage?"

"Sir?" Hugh responded politely, but Crandall saw something flaring in his dark eyes.

"I said, what is this Pa-ha-sa-pa garbage?"

When he set out to intimidate someone, Crandall had a way of peering over the top of his wire-rimmed spectacles so his piercing blue eyes seemed to look right through his victim. He was doing it now, but Hugh did not intend to be intimidated. He set down the composing stick with the line of type he had been working on before he spoke.

"I believe you asked me to compose an article promoting the Black Hills to fill out the front page."

"That's just it," Crandall sputtered. "An article promoting the Black Hills, not a theological discussion! Not 'Sacred Hunting Ground of the Sioux' and," he snatched up the newspaper and scanned the article as he talked, "and questions of right and wrong. *Never* questions of right or wrong! We're putting out a newspaper here, not writing lit-er-a-ture!" He threw the paper back down on the job case.

Hugh picked it up and studied his article. He

remembered how much he had enjoyed writing it. He had savored the word, *Pahasapa*, saying it over and over to himself. The word seemed to evoke images of mysterious, beckoning mountains wreathed in fog, deer grazing at the edge of meadows, valleys with clear, sparkling creeks where the sunlight caught the gleam of golden nuggets. The longing that came to him when he thought of the forbidden lands was sharp. It was as if, although the area was off-limits to whites by treaty, something was calling him there. He felt something great would happen there and he longed to explore this last frontier.

"What are you doing, boy, dreaming!" Crandall's voice broke his reverie. "You see! That's what I wanted to get on you about! Dreaming all the time. You think too much. Sacred Hunting Ground—nonsense! Whose side are you on, anyway?"

"Naturally I'm for opening new lands to civilization," Hugh measured his words carefully, so his anger wouldn't keep him from making his point, "but until the government succeeds in negotiating for the Black Hills, the Treaty of '68 clearly—"

"The Treaty of '68? You're talking like a bleeding-heart, pap-sucking Quaker, and there's enough of them in this world without a responsible paper like *The Sentinel* admitting the Black Hills belong to the Sioux."

"But the point is, they do—"

"The point is the goddamn treaty commissioners in Washington have to be made to get off their fat asses and write a new treaty and take that land away from those heathen redskins!"

"You talk like a—"

"I talk like a realist. That's what I am, and that's

49

what you're going to have to be if you want to get along in this world. Your father got you over-educated, that's your trouble. I warned him about it, but he didn't listen, and now he's dead and you're writing about the Sacred Hunting Ground, for God's sake!"

"Listen, Crandall, if you didn't like it, then why—"

"Then why did I let it go to print? Is that what you're asking? Not because I didn't see it. No, it's because—because I like you and want to see you get ahead. Figure I owe it to your father. That's what I told Hornbringle when he joshed me about your little essay. 'He'll learn,' I said. 'He'll learn running a paper is a business. The gold rush is important to a hardware man like Hornbringle, and we have to be loyal to our advertisers.' "

"You make it sound as if the whole gold rush is nothing but a business opportunity!"

"And what do *you* think it is, boy, a goddamn crusade? You've got to learn there's nothing wrong with business. It's the free enterprise system. Why, if enough people invade the Black Hills, and the goddamn government can be brought into line to protect the rights of its law-abiding citizens by wiping out the Indians, then a whole new land will open up right on our doorstep. Can you see what that will mean for us? For the railroad and for Nebraska?"

"Crandall, I think—"

"Civilization! That's what it will mean! Miners digging down and breaking rock and getting all that gold, and timbermen cutting down all those trees, and farmers clearing the land and people building houses and barns and chicken coops!" Warming to his subject, Crandall struck a pose with one hand on the type case s if it were a podium and the other hand hooked in he front of his vest. He looked senatorial with his atty suit and his snow-white mutton-chop sideburns etting off his bald dome. "What would be a more itting way for this nation to celebrate its Centennial han by opening a whole new territory to the free nterprise system? Think of it, 1776 to 1876 and undreds of new businesses—livery stables, hardware tores, hotels, boarding houses, and brothels, and even ewspapers! Why there might be an opportunity for ome enterprising entrepreneur to own a whole chain f newspapers! Progress, that's what it is!"

"But what about *truth*?" Hugh demanded as Cran-lall paused for breath. "Don't we have some obligation o inform people of the truth? Don't they have the right o know about the moral issues and the risks involved n attempting such an expedition?"

"*Truth*? Now where did you get a fool idea like that? No one cares about *truth*, boy. Not even the ministers. Why there wouldn't be a church in operation today if people cared about truth. No sir! What people care bout is economics. Business, getting on, surviving."

Suddenly Hugh could stand no more. He wanted to hug Crandall, get out of the office and keep going. He wanted to bust loose and follow the crazy idea that had been in his mind all week. He was sick of grief and esponsibility and Carpenter, Nebraska, and moral lecisions.

He ripped off the sleeve protectors and the black ypesetters apron and threw them on the floor. No nan should have to wear an apron.

"What are you doing?" Crandall demanded.

Hugh hesitated. He had no plan and from some-

51

where inside him a voice was saying, *remember Luther Take care of your brother*.

Crandall was staring at him accusingly. Hugh fought for control. He told himself he was a civilized man and he must behave logically. He needed time to think. He spied the empty coal scuttle. "I need some fresh air," he said. "The bucket's empty. I'll get some coal." Without waiting for Crandall to reply, he grabbed the scuttle and stormed out.

Outside, Hugh took deep breaths of the cold afternoon air. The air held just the promise of spring in it. It was the second time in as many weeks that he had come to the point of telling Crandall off. The first was shortly after the funeral when he asked Crandall to set a value on his father's share of the partnership.

"Did he mean in dollars and cents?" Crandall asked. "What else is there?" Hugh replied. "Well, there's good-will," Crandall said pleasantly, "and loyalty and reputation. Intangibles built up over the years of a partnership." "In dollars and cents," Hugh had persisted. And then Crandall had told him.

Nothing.

His father's share of the partnership, which Hugh had assumed would be sufficient to keep Luther in school and allow Hugh to return to the law, was worthless. "It has not had a cash value for some time," Crandall went on explaining while Hugh, through a red mist of controlled rage, saw his dreams slipping away.

Hugh could not believe it and said so. According to the banner on the masthead, *The Carpenter Sentinel* was "Nebraska Territory's Leading Bi-Weekly." How could his father's share be worthless? With a great show of affronted dignity, Crandall produced evidence in ledger after ledger that the sizeable investment his father made in the partnership six years before had dwindled away. In Crandall's precise script was the record of dozens of withdrawals of capital made when his father's illness had prevented him from earning his salary and he still insisted, Crandall emphasized, on providing his sons with the luxury of education. Hugh's certainty that Crandall had cheated his father was shaken by the old man's implication that the family's financial ruin was somehow not his fault but Hugh's.

"I knew it was your responsibility to take over. I told him to call you home months before he did."

"If only I'd realized how sick he was. His lungs had been bad for years, but we somehow never expected—"

"Ah, if we could only pierce that shroud of mystery, son."

Hugh shut out the words as best he could while Crandall launched into a sermon about the mystery of death and what a blessing it was that his mother had followed her husband in death to be his helpmate in the beyond. Hugh wanted to believe all the platitudes about death, but he was filled with doubt. With all he'd been through by the age of twenty-two, he thought he should have discovered some answers to the meaning of life and death, but he had not. He avoided thinking of the deaths of his parents, deaths which had thrust upon him the responsibility of his brother, Luther.

Crandall had reminded him of his responsibility. "How old is Luther now?"

"Sixteen."

"Ah, yes, sixteen. Well, some are men at that age and some are not." He peered at Hugh over the tops of his spectacles. "It is my impression your brother is not exactly settled yet?"

Luther. Hugh frowned when he thought of his brother. He supposed a certain amount of rivalry and resentment between brothers was natural, but Luther was always out to prove there was something he could do better than Hugh and then getting hurt and angry when he again came up against the fact that Hugh was the smarter and the taller and even the better-liked of the brothers. He did not regret his promise to take care of his brother; he loved him. He only wished he could *like* him a little more. None of this was Crandall's business, however, so he replied only that Luther was still in school.

"Then you will need to provide for him as well as for yourself? Had you planned to go on reading for the law?"

"I don't see how I can afford to now."

"I don't either," Crandall said cheerfully, "and that is why I am prepared to make you an offer."

The offer was for Hugh to take over his father's duties at a figure so low Hugh could not trust himself to answer, but Crandall had assumed it was all settled, and that Hugh would spend the rest of his life as the all-around work horse of the *Sentinel*. It should have been a simple matter to tell Crandall off and quit, but Hugh was only too aware the whole country was still feeling the effects of the depression which had followed the Civil War. Thousands of families like his had followed the new railroad lines west, but the lands they took up had often proved barren and worthless.

Throughout the western territories men were looking for work or waiting for the spring thaw to clear the land so they could make a try for the Black Hills, which seemed to be hope's last frontier. Hugh wanted to go himself. Sometimes it even seemed as if it was his destiny to go. But he told himself such feelings were irrational and he, an educated and rational man who knew better than most the risks of such a venture, could not go off chasing a will-o'-the-wisp. Especially not when he was responsible for his brother and any decision he made would affect Luther's future as much as his own.

There has to be a reasonable solution to this, Hugh thought, standing with his filled coal scuttle in the alley behind the office he never wanted to enter again. *I can't be as trapped as I feel.* There had be to some compromise between what he wanted to do and what he felt he had to do. Some way he could take care of Luther and still have his adventure. There had been an idea in the back of his mind ever since he wrote the Pahasapa story, and now it surfaced and seemed suddenly reasonable. He would talk Crandall into sending him into the Hills as some sort of special Black Hills correspondent. He'd send back reports of what was really going on. Luther could board with someone in the meantime, and Hugh would send for him when he was established, or he'd come home rich. And then if the gold rush proved false, he'd at least have a job to come home to.

He decided to take action before he had time to think about it any more. Resolutely he strode back into the office. Crandall was sitting at his own desk, but he had taken the drawer of type with him and was finishing the galley on which Hugh had been working. He looked up as Hugh came in. "Well, it's about time you came back to work. Get to setting this type. My eyes aren't as young as they used to be."

Hugh knew Crandall was expecting him to pick up the drawer of type and take it meekly back to the job case to finish. He wanted to keep the old man happy, but he didn't want to make another submissive gesture. He busied himself with picking up his apron and sleeve protectors.

"Crandall, there's something I'd like to talk over with you."

"Of course, son." Crandall was obviously expecting to be asked advice.

"I'd like to go to the Black Hills. I've been thinking it over and I was thinking the *Sentinel* really owes it to its subscribers to discover the truth of this gold rush thing, so I was thinking if you could outfit me, I'd—"

"The Black Hills? You can't be serious. Only a fool would do that."

"What's so foolish about it? The paper's been urging people to go for months."

"People with nothing to lose. People who don't matter. People who can be used to open up the lands. Not someone like you."

"Why not? Why not me?"

Seeing he was serious, Crandall stood up and walked toward him. "Because you have something. You have prospects."

"Prospects? What prospects have I?"

"Why I told you, boy. You can work for me. I'm going to train you up in the business. Just like you were my son."

"Son? Don't call me your son! And don't ever call me *boy* again. I'm twenty-two and I'm a man!"

"Not while you've got such fool schemes in your head. What do you think you'll accomplish by going? What do you think you'd find there?"

"I don't know — something!"

"Wealth? Power? Land? Adventure?"

"Yes! All of those! Gold! I'll find gold!" Even as he said it, Hugh felt foolish. It was something more than gold he sought, but he couldn't put a name to it.

"You really think you'll find gold? That it's just lying there waiting for you to strike it rich?"

"Is that so crazy? To want to stake a claim? Why shouldn't I go? At least there I'd have a chance for something!"

"Dreamer! That's what you are! A fool dreamer like your father!"

"I'd rather die a dreamer like him than spend my life slaving away here for you."

"You'd hardly be a slave," Crandall said, backing away from Hugh's anger. "I was thinking of making you a partner one day. I wasn't going to tell you yet. Was going to see how it worked out, but seeing as how you've been bit by the gold bug, I'll tell you now."

"A partner?" Hugh almost choked over the word.

"There now, son," Crandall moved closer to him. "I knew that would make a difference. Can't turn down an opportunity like that, can you?"

"A partner?" Hugh sputtered. "You'd make me a partner!"

"Just like your father," Crandall beamed and picked up the drawer of type from his desk and offered it to Hugh as if it were a gift. "Now you take this type back over to your case and finish setting the copy and we'll discuss the details later."

"Shove it." Hugh said evenly.

"What?" Crandall blinked from behind his glasses. He held the drawer before him, suddenly wary.

"I said you can take that drawer of type and shove it. And you can take the whole damn *Sentinel* office and your goddamn lousy job and do the same."

"You've gone crazy." Crandall backed away.

Hugh saw his fear and took a step forward, enjoying it. And then it happened. As he retreated from Hugh's anger, Crandall clutched the drawer to his chest, and the type rained down like hailstones.

"Look what you've done!" Crandall shouted. "Now look what you've done!"

Hugh had to laugh as he watched the little editor drop to his knees and begin frantically to gather the type. Some had fallen between the cracks in the floor. He'd never get it all back.

"Don't just stand there, boy, help me!"

"I'm sorry, Crandall, *Sir*," Hugh had turned the word into an insult. "I'm sorry, but I've got better things to do. I'm going to the Black Hills."

"And what about Luther? Have you forgotten your brother?"

Hugh hesitated. He had. Just for a moment.

"Will you take him with you to face the Sioux?"

"Yes! Why not? It'll make a man of him."

"You've gone crazy," Crandall muttered, still down on his knees gathering the type. "You're crazy and you're a fool. You'll be sorry, mark my word."

"Maybe."

"You're a fool, but you'll have to find out the hard

way. Remember I said that! You're a fool!"

"Maybe I am," Hugh said evenly. "Maybe I am. But there are some things a man has to find out for himself."

Chapter Four

Afterwards, whenever Hugh or Molly would think of that meeting in the camp on Lodge Pole Creek, and they would think of it often, they would wonder if it was fate that brought them together. In their dark moments, and there would be many, Molly would think of the meeting as something arranged by God to test her strength and honor; while Hugh, although he too wondered about God's will, was more likely to think of their meeting as a joke planned by malevolent gods who found pleasure in watching humans struggling in the tangled skein of emotions set in their paths to torture, confuse, and tempt.

In those moments when there seemed a rightness about their being together, the thought that *they were meant to be* would triumph, but it was always followed by the fear that such thoughts were only a way for their troubled consciences to justify what they allowed to happen.

In truth, it was not the will of God, nor the malevolence of evil spirits that brought them together; it was the goodness of Jake Lewis. None of it would have come to pass had not Jake been feeling so good about himself, his prospects, and the Black Hills, that late April day as he sat around a campfire with the other members of Hobart's party in their camp just outside Sidney, Nebraska, to plan the expedition that would begin the next day.

Jake had quite forgotten that going to the Hills had been Molly's idea. He had also forgotten that he was a man cursed by bad luck and failure. Had pushed aside the knowledge that he was once again beholden to Sam Tuttle for buying his homestead and all his farm goods for his eldest son, and that besides his wife and child, a team of mules and a wagon and supplies, he had not a thing in the world to call his own.

For it was a fine team and a fine wagon. Not, of course, the heavy wagon of the freighters, but a Studebaker, and as good as could be had in Sidney, the jumping-off point for the Black Hills. And he had plenty of flour and beans and bacon stowed away in the wagon, along with Molly's trunk and a few sticks of furniture, broken up and cached away so as not to advertise the fact he was taking a woman and child into Sioux country. And he had a pick-ax and gold pan, prominently displayed for all to see, though he would not need it for weeks until the party reached Custer, the gold camp on French Creek named for the man who had proved the existence of gold in the Hills and begun the invasion of Sioux hunting grounds.

He had forgotten that it had taken Molly hours to persuade him to join the gold rush. In the days it took to sell their possessions and arrange for train transport to Sidney, he had become as consumed by the promise of good fortune in the Hills as any other down-and-out farmer in the territories. Nor did his optimism fade when they reached Sidney and saw how many were, like them, selling what little they had to outfit for an expedition. Nor was he discouraged by reports that not only would they be opposed by the Sioux in entering the Hills, but the U.S. Cavalry would be under official orders to stop and turn back anyone suspected of entering reservation lands in violation of the treaty Custer and his official expedition had already broken with governmental sanction.

He felt his luck had changed. That rare good fortune was finally coming his way. His optimism was reinforced when he succeeded in being accepted by the group the outfitter assured him would be the strongest and best-armed party to enter the Hills that spring, the Hobart Expedition. Jake was not a man easily impressed by other men, but Emmet Hobart impressed him. He had the look of a true frontiersman. Jake had seen plenty of men on the streets of Sidney who tried to affect that appearance by wearing buckskins and carrying heavy cartridge belts across their chests even in the city, but who somehow revealed in their manner or their grandiose speeches about their deeds on the frontier that their appearance was largely an act. But Hobart wore his buckskins as if they had grown on him, and he was almost as taciturn as Jake himself. It was from others that Jake learned Hobart had served the North bravely with the 43rd Wisconsin Volunteers and, after the war, had done it all—fought Indians, killed buffalo, and built a railroad.

And not only was their leader a real frontiersman, but his expedition would have the benefit of an experienced guide. Donnelly was a fat Irishman who told bad jokes and looked like he'd be more comfortable tending bar than riding a horse, but he had wintered in the Black Hills and knew the way to Custer City. It would be a fine expedition. There would be about a dozen wagons and at least thirty-five men armed with single-shot, but reliable, needle guns, or even with repeating rifles. The party was small enough to travel fast, but big enough to impress the Sioux who, it was generally agreed, never organized to defend their territory, but only banded together in small war parties which struck only the stragglers who promised easy scalps.

Jake felt good about easily winning acceptance as part of such a party. Hobart and Donnelly and Pearson, another man whose position in the party was not clear but who seemed to have taken on for himself an aura of leadership, looked over his wagon and team.

They remarked that he seemed to have plenty of room in his wagon and wondered if he planned to freight some goods for men who were walking or on horseback. He said yes, that was what he planned to do, avoiding mention of the fact the extra space in the wagon was for Molly and the boy. No one had thought to ask him if he had a family along, and he had not volunteered the information.

His secret was the source of some uneasiness as he hung around the camp that day, listening to the men's tales of previous adventures and plans for the one that was to begin with the next dawn. Molly and the boy were waiting in the hotel back in town, and he figured he'd just show up with them in the morning, maybe even keep them down in the wagon until the party was underway. Once they were on the road, he didn't think they would make him turn back. He hoped not. He desperately wanted to continue to be part of this expedition. For once in his life he was as good as anybody else. Had as much hope and chance for success as anyone. It made him feel bold and generous and a little bit testy. And that was why he acted as he did when the Everett brothers showed up. That and—perhaps—destiny.

It might seem strange that the men so easily accepted Jake into their group, yet questioned the addition of the Everett brothers. But Jake, though he was a farmer and not a frontiersman, was clearly one of them. He, by the leather look of his skin and the hardness of his palms when he shook hands, had worked all his life outdoors. His clothes were work-stained and old. He spoke like them, simple, direct, uneducated. The Everett boys were different. Anyone could see that, even as they approached the camp from a distance that day. Their clothes were rugged, but so new the creases showed, and the young one was wearing Napolean boots so stiff they must have hurt, with kneehigh fronts, more suited to riding than walking. The boys, the Hobart Party thought of the newcomers that way, although the tall one was obviously a man—were tanned, but not leather-skinned, and their hands when they shook hands all around, were firm, but not horny with calouses.

So the boys got off to a bad start by looking wrong, and Luther compounded his youth and ignorance by blinking nervously and acting like a kid ready for a day at the circus instead of a man wanting to join a dangerous expedition. But had they looked like wilderness scouts, they might have been denied admittance to the expedition solely because they arrived late.

64

Hobart had been encamped on Lodge Pole Creek for a week while he recruited the best outfitted of the men who gathered in Sidney. The others, even Jake, the last to join, had been there since early morning forming their plans and forging their group. They had named the expedition officially, decided on a line of march, and agreed to set out at dawn the next day. They were a unit, the Hobart Expedition to the Black Hills, and there is no better way for a group to solidify its identity than by excluding some Johnny-Come-Latelys, some greenhorns, and that was how they saw the Everett brothers.

"Well, look what's coming down the road," Jake heard Pearson sneer as he looked up from a cup of coffee liberally laced with a shot from Donnelly's pocket flask to see two young men entering the camp. One was exceptionally tall and the other short, plump, and limping a little. The smaller one carried a needle gun over his shoulder and, although it was a man-sized weapon, Jake had the fleeting thought that he looked rather like Edwin did when he was playing soldier with a wooden gun.

"Faith," Donnelly joked. "It must be the schoolmaster and his star pupil come to see us off." But Hobart rose from the group to assume his proper role as leader, and the tall young man, the fine-looking one, stepped into the group and offered his hand to Hobart.

"Emmet Hobart? We've been looking for you. I understand you have an expedition leaving for the Hills tomorrow."

Hobart merely nodded. Jake felt a subtle shift in the attitudes of the men who had been lazing around the fire. Donnelly and Pearson both stood up and moved closer to the newcomers, and the others tensed forward a little as if not to miss anything. Jake stood up too, but took a position behind the others.

"I'm Hugh Everett, and this is my brother, Luther." There was a general shaking of hands among those standing and friendly nods to the men still sitting around the fire.

The men were responding cooly, and Jake could tell by something that flashed in the tall one's eyes that he was aware of it, but he went on as if undaunted, while his brother stood blinking and cradling his rifle across his stomach and managing to look generally foolish.

"I don't know what it takes to join up with you, but we hear you've got the strongest party ready to go, and we'd like to be a part of it." Hugh said, and Jake thought that was good enough, but the young one had to pipe in, "We'd sure like to ride along with you!"

"Ain't no riding," Pearson said, standing a little apart from the rest, his broad-brimmed Mexican style hat almost obscuring his face. "Ain't no riding along. This is a freight outfit and we mean to make time."

"You might find someone to transport your gear," Donnelly said, "but you'd have to walk. That is, unless you want to wait a few years until there's stage service to the Hills."

"Walk all the way?" Luther blinked.

"That's right," Hobart spoke at last. "Some three hundred miles and the last of it all uphill."

"We can walk," Hugh said. "And we'd like to travel fast."

"Sure you would," Pearson said. "You and your little brother."

The boys tensed then, and Jake almost expected

something to happen, but Hobart subtly moved in and let it be known by the tone of his voice, that if anyone was going to turn away the newcomers, it would be he.

"There are other expeditions," he said pleasantly enough. "Expeditions which are still forming. On down the creek. You can probably find a place in a day or two. We're ready to pull out in the morning."

"We can be ready," Hugh said. "We've all our gear waiting at the store. We want to go as soon as possible. We want to be among the first."

"Well, you're already late for that," Donnelly interjected. "Miners have been sneaking in there all winter. The choicest spots are filling up fast. I've already staked my claim, but the rest can't waste time."

After Hobart moved in, Pearson had settled back against a wagon wheel and begun to whittle as if he were no longer concerned, but now he spoke again, his voice snaking out at them.

"How old's your brother?"

The men turned their attention to Pearson. He kept his eyes on his whittling as if he wasn't really interested in the answer to his question, or as if he wanted the men to notice what he was doing. Jake noticed the knife. It was not the pocket knife most men used for whittling. It was not even a standard hunting knife. It was a weapon known as an Arkansas Toothpick. It had a long, thin blade and was a fighting knife, useful only for sticking pigs or other men. Or, Jake thought, making men *think* you were a fighter. He figured Pearson was the kind of runty little man who concealed his weakness by looking and acting sinister. He was interested to see how Hugh would react.

"Seventeen." Hugh stood his ground and answered

straight out, but something in the way the brother looked made Jake think he had exaggerated by at least a few months. Well, sometimes a man had to lie a little.

"Seventeen," Pearson snorted, twisting his knife so a long sliver of wood curled around the blade.

"Frank's trying to point out," Hobart interjected, "that this is a dangerous expedition. Or at least it will be if we don't stick together. We can't have anyone turning back. The Sioux won't bother a party of any size, but they'll pick off stragglers."

"We won't turn back" Hugh said evenly.

"Well, I don't like to turn anyone away," Hobart said, "but your brother seems awfully young, and you don't either of you look like you've spent much time outdoors."

"I've been working as a reporter, and Luther's been doing farm work. He's harder than he looks. And we're neither of us greenhorns. We've grown up hunting, and we're good marksmen, and we're well supplied."

"And well-armed!" the kid interjected, brandishing his needle gun.

"Hurrah for you!" Donnelly chimed in and Pearson snickered.

"We both have new needle guns," Hugh seemed to be speaking only to the leader. "I can't see where having two more armed men can hurt your party. We'll find another party if we have to, but we'd prefer to go with you."

"We'll go by ourselves if we have to," the young one said, and Jake couldn't help but grin. He figured Luther'd catch hell from his brother later.

"I don't like to turn anyone down," Hobart began,

"but—"

"But it's no Sunday School picnic," Donnelly finished for him.

"We ain't got time for nurse-maiding no kids," Pearson wiped the blade of his knife on his pants leg, and Jake suddenly felt the urge to say something. He was debating what it should be when Hobart turned to the men around the fire.

"I say this is really a group decision. It's up to you men. Anyone here willing to freight their goods and take them along?"

There was an awkward silence as the men looked at each other and shrugged. Hugh faced the group squarely. He looked to Jake like a good man to have along on a fight. And a decent sort who would not be a trial to Molly.

"They can freight with me," Jake said.

"Well, then I've no real cause to object," Hobart said. "So long as you boys know the danger."

"We do," Hugh said and stepped forward and shook Jake's hand.

"We've already divided into messes," Hobart said. "You'll have to find someone to share cooking chores with."

"They can mess with us," Jake said.

Hobart nodded, turned as if to walk away, then came back. "Did you say *us*? You got someone else in your party?"

"My wife and son," Jake said levely. "They're waiting in town."

Hobart frowned. Hugh looked at Jake in surprise. Tension seemed to gather and ripple through the group. Pearson stopped whittling. "You got a woman and kid along?"

Jake nodded.

"How old's the lad?" Donnelly asked.

"Edwin's going on six."

"Lord have mercy."

"Why didn't you tell us this before?" Hobart demanded, his voice angry.

"Didn't know it was important. Nobody asked." Jake took his pipe out of his pocket and began, very deliberately, to fill it. "I got room in the wagon for them to ride. There's been women in there already, ain't there? They had to go in with someone."

"Not decent women," Pearson said, whittling with a fury.

"Decent women don't take up any more room in a wagon than the other kind," Jake replied.

"If there's one thing the Sioux hate to see," Pearson snarled, "it's women and children. That means permanent settlement to them. They'll tolerate folks passing through, but if they think a party's come to settle, they'll fight for sure."

"We'll be ready for them!" Luther hefted his rifle.

Hobart was still frowning. "I don't like it."

"I've nothing against women myself," Donnelly said, "but there's no sense in tempting the heathen red devils."

Jake didn't like the way it was going. He would fight, if need be, for the right to take Molly and Edwin along, but he didn't know how to argue the matter reasonably. And then Hugh spoke.

"It's smart to take them," he said. "Women and children must be included if we are ever to occupy the Black Hills. As long as no one but prospectors goes in,

70

the country will see us as no better than trespassers. Families going in will make us *settlers*, and the government will *have* to offer military protection."

Jake was surprised and grateful that the young man had interferred. The others were quiet until Hobart spoke. "It makes sense. Still, I don't like it. I wouldn't risk my wife that way."

"It was her decision," Jake said. "She knows the risk, and she's willing to take it."

"Women got no business making decisions," Pearson muttered.

"I don't like it," Hobart repeated. "I didn't plan on being responsible for a family when I let you join."

"We already shook on it," Jake said, "and it's my responsibility."

"All right," Hobart sighed. "I won't go back on my word."

They shook hands all around. All except Pearson, who threw down his whittling and slipped his knife in his boot. As he straightened up, Jake finally got a good look at his face. There was something narrow and twisted about it, but it was to Hugh that Pearson seemed to direct his parting shot. "Women always make trouble."

Hugh looked strangely at Pearson, as if aware he had made an enemy, but he said nothing, and soon they were busy making arrangements for the next day. Jake agreed to give the boys a ride to town and load up the gear they'd left at the hardware store. The boys wanted to spend their last night in town, but he figured now that the fuss over Molly had passed, he'd move her out to the camp. It would be easier for her to spend her first night of camping within the reaches of

71

civilization. They had all piled into his wagon and were driving away, when Donnelly, too,, felt the need for a parting shot.

"Be here at dawn with the women and children, or we'll leave without you!"

Hugh kept silent and Jake approved of that, but then he looked around Hugh to where Luther sat muttering on the wagon seat.

"Children," he said. "Donnelly called us women and children. Well, I'll show him. I'll show all of you."

That made Jake wonder if he'd done the right thing. The kid was going to make trouble, that was for sure. But, hell, what real damage could he do? A few days on the trail would settle him down. Jake's feeling of optimism returned. He'd done right. He was sure of it. Luther would be a companion for Edwin. There would be two more guns protecting his family. Molly would appreciate that. And she would like Hugh. He was sure of that.

Molly was horrified. Not at the thought that she was to see Hugh again, but at the thought that she would imagine such a thing; that she was so foolish a woman that after all the years and all the miles that must be between them, that the very mention of a name that sounded like his, of a description that could have been Hugh, the boy she had loved, turned man, she would blush and grow faint with fear and wonder that it was indeed he.

Oh, she had always thought they might meet again. Someday when she was a lady and back in Pennsylvania and old, perhaps, and past the remembering and the wondering; so that when he came to call back to her parents' farm, on a visit East, they would meet as civilized people at a time when they could reminisce sweetly of childhood love without ever speaking of what had passed between them, and she would only acknowledge the meaning of his coming back to see her after so many years by taking down a tintype of Edwin, a grown man to be proud of. She would speak of her son and send him away finally, wondering and wishing it had been different.

But here? Now? With her in faded gingham and Jake beside her, and her heart already tripping with the thought of giving up everything to face the Sioux? It was crazy. It was crazy of her to even think such a thing because the name sounded like his, though Jake never got names straight, and she couldn't question him too closely because then he would suspect something and then what? What did she say? How could she speak now of what was never spoken of between them?

She never seriously thought it might be true. She thought only that she had strained her nerves with preparing for the journey so soon after childbed. Lizzie had warned of that. She would push the thought aside. She would think only of the journey.

The prayer she never dared speak but had formed with half the breaths of her body had at last come true. It was Hugh standing before her the next morning as she stepped down from the wagon and faced him in the dawn. She thought him for a moment a vision, haloed, as he was, by the sun behind him.

She was faint, the world misting around her, Jake and the others a blur.

"How do you do, Mrs. Lewis?" he spoke. Odd to hear his familiar voice. The formal words. Then his voice broke and stumbled, and she knew he had truly seen her. She had to think quickly. Had to react properly. What was she to do? What did one do in such a case? There was a boy behind him. The brother perhaps. The brother she had never known. He would not give them away. Unless Hugh did first.

She knew what she had to do. She thrust out her hand and shook his, very quickly, very formally.

"I'm very pleased to meet you, Mr. Everett."

She saw his confusion and tried to think how to signal his silence. She was aware of Jake to the side, looking pleased and cordial, showing off his wife.

And then Edwin was clamboring down from the wagon, wailing something about lost suspenders. She pulled him to her, letting him bury his face in her skirts for just a moment and then turned him and held him out for Hugh to see.

"This is Edwin," she said. "Our son."

She hoped he understood.

Chapter Five

There was no time to think or to react. Even as they stood staring at each other dumbly, Emmet Hobart galloped up on a big roan horse shouting commands. "Day's wasting. Line 'em up and move 'em out."

And then Jake was hustling her back up into the wagon and there was a flurry of activity around them as men shouted and swore, kicked out their campfires, and stowed their gear in wagons. In the confusion she did not know if Hugh understood about Edwin, did not even know if she wanted him to know, but she did see that he understood she wanted him to be silent about the fact they had met before.

Sitting on the wagon seat trying to hold Edwin close to her, despite his excitement as they took their place in the line of march, she wondered if she had done the right thing. Should she have acknowledged knowing Hugh? Tried to pretend that they had been only friends? Should she now turn to Jake and confess the whole thing?

She looked at her husband and knew it was impossible. In all the years they had been married, he had never once alluded to the fact he was not Edwin's true father. He had assumed, she knew, that she had been taken advantage of, that she was not responsible for the predicament he had heard her parents whispering of. She knew that when he came with his hat in his hand to ask her father for her hand, saying that he understood there was a problem and he wanted to go West and needed a wife, that he thought of her as a woman wronged. He did not know it had been as much her doing as the boy's, that one sweet time, and that she had lain awake and cried for her lost love all the night after she told her father she would accept Jake's offer and his promise never to "hold it up to her." Her husband did not know either how to speak of love or of the act of love, though he had shown his devotion to her in many ways. How could she now tell him the identity of the man he had befriended, or of how she had felt when she stepped out of the wagon and saw who it was?

They journeyed in silence.

As for Hugh, he wanted desperately to talk to Molly, to try to understand what had happened, if what she had implied about the boy could possibly be true, and if she really intended not to acknowledge even knowing him, but there was no opportunity, as the wagons rolled along and he and the other men on foot scrambled to keep up. He thought at noon he might have the chance to draw her aside, but when they camped for dinner they were joined by another party which met them coming back toward Sidney and civilization. It was part of the backwash of men who had been to the Black Hills and given up. Needless to say, their presence put a damper on the high spirits of the Hobart party. They had the look of failure about them and seemed determined to spread their discouragement among the new pioneers, telling horrendous tales of death and scalping at the hands of the Sioux. Yet, when pressed, not one man could say he personally had seen an Indian fight. Hugh had the feeling they had gotten together on their stories so as to justify their quitting; most of them had not even reached Custer.

Hobart did not let his party tarry with them, but hustled them through their meal and got them moving again so fast that the only contact Hugh had with Molly was the exchange of another dreadful, confused look as she handed him his plate of cold bacon and biscuits.

There was a critical moment as the two parties separated, with some of Hobart's Expedition looking uncertainly at the road leading back to Sidney, but Hobart paraded on his roan before them like the commander of a battalion, delivering the words which would inspire them to go on. He dismissed the party trailing back toward Sidney with one contemptuous word. *Greenhorns*.

They were different, he told them, stronger, better, well-informed and well-armed and properly outfitted. Hobart's confidence was contagious; he made it seem as if only a fool would have doubts, and they believed him because they wanted to. Each of them had already cut himself off from home in some way; there was no easy retreat.

And then, after they were once again underway, they heard a strange sound. It was a train whistle, mournful, faint and thin on the morning air, reaching them all the way from Sidney. It seemed impossible that it could be heard all that way, but there it was. A train whistle.

Hugh looked up from his place beside the Lewis wagon and saw Molly tilt her head to listen. And then from the other party, the one returning to Sidney, he heard another sound. The sound of cheering. He looked back. The men were jumping up and down, throwing their hats in the air, whistling and shouting. All for the sound of a train whistle.

It was their first sign of civilization, Hugh realized. *And our last.* He looked again at Molly. She had turned white.

Molly had avoided talking to Hugh at noon, glad of the interruption of the other party and so preoccupied with her own emotions that she was, until the moment with the train whistle, almost oblivious to the meaning of meeting the men who had not found the new Mecca in the Black Hills, even as they themselves set out with hope in their hearts. She was in that moment afraid, but afraid more of the confusion in her heart than of the danger of the journey.

By evening, they all gathered together around the campfire for the evening meal. She almost choked when Luther, making small talk over dinner, asked Jake conversationally, "So, where you folks from originally?"

"Back East," Jake said. "Pennsylvania."

"No kidding," Luther said cheerfully and turned to his brother. "Didn't we live there for a time?"

"Just briefly," Hugh said quickly. "We were from New York state. Moved west because of our father's

78

health."

Molly realized that he was giving her a pointed look. She knew he was asking if he should mention where they'd lived, so that they might pretend to suddenly "recognize" each other.

No! she signaled him with her eyes, and he swiftly launched into a lengthy and maudlin description of his father's health and the death of his parents, obviously to distract his brother from further questions. But when he paused for breath, Luther interrupted.

"So, Jake, how'd you come to move to Iowa?"

"Homestead," Jake answered. "Always wanted to homestead."

"And you, Mrs. Lewis?" Molly was startled to realize Hugh was speaking to her. "What did you want?"

"Me?" What a foolish question to ask a woman. She could not remember anyone asking what *she* wanted. "I wanted what my husband wanted."

Hugh seemed satisfied by that, but something perverse made her add, "I wanted to be married."

She felt herself blushing. It was not the sort of thing a woman said. But he had asked her a foolish question. A leading question. He left her no choice. And he had left her no choice then, either, however innocent it had been. What gave him a right to ask her such a question now? He seemed taken aback by her answer and was quiet, letting Jake and Luther, mostly Luther, carry on the conversation with dreams of what they would do when they struck it rich in the gold fields. Luther was rattling on about buying himself pearl-handled revolvers and dozens of pairs of fine boots, when Hugh turned to her again.

"And what will you do, Mrs. Lewis, when you strike it rich? What do you want *now*?"

It was a question she could answer. "I'll go home."

"To Iowa?"

"No!" She almost laughed. She stood up, still hanging on to her tin coffee cup, and stared into the dying embers of the campfire. "I'll go home to Pennsylvania, and I—we'll buy a house on a street with trees, somewhere near my family and I'll have a piano and put Edwin in good schools and—I don't know—What do rich people do? Go to dances and parties, I suppose."

Dances and parties, she thought. But she would be too old for that. Those were things for maidens and she had lost all that. Because of him. And he was free. Or was he?

"And you?" she asked. "What will you do when you get your gold? Have you a sweetheart waiting?"

"No," he said simply. "No sweetheart. No one waiting."

She felt foolish and vulnerable for having asked, yet vastly relieved. She could not meet Hugh's eyes, but stared into the dying campfire and found a shred of girlhood vanity left inside her that wondered if the firelight was flattering to her face. She wondered at the picture she made before the fire with the barrenness of Nebraska behind her and the hope of the Black Hills before her. She wondered what Hugh felt for her. If he, too, remembered. And then Jake stood and in a word shattered the moment.

"Bedtime."

He said it as he had a thousand times before. Each night when the day's work was done. That was all it meant. It signified nothing between them, but that it was the end of the day and a woman's place to be beside her husband. But that night she looked at Hugh and thought she saw something awful in his expression, and when she took Jake's arm and turned back to her place in the wagon, she felt suddenly disloyal to Hugh. She and Hugh had exchanged promises. They had said words never spoken between her and Jake. But Jake was her husband.

She climbed into the wagon and did not look back. She felt infinitely weary.

They made a long drive the next day. Most of the men seemed to have recaptured their enthusiasm for the journey, but Hugh noticed the closely cropped grass alongside the trail and thought about how many must have already passed before them. They were in a race that would go to the swiftest, and they were already late. And Molly's presence had changed everything. Molly beside her husband on the wagon seat. Molly in the wagon with him at night. Molly—another man's wife. Molly avoiding him and neither confirming nor denying what she had implied about the boy Edwin. Edwin, darting ahead of him on the trail, peeping out at him from the wagon. Edwin, whom he hardly dared to look at, not dark like Jake, but blond. He had to talk to Molly alone.

Molly knew she could avoid Hugh no longer. She did not know what his questions would be or if she had answers for them, but she knew he had a right to ask. So on the evening of the second day when Luther and Edwin followed Jake to stake out the mules for the night's grazing—a chore she knew would take Jake some time as he liked puttering with his mules — and Hugh offered to go with her to fetch water from the creek, she knew the time had come.

"I have to talk to you, Molly."

She said nothing, but took a seat on a fallen log, feeling almost faint with the knowledge of what was to come. He sat down on the other end of the log, not facing her. They both watched the men in camp. No one was noticing them, but if anyone did, they would appear to be two people resting and chatting after a long day's journey.

"You didn't answer my letters," he said.

She was surprised. It was almost an accusation. He was angry at her, after what had happened. But, of course, he couldn't know that.

"There were only three," she said. "And no address on the first two. You were on the road and no way to write you and then later there seemed no point. You were gone."

"I didn't want to be, you know. I had to stay with my family. Dad was sick. They needed me."

"I know that."

"I thought of seeing you again. I always thought I'd come back someday and see you again."

"Did you?" She felt a rush of pleasure.

"Molly, we may not have much time. We must talk."

She nodded. She knew it was coming. The moment she had both prayed for and dreaded.

"I have to know. The boy, Edwin. You said — is he — "

"You know. Please don't make me say it."

"My God."

It was a moment before he spoke again. Then,

"Why didn't you write me? Why didn't you let me know?"

He looked as if he really cared, as if he was hurt. Yet it seemed such a foolish question. He looked more like the boy she had remembered as he turned to her with his frowning question than the stranger he had become.

"It was too late," she said at last. "It was months before you were settled in Nebraska and there was an address for me to write to. By that time, I was —" She paused. She had never talked of such things with a man before. "It was too late. It would have taken weeks to hear from you, and what could you have done, anyway?"

"I would have married you. I would have come back if I'd known."

"How? How could you have married me? I was sixteen and you weren't much older. A schoolboy. You had no way to take care of a wife and baby."

"I'd have found a way."

"You say that now, but you have to remember how it *was*. We were so young. You've just had a few minutes to think about this. I've had *years*. Months and months of trying to decide what to do and wanting to die. I figured your folks would try to keep you from coming back, even if you wanted to, and I didn't know if you did. You say you would have, but you were young then and free. Free as you should have been. You were a boy, and I had become a woman. I remember your letters. Three letters. They were sweet, but they were a schoolboy's letters, full of longing and promises and pretty words, but I needed a husband."

"So you took Jake."

83

He made it sound as if she had cheated someone. Again, she felt a strange mixture of anger and guilt and another emotion she could not name, but which filled her with anguish and made her talk too fast.

"He worked for my father, and he had known me since I was a child. He was a good man, and he'd always liked me, and when he heard about my trouble, he offered to marry me."

"The hired man. You had to marry the hired man!"

"Don't you say that! Don't you ever say anything against Jake! And don't you accuse me. I never lied to Jake and I did what I had to do!"

"I didn't mean it that way. I just meant—my God, I did *that* to you and you had to marry the hired man and—Molly, did you love him at all? Did you *care* for him?"

"Oh, Hugh," She gave him the same smile she gave Edwin when he was being foolish. "It wasn't important how I felt about him. I was four months gone and the neighbors knew. He said he was going west to homestead and told my father he'd marry me and take the child as his own and never hold it up to me. And he did. He did all of that."

"He's been good to you then?"

"Yes."

"You've been happy?"

"Happy? The questions you ask! What is happiness? I've been safe, protected, loved, in a way. I guess I've been happy enough. As much as I deserved. It's not easy homesteading. And we haven't been lucky."

"You don't—" he started to say something and then couldn't get it out. She knew what was coming and she faced him and he finished, "You don't have other

84

children."

It was a question. She knew she was blushing, but she kept her head up. "If you're asking me if I've been a true wife to him, I have. I've tried. I lost two babies. I probably can't have more."

"I'm sorry. I'm sorry. For everything."

"It was God's will. I sinned and I was punished."

"Don't say that. You never sinned."

"What would you call that day in the barn?"

"Beautiful. I thought it was beautiful, the way it happened. The first time for us both. I thought it was as God intended."

She could not look at him then, she felt such a rush of emotion. She had thought that, too, thought it a thousand times, but it was not what a woman wronged should think. Not the way it had proved to be for her with her lawful husband. Not the way it had ever been again. She could never say that that one perfect hour of making love with Hugh had been beautiful, but *he* had said it and she was full of joy that he remembered her that way. A sudden thought came to her and she had to ask.

"Have I changed much?"

Hugh was touched. It was such a feminine question. She was, of course, the most feminine of women. He was glad he was not sitting too close to her on the log. He might not have been able to resist the temptation to reach out and touch the strand of golden hair that had escaped its knot and lay along the curve of her neck. She had changed. Her youthful prettiness was gone, but she was still beautiful. He didn't know what it was exactly that made her so, the hair maybe, or her eyes. She had pale blue Scandinavian eyes—cool and far-away looking, but there was about her mouth with its full lips, a hint of sensuality. Did she want him to tell her she was beautiful? Did she want him to make love to her again even though she was another man's wife? Would he, if she did? Or did she only want a reassurance that she had not been robbed of everything in her that had been fresh and lovely?

"You're just the same."

"That's not true," she said to keep in check the thrilling surge of emotions his words had given her, "but thank you for saying it. Life's been hard on me. I'm not the pretty girl I was then. I'm not the girl—" She looked down at her work-worn hands, suddenly ashamed not just of how she looked, but that she had been foolish enough to speak of such things.

"I have Edwin. I have a fine son and that's all that matters."

"He *is* fine. He's a beautiful boy. And smart too. You've done a fine job with him."

"I always wanted you to see him. I always thought that someday you'd come back and know the truth." *Know that I never stopped thinking of you*, her heart longed to add.

"If only you'd let me know."

"Would you have been happier, knowing?"

"It would have driven me crazy."

"See then, I was right. It was better to forget."

"And did you?"

"Did I—?"

"Forget."

"Don't. Don't ask such questions. We have no right to talk that way. It's over. I don't know why we've met again, why God let this happen. Maybe it was meant

86

that you should see your son, but there is nothing between us. It's over."

"How can it be, Molly? How can it be over when you have my son, when you're—When I feel so—"

"Stop!" She shouted at him, suddenly terrified, not just by his words but by her own surging need to be in his arms and give in to the desire she saw in his eyes. "Don't talk that way. He's not your son!"

"What?"

"Forget I told you. Forget all of it. He's Jake's son. Jake was the one that helped me birth him and raise him. Jake walked the floor when he was sick, and it was Jake who taught him to ride a mule and behave like a man—all that counts for something! He's as much Jake's son as yours—more Jake's. And I'm Jake's wife. It doesn't matter what happened between us once. So don't you think you can come along after all these years and change things!"

"Don't think I *want* to!"

"What?" His sudden anger seemed to pierce her. Couldn't he see that she had no choice but to push him away, so fierce was her own need?

"Don't get the idea because I had to know about you and the boy that I still—that—that I want anything from you. I came to the Black Hills to look for gold, not to look for you."

"I know that. Don't you think I know that? Don't think I want anything from you. Go off on your adventure then. It doesn't change anything."

He looked like he wanted to hit her, and she wanted to scream at him, to throw things. To push him forever from her. They faced each other with their sudden and terrible anger. Hugh stood up and she was afraid he

87

was leaving her forever, and then, as if he saw that fear, his expression changed.

"Of course it changes things. Of course, I feel different *knowing*. Knowing I'm responsible for what's happened to you. For Edwin. But what can I do now? You're right, you—the boy—you're Jake's now."

"I didn't expect it to be otherwise. To be your responsibility."

"Don't make it sound that way. As if I wouldn't take responsibility. I would have then and I would now, but what can I do? I think it's better if I leave."

"Leave?" She spoke quietly and calmly feeling as if a shroud had settled over her at the prospect of losing him again.

"The party. Leave the party and go off alone somewhere."

"You can't do that," she was terrified. "You can't leave the party. You can't just walk back and you can't go into the Black Hills alone."

"I'll steal a horse if I have to. I'd do what I have to do. If you can't stand to have me around. If it's going to hurt you and Jake. If you want me to leave—"

"I don't want you to go. I want you to be here. To get to know your son."

"Make up your mind, woman."

"Don't leave the party on account of me. You can't go on alone and going back now might mean you'd never make your strike. Have your adventure. Stay on. We can handle this. Jake won't be hurt. He'll never know there was anything between us and they'll be nothing more, except—"

"Except?" He stared at her, his dark eyes intense and searching. "What would you have of me now?"

Molly was confused by what she thought she saw in his eyes, by the implication of the question. What did she want from him? What did she want that she could have? There were so many barren spaces in her life, but she could not put a name to any of them. She had learned to live only for her family. For her child. She could, she would, think only of her son. She refused even to acknowledge her own need.

"Edwin. You could help me with Edwin."

"Edwin?" he pulled back a little, his expression changing, losing its intensity. She felt relieved and rushed on, the words tumbling out. "You could help me with Edwin. Pay attention to him. Talk to him. Teach him his letters. You're an educated man. You could do things for the boy his father can't."

Hugh seemed to hesitate, as if he sensed some fallacy in what she asked. But it was true, she told herself. She was not being disloyal to Jake to admit he was not an educated man. And then, as if on cue, Edwin came running up, complaining that Jake and Luther had sent him back while they stayed to play cards and talk with the other men.

Hugh looked from the boy to her as if he were pondering something. Probably wondering about his freedom, she thought. His adventure. He'd avoided Edwin so far. Not wanted to be involved, she suspected, or to acknowledge what she'd implied when they met. She held her breath, sensing the importance of the moment, and then Hugh squatted down and spoke to the boy.

"Edwin, would you like a piggy-back ride? When my brother was little, he used to like to climb on my back. Would you like that?"

Edwin nodded solemnly and Hugh indicated he should use the log as a mounting block. With the boy on his back, he turned back to Molly.

"It's only until Custer City," he said. "When the wagon train reaches Custer, we'll disband. It's only for this little while. Till you're safe in a city again."

"I know," she whispered. "Just for a little while."

She was glad to see Edwin clinging happily to Hugh. The boy looked right with his father. She told herself not only in that moment, but later when she was forced to face the consequences of that evening, that she had done it for her son. She would tell herself that her mistake was not in getting Hugh to stay, nor in letting the boy climb on his back. It was in not turning away soon enough, in taking just a moment to stand there beside Hugh and Edwin and allow herself the tiniest fantasy that they were a family. For in that moment that the three of them stood together with the setting sun lighting their fair hair, they looked like a family.

And it was then that Frank Pearson rode up.

He had a brace of jack rabbits slung over his saddle horn and his rifle cradled in his arms. He reined up and looked at the three of them for a moment. Then he seemed to relax, and his scarred face broke into a grin that revealed yellow jagged teeth. He acknowledged Molly with a fingertip touch to his sombrero.

"Evening, Mississ. I brought you some rabbits. Didn't know if your *man*," he looked at Hugh pointedly, "had any luck hunting."

"Mr. Lewis has been occupied with his mules," Molly said cooly. "Mr. Everett was about to g*ive Edwin a piggy-back ride*."

90

"I see that," Pearson said, then turned to the boy. "How'd you like to ride a real horse, son? You can climb right up here behind me."

Edwin had been riding astride with one man or another for most of the day, but he hesitated, even as Hugh took a tighter grip on the boy's legs.

"Thank you," Molly said. "But it's his bedtime."

"Ma!" Edwin whined, but Molly cut him off with a sharp word. "Do as I say, Edwin. It's past your bedtime now."

Hugh didn't give Edwin another chance to argue but took him to the wagon, feeling both foolish to be seen toting the boy and irrationally annoyed at Pearson's efforts to be friendly with Molly. When he returned, he found Pearson staring at Molly with a look he did not like.

"You know," Pearson said suddenly, "That boy's the spitting image of you!"

Hugh was stunned; then realized Pearson was talking to Molly.

"What a terrible thing to say!" Molly had made the same mistake.

"Huh?" Pearson cocked his head and stared at Molly. Hugh started to step forward to try to shush her, but it was too late.

"What a terrible thing to *imply*. How dare you!"

Pearson's eyes flickered between them. He grinned suddenly. "Why, I meant he looked like you, Mrs. Lewis. I wasn't even thinking of Mr. Everett, but now that you point it out to me, there is a sort of resemblance."

"I—" Molly sputtered.

"You folks neighbors back in Iowa?" Pearson

sneered.

"Of course not," Hugh said, trying to keep his voice even and the situation under control. "That's a poor sort of joke." He wanted to swing at Pearson and drag him off the horse and shut him up, but reason told him the man could know nothing, and he would only make the situation worse by overreacting.

"Sorry," Pearson grinned. "I was just making conversation. Didn't mean to offend. Never like to hit a nerve, especially with a lady." He jerked at the horse's head and turned back toward the other wagons, then swung back toward them. With a smooth gesture, he swung the rifle into its scabbard and held up the brace of rabbits tied together by their hind paws.

"Forgot to give you your rabbit." From nowhere he produced his knife and separated the brace by slashing through the haunches of one rabbit. He let it drop to the ground, spurred his horse, and, with a grin over his shoulder, rode away.

Hugh was livid. "I'll get that ba—"

"Stop it, Hugh." Molly grabbed his arm.

"I'll shut him up."

"Stop it, Hugh. You'll only cause trouble. You'll draw attention to us."

"You heard what he said! Saw how he treated you!"

"He didn't mean anything. I took it wrong. It was all my fault. I thought he meant Edwin looked like you and—"

"But he's got to be shut up."

"No, no. I don't think he'll say anything to anyone. He's got no proof. No one has ever doubted Edwin was Jake's before. We just have to act like nothing happened, and Pearson will forget it."

"I'll make him forget it."

"No, Hugh. You mustn't. Please listen to me. I know."

So he agreed finally. She persuaded him just as she had persuaded him to stay with the wagon train. He even cleaned the rabbit for her, though she insisted she could do it herself. He told himself she was a lady who needed to be cared for. He told himself he was doing it for Edwin. And that it was all a temporary interlude, and he was still off on an adventure to the gold fields and could leave her behind at any time.

He told himself that nothing had changed.

Chapter Six

When Austin Avery came back at the end of the week, the green velvet dress was finished and hanging on the rear wall of the shop. Emerald had just pulled out the last of the basting threads. He came into the shop as suddenly and as unexpectedly as he had the first time. Her mother had just left; it was almost as if he had been watching, though Emerald did not think him to be so calculating. They were alone.

He was as handsome as she had remembered. He was tall and elegantly dressed. His hair was as black as her own, but his eyes were dark while hers were green. His skin looked to be the kind that would tan deep and rich if he had been the kind of man who worked outdoors, but it was obvious he was not that kind of man. She was a small woman, petite and round, and she had the feeling he might simply pick her up and carry her away.

It was not just the way he looked that struck her as he walked into the shop. It was the moment. The possibilities. The scene they made together, he darkly handsome, elegantly dressed and she, round and pretty, her black hair piled in curls on top of her head, her eyes flashing, her cheeks flushed from pinching and the excitement of the scene. She had raised one hand to the throat of her blouse spontaneously, but now she kept it there, aware on some level that it symbolized the uncertainty she wished to project. An uncertainty she did not feel.

For a long time they just stood and looked at each other. She was trembling within but at the same time aware of the scene it made, the play that was about to begin. She knew, too, when it was time to begin the action. She tore her eyes away from his and pointed dramatically to the dress. But he only nodded and held out his hand, offering her a small box. Wondering, she took it and opened it to find the emerald ear bobs she had admired in the shop window. They were so beautiful they made her dizzy. How had he known she coveted the ear bobs? It seemed a sign. Something wonderous had begun. Something that was meant to be.

"For you," he said at last, only the hint of a smile playing about his eyes and never reaching his lips. "The dress too."

This she had expected; she was ready. She kept a hold of the box, but tilted her head up proudly and met his steely gaze as she said coyly, "And what, sir, do you want from me in return?"

"Everything."

Everything. It was just the line she had hoped for. The part she would have written for him, and she smiled secretly inside even as she shrank back as if he had frightened her. It was delightful that it was going as she had planned. He would be visiting the shop often when her mother was gone, bringing her little gifts and begging her to become his mistress.

"I want you to come with me tonight."

"What?"

"I want you to come away with me tonight. I'm taking the Mississippi Belle up river on my way West. I plan to be gone some time securing mining interests in the Black Hills. I want you to come with me."

"Tonight?"

"Tonight?"

Emerald's jaw fell open. She knew it was an unattractive gesture and quickly bit her lip, then realized that was no better. She was stunned. She had expected him to ask her to be his mistress, but to *leave* with him, to go away *tonight* on a riverboat, it was not as she had planned the scene. He had taken the control away from her, and that was something she had not expected. She had always known she could control men, send them away dejected or blushing with hope with one look from her eyes or the tilt of her chin. She had thought this man would be the same, only challenge her to greater efforts with her play acting. Now she realized that if she went with Austin Avery, she would be giving herself up to a will stronger than her own. Or was he stronger? Could she control him? The thought was exciting, as was the thought that somehow in giving in to his will something unexplainable and delicious might happen to her.

"I don't know what to say, sir. Your suggestion is very bold." She did not especially like the line, but she was playing for time, trying to sort out her emotions.

"The dress and the ear bobs are yours whether you

choose to come with me or not. They were meant for you."

She had, of course, never considered giving them up. But would they be enough in themselves? Could she win with them another man, with the qualities of stability and responsibility her mother would urge on her? She clicked off the possibilities in her mind. Could there be another man somewhere in the world who would be more satisfying to win than Austin Avery? She doubted it; she doubted there could ever be a man as exciting and as mysterious and as challenging as the dark-haired stranger who stood before her, waiting for her answer. He had, after all, *known* that the green velvet and the emerald ear bobs were meant for her. He had *known* what she wanted him to say. As young and inexperienced as she was, Emerald O'Brien realized a great truth. There are few men in this world who ever *know* what is in a woman's heart.

Emerald made up her mind. There had never been any real doubt about it from the moment Austin Avery first walked into her shop the week before. But she intended to play out her scene.

"You have overwhelmed me, sir. To walk in here and make such a suggestion. To ask me to leave my poor widowed mother and my brothers and sisters, to—

"You don't have to decide now," he interrupted her and spoke, she thought, a bit too brusquely, especially when she was about to manage a few tears which would have set her eyes off nicely.

"I realize you have many things to think over," he said cooly. "I am sorry I cannot make my proposal in a more traditional way, but my business interests in the Black Hills will not allow me the time to court you in the more leisurely manner of the old South."

She allowed him a smile. She liked the turn of the conversation. He was talking of courting and proposals. It was on the tip of her tongue to ask just what his intentions were, when abruptly he picked his wide planter's hat from the counter and tipped it to her before putting it on his head.

"So, Madam, the choice is yours. If you wish to take a chance, then be at the dock at 8 o'clock tonight. When the Mississippi Belle leaves, I will be on it. With you or without you."

He turned and, before she could speak, was gone.

It did not take her long to decide. She knew this was it—her chance to get away from her mother and all that was dull and dreary about the Mississippi waterfront town. More than that, this was her chance for something she could not quite put a name to, something that was wondrous and exciting and made her feel she herself was glamorous. She had always expected inside that she might be beautiful and she had noticed that she turned men's heads, but never until she saw herself in that mirror as Austin Avery saw her did she have any sense at all of the woman she was or could become. This was her opportunity and she must grab at it. If she did not, she would deserve to be the same woman forever.

True, Austin Avery had not mentioned marriage directly, nor even love, but he had hinted at it, and surely those things would come later. She was not without wiles.

Emerald wove herself a fantasy of a life with Austin Avery. She made of it a tapestry even richer than the green velvet. It was a tapestry threaded through with stately houses, elegant clothes, rich foods, all sorts of exciting and theatrical events. In her fantasy admiring eyes were always on her and she had power. Never again would she have to bow her will to that of her mother or to the whimsy of customers who envied her youth and beauty.

Her dream ended with Austin Avery regaining his fortune in the mines and returning to the South in triumph to buy back the old plantation. She would reign there in splendor, as his bride, wearing the emerald earbobs and, at her throat, a matching choker. How people would stare at her then!

Her fantasy was not one of love. She had known so little of that in her life, she could not know how it would feel to love or be loved. She sensed a man could give her back the feeling she had lost when her father went away, the satisfaction of knowing she came first in his affections, for she could always win his smiles and hugs away from her plainer sisters with her little songs and dances and pretty ways. To Emerald, love meant attention.

She did not, of course, articulate these thoughts. She knew only that she had been waiting all her life for Austin Avery or someone like him who would choose her, and only her, and in that moment decide her fate. He was so unlike every other man who had noticed her. Other men she could turn to jelly with the merest frown or tilt of her chin, but Avery had known instinctively what it took to win her — a fantasy, a dream, a play in which she would star. He would know how to play out the drama. He would make love to her. And she knew that it would be done well.

And so, it did not take her long at all to decide to

run away with Austin Avery.

That night for a few hours, the fantasy came true. The Mississippi Belle was like a floating wedding cake, or a fairy castle with she the princess. She had often watched the steamboats churning up and down the river and dreamed of someday escaping on one. She was not disappointed, for inside it was a palace of carved wood, gilt and scarlet paint and red plush. There were servants to wait on her, gentlemen to admire her, and women to peer at her with envy. And the food! Seven kinds of meat and three soups and fishes and dozens of desserts all cunningly displayed with raisins and bananas and oranges and figs and pineapples — foods she had not known existed. And the drinks! Champagne in goblets so thin and clear and delicate she was almost afraid to pick them up. She tasted everything and thought she would never get enough.

And through it all, Avery's eyes upon her. And saying *such things* to her across the table.

And then late that night, she and Avery alone in his state room. Avery unbuttoning her green velvet dress. Avery kissing her lips, her neck, her breasts. She was trembling and afraid; her mother had warned her men did terrible things. But then he looked directly at her with the closest look to a smile she had yet seen on his lips. She admired his white skin and the dark lock of hair that fell over one eye making him look devilish, yet familiar. But most she looked into his eyes, for it was in his eyes that she saw herself reflected and found that she was beautiful. It was for that she loved and needed him — for the image of herself that danced within his eyes.

She did not wonder in that moment if what he saw reflected in *her* eyes that *he* loved was Austin Avery himself.

She only knew that by the time he slid the green velvet dress from her hips and carried her to the bed that she was ready for something wonderous to happen.

It was that moment she would remember later. Austin Avery carrying her to the bed. It would take her some time to appreciate what happened next, though appreciate it she would in the days and weeks to come. But that moment of giving herself to him she would always remember as perfect. For in giving herself to Austin Avery, she felt a tremendous and wonderful surge of power. For she recognized that in that moment she was the whole world to him.

The feeling of mattering to Avery did not last long, although she was always able to recapture it in other moments when he made love to her. He took her again and again that first night as the riverboat chugged up the Mississippi and her body cried out in pain that was mixed with the beginnings of a pleasure she had only dreamed existed. That he stayed with her all night the first night did not seem important.

But it seemed very important that the next night was different. He insisted she wear the emerald green dress and watch him gamble. She enjoyed the glances she received from the other men at the gaming table, but she was aware that Avery hardly looked at her all evening. Still, it was exciting at first. He won over a thousand dollars that night and when they finally returned to their cabin at three in the morning, he made love to her, calling her his lucky charm.

Then, to her utter amazement, he got up and dressed and went back to his game. That night set the pattern of their life together, but it was only after he left her bed night after night to play cards until dawn in the Texas room of the great steamer, that she finally admitted to herself that he was what she had suspected him to be all along—a professional gambler.

She had given him her whole life; he had something else.

Chapter Seven

Hugh stood on the shore and stared at the river. The North Platte was a challenge at any time, but Hobart's party had arrived to find it flooding, sweeping dirt and debris along and overflowing its banks in great swirls of muddy water. It seemed an impossible barrier. Donnelly said they must camp and wait; eventually the river would recede. The others used the time to secure the wagon loads, rest the stock, and practice shooting; but Hugh returned again and again to stare at the river and brood.

In the three days the wagon train had traveled since leaving Sidney and the day they had camped by the river, it seemed to Hugh that not only the country but something within him had changed. He had grown harder and leaner with the journey and had stopped shaving, so that when he touched his face he was surprised at the coarseness of his growing beard. He seemed more a man, but a man he was not sure he could like, for Molly's innocent suggestion that he stay with the party for Edwin's sake was causing him increasing uneasiness, as if something in his gut was being slowly twisted and tightened.

There was another party waiting to ford the river, a freight caravan of a dozen bull whackers, their heavy freight wagons and herds of oxen. Somehow the presence of the bull whackers and their beasts seemed to intensify Hugh's conflict.

The bull whackers were crude men who talked of killing Indians and slaughtering buffalo with equal nonchalance. They welcomed Hobart's party to their campfires and regaled them with their tales. Most of them had begun their careers on the frontier as buffalo hunters, and their talk was of slaughter. Hugh was disturbed to learn their killing of the buffalo — as many as a hundred head per man per day — had been part of a sanctioned, if not official, government policy of destroying the Indians' way of life; but the others seemed to regard the killing of men and beasts as equal sport.

"I wish I could have killed me a buffalo," Edwin said, and Luther ruffled his hair and replied, "Don't worry, you'll get you an Indian."

Hugh was stunned at his brother's attitude, even more stunned when he tried to talk reason to him, admitting that although the Indians had certainly killed many a homesteader, the white men, too, had been at fault. Luther conceded no trace of humanity to the redman, but said he intended to notch his gun for every Indian he shot.

Hugh talked then of white men's sins. Of Chivington and his men's slaughter of innocent women and children, and Luther came back with "Nits make lice."

And then Jake had laughed as he caught the meaning. "Papooses make Indians! I get it. That's a good one."

Edwin laughed with the men. Hugh did not like it, but felt powerless to say more. Afterwards Molly managed a few words to him away from the others.

"You see? You see how it is with these Western men? I've got to get Edwin back to decent folk. I can't have him raised out here with people who make a joke out of killing."

He had no answer for her. It was no place for a child. Or, for a woman; he could see that.

"I'm afraid, Hugh," she said to him. "I'm afraid of this place and what's going to happen to us. Promise you won't leave us. Promise you'll stay and protect us from the Indians and from men like that."

And so, once again, he had made a promise to her and now, facing the river with a cold breeze blowing over it and chilling him, and the laughter of the bullwhackers coming from the camp behind him, he wondered how he could keep that promise.

Though the river had barely receded, the bull whackers were to attempt a crossing the next day, and Hobart said if the bull teams succeeded, his own party would cross next. Pictures of Molly and Edwin adrift in the wagon and careening down river tormented Hugh, but other pictures arose in his mind which troubled him more. Molly as he remembered her, young and unafraid, laughing and blushing as she walked beside him, turning to him, her cool blue eyes suddenly merry; Molly, warm and yielding in his arms. He tried to crowd out these images with thoughts of loyalty to Jake.

So he faced the river, knowing that whatever happened, whatever dangers they faced, and whatever

105

ways Molly and Edwin and Luther were affected by crossing into the forbidden land, the responsibility was his. He had by his own foolishness brought them all to this. And if Molly or Edwin was hurt, or Luther became a man who lived by the gun, the fault was his.

And what of yourself, he wondered, touching again the new stubble of his beard. *What of the beast within you? Are you sure you can cross that river yourself and still remain a civilized man?*

As Donnelly and the bull whackers had predicted, the waters slowly but steadily receded, and the next morning the freight teams began their crossing. It was an impressive sight. Three freight wagons were usually hooked together and pulled by a team of seven yoke of oxen, but to test the river, the trail wagon was unhitched, part of its cargo stacked upon the other two wagons, and three teams yoked to the lead wagon. That made forty-two oxen to pull the two wagons. It seemed impossible that the bull whackers could handle such a large number of the great long-horned beasts. But they did.

Although they usually walked beside their teams, the bull whackers were mounted on horses to cross the river. Each swung a long buckskin bullwhip over his horse's head. The popping of the bullwhips was accompanied by a profanity so rich it made Molly blush. The line of oxen was stretched nearly across the stream before the first wagon slid down the muddy bank and into the swollen river. Hobart explained how the long team would keep the wagons moving even if one ox should fall or flounder in quicksand. If the heavy wagons stopped for an instant, they would quickly sink to their hubs. It seemed to Hugh that Hobart knew everything about pioneering, and he was ashamed of his own ignorance.

The crossing took most of the day as the huge team of oxen had to be driven back across the river several times to fetch the remaining wagons. By late afternoon, however, the freight train had moved on out of sight; the flood waters had receded farther, and it was their turn.

After all Hugh's dread and anticipation the crossing of the North Platte was anticlimactic. It was not that it was so easy, it was just that he had no real part in it. The crossing was the responsibility of the mule drivers. There was nothing for him to do but climb into the wagon beside Luther and let Jake do his job, which he did expertly. The mules struck into the water surely and even when the current seemed to lift and sway the wagon they did not falter, but at Jake's urging only leaned harder into the traces.

And yet something did happen at the crossing of the North Platte, something that marked a change in Hugh, as if he had, indeed, left behind the civilized man.

It was after Jake had driven the wagon across. Hugh helped Edwin and then Molly down from the wagon so they could watch the other wagons cross. Hugh had helped Molly in and out of the wagon a dozen times before, one hand at her elbow or hand and the other at her waist in the stiff and polite gesture of a gentleman, never giving in to the urge to grasp her to him for an instant as a man will with a girl he is courting or seducing. Yet even in this most formal of touching,

Hugh was always sure that something seemed to pass between him and Molly, and he had been concerned that someone else might see them and know.

And that day after they crossed the North Platte, it happened that as Hugh helped Molly from the wagon, Pearson rode up. He sat there silently on his horse and saw the smile Molly gave Hugh and the way their hands touched for just a moment longer than was necessary. He saw the way Hugh stared after her as she followed Edwin down the bank where the others were gathering to watch the crossing. And then when Hugh turned back to latch the wagon tail, Pearson sat there on his horse, his sombrero tipped back to reveal his grin.

"So," he said, "you did it, didn't you? You got some of that."

Hugh was startled. He had not expected to see Pearson; he had just been thinking how foolish had been his premonition of danger at the crossing of the Platte. It took him a moment to react, not believing at first that Pearson would dare to taunt him with such a remark.

"Can't say as I blame you for getting into her, even if Lewis is your friend," Pearson continued, tilting the sombrero back down over his face and jerking his horse's head around with his reins. "I wouldn't mind having some of that myself."

Hugh reacted then, lunging forward to jerk Pearson off his horse, but even as he did it, Pearson gouged the animal with his spurs, wheeled and rode away.

The hooves of Pearson's horse sent a spatter of mud into Hugh's face.

Pearson laughed as he rode away.

I'll kill him, Hugh thought. *I'll kill him. I swear it.*

And so after the crossing of the North Platte, it was not just the threat of the Sioux that caused Hugh to keep his gun always at his side. One part of him burned to seek Pearson out and shut him up, but the more logical side of his nature argued that if he fought the man, Pearson's accusations might come out in the open. In a way, he would have been glad. He hated the lie he and Molly were living, but he knew he had no right to expose Molly and Edwin, nor did he wish to hurt Jake. He knew it was better to keep quiet, but at the same time he resolved to take no more of Pearson's insults. His anger was intense. He had not known he could hate so much. He wondered how long he could lock up his fury.

As if sensing Hugh's mood, Pearson avoided the Lewis wagon.

The Indian danger was real now, and Hugh noticed the entire party seemed to grow more tense as they ventured farther into the forbidden territory. Hobart took to swinging his big roan back through the line of march several times a day, reminding them to keep together. The country was dreary, the trail, tedious. But none of them was really afraid until they reached the first and last outpost of civilization on the trail to the Black Hills, the Red Cloud Indian Agency.

They had all looked forward to stopping at the agency, hoping to hear some good news of the government's negotiations with the Sioux, expecting even to learn that the Black Hills had been officially opened to white settlement and they could expect military protection on the rest of their journey.

They were to be disappointed.

The Red Cloud Agency was situated pleasantly enough on a fine bit of bottom land near the White River. Behind the agency were extensive buttes of sandstone rock. But the agency, and especially the agency store, was a dreary place. The store stocked only the most basic of necessities. Hugh bought Edwin a piece of horehound candy, but there were so many Indians loitering about the place Molly kept the boy close by. Jake tried to make a joke of it. Hadn't she expected there to be Indians at an Indian agency? Donnelly told her there was nothing to fear from the agency Indians. They were tame. It was the wild bands of northern Sioux they had to fear. Hugh joined the others in attempting to reassure her, but he had to admit Molly was right about one thing. The Indians seemed sullen. Even the squaw men, white men who lived with Indian wives, seemed hostile. Hugh did not like the way they eyed Molly. Like the Indians, the squaw men seemed fascinated by her fair hair. They were strange men with strange accents. French, Hugh guessed. They all said the same sort of thing, *Go back. Trouble for you if you go on. No young mans here. Old mans yes, squaws, papooses, yes. What that mean? Trouble. All young men leave agency. Go north to Sitting Bull. I see fresh scalps two days ago. White scalps. You go back now.*

Hugh didn't like being threatened, especially by whites who drew government allotments for their wives and half-breed children, moved freely on agency lands, and then tried to intimidate other whites, keeping them from entering the Black Hills. But still, he felt a chill when they spoke. They were right. There were no young men at the Red Cloud Agency. Hugh knew Hobart and the rest were wondering the same thing. *Where were the warriors?*

There were soldiers at the agency. They came from nearby Fort Robinson and, like the Indians, loitered about the store. Donnelly told Hugh Fort Robinson had been built four years before to protect the Indian agent and his family from the supposedly tame agency Indians, but there had been times in those four years that the agent had been a virtual prisoner of the Sioux. It made Hugh wonder. If the government couldn't control Indians who were supposedly at peace, what protection could it offer from the renegades?

"What are your orders?" Hugh boldly asked a young lieutenant. "Will you try to keep prospectors out of the Black Hills?"

The lieutenant looked at the other soldiers uncertainly. As ranking officer, it was his place to talk. "A few months ago," he finally said, "our orders were to remove all whites except government employees from the Hills. That order has never been rescinded, but we haven't any *current* orders to remove anyone. So we've been standing by and watching parties go in. There's too many to stop without declaring war on the civilian population."

"Then the army won't try to stop us?" Hugh asked.

"No, but—"

"But?"

"But we don't have orders to *protect* you either. You're on your own."

The others seemed to think that was good enough. Hugh might have thought so too, if Molly and Edwin hadn't been along. He wished the army would offer

111

protection. His uncertainty was growing. He felt they needed more information. He asked if anyone there had actually been to the Black Hills. The squaw men looked at each other and smiled, but none would talk.

There was, however, one young non-commissioned officer who was terribly excited about their expedition. He said he had been in the Hills with Custer in '74 and was convinced there was gold in the region. It was, he declared, the most beautiful country he had ever seen. When the squaw men heard the name of Custer, a ripple seemed to go through the group. "You know what the Sioux call Custer's trail to the Hills? The one you'll be following?" a squaw man said, spitting. "The Thieves' Trail, that's what they call it. They figure Custer's the biggest thief of them all, but all white men who come to the Hills for gold are thieves and deserve to die."

The remark angered Hugh, but he ignored it and persisted in questioning the soldiers, asking about the present location of troops in the field. The soldiers hadn't much information to give. General Crook had been in the field since March to round up the Sioux and bring them back to the reservation. There was also a rumor that Terry and Custer and the Seventh Cavalry were to be campaigning that summer. If so, they were certain to meet the Sioux in a battle that would once and for all settle the question of the Black Hills in favor of white occupation and civilization.

This news made everyone feel better.

They camped that night within sight of Fort Robinson, but they drew no sense of security from the fort, for it, too, was a disappointment. It seemed inadequate to offer protection, but when Hugh said as much to Hobart, he made a little speech about the fort and the agency it stood to protect.

"Fort Robinson is as good as most army posts. It serves its purpose. The agency permits a lot of white men to profit off the government by cheating the Indians, and the fort is an efficient agent for spreading contamination and disease — cholera, diptheria, small pox and others; all of which serve to effectively reduce the Indian population."

Hugh had learned that to argue with Hobart would be to argue with years spent on the plains living kinds of experiences Hugh had only read about. Still, he thought Hobart unduly cynical. Despite all Hugh had learned since leaving Nebraska, he did not want to admit the government was engaged in a systematic program to wipe out the Indians. Hugh had left Nebraska with the notion the Sioux would be peacefully persuaded to adopt an agrarian life which would allow civilization to proceed. Now he was beginning to see that a solution to the Indian problem would not come so easily. He felt himself growing angry and did not know if he was angry at the government for trying to impose civilization upon the Indians, at the Indians for refusing to accept it, or at himself for becoming part of a movement that seemed destined to lead to war.

When they lined up the wagons to move out the next morning, they were five men short. Hobart got them moving before they had time to think about the desertions. It was the strong who remained, he assured them. They did not need cowards and weaklings on their venture. They were better off without them. It was only five men, after all.

But Hugh knew it was five fewer guns and that worried him. To turn back now would have made him feel a weakling and a fool. The sort of man who deserved to grow old within the limits of Carpenter, Nebraska. But for Molly and Edwin, he was afraid. Jake's confidence seemed unshaken and Hugh wondered if he should try to persuade Jake to take his family back to civilization, but he did not try. Later, he would admit to himself that it was Molly and not just his dreams of pioneering and gold that he was unwilling to give up. That day he concentrated only on walking and trying to talk the others out of their discouragement.

By the end of the day, he seemed to have convinced not just the other men, but himself. Their spirits were higher, although, as always happened in the afternoon, their line of march trailed far behind the wagons.

Hobart galloped back to them to urge them to keep up. He had Edwin riding behind him, clinging to his back and grinning happily at the treat. Hugh was both relieved and frustrated at the way Edwin had become the camp pet. He wanted to be close to the boy, but reason told him not to care too much for a son that belonged to another man.

While Hobart rode alongside, the men walked faster, but once he and Edwin galloped to the head of the column, they again fell behind the wagons. Hugh paused to let Luther catch up with him, and was suddenly pleased at the sight of his brother. The journey had been tough on him at first; his new boots had worn blisters on his feet. But now he was thinner and tougher-looking from all the walking, and Hugh had the pleasant thought that the journey was making a man of him. He had not been wrong to bring him, after all. He felt happy. They had not let Red Cloud get them down.

He was whistling when he saw them.

Horsemen topping the ridge to his left and boldly riding down to the wagon train.

There was no mistaking them for another band of discouraged Black Hillers, nor for the ragged agency Indians.

These were the Sioux.

Chapter Eight

There was no comfortable way to ride in a wagon,
Molly decided. She preferred walking, but walking
was likely to bring her into contact with Hugh, something best avoided. Being near him brought both a
persistent, nagging sense of loss and a wild rushing
joy. Both emotions disturbed her. She found it ironical
that she should be cooking for him; and as she
struggled with the unfamiliar task of preparing meals
over an open fire, she told herself it was Jake and
Edwin she was "doing" for. Yet when she handed
Hugh his dinner plate or when their eyes met over the
campfire or their hands touched as he brought her
wood or water or helped her in or out of the wagon,
she could not control her blush. Her fair skin, so quick
to signal her emotions, had always been an embarrassment to her; now she was sure her flaming cheeks were
a beacon to the rest of the camp.

She would find herself staring at her own reflection
in the scrap of mirror she kept in her trunk, trying to
find a composed expression for her face, one she could
wear even when a look from Hugh sent her heart
pounding. Then she would find herself wondering if

she was still pretty and knowing that she had no business wondering such a thing would send her to blushing again.

She told herself she had asked Hugh to stay only because it was dangerous for him to go on alone and because she needed his protection and help with Edwin. Having denied her memory of him and her own feelings for so long, it was possible to convince herself she was thinking only of what was best for the others.

Trying to sort out the meaning of Hugh's presence occupied most of her thinking time, but on the day the party marched away from Fort Robinson, she had succeeded in freeing her mind from her worries long enough to take a nap in the back of the wagon. Hobart had taken Edwin off on his horse, and it was good to have no responsibility, but to doze in the wagon, warm from the day's sun. When Jake stopped the wagon she awoke with a start, surprised that it was already time to camp. Then she heard Jake's shouts.

"Indians! Indians coming!"

She thought he must be joking, though he was not a joking man. She started to climb out onto the wagon seat, but Jake held her back. She could see only the wagon ahead of them, but Jake's manner told her something was wrong. "Edwin!" she cried. "Where's Edwin?"

Just then Hobart galloped up beside their wagon. Edwin was not with him. "Don't get excited, Lewis," he said as he reined in his horse. "It's a party of braves, but I don't think they'll want to fight. We're too evenly matched. I stuck Edwin in the lead wagon with Morris soon as I saw the Indians. I don't want them to see the

117

boy or you, Mrs. Lewis, so get back in that wagon and keep out of sight!"

"I have to get Edwin!" She struggled to get past Jake.

"Stay down!" Jake commanded.

"Get in that wagon and shut up!" Hobart shouted, drawing his horse up so it almost hit against the wagon. "The Sioux are going to be swarming all over the place in a few minutes. We'll try to keep 'em away from the wagons, but we don't want to provoke a fight. They'll probably just look us over, palaver awhile, maybe do some trading. If they see they can't scare us, chances are they'll move on."

"But Edwin?"

"I can't bring him back now. Morris will keep him safe. Besides, Morris has a gun, and you don't." He wheeled his horse, but reined him in long enough to say, "Lewis, you get her stowed in the wagon and come on with the men. The more guns they see, the sooner they'll stop trying to buffalo us."

As frightened as Molly was, she would have gone after Edwin, but Hobart made her feel helpless— helpless and a little angry. She told herself the men knew best. Jake jockeyed the wagon into the middle of the knot the others were forming and then poked his head inside long enough to announce he was joining the others.

"Stay with me, Jake!"

"Can't. All the men got to be there." He dropped the wagon flap and was gone.

She had never felt so alone. She hoped Hugh might come, but realized he would have to take his place among the men. She tried to control herself. She was a

118

grown woman; she must be brave. She tried not to think of what was whispered that Indians did to captured white women. She tried to peek out from under the canvas wagon cover, but she could see only grass. In the distance she could hear shouts, but could make no sense of what was happening. Then it grew quiet. She was reassuring herself that there would be no fighting when the shooting started.

She could not believe it at first. Hobart said the Sioux would never attack a well-armed party. Now she feared she would be killed, but even stronger than her fear was her need to protect her son. She started to climb over things to get out of the wagon. She would get to him, no matter what. If they were already fighting, it couldn't matter if the Indians saw her.

She had reached the end of the wagon and was about to pull aside the flap when it opened.

She jerked back, gasping. The Sioux were coming for her.

"Howdy, Mrs. Lewis, how you doing in there?"

It was Frank Pearson.

"Oh! It's you." She was faint with relief. "I thought they were coming to get me!"

"Who? The Indians?" He grinned, stepping up on the back of the wagon.

"Yes." She didn't like the way he was looking at her.

"Did you think a big naked buck was going to come in here and do it to you? Is that what you thought, Mrs. Lewis?"

He was climbing into the wagon. She backed up a little, clutching at the collar of her dress. She could see what was coming.

"Now that's something for a lady like you to be

thinking about, ain't it? Imagine you thinking about some young buck putting it to you. Just goes to show, you're the kind that can't get enough. Just like I figured. Just wanting it all the time, ain't you, Mrs. Lewis?"

"Get out! Get out of my wagon!"

He was through the flap and crawling toward her.

"And leave you all alone? With all those bad Indians ready to tear your clothes off? They'd take your scalp too, Mrs. Lewis. You wouldn't like that would you? But they'd love all blond hair. How does it look down, Mrs. Lewis?" He reached for her head. "I been wondering ever since I first saw you."

She had backed up as far as she could go. She told herself to keep calm and try to talk him out of it. "Please get out and leave me alone," she said, but she was crying. She didn't mean to cry.

"It'll just take a minute, Mrs. Lewis. Just a quick in and out. I'll be real careful not to tear your clothes or anything, you being such a lady."

"I'm going to scream!"

But he already had his hands on her. One holding her mouth closed and the other pulling at her hair, jerking the pins out savagely. "You can't scream, Mrs. Lewis. You'll bring the Sioux down on us. Unless, of course, you'd rather have all those bucks do it to you. I don't think you'd like that though. Even a bitch like you that pretends to be a lady wouldn't like how the Sioux do a woman."

He had her hair down now and had pulled her around so her back was against his chest. He kept one hand over her mouth so that she could hardly breathe. With the other hand he began unbuttoning her dress.

She began to struggle frantically, digging her finger-nails into his hands.

"So you think you ought to fight a little, just to make it look good? You don't have to put a show on for me. I know you're no lady. You done it with that Everett kid. And he ain't half the man I am."

She couldn't believe he was saying it. His other hand was on her breast now, squeezing it. Hard, too hard. She couldn't get enough air, and his hand covering her mouth smelled bad. She was afraid she would gag and then choke on it.

"I can't wait," he breathed. "I can't wait any longer, Mrs. Lewis. I got to put it in you." As he turned her around and laid her down, his hand came away from her mouth.

She looked up into his eyes. Dark piercing eyes that looked right through her. She twisted her face away from him. His breath was foul as he brought his face down and tried to kiss her, slobbering on her and scratching her face with his whiskers. She would scream. Jake would keep the Sioux from getting her. Pearson had his mouth on her breast now, wetly biting and sucking at it. She kept trying to push him away, but he was so much stronger than she.

"I'll tell," she said, shoving at his greasy head, grabbing his hair and trying to pull his head away from her breast. "I'll tell my husband, and he'll kill you."

He grabbed her arms and pinned them down as he raised up a little and looked at her. "No you won't." He grinned. "I already figured that out. I've had lots of time to plan this since I figured out you and Everett done it. You won't ever tell your husband what I done to you, Mrs. Lewis, cause if you do, I'll tell him you done it with Everett. He don't know that, does he? He don't even know the kid ain't his. That would be a shock, wouldn't it? For him to find out you got your lover boy along on this outing? How do you think he'll take that, Mrs. Lewis? Who do you think he'll try to kill first, me or the one that's been putting horns on him right in his own wagon?"

"You're lying. Those are all lies. Jake wouldn't believe—"

"Wouldn't he? You want to take a chance? Maybe you want to get him killed, is that it? You think your lover boy could kill him in a fight? Would you like that? Which one of 'em do you want to get killed?"

"Jake wouldn't do that, he's —"

"But you said he'd kill *me*, didn't you? And he'd have to *try*, wouldn't he? He'd be honor bound to defend his property. Has your husband ever killed anyone, Mrs. Lewis? I have. I've stuck a lot of men with my knife. I'm real good at it. So you tell him, and we'll fight it out, and if I kill him, then you and me can—"

"No, no, stop it!" She moaned, but all the time he had talked, his hands had been using her. She closed her eyes. There wasn't time to think. He would kill Jake. She could see that. Jake had never been in a knife fight. He wouldn't stand a chance. She was so tired of struggling.

"That's right. You just relax and enjoy it, and if we're lucky, we can figure out some way I can visit you regular all the way to the Black Hills."

He kissed her again, his tongue in her mouth, gagging her. He was pulling up her dress. She had to try to fight him again. She couldn't let him—

He raised up for a moment, and she opened her eyes. Maybe he was going to stop.

He was unbuttoning his pants.

Hugh had seen Indians before. He had seen the Poncas, Pawnees, and Omahas in their tribal dances, and he had seen the squaws and the old men at the agency. But he had never seen Indians like these. These were the Sioux. And even though they had ridden their ponies to the edge of the trail without raising their weapons or uttering the shouts that would signal an attack, it was evident this was a war party. There were twelve of them. Eight men and four half-grown boys, as confident in their bearing as the warriors. Only twelve. There were twice as many white men, all well-armed; yet there was something about the Sioux that Hugh found awesome. They rode their horses as if they were part of the animals, controlling them with only a rawhide cord around their jaws.

The war party had stopped about a dozen yards from the first wagons and sat there on their horses, stoic and calm, while the mule drivers sweated and cursed as they maneuvered the wagons into a cluster. Hugh and the other men on foot ran to catch up to the wagons, and Hobart and O'Connell galloped up and down the line of wagons issuing orders.

Luther was puffing beside Hugh as they ran to the wagons. Hugh wondered if Luther was afraid, but there wasn't time to ask. Hugh spotted Jake leaving his wagon and cutting over to where the rest of the party was forming a line confronting the Sioux. Hugh caught up to Jake before they reached the others.

"Where's Molly and Edwin?" he asked.

"They're oaky," Jake answered. "Hiding in the wagons. Hobart told 'em to keep out of sight. Edwin's in Hobart's wagon with Morris."

"Is there going to be a fight?" Luther asked as he joined them.

"Hobart says not," Jake said. "We got 'em outnumbered. He claims they'll just want to palaver—whatever that is. Talk and trade, I guess."

"Well, I aim to have a fight," Luther dropped to one knee and raised his needle gun.

"Damn it, Luther," Hugh stepped in front of his brother. "Stop that before they see you and you get us all killed."

"There's twice as many of us as them!" Luther shouted. "We can take them."

"Your brother's right!" Jake joined Hugh in blocking Luther from the view of the Indians. "We don't want to start anything."

Luther lowered his rifle reluctantly, blinking rapidly.

"You can tell by the way they're lining up there, they aren't going to fight." Hugh gestured to the line of Indians still sitting stoically on their ponies facing the Black Hillers.

"Hobart's talking to them," Jake said. "Let's get closer and find out what's going on."

Hugh grabbed Luther's arm. "Keep hold of yourself. Think of Molly and Edwin back in the wagons. If we start a fight, they might get hurt."

"I won't start anything." Luther still brandished his rifle. "But if those heathen redskins start anything, you can bet I'll give 'em what for."

Keeping an anxious eye on Luther and a tight grip

124

on his own rifle, Hugh followed Jake to the cluster of men confronting the Indians. Emmet Hobart was a little in front of the others talking to an Indian Hugh saw immediately must be the chief.

"What's happening?" Hugh asked the man nearest him.

"Hobart and the chief been talking it over. Or rather the chief has been threatening and Hobart's been listening, trying to cool him off."

"What did the chief say?"

"Said we better keep out of the Black Hills. Says many whites will die. Said he dreamt it in a vision quest or something like that. Seemed real certain about it. Wasn't much Hobart could say."

"We're not turning back!" Luther wailed.

"Course not," the man spat. "They can't stop us and the chief knows it. But he's going to make it tough on us. Besides, it gives 'em credit, facing an enemy like this. They can go home and brag on it."

Hugh knew Indians considered it a mark of bravery to touch an enemy in battle, and as he studied the line of warriors, he could see the men all wore marks of honor to signify the times they had counted coup or killed an enemy. Several ponies were painted with a red hand, and the same mark appeared on the clothing of several men. Hugh knew the mark had something to do with killing an enemy in combat as did the crosses painted on their leggings. Hugh knew the eagle feathers they wore in their hair signified the times they had counted coup and the angle at which the feather was worn also had significance.

In contrast to the marks of their bravery and their quill-decorated buckskin shirts, leggings and moccasins, the Indians carried or wore government-issued blankets, signifying they had made at least a paper peace with the whites. The boys were armed with bows and arrows, but all the men had new rifles. They were Henry's and Winchesters, fine repeating rifles, better than the single shot guns Hugh and most of the others carried. Hugh wondered if the rifles, too, were government issue.

One look at the face and bearing of the chief and the others as they warned the Black Hillers to stay out of Sioux lands tore away all the theories Hugh had held about educating the Indian to the white man's way of life. He saw these people were as much a part of the plains as the buffalo and the sagebrush. They could no more be tamed than could a timber wolf.

Hobart seemed to have reached an impasse with the chief. The Indian sat on his pony, seeming to stare beyond Hobart, his face impassive, one hand resting on his rifle, the other holding up a lance. Hugh couldn't help but admire the warrior. He had the wide-spaced narrow eyes, reddish-brown skin, blue-black hair and hooked nose that marked his people; but he was nothing like the Indians Hugh had seen loitering about the white men's towns or Indian agencies. One of his braids was bound in red cloth; the other flowed free over his shoulders. He wore three upright eagle feathers in his scalp lock, one dyed red. There was a shell choker around his neck, and a bone breastplate covered his chest, while his buckskin shirt was decorated in quill embroidery over his shoulders and down his arms. His shirt, unlike that of the other men, was fringed with hair, and Hugh wondered uneasily what this meant and if the hair was human.

Hobart was talking to the chief, admiring his gun. It was a Sharps forty-five, as fine a rifle as was made. The chief refused to look at Hobart. He stared ahead as if he didn't hear what the wagon master was saying. Then suddenly, he handed his lance to the warrior next to him. As he did, Hugh realized with a shock the lance was decorated with scalps, and one of them was blond.

The Indians backed off a little as if to give the chief room. Something was about to happen. Hugh felt his hands on his rifle growing sweaty in anticipation.

With a deliberate broad sweeping gesture, Steals-Many-Horses pointed to a tree some distance away. A magpie sat on one of the branches. Slowly and with a great air of showmanship, the chief raised his rifle and sighted on the bird. Hugh was just thinking it an impossible target when the shot rang out and the magpie fell. The Indians did not react visibly, but a little murmur of awe and confusion passed among the whites followed by a deadly silence as the old chief challenged the whites with his eyes.

Hobart stepped into the silence and, with a show-man-like flourish, pointed out a little white spot on a boulder near the foot of the tree, raised his rifle and fired. The sound indicated the shot had hit the boulder but the white spot remained, so one of the Indians galloped over to check. Without waiting to see what he would report, Hobart picked a stick from the ground, took out his pocket knife and notched the top of the stick. Hugh moved closer to see what he was doing. Hobart stuck something in the notch and one of the men nearer him passed word back that it was a nickle. Hobart stuck the stick in the ground and walking up to one of the young boys, pointed at the stick and made a gesture as if he were shooting with a bow and arrow. The boy's face showed a trace of a smile as he looked to the chief for permission. The old man nodded imperceptibly, and the boy kicked up his pony, galloped away, then wheeled and raced toward the stick, taking aim with his bow and arrow. While still some distance away, he shot, trailing the arrow and dislodging the nickle with its shaft. He gave a little cry of triumph and leapt from his pony to retrieve the coin.

Hobart quickly picked up the stick and affixed another nickle, gesturing to another boy. Hugh saw what the wagon master was trying to do—defuse the anger of the warriors; yet allow the Indians to save face and show their skill and bravery. Hugh had to hand it to Hobart; he knew how to handle a difficult situation.

At this point, the chief dismounted and pointing to the rock, sent another brave to set up a target.

Donnelly came back through the group grinning. "Okay, boys, the best marksmen among you get out there and do your stuff. But don't start gambling because they'll take us for all we're worth. Just put out some nickles for the kids and act impressed when they do their stuff."

It was a strange shooting match with no comradery about it. Yet, as they took their turns and fired, the tension of the Black Hillers eased a little, and the Indians too became less silent as they acknowledged an especially good shot by one of their braves with a little hup of praise.

Hugh and Luther took their places in line and shot when their turns came, but it was evident to Hugh that even among the whites, they were far from the best shots. Hugh dropped out of the shooting and let Hobart, O'Connell and Luther continue the challenge. Finally Luther had to admit he was outclassed. Pearson quit at about the same time. Hugh wondered about it, for he had noted uneasily that Pearson was an excellent shot.

Hugh was also uneasy about the amount of ammunition they were wasting. He turned his attention to the young boys who were still shooting at the sticks with their bows and arrows. He marveled at the way they maneuvered their ponies as they rode about in circles, sometimes hanging off the side of their mounts as if to show how difficult a target they would present in a real battle. He wished Molly and Edwin could watch. He considered getting them out of the wagons, but if Hobart was right, the sight of a woman and child might unleash the carefully controlled anger of the Sioux. No one doubted each time the Indians shot, they were pretending it was one of the trespassers who was hit. Although on the surface, the shooting match was friendly, Hugh suspected it was having the desired effect on their party, for he saw reflected in more than one face his own awe at the skill of the warrior Sioux.

He decided against bringing Molly and Edwin out to watch. Besides, he realized it would have been Jake's place to fetch his family, and Jake was completely involved in watching Hobart and the chief shoot it out. He wondered if he could slip away and reassure Molly and Edwin or perhaps shift them around so they could see something of what was going on. He hesitated, not wanting to draw the attention of the Sioux to the wagons. He decided if he could manage it, he would find Edwin and sit with him, sending Morris to watch the shooting. He looked around for Pearson. He didn't want Pearson to see him going to the wagons. Ever since Pearson had stumbled on the truth about him and Molly, Hugh had been watching the faces of the men to see if he had spread his gossip, but so far there had been none of the sly grins that would prove he had not kept his suspicions to himself.

He couldn't spot Pearson in the crowd. It made him uneasy. Since Pearson's threat at the crossing of the Platte, Hugh had made it a point to keep track of the man and make sure he never had the opportunity to annoy Molly when she went out alone to gather wood or attend to her personal needs. But now he couldn't find Pearson. It hadn't been long ago that he had been shooting, but now he wasn't even among the crowd watching the match.

Hugh spun around and scanned the wagons again. Surely not, he thought. Not in the middle of a confrontation with the Sioux. Even Pearson wasn't so low or so crazy. He could not believe it of another man. Hugh began to walk toward the wagons, then broke into a run.

It seemed to take forever to get there. He kept his right hand gripped around his gun and with the left pulled himself onto the wagon and jerked open the flap. Even as he did it, he could hear the muffled moaning and the sounds of struggle.

He saw only that Pearson was on top of her. There wasn't room to shoot. He threw down his rifle and with an angry roar pulled himself into the wagon and charged Pearson, wrapping both arms around him and jerking him away from her and then throwing Pearson and himself both sideways back across the end of the wagon. He pinned Pearson to the wagonbox with one arm and with the other rained blows into his side while Pearson struggled to free himself. Hugh couldn't really get at him within the confines of the wagon, and he wanted to kill him. So he got his arms around Pearson and with a mighty heave let his anger carry them both over the end of the wagon and onto the ground.

It was a mistake. Outside the wagon, Hugh lost the advantage of his size and strength. Pearson landed cat-like on all fours while Hugh was stunned from the fall. Hugh was too blind with rage to take time to think it out and compensate for Pearson's agility. So when he threw himself toward Pearson again in a bull-like charge, the greasy little man simply backed himself against the wagon and grabbing the sides, met Hugh's charge with both feet up in a sudden kick that knocked the wind out of Hugh.

Hugh regained his balance as fast as he could, but Pearson was already crouching and reaching into his boot for the knife. He brought it up and snapped his wrist back and forth so that Hugh could hear the blade as it cut through the air. It gleamed wickedly. Pearson grinned, and with his other hand beckoned Hugh to him. There was something in his eyes that was almost hypnotic; like a king cobra in his death-dance.

Hugh could hear Molly somewhere behind him in the wagon as he and Pearson began circling each other slowly. Hugh pulled his hunting knife from its sheath. It seemed a thick and clumsy weapon compared to Pearson's, but he was too angry to be afraid. He wanted to taste blood.

Pearson was still beckoning him forward, grinning. Hugh knew he was no match for an experienced knife fighter and he should play for time, holding his body sideways to protect his vital organs, but his anger was stronger than his reason, and he charged holding his blade like a knight's lance.

At the last moment, Pearson simply stepped aside and Hugh buried his knife in the soft wood at the end of the wagon. Hugh started to pull it out, but Molly's scream above him warned Pearson was striking, and he swung himself to the side so that the blade only knicked his arm. He came up swinging and felt a blow collide with Pearson's face, but it did not land solidly and only served to separate them.

They began circling each other again. Pearson seemed in no hurry to make the kill. Hugh flashed his eyes between Pearson and the ground looking for a rock or some sort of weapon. He felt Pearson was delaying his move, playing with him, enjoying it.

Then Hugh saw his gun lying where he had drooped it when he climbed into the wagon. There wasn't room to get the long barrel up for a shot. Pearson would have him in the belly while he cocked it, but maybe he could use the rifle as a club. He dove for the gun and had it by the barrel before Pearson realized what he was about. Pearson made a jab with the knife, but it went too high and then Hugh had the rifle barrel in both hands and was ready to swing it.

Pearson looked startled, then almost happy, like it would make a better fight. Pearson was licking his lips, the white scar across his face ugly and his dark eyes gleaming. Hugh raised the gun over his shoulder. It was heavy and awkward, but he gave a mighty swing. He had telegraphed his intentions, and Pearson ducked smoothly. Enraged, Hugh swung the gun back with the vicious strength of a medieval battleaxman. Pearson stood up just enough so the stock hit him squarely in the side of the head.

Pearson looked startled. His grin grew wider, and then he fell forward in the dirt.

The knife was flung far from Pearson's fingers and, still clutching his rifle, Hugh grabbed it and waited for Pearson to get up. Then, seeing the man was out cold, he turned back to Molly in the wagon.

"Are you all right?"

Her eyes were wild, her face flooded with color and her hair tumbling around her shoulders. She was cupping her exposed breasts with one hand and holding onto the wagonbox with the other like she might fall out. He wanted to touch her, to reassure himself she was safe.

"Did he . . . he didn't *hurt* you did he?"

She seemed for a moment unable to speak. Then as she managed to pull her dress closed whispered, "you came in time."

"Are you sure? He didn't—" He couldn't say it. As he stepped toward her, Molly seemed to shrink away from him. She glanced anxiously toward the clearing where Hugh realized from the sound of firing, the shooting match was still going on. Only minutes had passed. It seemed like hours.

"Did anyone see?" she asked, still clutching the dress closed.

Hugh stepped back a little so he could see the men and still keep an eye on Pearson. "No, they're still busy with their shooting match."

"Shooting match? They're having a shooting match?"

"They've set up targets and are trying to outshoot the Sioux."

Molly seemed to fall apart. "A shooting match! And all this time I thought they were fighting and Edwin was maybe being killed while I was—"

He saw she was on the verge of hysteria and putting Pearson's knife in his belt, he started toward her, but again she pulled away from him. "What are we going to tell people?"

"What?"

"Jake and the others. What are we going to tell them about Pearson?"

Hugh looked at Pearson still lying spread-eagled on the ground. "I guess we'll just tell the truth, that he was trying to—"

"My God, you can't do that! He'll *tell*. He said he'd *tell*!"

"You mean about us?"

"Yes! He said he'd tell Jake and everyone about you and—"

"No one would take him seriously. Besides, I'll kill him if—"

"Hugh?" Molly's voice was suddenly small like that of a little girl's. There was something in her eyes that alarmed him. "Hugh, he isn't moving. Are you sure you didn't—"

"He's just out cold," Hugh swung the rifle around and gave Pearson a poke with the barrel.

Pearson didn't move.

Hugh put the rifle down and pulling his knife from the wagon kept it handy as he knelt beside Pearson and turned him over. He seemed very still, like something had gone out of him. Hugh didn't believe it.

134

Molly said it. "I think he's dead."

"No! You're overwrought. He's just out cold. I didn't hit him that hard."

"You caught him in the temple."

Hugh picked up Pearson's wrist and felt for a pulse. "I couldn't have," he groaned. "I was mad enough to, but I'd never—"

Molly disappeared in the wagon. Hugh couldn't get a pulse. He told himself he didn't have the right place and kept trying. He looked to where the men were still gathered. Hobart would know what to do.

Molly climbed out of the wagon.

"I'll get help." Hugh stood up.

"No, wait." She knelt beside Pearson. She was holding something in her hand and Hugh almost laughed when he saw it was a mirror. She looked like a little girl kneeling there with her hair streaming around her shoulders, holding the mirror beneath Pearson's nose.

"Molly, that won't prove anything," he began and then was fascinated by what she was doing. The minutes passed silently and slowly. Even before she held up the mirror to show him, he knew. It was unclouded.

"Oh, my God," he groaned. "I didn't mean to—I never meant to—He was hurting you and I got so mad and—"

"I'm glad. I'm glad he's dead!"

"Molly!"

"He was going to give us away. Jake would never understand if he found out now. He'd think—he'd think there was still something between us. He'd think I still want you. I'm glad Pearson is dead."

Hugh stared at her. Her face was flushed and her

eyes glittery. She was both beautiful and terrible to behold. He didn't know how to deal with the change in her which was so startling it seemed almost more important than what he had done. He'd better get Hobart.

"Where are you going?" she asked as he turned to leave.

"I'd better get the others."

"You can't do that!"

"What else can I do? He's dead. I've killed him. It was self-defense. They'll understand that. Besides he was going to hurt you."

"You can't *tell* them. You can't let anyone *know*. They'll banish you from the wagon train. They'll do that even if they believe it was self-defense. You and Luther will be out there alone with the Sioux."

"They wouldn't do that. That would be murder, sending the two of us out against the Sioux." Even as he said it, he knew it was true. Banishing him would be the only way the wagon train could deal with his act. "Luther's done nothing wrong," he finished lamely.

"Get rid of the body."

"What?" He couldn't believe she had said it.

She looked around frantically. "No one's seen anything yet. Do it now. Quickly. Drag him out there to that rocky place. Out beyond the camp."

"I can't do that!"

"You have to. It's the only way. Hurry before someone comes this way."

"But they'll notice he's missing. They'll look for him. I haven't time to bury him and the ground's too hard. They'll find the body."

"It's getting dark. No one will find him until morning. They'll think the Sioux got him. They'll think he wandered off from camp and the Sioux got him."

Hugh stood there a minute. What she said made sense, but it didn't seem right. "No, I'm going to tell the truth. I'll take my medicine like a man. I think they'll let me stay with the party."

She grabbed his arm. "And what about me?"

He looked at her.

"Do you think I want the whole party knowing what he tried to do? Do you think I want them all looking at me and wondering if he succeeded? Do you think they'll believe he didn't?"

"They wouldn't—"

"They would, Hugh. They'll all say he had me. Even Jake. My God, don't you think I know how people talk? How they stare? I went through that once. And it was because of you! Would you ask me to go through it again?"

Her eyes were wild, her half exposed breasts heaved with her ragged breathing. He had brought shame on her once. He couldn't do that to her again.

He walked to the body and picked up Pearson's booted feet. "Get back in the wagon and mend your dress," he told her. "I'll take care of this."

Slowly he dragged the body away from the wagon, keeping his eye on the men in the clearing, sure he'd be discovered at any moment.

Even as he did it, the shooting stopped. The Indians mounted, shouting and brandishing their lances. It was almost dark. If the men would just be occupied with the Indians a few minutes, he thought he might make it.

He was out of sight of the camp now, but on rocky

137

ground, so it was harder to drag the body. It kept catching on things. He figured he'd better go where he wouldn't leave tracks. He'd have to cut a piece of sage and try to brush out the track where he had dragged the body from the wagon. There was sure to be a search in the morning. Maybe they wouldn't look too hard; they wouldn't dare to spread out too far with the Sioux still watching them. But he couldn't take too long hiding the body. His absence in the clearing might already have been noticed.

He saw a little gully, as good a place as any. He rolled the body down it. Pearson landed face up. Hugh remembered to put Pearson's knife back in his boot. The dead man's fly was still open, but Hugh decided it was just as well. If someone found him, maybe they would conclude he had stepped out to relieve himself and an Indian had picked him off silently with a war club. Pearson's eyes were open. He seemed to be staring at him. Hugh reached down to close his eyes and then stopped. The Sioux wouldn't do that. It had to look like he had been killed by Indians.

He realized there was something else he should do. Hugh hesitated for a long time. Then, suppressing a shudder of revulsion, he took out his knife.

Chapter Nine

No one missed Pearson until morning. When the Indians finally galloped away, still brandishing their lances and muttering threats, they camped less than a mile from Hobart's party. The glow of the Sioux campfires was barely visible once they had their own fires lighted, but the sound of their drumming seemed to fill the air. It went on all night, the drumming and the yelling; and although everyone agreed the Indians wouldn't attack, the rhythmic pounding of the drums was almost more than nerves could bear. Hugh realized it was a lucky break for him the Sioux were continuing their harassment of the party. No one wondered why Molly was pale and trembling or why he paced restlessly back and forth. And no one missed Pearson.

The next morning the sun came out, the drums were silent, the Sioux gone, and once again there was the sound of easy conversation and laughter over breakfast. But as Hugh was busying himself helping Jake to hitch up, Morris came around wearing a worried expression and announced that Pearson was missing. No one could remember seeing him since the shooting match, but when he had disappeared no one knew, since Pearson had no friends. His horse was picketed with the rest, so something must have happened to him. Morris asked Jake and Hugh to join in the search. With a glance at Molly, Hugh picked up his rifle and followed the men.

They formed small groups for the hunt, staying near the camp. Pearson would not have gone far, they reasoned. An hour passed and the mule drivers became restless. No one wanted to stay long in the place they had been threatened by the Sioux. They were about to give up the search when Morris let out a yell.

Hugh followed the others to the edge of the gully and reluctantly joined in looking down at the corpse. Morris had thrown his coat over Pearson's head. Hugh was glad he did not have to look on the dead man's face again. A few clamored down the gully to examine the body. Hugh remained behind. Hobart appeared and strode down the gully, sending little avalanches of gravel toward the men as they stepped back to acknowledge his leadership. Morris jerked the coat off Pearson dramatically and Hobart knelt over the body for what seemed to Hugh like a long time. Finally Hobart stood and motioned for Morris to replace the coat.

Hobart's expression as he climbed the gully was carefully composed. "Indians?" the waiting crowd asked as if one man. "Did the Sioux get him?"

Hobart nodded. "Indians all right. He must have gone out to take a leak and some bloodthirsty redskin picked him off."

"You sure?" Donnelly asked as Hugh clenched his fists involuntarily. "Pearson was never shy about piss-ing in the middle of camp."

"It was Indians all right," Hobart seemed to be looking directly at Hugh as he said it. "The heathen redskins got his scalp."

No one was anxious to linger so they planted Pearson in the same gully in which he'd been found, covered the place well with rocks, said a few words over the mound and marked it with a cross, and were on their way by noon. When they had gone a little distance up the trail, Hobart rode to the end of the column and sat on his horse a moment looking back. He remarked that it was the kind of place one could never find again. But Hugh looked back along the same trail and then down at his hands, and knew he would never forget the place or what he had become there.

In the days that followed, the country began to change, growing more rugged. They began to see antelope, small bands at first, then great herds which bounded away as their wagons approached. They all itched to hunt, but after Hobart expertly picked off two bucks and distributed the meat, he forbade the rest to hunt, warning them again to stick together. Subdued by Pearson's death, the men followed orders, although Luther was not the only one to complain. They were basically all city dwellers. Even those who drove the mules had come once from some choked-off city place where they felt stifled and edged in by the rules and limitations of other men. They had come to the frontier not just to find gold, but to cut loose in some way, to explore and build and destroy, and somehow be their own men. They all knew they had come too late for the buffalo, and now they were told they would miss the antelope too. The restriction chafed them; yet they were afraid of meeting Pearson's fate. Life is as unfair to men as to women. A man can yearn and fight and die and get put down without ever finding whatever it was he was looking for or even knowing just what it was. Women don't often get what they want either, but they more often know what they seek.

Hugh was too preoccupied to pay attention to Luther's grumblings. He longed to talk to Molly alone, thinking that this would somehow purge him of the terrible guilt he felt about Pearson's death. But there was so little privacy on the wagon train, and she seemed to avoid him, sitting stiff beside her husband on the wagon seat days, and nights around the campfire, keeping Edwin always at her side. The sight of another band of Indians, this one containing women and children, reminded them of the need to stay together. They felt the constant pressure of Indians around them.

It was the first week of May, but cold drizzling rain mingled with spurts of snow made them miserable. Hugh and Luther had no tent, so Jake insisted they spread their bedrolls under his wagon at night to stay dry. There was no way to decline without drawing questions, but it was agony for Hugh to sleep so close to Molly that he could hear her turn and moan during the night. He lay awake, listening to the night sounds, trying not to imagine Jake taking his rights with her. He had been enraged to the point of murder by Pearson's lust; now he wondered if his own feelings were any more civilized, for, though he tried to deny the feeling, he knew he wanted his partner's wife.

Inside the wagon, Molly was equally tortured. She could not seem to stop herself from the endless remembering of how it had once been between them.

It had been raining then too. A sudden spring thunderstorm that sent them from their meeting place in a hillside meadow in search of shelter. Hugh knew of an abandoned barn, so old the smell of horses was only a memory. The roof was broken at one end and pine needles had drifted in. Hugh piled them into the remains of a box stall where the roof still held, and here the two were as dry and safe as if they existed only in their own special world.

She wore a blue dress and her hair hung loose about her shoulders. His shirt was a bit short in the sleeves and she thought she might make him a new one. Then when he rolled up the sleeves and she saw the fine blond hair on his strong arms, she longed to touch them and felt a strange aching need within her. She wondered about their bodies being so different when they were alike in so many ways, and she started to ask him about that, realized she could not; then wondered why such things had to be secret. He looked at her strangely, and somehow she knew they were thinking of the same things.

She laughed nervously then and set to arranging the straw, talking of playing house. It was childish talk, but she said she had dreamed they might one day share a house. And then he said the thing which broke her heart.

He was leaving. He had learned the news that morning but kept it from her to give her one more happy day, but now he could not hold back his grief. The Pennsylvania climate was no better for his father's lungs than that of the coast from which they had come. They would move west immediately. She began to cry and was surprised to see tears in his eyes, tears he held back with the boy's need to be a man. He declared he would stay with her. She reminded him of what he knew: he could not leave his mother with his father so ill. Duty came first, they agreed.

But they had only just found each other! Only yesterday they first dared to kiss and speak of love. Now they clung together, frantically willing the moment to be a lifetime.

And then it began. The touching that was so strange and so unreal and so infinitely tender. They explored each other with a touch of innocence, wondering at the beauty they found in each other's bodies and unaware at first of the passion, never connecting something so sweet with the sin they had been warned against. They wanted only to share and to give as a special, secret token of their love. They thought only of the wonder of it, discovering passion together from the first taste to the last sweet shuddering sob. Even afterwards, they felt no guilt but only a closeness as if their bodies were still joined. She had been the first for him and he for her, and they swore it would bind them together for all time.

And now it seemed they were indeed bound together, but in such a tangled knot Molly was certain she would never sort it out. The future was so clouded, so emeshed with emotions she could not admit feeling, that Molly could find refuge only in the past. How she felt about the present Hugh, the man who had saved her from Pearson, who walked beside her wagon days and slept under it nights, and seemed to want her if she could believe his eyes, she could not say, even to herself.

The trail to the Black Hills steadily grew more difficult. The rain and sleet were dreary, and the men actually found themselves praying for snow so the ground would freeze. Anything seemed better than the mud, a thick gumbo that gathered on the wagon wheels so they had to stop often to scrape it off. The men's boots were so heavy with it that sometimes they could hardly lift their feet to take another step. Molly and Edwin had to stay inside the wagon all day, and Hugh alternated between chafing that there was no opportunity to see Molly alone and relief that he was spared the opportunity to make a fool of himself by saying or doing something so rash he would offend her.

Someone suggested they camp a few days until conditions improved, but Hobart reminded them there was neither wood nor water so they might as well push on.

Then after nearly a week of dreary discouraging weather, it began to clear almost magically. There was a sudden break in the clouds, the men found themselves leaning forward in anticipation and then, through swirling mists, they caught their first glimpse of the Black Hills, looking like some sort of enchanted land. The Black Hills, they discovered, were really shades of deep muted blue, lovely but forboding. The land before them seemed cold, dark, and mysterious; menacing, even as it beckoned.

For two days the Hills appeared and disappeared through the clouds, each time appearing a little closer.

Finally the party began to climb the first pine-dotted slopes, following the low places between the foothills so they were barely aware they were climbing except that as the trail wound higher, the grass became more lush and the air colder and the clouds seemed to settle in a light fog all around them. The weather had never cleared entirely and now it seemed to grow more miserable with each step they took; their spirits were so low no one bothered to comment they had left the barren plains behind at last and were actually entering the Black Hills.

Finally they camped at a place called Buffalo Gap and the next morning awoke to sunshine and the sound of singing birds. The sun changed everything. For a week the men had been surly; now Hugh heard snatches of conversation and even whistling. He and Luther bickered good-naturedly as they had in the old days, and for the first time they were aware of the fragrance of the pine forest and the beauty of their surroundings. Molly was talkative as she cleared up the breakfast things, saying how the sunshine had changed the world and that she felt certain the worst of their journey was over. Hugh agreed, realizing that the burden he seemed to have carried since Pearson's death seemed lighter.

Molly wanted to walk and to talk. She was sick of riding in the wagon, weary of Jake's silences, but he told her now that the grass was too wet, she'd soak her shoes, so she stayed on the wagon seat that morning, chafing at the restraint, wanting suddenly to laugh and even dance, so light had the sun and the clear mountain air made her spirits.

Then, late in the afternoon, Jake finally stopped the

wagon and let her down. She stood in the deep, lush grass for a moment, watching him drive on, suddenly glad that Edwin had fallen asleep, feeling free and very aware that their wagon was the last in line and behind her Hugh approached, also alone. She would not have planned it this way, but did God require her to stay always beside her husband? Could she not take joy in this spring day? It seemed so right to wait for Hugh, to see the way his face gladdened at the sight of her.

They walked along together silent for a time, aware of sudden flowering of the land about them, the beauty, the scented air, the goodness of their being together. Then Hugh began to speak of incidentals. He had wanted to talk to her of Pearson's death and what he had done to the body to protect them both from discovery, but it now seemed unnecessary and foolish to bring up the past. The day was beautiful. A new beginning.

"And how do you like the Black Hills now?" he asked her.

"Beautiful," she said with a smile so lovely it hurt him. "They're so beautiful they make my heart want to sing."

Beautiful is what you are, he wanted to say, but he did not, though she, looking at him, knew his thought, and blushed and wished the moment could last forever. She wanted to hear him say it.

The thread of a trail the party followed narrowed until they found themselves surrounded on either side by the fragrant pine forest. The trees seemed to form walls beside the trail, but the effect was not unpleasant. They were still close enough behind Jake's wagon and the others to hear their slow progress. She savored the forest smells and the sunlight flickering through the trees in little patches of gold. She could hear water tumbling over rocks and knew they were near a brook. Two dragon flies danced by, locked in an embrace.

Suddenly Hugh stopped and stared at something off the trail. He put his fingers to his lips and motioned her to come. She followed him to a little clearing barely screened from the trail by a scattering of young aspen, and there she saw a doe and her fawn. The others had driven past without seeing the deer who stood calmly watching Molly and Hugh, their heads alert, the black muzzle of the doe sniffing the air. Molly realized they must be innocent of humans to stand so calmly. Finally the breeze changed and brought their scent to the doe and she turned and bounded away, the fawn leaping after.

"I've never seen deer so close before," Molly whispered, as conscious of Hugh's nearness as of the beauty surrounding her. Their shoulders were touching now, by accident surely, but touching, and they dared to prolong the moment as they had never dared in the past when they accidentally touched and discovered that the slightest contact meant temptation.

For a long moment, neither moved nor spoke. It was as if the gods had turned them into two marble statues transfixed in the forest, caught in the spell of a moment alone; the very air pregnant with all that was unsaid and forbidden between them. She kept talking, telling herself the moment was innocent and could be savoured and prolonged.

"How graceful the deer were," she said, knowing that to speak of beauty was an invitation. "I've never seen anything so beautiful."

"I've never seen anything so beautiful as *you*." He turned to her with bold eyes, devouring her eyes, her lips, her breasts. "There is no other beauty when you are near me. You are more beauty than my eyes can hold."

He spoke rather formally, as if it were a speech rehearsed, or words said so often only to himself they had become a prayer. Astonished that mere words could have such effect, she felt transfigured from marble statue to glorious being and faint with joy that he did, indeed, still find her beautiful. She closed her eyes to hold herself strong against the overpowering pleasure of the golden sunlight, the lush awakening of the spring woods and the glory of such words and such a moment. It was already beyond anything she had dared dream.

Hugh, too, was overcome by emotions long held prisoner by the demands of the trail and by honor, but unlike Molly, he was not content with meaningful looks and tantalizing words. His desire was as demanding as that of a young stag's and clamoured for fulfillment with the woman he adored. Touch, he must. His hand found her face almost without his willing it.

Her face was as soft and dear to his fingertips as the most tender memory of childhood. He had so often longed to touch her just so, to soothe away her fears of the trail, to protect and cherish her. With her eyes closed and her lips smiling, she looked like a Madonna, and his caress was gentle. To Hugh, the touch was but a promise, but Molly was astonished by the way it stirred her with instant recognition of his need. He was not a man who could easily be held in check.

Her own response was even more disturbing, so disturbing that she instantly denied feeling anything but tender nostalgia for that other time of glorious love-making so many years and miles before. She held his hand against her face for a precious instant. She had so often longed that Hugh might touch her just so, knowing that only his touch could truly comfort her. And then, knowing the touch was only a beginning, she pulled his hand away and grasped it between her own to hold them both fast against temptation. But his hand between hers sent shivers of delight throughout her being, and she found she could not release it but must press it to her and hold him locked against her heart.

Again they stood as statues, neither daring to move, so intense was their realization that in lingering together they risked more than discovery by the Sioux. For the Sioux would make a swift end of them; but another touch, another promise would bind them in a sweet prison of desire from which there was no escape. She longed to see again the unashamed love in his eyes, but knew she must not meet his gaze lest he capture her lips and so flood her body with a desire that would damn them both.

And then Hugh pulled his hand from hers, and brought hers to his lips; then let go her hand and taking the mist of golden hair at the nape of her neck, raised her face to his.

She could not help but meet his lips and revel in his kiss. The memory of that long-ago kiss had haunted a thousand of her nights. Now past and present, time and eternity joined and soared so that they seemed to stand not in a forest filled with both wonders and dangers, but in a swirling cloud that hid them from this world and carried them to another where nothing mattered except that destiny had promised them to each other. On and on went the kiss in a myriad of variations that seemed a symphony of sensation, first tentative and gentle, then tormenting with need.

Passion consumed Hugh. All reason abandoned him and he thought only to be one with Molly. His hands sought the rich fullness of her breasts and hips, and he rejoiced in their womanliness. She seemed to offer an earthly paradise richer in the winning than the tantalizing promise of gold-washed streams and unknown lands that had led him to defy the Sioux to enter their sacred and forbidden place. He sought to lift her so that there in the woods, he might take her. He forgot Jake and the wagon train, and when he remembered for an instant that the Sioux might discover them thus, he thought that if a war lance found his back, he would die happy if only he gained the treasure of her surrender.

His urgency was too much for Molly. Though she herself swelled with emotion, she could name only her fear and could not accept her desire; she was no match for the demanding young stag who surged against her.

"No, Hugh, stop." She struggled against both the unleashed power of his body and her own awakening need. At first he did not heed her trembling protest; so that her fear grew, and she beat frantically against him with her fists, even as her spirit joyously protested that it must already be too late.

He hesitated just long enough to caress again her face, and when he saw the fear and confusion there, he was shocked. His senses returned and with an anguished groan he pulled away.

They stood facing each other and she saw he was as stunned as she by what had happened. She felt herself on the edge of a precipice, as if she took one step forward they might fall together there in the grass like beasts in a field. She felt her chest heaving with her emotion and knew her hair had tumbled down. She must stop this.

"We can't do this, Hugh. We have no right."

"We do have a right. I'm the father of your child. We're meant to be together. Don't tell me you don't feel that."

"No. It's not so."

"But you wanted to be alone with me. You wanted me to tell you I found you beautiful. I know you did."

"That. But only that. Because of what's passed between us. That time, I'll never forget, but there can't be more."

"What do you want? To keep me hidden away? Like a locket made out of the hair of a dead man? Something that you take out to admire and remember your lost love?"

It was too close to the truth. An image flooded through her mind. A picture of the Hugh of her memories, of her thousand fantasies of winter nights in the homestead; a memory that was full of golden sunlight and encased in glass, preserved always the same. A memory she could cherish and control. Not this very real man before her. Not this man with his passion and needs. His demands.

He was moving toward her, still reading her mind. "I'm here now, Molly. And I'm real and I need you. I want you."

"No, Hugh, stay away."

"I just want to hold you again. Just for a moment. I know there can't be more now. Until we work it out with Jake somehow."

His arms were open to her, gentle, beckoning, and she pictured herself inside them, and was terrified by what she felt.

"Don't touch me," she screamed. "Don't say those things to me. You're—you're acting like Pearson!"

He was shocked, hurt and angry.

"How can you say that to me when I—"

"Killed him!"

"What?"

"Yes, you killed him. You know you did."

"To protect you. You know that. It was an accident, you know that!"

"And the other thing?" Even as she said it, she hated herself, but she must keep him from her, drive him away. "What you did to Pearson's body," she spat out the words. "Did you do *that* to protect me? Was *that* an accident?"

He reeled back as if she had struck him, and she was instantly sorry she had said it. But he had ruined her memory of love. He had taken the memory of the Hugh she had loved and cherished, the sweet, silk-wrapped memory of a boy who had loved her gently and tenderly, and turned it into something wild and passionate, something connected with blood—Pearson's blood, and the blood of childbirth, a dark reality that terrified her. This was not the kind of love she remembered and longed for. There was no poetry in this, only a wild rush of emotions that must be denied.

She held herself away from him; then saw the defeat

153

and hurt in his eyes and knew he was no threat to her. That he would not force himself on her. That he was torn with guilt over Pearson and was a civilized man, almost as bound as she by right and wrong.

She was about to reach out to him then. To tell him she had not meant it, that she understood; but they must somehow bridle their feelings and not tarnish the memory of what had passed between them, when she heard in the distance a sound that was familiar, yet in her present state, unrecognizable. Hugh spoke.

"Gunshots. Someone's shooting up ahead."

And then suddenly Luther was crashing through the brush towards them, shouting and brandishing his needle gun.

"There you are! My God, come quick. There's shooting ahead. The bloody Sioux have ambushed a party."

Chapter Ten

There were three of them. Two men and a woman. Dead, scalped, mutilated. Hugh hadn't realized Indians did so many awful things to a body.

Lingering as they had been at the end of the wagon train, he and Molly had been the last to see. By the time they got to where everyone was, the massacre had been pretty well discussed, and the men were standing there silent, just looking at the bodies. The Indians had killed the oxen too. Hugh had the irrational thought that after all their days of traveling single file on the narrow trail, it was nice they had found the bodies in a clearing. It made it real handy so they could all stand around and gawk. He was angry at the others for staring and at himself for not knowing what else to do.

Finally someone spoke. "They killed the oxen too. You'd think Indians would take a good team of oxen like that."

Hugh nodded, thinking there was an awful lot of blood in an ox.

"Mother of God," Donnelly spat. "The bloodthirsty heathens have no use for oxen. Unless they're hungry and these weren't. They didn't even take the food. Just scattered it around and fouled it so no one else could use it."

"They didn't do this because they were hungry," Hobart broke in. "No matter what your bleeding heart liberals would say. These Indians been eating off Uncle Sam all winter so they could go off in the spring and kill honest folk."

"They did it for meanness," Donnelly agreed. "Pure devilishness."

"They did it for a sign," Hobart said, "to let us know they want to keep us out of the Black Hills."

"You mean they knew we were coming?" Hugh asked.

"Sure," Hobart said. "This party was just far enough ahead of us that the Indians knew we could hear their shots. They probably been stalking us for days, but we're too big a party to take on, so they were just waiting for someone to wander off so they could pick up a couple of easy scalps."

"God." Hugh said as the realization sunk in. It could have been them. He and Molly, murdered even while they embraced.

Molly, standing behind Hugh, thought how awful if they had died with Hugh thinking she hated him.

"Our coming scared them off," Donnelly said. "That's why they didn't take time to set the wagon on fire and mutilate the bodies."

"That's not mutilated?" Hugh stared at the bloody mess. *That woman raped and murdered could be Molly. And it would be my fault for trying to get her alone.*

"Hell, no." Donnelly laughed. "They're laid out real nice, Sioux style. Mutilation is cutting off hands, arms, fingers, what-have-you."

Hugh felt sick with rage at the brutality of it. He clenched his fists, holding back his anger. How could Hobart and Donnelly take it so cooly?

"Let's go after them," Luther shouted, brandishing his needle gun. "Let's get after them and make them pay for this!"

Hugh was ready to go.

"You think they're waiting around for you to get a shot at them?" Donnelly laughed. "They'll be miles away by now."

"He's right," Hobart said. "Nothing we can do now but bury these folks. We can't be more than a day from Custer City now. We can see if they have any letters or anything on them to identify them and we can leave word in Custer."

Hugh kept staring at the bodies. Hobart was right. Going after them would be both futile and foolhardy, but he still wanted revenge.

"Well, let's get them planted then," Hobart said.

"No need to cover 'em over too fancy," Donnelly said. "Let's just roll them into a gully somewhere and pile some rocks on to keep the coyotes from dragging the bones around. If they got any kin, probably someone will come out from Custer later and bury them proper."

Several of the men nodded assent and one stepped forward, grabbing the feet of the less bloody of the male corpses to drag it away. Another stepped up to the woman. Someone had already made an attempt to cover her exposed body with a coat. With an effort, Hugh turned his thoughts to the burying.

"Faith," Donnelly said, crossing himself as he uncovered the dead woman. "Judging by the paint and clothes on that one, the Indians didn't get anything she hadn't already sold to half the miners in Custer."

"There's a gully over here that should hold them all," someone shouted. Donnelly began to drag the woman away.

"Stop this. Stop this right now."

Hugh looked up, startled. It was Molly speaking. He hadn't realized she was still there. She should be in the wagon. This was something a woman shouldn't have to see. But Molly was elbowing her way to the front of the crowd. She kept her head high like she didn't want to look at the bodies, but her voice was steady as she confronted the men.

"We're going to give these people a decent burial. Just because we are in this god-forsaken place doesn't mean we have to be as uncivilized as the Sioux."

The men shuffled uncomfortably. Several began to nod. They kept their eyes downcast. Hugh was ashamed. She was right. They were behaving like savages thinking only of revenge and wanting to dispose of the bodies and be on their way. And he had been no better than the rest. He stepped forward to help her, but Molly was in command.

"Now I want several of you to start digging," she said. "We will want three graves. Three *separate* graves. I think under that tree over there. And you will please make them deep enough so there will be no worry about animals."

She hesitated then, glancing quickly down at the half-naked bodies and then back at the circle of men. "These people are not decently clothed. Will the rest of you look around the trail where the Indians scattered

158

their belongings and see if you can find enough to cover them decently?"

"Everything is pretty well torn up," Hugh said.

"In that case, if you can't find enough clothing, perhaps some of you have something you can spare." She glanced down again and seemed transfixed by the scalped head of the woman. "If you can't find her bonnet, I will give her mine."

The men began to move.

"And look for identification too, as Mr. Hobart said, so we can notify the families."

The men started picking up bits of clothing. Someone got a shovel out of a wagon.

"Wait," Molly added. "I will need some water. Would two of you bring me some buckets of water and—" she paused, biting her lip, then holding her head high and speaking with the voice of authority said, "Jake and Mr. Hobart, will you please wash the bodies of the men and dress them for burial?" She paused and seemed to be steeling herself. "I will wash and dress this poor woman."

Jake touched her arm. "I'll tend to it, Molly. You never laid anyone out before."

She hesitated. Hugh thought she had never looked so fragile. He wanted to shelter and protect her from this. He was stepping forward when she shook off Jake's hand.

"It's woman's work," she said. "I can do it. It has to be done. This poor woman is going to be laid out decent. I don't care what kind of a woman she was. That's not for us to judge."

Jake nodded and stepped toward the body. "Where do you want her?"

159

For the first time Molly faltered. "I can't take her in our wagon. Edwin could wake up any minute."

Hobart stepped forward. "We could set up my tent."

"Thank you." She gave him a thin smile and then looked around anxiously. "I don't want Edwin to see until they're all laid out. Luther?" She found Luther in the crowd, then hesitated. "No. Where is Hugh? There. Hugh, would you go and sit in the wagon and keep Edwin in there in case he wakes up?"

Hugh hesitated. It seemed so little to do. He wanted to dig the graves. It would be good to feel the shovel bite into the earth. It was man's work that would still the turmoil with him. But she was right. Someone had to be with Edwin if he woke, to keep him from seeing and try to answer his questions.

"All right." He started to leave, but he felt she was trying to tell him something with her eyes. "Is there anything else I can do?"

"Yes," she said. "Do you have a Bible?"

"Not with me."

"You'll find mine in the top of my trunk. Get it out and choose something to read at the services."

"We didn't do no Bible reading for Pearson," Donnelly said. "Hobart said a few words over him and that was good enough."

"I didn't think about it then," Molly said, keeping her eyes on Hugh. "Besides, I'm not sure Pearson was a God-fearing man, but these innocent people have been cruelly murdered by savages and we must do the best we can for them. Hugh, will you do it for me? Will you conduct the service."

His immediate impulse was to turn the job over to Hobart. He would feel like a hypocrite conducting a service, but then, searching her face, he saw she was trying to tell him something. Perhaps it was her way of saying she understood about Pearson and forgave him. Surely she would not ask him to read from the Bible if she thought of him as a murderer. He nodded his acceptance and started for the Lewis wagon, feeling his guilt eased. Then he noticed Luther was still standing in the clearing, not joining the men who were going to dig, nor helping those who were moving the bodies and setting up the tent. "What are you going to do, Luther?"

His brother shrugged. "I'm tired."

"We all are." Hugh tried to keep his voice even. "We have to keep a hold on ourselves. Mrs. Lewis will be wanting some sort of a marker for the graves. Do you think you could make something, a couple of sticks tied to make a cross?"

Luther just stood there. Finally he sniffed and wiped his nose with the back of his hand.

Without waiting for a reply, Hugh said, "I'll get you an ax out of the wagon."

"You're getting just like him."

"What? Getting like who?"

"Like Hobart. Always telling people what to do. You've got no power over me."

"Damn it, Luther," Hugh felt the anger he had suppressed in the clearing boiling to the surface. "I wasn't trying to shove you around. I just wanted a headstone for the graves. I thought you'd want to help Molly."

For a moment the two brothers stood, face to face, their fists clenched. Hugh decided it was time he showed his brother who was boss. He was about to jerk

161

the boy up by his shirt fronts and lay into him when Luther blinked again and Hugh saw the softness and vulnerability in his face. His brother would be no match for the anger Hugh might unleash. And then he saw Luther was going to back down.

"Oh all right. I'll do it. But I'm warning you, Hugh. I'm sick of you treating me like a kid. You're no better'n me. And if I hadn't found you and Molly in the clearing, the Sioux would have got you too."

Hugh had never before felt the calling to preach and he never would again. But that night at the burying, he had opened the Bible and wished he could make his words as strong as the feelings that were welling up within him. Later, lying in his blankets and staring up at the stars with Luther snoring beside him, he wished he had done a better job. He had wanted the burying to be done right. Not just for Molly, but for all of them. He knew they were disheartened by the massacre, and he wanted to give them hope, but his words seemed not as strong as his emotions. And he could not help but feel a hypocrite to stand before them holding a Bible in hands stained in a man's blood.

Even though they didn't know those they were burying, he had begun, they knew these people had come to the Hills with hopes and dreams before they became discouraged and turned back. This should not be a sign, for perhaps if they had just stuck it out a little longer, they would have been rewarded. Yes, it was a temptation to turn back, for they had all learned going to the Black Hills wasn't just an adventure, but a test of their strength and courage. The important thing was to have faith and keep going, to keep searching for the stuff of their dreams and let no man call them fools for dreaming.

Then he read from Isaiah 2:4, the part about beating swords into plowshares, and prayed aloud that soon they would be turning from war to peace. For they were nation-building. They had not come just to find gold, but to win a new land. Some of them were destined to live out their lives in the Hills, bringing civilization to the wilderness. And maybe they would be remembered as pioneers.

Even as he said those words, he had looked across the open graves at Molly standing there with her husband and son, her hair pulled back and her face solemn and pale, and found her magnificent. He had a thought then — one he could not speak aloud — for he had no right to speak of another man's wife, but one which came to him again that night, lying under the stars. For looking at her over the open graves, he had seen growing in Molly a remarkable strength and spirit and had known that if any of them was ever to be remembered or spoken of as pioneers, it would be Molly. Molly Lewis, who said she wasn't the pioneer type, who dreamed of home and pianos, but who had taken charge of the men and given a proper burial to the gold-camp whore.

Chapter Eleven

In Custer City Hugh bought a small ledger book. He felt the need to keep a record of his pioneering experiences, for increasingly he felt they were part of history in the making. It was also as if by filling the ledger pages with his careful writing, he might somehow control what was happening. He wondered if Crandall could be right, for while part of him raged to be free, he sometimes found himself yearning for the order of his life in the *Sentinel* office. Perhaps man did need the restriction of civilization to keep himself in check; perhaps keeping accounts that balanced and recording words in rows of black ink could somehow bring order to a troubled soul.

He had only so many sheets of paper in his book, and he had left some at the beginning blank, so he could record his impressions of the journey that had finally brought them to Custer. As he wrote his first entry, the story of their great disappointment at reaching their goal, he was not pleased with his words. They seemed stilted and did not convey the mixture of enchantment and disappointment he felt at reaching

164

what was to be the end of their journey. But there were not enough pages to allow for revision and he sensed the journey had only begun.

We arrived at our destination, Custer City, after nearly three weeks of arduous travel to discover no more than 100 residents remaining in a city we were told only days ago numbered 10,000. A large hotel stood half-completed and the city's most pretentious building, a theatre, had likewise been abandoned after one night of merriment. Even the sawmills, with one exception, have been rolled away by a population bound for a new stampede in the northern diggings to a place they call Deadwood.

The demise of Custer seems tragic for it is most attractively located in a beautiful parkland, surrounded by mountains of considerable magnitude. The city seems destined to become a center for farming and ranching once the Indian problem is settled.

Massacres in this vicinity have occurred almost daily. Just before our party reached Custer, it was our unfortunate duty to bury three victims of an Indian attack. We were unable to ascertain their identity, but gave them Christian burial. There are many such graves in these Hills, bearing only the fading legend "Unknown Man, killed and scalped by Indians."

Burley Bemis, the city's first, and possibly last, mayor urged us to remain, assuring us the population would soon return, but the Hobart Party has deemed it more expedient to throw our lot in with those who have stampeded to the new Mecca of Deadwood.

Here Hugh found he could write no more. He was not sure he and Luther would any longer be part of the Hobart Party. It seemed foolish to remain in Custer and foolhardy to venture on alone, but when the others decided to move on, he held back, suggesting that he and Luther might linger a few days. He had promised Molly only to remain with her until Custer. He did not want to leave her now, but they had not spoken since that terrible scene in the clearing, and it seemed the most sane thing to do would be to end their relationship while he still had some control over himself.

Custer was a disappointment for Molly too, but a disappointment of a more personal, womanly nature. She had been so delighted by the sight of a city of hundreds of log and frame cabins, that she hardly noticed the lack of population, and when Jake remarked that there was something mighty strange about their being greeted personally by the mayor and told to take their pick of cabins to use until the owners returned from the northern diggings, she thought him unnecessarily suspicious.

She found great joy in settling into one of the abandoned cabins, unpacking the wagon, doing a wash and baking bread. By the time Jake returned from a day of what he called "reconnoitering the situation," she was thoroughly settled in. She took it badly when Jake told her they must move on. Why? she asked. Why when the spot was so pretty and they had a cabin for the taking?

Because the stampede had moved north, Jake said, and when she demanded to know why they could not look for gold in Custer as well as anywhere and accused him of having the wanderlust, he patiently tried to tell her things he had only learned that day about what it took to mine gold.

Water, he said. There was not enough water in Custer City. And when she had protested that French Creek was the loveliest little stream she'd ever seen, he tried to explain to her about the need for fast-moving water to wash the gold from the gravel dug on the creekbeds and processed through crude homemade rockers. He told her they were no longer hoping to find gold nuggets—the first to come had found all those—but to find placer gold they could wash from the gravel until it led them to the mother lode, the hillside vein into which they could sink a shaft to take the gold from the heart of the mountain.

He told her something else. Of a kind of gold she would hear of again and again in the weeks and months to follow until she would curse the name itself.

Poor man's gold. Gold to be found in a place they called poor man's diggings. A place where the gold could be found on the surface, washed down in the stream beds, so that it could be mined with placer methods, a sluicebox and rockers or even a simple gold pan. Gold that could be mined with hand labor and no investment of capital in machinery to go underground. Gold that could be won by a man with only his hands and his labor, a poor man who would become a rich man.

This is what the 10,000 residents had abandoned Custer to seek. Poor man's gold in a place they called

Deadwood.

She thought it sounded insane, but she was ready to follow Jake like a good wife if that was the decision reached by Hobart and the rest. She respected Hobart's judgment and would have asked no more questions, had not Jake said something else which shattered her calm.

"Everyone's going on in the morning but the Everett boys."

"What? Hugh and Luther aren't going with us?"

"Nope. Hugh said he figured they could move on faster in the mountain country without the wagons. Could be he's right, though it would be a risky business. Anyway, he said to tell you he hoped you'd understand that they had best go on alone."

"You mean he's leaving? Just like that, without saying goodbye?"

Jake shrugged. "Oh, I expect he'll be by before we push out. I think he figured it was too much trouble for you cooking for them and putting up with Luther."

"Didn't you tell him it wasn't? Didn't you ask him to stay?"

"Course. But you can't tell a man what to do."

Molly was stunned. She sat picking at her dinner, trying not to let Jake know how upset she was. Just that morning she had been so full of hope. She felt that if she could make the cabin into some semblance of a home, then she might once again be at peace within herself, that she could return to the feeling she had when they lived in the soddy. She hadn't been happy, but she had known her place, seen her duty, done each day the chores that make a place home. Women's work had been enough to make her believe her life was in order. Now what was the good of trying to do right if Hugh was going away and there would be not even the hope of love? If he robbed her of even the passion-tarnished image of the innocent love she had cherished and clung to? In the sod house she had been able to tell herself her feelings did not matter; that if she never again felt that sweet surge of tender love it would not matter; that it was better to have the loyalty she felt for Jake. But now, having known again the trembling excitement, the life that came to her when she was in Hugh's arms, she did not know if she could ever again make a life of baking Jake's bread and ironing his shirts and doing for him when he was not even aware of how much of herself she gave up to be a wife to him.

She looked at Jake, wanting desperately for him to be aware of her distress and come to her and put his arms around her and be the father to her he had always been.

But Jake was busy wiping up the last of the stew with his bread and seeing him, she could not hold back her anguish. "I don't want Hugh to go on alone. It's too dangerous."

"Then go to him."

"What?"

"Go to him. Tell him to come on with us. He'll listen to you. He likes you."

She put her head down in her hands. If only he knew what he was saying to her.

"Go on, Molly. Their cabin is just down the trail. Take Edwin with you. He can finish gathering the kindling tomorrow."

Still she hesitated.

"It's going to be dark soon. If you don't go now, it

will be too late. If they push out before us, you won't see them again."

Not see Hugh again! It was too much! She could not let him go without even saying goodbye. She could not let him go thinking she hated him for what he had done to Pearson's body, for what he had done to her in the glen. She rose from the table. She would persuade him to stay to keep him safe, or if he insisted on going on alone, at least she would send him with the truth.

She got her shawl and walked to the doorway, and then as she pulled aside the hide that closed in the cabin and felt the sweet, cold mountain air, she knew she was doing something that risked all her security and sense of right and wrong. She turned back to her husband.

"Jake?"

"What?" He was lighting his pipe.

"Come with us?"

"You can go that far alone. Don't be afraid."

"Please?"

"I got to tend my mules."

Suddenly he looked different to her. It was difficult to believe he was really her husband. It was as if she was seeing him for the first time, or perhaps the last.

She stepped out of the door.

Molly had come to him. It amazed Hugh for he had believed she hated him when she pushed him away saying he was no better than Pearson. He had known it was a coward's way out, simply to leave the party at Custer without even saying goodbye to her; but he had known he would feel just as he felt now at seeing her standing before him: that he could not say to her face

170

that he would never see her again. That was why he had decided to walk out of her life. He knew he could not forget her but he thought if he went away and got on with his adventure, threw himself into the search for gold, then at least he would be free. Hugh was not a coward but the depth of his feelings for Molly made him afraid — afraid more of himself than of anything. Sometimes he feared the beast within him, believing he might lose control of his passions and do something terrible. And sometimes he feared something else that was within him, a great well of love that ran so deep he might be drowned in it and never again be his own man. Often when a man senses himself on the verge of such an all-encompassing love, he pulls back, runs away, or does something to push away the very love he yearns for. Hugh had resolved to leave Molly and, had she let him go, it might all have turned out quite differently. But she had come to him.

He'd been amazed to look up from where he and Luther were organizing their gear before the cabin to see her approaching with Edwin beside her, and surprised at the way she had taken charge of the situation. She had let Edwin beg them to continue with the expedition, listened while Luther made a great show of protesting the high-handed treatment he fancied he'd received from Hobart while all the time his nervous blinking betrayed his insecurity at striking out alone, and then, while Hugh was still trying to think of some excuse to talk to her alone, Molly had reached into her pocket, produced a penny, and asked Luther to take Edwin into town for some candy.

"I had to talk to you alone," she said as they watched Edwin and Luther disappear down the path to town.

He nodded, wanting to make it easier for her, but being without words.

"You aren't really leaving, are you?"

"Yes. I think it best."

"Why?"

"God, Molly. You know."

"Is it because of what I said back there in the trees, about Pearson?"

"Partially."

"I didn't mean it, what I said about what you did to his body. I understand. I know you did it to protect me."

"It's not just that, Molly. There's more. You know."

"Because of what happened there."

"Because I kissed you. Because I can't keep my hands off you. Why pretend, Molly? I made a fool of myself. I was an animal. I was like Pearson. You said it yourself."

"I shouldn't have. That's what I had to tell you. I acted like I hated you and then later when I realized it could have been us the Sioux got, when I heard you preach at the funeral, when Jake told me you might be leaving, I couldn't let you go without telling you—" her voice trailed off.

"Without telling me what?"

She was confused, afraid. She pulled her shawl closer around her, bit at her lower lip, and could hardly get the words out. They came at last in a whisper. "Just that I don't *hate* you. I don't hate you at all. I never could. I forgive you for what happened to Pearson and—for what happened to me back home and—and I could never hate you."

It was not enough. It was just not enough. Something inside Hugh sensed what Molly was driving at, even knew why she could not say more, but he wanted more. He sensed that he might win her. That she had come here to keep him and that if he were cautious, if he played her gently—but he did not want to win her by subterfuge. He wanted her to come to him of her own volition and it made him reckless.

"You're trembling, Molly. It's cold. Come inside the cabin. I'll light a lantern."

She looked alarmed and although the hand he reached out to her never touched her shoulder, her trembling increased. "No, I can't come in. I have to get back. It's getting dark. I just wanted to ask you not to leave the party because of me. Jake wants you to stay partners and it's not safe for you to go on alone, so please, please just forget what I said because it wasn't true."

"You don't hate me."

"No, not at all. It was just that I was upset because, because—"

"Because I kissed you. Because I love you."

"Don't say it, Hugh. Please don't say it."

"It's true."

"Don't you see? If you say it then we really can't go on."

"And if I don't say it, then we can go on? Is that how you manage, Molly? Not saying things? Not admitting things? Do you think if you never say that we've been lovers, if you never admit it even to yourself, that we can pretend to be just friends? Is that what you want? To be friends?"

"Yes, friends."

"Oh, Molly, can't you see I can't go on like this? If

you won't leave Jake and come away with me, then I've got to get away from you."

"Leave Jake?"

"Yes. You don't love him. You can't possibly love him, so come with me."

"How can you say such a thing? How can you even think it? How could we do that to Jake?"

"He's strong. He'll get over it. We'll explain about Edwin and that will make it easier if he knows I'm Edwin's father."

"Take Edwin away from him? I couldn't do that. I could never do that. He loves Edwin. He raised him. Hugh, can't you see? Jake is my husband. We were married in a church."

"Because you had to. But just because it was right for you then doesn't mean you have to stay with him forever. I know it's hard, Molly. I like Jake; he's my friend. I don't want to hurt him, but—"

"I won't hurt him. I won't ever hurt Jake. He's my husband and, and—"

"And you love him? Tell me you love him."

She backed away from him, looking helpless and he pressed his advantage, grabbing her roughly by the shoulders. "Say it, Molly. If you won't say you love me, then tell me you love Jake."

"I love . . . Jake. Jake Lewis is my husband and I love him." She said the words with her eyes closed and her whole body trembling. He could sense the tension in her body. It was as if she might break any moment and he knew he could not love her and hurt her any more. He let go of her shoulders and she slumped against him weakly. He stood there holding her ever so gently while she sobbed.

"I'm sorry, Molly. I'm sorry, sweetheart. I don't know why I'm doing this to you."

She looked up at him. "It's so confused. Oh, Hugh, I hurt so. I never hurt so badly before. I don't think I can stand it if you go away. I'm so afraid. I'm so afraid."

He held her in his arms, wiping away her tears, comforting her like a child.

"What are you afraid of, Molly? The Indians?"

"Yes, no . . . I don't know. I don't know. I'm just so afraid."

He wondered then if she could fear the same things he feared. The beast within, the thing that might cut loose and wreak havoc. Or was it the great whirlpool of love that might suck one down? He thought a woman's fears must be different, that it had to be the Indians or Jake's finding out or something terrible and unknown outside of her that made her tremble, and so he told himself he must protect her.

And she, sensing perhaps the one thing that would make him stay, looked up at him and said, "Please don't leave me, Hugh. Take care of me."

He said nothing more then but only held her close, knowing she would soon withdraw from even this chaste embrace. He knew if he followed her to Dead-wood, he was lost.

"I won't ever leave you again," he said.

175

Chapter Twelve

"So if it's this Deadwood place we're going to, why don't we go?" Emerald asked. She was dressed only in a chemise and underskirt and had arranged herself artfully on the great mahogany bed so the soft swell of her breast was revealed in a manner that was seductive without being bold. Austin Avery seemed to like her best when she was just a bit coy. "I'm bored to death with hanging around Cheyenne," she added, but Avery seemed bent on ignoring her. He was dressing to go out and intent on studying his own reflection in the beveled oval mirror of the ornate mahogany dresser.

Emerald lowered her chin and stared at him with wide eyes. She felt the emerald earbobs jiggle against her neck and hoped the light was striking them so they brought out the green in her eyes. Sooner or later he would look at her and she would be ready. She had asked the question petulantly, more to attract Austin's attention than to gain information. He was dressing to go out and she was bored to death with watching him gamble; nor did she fancy another night alone. She did not have any illusions that Dakota territory would be any more pleasurable than Wyoming, but she figured the sooner Austin Avery struck it rich in the mines, the sooner they could be back on a riverboat steaming back to the luxuries of civilization. She decided to rephrase the question; this time taking a strand of her long black hair and twisting it around her finger as she spoke. "I said, when are we leaving for Deadwood?"

She studied the curl, keeping her eyes down so Austin would notice the lushness of her eyelashes. That way when she looked up at him, the effect of her wide green eyes would be even more devastating. In the weeks she had been with Austin Avery for hours at a time, there had been little to do but sit in hotel rooms and look into the mirror, seeing each time less of Emma O'Brien, shop girl and dreamer, and more of Emerald O'Brien, woman of the world.

"I told you, we'll go when I say so." Austin finally acknowledged her presence, though he kept his eyes on his own reflection in the mirror. After shaving he had splashed himself with Bay Rum so generously that Emerald caught the scent from across the room. It was delicious. He applied just enough lacquer to his dark hair to make it gleam. Now with a tiny scissors he trimmed a stray hair from his luxuriant mustache, then tossed his head back to check for offensive hairs in his nostrils. There were none. He smiled at himself in the mirror, revealing his well-polished gold incisor. Sliding open one of the drawers which framed the mirror, he selected a set of diamond studs and began arranging them in the front of his ruffled shirt.

Emerald shifted on the bed in annoyance, then arranged herself so her ruffled underskirt appeared to have inched up by accident revealing the inside of one black silk-stockinged calf. She had kept her shoes on.

They were new, after all.

"I just don't understand what we're waiting for! We came all the way to this god-forsaken town just to go to the Black Hills, and everyone in Cheyenne is packing out every day like there's some kind of a race on, and we're just sitting here. Why, all the gold mines will be found before we get there!"

"Precisely, my dear," Avery said, slipping into a brocaded vest.

"But you told me you intended to acquire mining interests. That you owned mines in Montana before you sold out to go back down the Mississippi and you were going to the Black Hills to acquire more mines. So why are we just sitting here in Cheyenne while everyone else finds all the gold?"

"Emerald, darling, that's the point." He turned to her at last, almost smiling. "There are much easier ways to get gold than to dig for it. I thought I'd taught you that by now."

So he was going to the Black Hills to gamble. She should have known that, yet somehow she'd pictured him in the mountains with a pick and shovel. Of course Austin would never get his hands dirty. She had no doubt he could acquire a mine by gambling. She had seen him win over a thousand dollars in a night. It was just that it was still hard for her to admit that gambling wasn't a mere diversion with Austin Avery, it was a whole way of life.

"Of course I knew you'd be gambling," she said at last. "But I think we should get going. They're leaving Cheyenne by the hundreds every week."

"All in good time, my dear. We want to be sure this new Deadwood digging is the mother lode. We'd have risked our scalps going to Custer for nothing. Then we want to give them time to get enough gold mined so the miners have some gold dust in their pouches and the urge to double it at someone else's expense. And, of course, we want to wait until a road's been built and things are a bit easier and safer. We wouldn't want an Indian to get that lovely hair of yours, would we? The Cheyenne route is notorious for that sort of thing."

She smiled at the reference to her lovely hair and ignored the remark about Indians. She wasn't afraid. Danger only made things more exciting.

"It's just that I'm so bored with Cheyenne I could scream."

"Are you now?" He seemed to be really looking at her this time. "Do you mean I'm not keeping you entertained?"

She cast her eyes down modestly, letting the tip of one finger caress her breast casually. "It's just that you come in so late when you gamble all night; I get so bored watching you, I just can't stay awake. You won't let me go anywhere in the evening without you and you won't take an evening off to go to the theatre with me. And then you sleep all day."

"Poor little Emerald," he said, studying himself in the mirror as he tied his flowing black silk scarf. "I thought you were having so much fun shopping. I see you have some new shoes."

At least he had noticed something. They were genuine French kid. She smiled and made the most of the opportunity to reveal the inside of her thigh as she showed off the shoes. When she noticed a quickening of his interest, she quickly pressed her knees together and pulled her underskirt down demurely.

"But, Austin, Cheyenne is such a dreadful place. A decent woman can't walk down the street even in broad daylight without some terrible man making a suggestive remark."

"A decent woman can probably manage quite nicely." A flicker of amusement crossed Avery's usually impassive face.

"Are you saying I'm not a decent woman?" She felt a twinge of conscience.

"Not at all my dear. I'm just saying there is a simple and well established custom on the frontier which makes it very easy to distinguish decent women from," he shrugged, "from the other kind. Nice women do not paint their faces. The . . . other kind . . . do. If you will notice, there is a certain type of woman in Cheyenne. They chalk their faces white and paint their lips scarlet and wear red feathers in their hats and walk little dogs on leashes. Therefore, my dear, if you wish to be distinguished from such, all you need do is wash your face and refrain from acquiring a little dog. Thus, you will be able to stroll the streets of Cheyenne or Deadwood, I'm sure when the time comes, without fear of molestation."

"Are you saying I don't look nice?" Emerald allowed her lower lip to tremble. She spent hours each day arranging her looks to please him and now this!

"My dear," Avery turned to study her. "You would not be here if I did not find you delicious. I did not mean to imply that your little artifices with the paint brush were in the same class with the painted ladies. I'm merely telling you how you may walk the streets without fear of being mistaken for an indecent lady."

"I was a decent lady until you came along."

"Come now, Emerald. You were ripe for the plucking. If it had not been me, it would have been some fat Missouri merchant. Is that what you want? Do you wish you were married to some respectable merchant and safe behind the counter of his drygoods store?"

"I wouldn't mind being married."

"Well, if that is the case, my dear, then I'm sure you will have no trouble finding some upstanding young man either here or in Deadwood who will be delighted to make an honest woman of you. I never promised you marriage and I can tell you right now, you wouldn't like it." He stopped talking a moment to arrange a diamond stickpin in his ascot, then turned toward her and looked her in the eyes. "You're bred for adventure and excitement, just like me. That's why I picked you out of that miserable little dressmaker's shop and brought you along. I'll tell you another thing, Emerald. I'm the right man for you. You might think you'd be happier with some man who would offer you marriage and respectability, but you wouldn't. Because it's all a game with you just as it is with me. We play parts for each other and I know the part you want me to play."

It was true. He did know somehow what she wanted and had known since the moment they met. But she had a power over him too. She sensed that.

"Doesn't it work both ways, Austin? Don't I know what you want?"

He seemed a bit taken aback. "Yes, you seem to. You've been most satisfactory."

"It's because I love you."

"No, you don't." It was the first time she had said the words and he seemed almost offended, as if he would forbid her to talk that way. "People like us don't need love. Love is like the promise of a hereafter. It's pie-in-the-sky for those who prefer to live their lives on earth in suffering. You and I take our pleasure where and when we find it. We make our own rewards. It's only those who believe in sin and eternal damnation who have to talk about love to justify their lusts or to justify the fact they get so damn little pleasure from their sanctified mating."

"But, Austin—"

"I know. You'd like me to tell you I love you. Well, I won't. I don't believe in it. Love's an illusion people work for themselves, like one of my card tricks or what magicians do on the stage. And it's the worst kind of a trick because it's a trick you play on yourself."

She opened her mouth to dispute what he was saying, although she hadn't quite sorted it out yet, but she was struck by something she saw in his usually impassive face. Even as he denied love and a need for it, his expression had shifted so that for just a moment he had a little-boy look of wistfulness about him. He looked at her for a moment as if now that he had said it, he wished it were not so. Then, just as she was wondering if she had really seen what she thought she had seen in his face, he regained his composure, his face became darkly handsome and he gave her a look she understood.

"Will you be a good girl and help me with my cuffs?"

She nodded, demurely, knowing what he wanted. He sat on the bed beside her, offering her his open hand with the tiny diamond studs. She was a little hurt by what he'd said. It was true that what passed between them never seemed quite real, but what was wrong with that? Their way was more exciting and beautiful than life. Life could be dull, even painful. People could be ugly, even lonely. With Austin Avery she was always beautiful, like someone on a stage. What she could not understand was why he did not wish to play the scene all the way and make the pledges and promises that would complete the fairy tale. She decided it might come later if Austin knew what she wanted, for he did seem to have a sixth sense about her, knowing what she wanted just as, at this moment, she knew he was beginning to desire her. She knew he wished her to be both seductive and coy. She would play the part because it was what she wanted, too, although she sensed it was better not to let him know that.

She took the studs from him and put one through his cuff, drawing out the action, knowing his eyes followed the top of her chemise where the swell of her breast rose and fell as she breathed. Pretending to be unable to fasten the stud, she slumped a little to allow her breast to just touch the top of his hand, then quickly withdrew.

He tore his hand from hers, sending the stud scattering across the floor. He put his hand to her breast roughly.

She looked into his eyes, still wanting to see adoration in his face, but again it was impassive. He pushed her across the bed, demanding. It was happening faster than she liked. She had lost control of him, but she felt her blood pounding in excitement. He kissed her neck and then began to tug at her chemise. His breath was hot and his moustache scratched as his lips moved down her body and found her breast. He smelled of Bay Rum and something else, hot and masculine.

Despite herself, she moaned.

He rose up and smiled into her face as if he had won something. She had determined never to let him know she had begun to enjoy the things he did to her, so she held him away from her.

"Tell me you love me," she teased.

"Tell me you want me," he countered.

"What?"

"Tell me I pleasure you, Emma. Tell me I pleasure you."

"No," she said, still holding him back.

"Damn you," he said, and then his lips moved down her body and words no longer mattered, so that in the end it was she who pulled up her underskirt.

Afterwards, while she was arranging her clothes, her face and breast hot and scratched from his mustache and her hair completely disarrayed, he rolled off the bed and began searching for his stud. It made her furious, especially when he straightened up after only a moment and held out the diamond, shouting, "Gambler's luck!"

"Don't tell me you're still going out."

"Certainly. It's the shank of the evening. And you just gave me my good luck charm, Emma."

"Don't call me Emma. Don't ever call me Emma."

"Why not? It's your name isn't it? Emma O'Brien?"

"It isn't! I don't know where you got such an idea." She burst into tears before she even realized how they might cause the smoky kohl with which she darkened her lashes to run. She looked up as she wiped her eyes on the bedsheet. Avery was concentrating on a speck of dust on the satin lapel of his Prince Albert coat. "Why are you so hateful to me?" she cried. "I do everything to please you, give up my family and everything and you treat me like this."

"You seemed to be enjoying it well enough a minute ago. I believe I called you Emma then and you didn't seem to mind."

"That was different." She felt herself blush unattractively. She had been out of control, had almost let him know how much he affected her. She sensed there was danger in letting him have too much of her. That first night, she had given herself to him totally, but now she knew better. He had the gambling. She had nothing but him. She must not forget she was Emerald O'Brien. *Emma* O'Brien could be hurt.

"Call me Emerald," she said quietly. He must have sensed she meant it for he murmured, "Emerald," and patted her breast. It was a gesture that she didn't particularly care for. It was meant, she supposed, to be conciliatory, but it gave her the feeling he owned her.

"Be a good girl and perhaps I'll bring you some little bauble, though there aren't so many men traveling with their wives' jewels as we found on the Mississippi. Still, perhaps I can win enough greenbacks to buy you something you fancy."

Emerald blinked back tears. She felt lost and alone. He was going out, and there was nothing more she could do to stop him. She turned away from him and curled into a ball on the bed. She felt him pat her fanny, but she did not see him tip his hat to her as he walked out the door.

Later, when she'd had her cry, Emerald got out of bed and went to the massive walnut wardrobe. Opening it, she rummaged around behind her valise and took out the beaded purse in which she kept her jewels. She knelt on the floor, spilling the contents of the purse out on her lap. She had an emerald-and-diamond necklace to match the earbobs, her first gift from him and the only one she cherished, two ornate gold watches with chains, a half-dozen diamond stick pins of varying quality, and an assortment of gold chains and jeweled clips. The jewels gave her no satisfaction. He had not given them to her out of love. Only the earbobs had been selected for her; the rest were gambling winnings. If he lost, which he seldom did, he would come to her and borrow back the jewels, replacing them when his luck changed, often the same night. She merely served as his bank.

She sat on the floor before the wardrobe and looked at her clothes hanging above her. Seeing the emerald-green gown, she reached up and stroked it, then impulsively, pulled it off the hook and into her lap. Avery had bought her a trunkful of dresses but she would never have another gown she loved so much. She buried her face in the soft velvet folds and would have cried, but she did not want to waterspot the material. Poor dress, it was already showing signs of wear.

It had all begun with the green velvet. It made her think of her poor mother. How she must have cried when she found Emerald's note. How she must wish she had her daughter back. For a moment, Emerald thought about going home. If she sold the jewelry she would have enough money to go, but she knew her mother would never take her back and if she did, would make Emerald's life a misery with wailing about sin and repentance.

As disappointed as Emerald was that everything was not going her way with Avery, she knew in her heart, the last thing she wanted was repentance. A life of sin was occasionally depressing but seldom boring.

What do I want? she asked herself, sitting there in her chemise on the floor of the frontier hotel room. She had dreamed of going back to the South as the respectable wife of a plantation owner, but Avery seldom mentioned his plantation anymore. She found it increasingly difficult to conjure those images which had only a few weeks ago seemed so attainable, images of herself on Avery's arm, beautifully gowned, gliding down an elaborate curved staircase and into the grand ballroom of the plantation, every eye upon her.

Now, thinking of how the men in her dreams stared at her, and how even in reality other men seemed to envy Avery and want her, she stood up and held the green dress before her. She looked at herself in the mirror and knew she could get what she wanted from any man, including Austin Avery.

But what was it she wanted? She remembered Avery's speech about love. He said they didn't need it. He never told her he loved her. He was determined to keep that emotion to himself, even as he teased her to say she wanted him.

Love will do for a starter, she decided. *I'll make Austin Avery say he loves me.*

Then I'll decide what I want next.

Chapter Thirteen

They were two days beyond Custer and camped within the luxuriant grasslands of the southern Hills when Hugh next had time to write in his journal. The Hobart party was making its last camp on level ground before beginning its climb into the rugged mountains in which Deadwood was supposed to lie. It was evening and Hugh had climbed a hill so he could be alone to write and watch over the camp, yet not make himself a target for Indians. Hobart warned that the Sioux, who were horsemen and plains fighters and avoided the narrow trails of the inner Hills, might take advantage of their last camp in the valley to make a raid. Heeding his warnings, many of the men cleaned their guns as they sat before their campfires. Jake was busy hobbling his mules and adding picket lines as a precaution. Luther and Caleb Dexter, the old prospector who had joined the party, were taking advantage of the last minutes of daylight to work their gold pans in the creek.

Hugh looked up from his journal, unable to concentrate. He had been keeping an eye on the Lewis wagon and saw Molly climb out, stretch and walk about as if to enjoy the evening breeze before retiring. Her hair was loose and hanging in a pale mist about her shoulders that made Hugh's throat tighten. She saw him and waved but returned to her wagon. Once she would have joined him, but the days of casual conversation between them were over. They had become "friends." Friends who did not trust themselves to be alone.

Hugh turned back to the map he was making of their journey, but he found himself wondering if it would have been different if they had met again in a civilized place. Would he be a better man if they were not two hundred miles from the nearest church? Or would he still promise to be her friend and burn to be her lover? It had occurred to Hugh that something might happen to Jake. Jake was a middle-aged man and they were in a dangerous land. He was angry at himself for the thought and angry at Molly for driving him to it. His only consolation was that, although he had already killed a man, he was not capable of premeditated murder.

He was also concerned about their journey. Custer had shaken him. The rows of abandoned buildings were stark reminders of the riskiness of their venture. His doubt was compounded the next day when they came upon Hill City. Donnelly remembered it as a thriving mining camp of over 100 cabins. Now it was a ghost town, eerie, abandoned; with doors standing open, dishes left on tables as if not a moment could be wasted by those who joined the new stampede. They were in a race, he realized; a race that would go to the swiftest and strongest, and the Hobart party was already very late. Increasingly he feared they were on one of history's greatest wild goose chases, and somewhere up that steep and precipitous trail to whatever waited in the mountains above them, he must abandon his hopes and dreams, or perhaps find his fate lay in yet another unmarked grave.

Yet, despite these gloomy realizations, more often Hugh was driven by a spark of hope, a feeling that he was among the chosen few. Like Pip in the Dickens' novel he had enjoyed the winter before, he persisted in having *Great Expectations*.

He wanted to write some of these thoughts in his journal, but the light was almost gone, so he returned to watching the camp. There was a movement by the creek and he reached for his rifle, then saw it was only Luther and the old prospector, Caleb Dexter, returning from their gold panning. Hugh wondered again what Luther found so appealing about the foul-smelling, bad-mouthed, perpetually drunk old reprobate. Luther caught sight of Hugh and waved. The old man beckoned Hugh to join them and pantomimed taking a drink. Hugh shook his head *no* and the old man toddered off cheerfully, but Luther came up the hill to press the invitation. Again Hugh declined, but Luther persisted.

"Come on, Hugh. He's got enough for all of us. I never got drunk before."

"There's no sense to be drinking when there's danger of Indians."

"You never want to have fun," Luther whined. "You spend all your time mooning around."

"We didn't join this expedition for fun."

"We don't have to get *drunk*. Just one drink. You can

come on and have one lousy drink with us."

Hugh refused again and this time Luther turned on his heel and marched back down the hill purposefully. He joined Dexter and they drifted out of sight. Hugh had the uneasy feeling he should have gone along. It reminded him of all the times in the past he'd rejected his younger brother's efforts to be buddies. He wondered if he had made Luther angry enough to go on a binge and started to go after him, then thought better of it. The damage was done and besides, he was not his brother's keeper. It was a role he had tried to fill on the trip but with every mile they traveled, he became more aware of the futility of trying to control or even influence his brother, for his efforts only increased Luther's resentment of his authority. Had he realized how immature and bull-headed Luther was, he would not have taken him along, Hugh decided, but in the same breath told himself the pioneering experience might yet make a man of Luther.

Of one thing Hugh was certain. Caleb Dexter was not going to be a good influence on this brother. They had picked up the old man in Hill City, and their first sight of him, holed up in a buffalo robe in an abandoned cabin, nursing a jug and as rank as a hibernating bear, should have convinced them he was not fit company for civilized people. But it seemed only decent to see if the old man needed any help, and before they knew it he had latched onto their party. It seemed he had been on a solitary prospecting trip when the Indians ran off his burro and almost got what little hair remained on his scalp. When he made it back to Hill City, he found the town abandoned, so he had holed up with his cache of jugs to wait for the next party to come along and transport him to the new diggings.

He wheedled his way into their party with offers of chaws of tobacco, snorts of his jug, and stories of his adventures in the gold camps of the West. He had been to them all, Cherry Creek in '58, the Comstock in '59, and Alder Gulch since '63, from which infamous diggings he proudly displayed his good luck charm—a gold nugget as big as a tooth.

And he looked the part. His mangy, graying beard almost covered his shirt, which appeared to be the top half of a set of once-red flannel underwear; his baggy pants were so patched with buckskin it was difficult to determine their original fabric; and his knee-high miner's boots had obviously seen years of wading in creeks and mud. Under their craggy brows, his eyes were bloodshot and crafty.

His odor was beyond description. Hugh doubted if the old man had bathed since leaving the California gold rush of '49.

It seemed the old man had been to every gold field there ever was, and knew everything there was to know about gold mining. He talked about flour gold, specimen gold, and conglomerate gold, the technical details of underground mining and hydraulic operations and capital investment, but he always returned to tell of the magic lure of poor man's gold, that beautiful bonanza of nuggets just waiting to be picked up.

The men shook their heads in wonder as the old man talked. It was obvious there was a great deal more to mining gold than any of them had realized. Hugh saw that himself, but he didn't know if it justified what Jake did. He invited Caleb Dexter to travel with them;

agreed, in fact, to haul his pack and remaining jugs for nothing. Luther was delighted, being somehow fascinated with him, but Hugh had great reservations. He wondered aloud why if the old man knew so much about finding gold, he had never struck it rich, and was met with tales of fortunes made and lost and hints of secret stores of wealth in eastern banks.

"It's the gold fever," the old man concluded. "Once the gold bug bites you, you got to keep searching; no matter how much you've got socked away. It's the thrill of the thing, searching for the big strike, always hoping to find the mother lode!"

The explanation didn't settle Hugh's doubts, but the decision was Jake's. Now as Hugh sat looking over the camp, he wondered again if Caleb Dexter's knowledge would be worth the trouble of having the old man along. His fears were confirmed an hour later when, as he spread his bedroll by the dying campfire, Luther came staggering up, obviously drunk. Hugh was annoyed, but he kept silent. The damage was done and in a way it was his fault for not going along to keep Luther in line.

Luther sat down on his pile of bedding and, grinning foolishly, attempted to remove his boots.

"Need some help, little brother?" Hugh felt a touch of tenderness at his brother's helpless condition.

"Don't 'little brother' me," Luther said in a thick voice. "I'm as much a man as you!"

The comment annoyed Hugh, but he decided it was not worth answering.

Luther, apparently sensed he had overreacted and, not able to manage the boot alone, thrust his foot out in a conciliatory gesture. "Okay, Hugh, if you wanna give me a hand, I am jus' a little bit tired."

Hugh helped him out of the boots and Luther studied them sadly before using them for a pillow under the head of his canvas tarp. "Poor boots, all ruined. Thas' the first thing I'm gonna do when we strike it rich. Buy me some new boots." He struggled to remove his belt and then gave up, curled up on the canvas and pulled his blankets over him. "You shud of come along. Me and my old pardner Caleb Dexter jus' had ourselves the best old time."

"I can see that."

"I knew you'd be mad," Luther said. "You an ol' Emmet Hobart are always telling people what to do. But I'm going to show you both a thing or two one of these days."

"Sure you are," Hugh took off his own boots. "Now get some sleep or you'll be sick in the morning."

"Already feel a little funny."

Serves you right, Hugh stifled the urge to say it aloud.

Just as Hugh was arranging his own bedding, Hobart came by on his evening rounds. "You boys got guard duty tonight?"

"Not tonight," Hugh wished Hobart would not call them boys, and hoped Hobart would not notice Luther's condition.

"Well, keep your rifles close by anyway."

"Sure thing, Mr. Hobart. Whatever you say, Mr. Hobart," Luther muttered, rising long enough to pat the needle gun at his side.

"I see you and Caleb killed another jug." Hobart said with a trace of humor in his voice.

"Wasn't a jug, it wuz a flask," Luther mumbled. "Flasks is easier when you're out prospecting."

194

"A flask then."

"You want to make something of it?" Luther sat up unsteadily.

"Not at all. It's a man's own business if he wants to get drunk I always say. Just stopped by to remind you about the Indians."

"Don't you worry about us. We're alert as hell."

Hobart grinned and walked away.

"It's a good thing he didn't want to make nothing of it," Luther told Hugh, " 'Cause I'm too tired to take him tonight. Besides, I think I'm gonna be sick." He began to vomit. Hugh moved away in disgust spreading his bedding about halfway between Luther's snoring form and the Lewis wagon.

He usually avoided sleeping near the wagon Molly shared with Jake. It had been miserable on those rainy nights he and Luther had slept under the wagon, but somehow tonight he took a morose pleasure in being near her. He lay awake, almost savouring his loneliness, and then was startled to notice a figure coming through the darkness toward him. Instantly he was alert. He recognized the lean and slightly stooped figure. "Jake?"

"That you, Hugh?" Jake whispered. "Sorry if I woke you. I've got the dysentery. I'll probably be out in the bushes half the night. Where's Luther?"

"Over there," Hugh pointed.

"Snoring got to you, huh? He'll really be sawing wood after what him and Caleb Dexter was up to." Jake laughed and climbed into the wagon.

Lord, Hugh thought, *there's no privacy on a wagon train*. He was chafed and annoyed by the evening's experiences and he had a difficult time getting to sleep. He realized it was strange to be away from the sound of Luther's snores, a sound he'd grown accustomed to in the years he'd shared a bedroom with his brother. Jake disturbed him coming and going on another trip to the bushes and finally Hugh picked up his blankets again and moved away from the Lewis wagon and back to his brother's side.

He was sleeping soundly when, as if from far away, he heard Luther's voice and felt a jerk at his shoulder. He was certain he must be dreaming, but he could hear Luther saying, "Wake up!" His eyelids flickered open. It was near dawn. There was just enough light to make shapes barely discernable. His eyes fell shut.

"Hugh, wake up! There's somebody sneaking around in the bushes. Must be Indians."

Indians! Hugh raised up on one shoulder, trying to force sleep away. His heart began to hammer and his eyes searched the dim light appearing at the edge of camp as the sun rose. There was a figure there all right.

He was reaching for his own rifle when he realized who it was. He turned to Luther. Couldn't his brother see? Was he still drunk?

Luther stood erect, his needle gun raised, taking careful aim.

He was about to shoot Jake Lewis.

Chapter Fourteen

Austin Avery had decided not to gamble at the Railroad House that evening. Although it was Cheyenne's largest hotel, it was never a good policy to work the hotel where you boarded. He tossed a coin to decide between the American House and the Inter-Ocean Hotel and was pleased when the Inter-Ocean won. The American House catered to the tenting crowd, and there would be more action and news of the Black Hills, but the Inter-Ocean featured fresh oysters and he was due for a replenishing of his vital juices.

Emerald had been amusing as usual that day. Of course, she could become a problem if her willfullness and pouting persisted, but so far her little shows of temper had merely served to whet his appetite. His impulse to take her along had certainly proven auspicious, he decided, but then things generally went in his favor when he trusted his instincts. Taking a chance on Emma O'Brien had been an excellent move. The girls available in gold camps were so often diseased. Enjoying their services was not worth the risk. He had seen enough disease to last him a lifetime, and it was difficult and unhealthy for a man of his capacities to abstain for long periods of time. He had learned that lesson well at Alder Gulch and so, thus far, his little traveling companion had been well worth the trouble and expense of bringing her along. He had chosen well. He had known she was the one the moment he entered her shop and saw her posing before the mirror, a shop girl with the reflection of a courtesan.

Of course she could become a problem. All that talk about marriage and returning to his old family plantation. He had been a bit startled when she first mentioned the plantation one night when he was lying in bed smoking a cheroot. He had almost forgotten telling her the plantation story. He had so many stories. Still, it was satisfying to him that she had so thoroughly accepted him as a Southern gentleman and a plantation owner, at that. It went well with the name, he had to admit. Austin Avery, a fine old name. Much better than the one he had used in Alder Gulch. And he needn't feel guilty about using it. It belonged to no one else. It was his. He had made it up himself.

He couldn't have fooled a real lady, of course. He knew enough about the Southern aristocracy to be sure of that. Nor would Emerald O'Brien ever be a real lady. But, decked out in the finery he had provided for her, she looked enough a lady to enhance his own appearance. She was, in fact, startlingly beautiful. Perhaps more beautiful than was necessary and perhaps more spirited, too. But he could handle her and he would never reveal his hand where she was concerned, not about the past nor about the present. A man must be in control of his emotions. If he ever let a woman know how much he needed her, she would win something precious away from him—his independence, his spirit, perhaps his very manhood.

Emma had her faults, he told himself, almost wishing there were more to enumerate. He liked a woman who had enough faults so that he could leave her with neither loss nor guilt because she laughed too loud or got drunk in public or did not accommodate his physical needs adequately. But Emerald was invariably pretty and charming and agreeable in bed. So he had to do some thinking to decide on the ways Emerald annoyed him. She was preoccupied with her own appearance. She had the annoying habit of always reaching out to touch his face or sleeve in a way that sometimes flattered him but at other times seemed wifely and demanding. And she was certainly not the best audience he ever had! She was far too concerned with her own performance to be totally engrossed in his, though she did seem to instinctively say, "Poor Austin" or "Brave Austin" at the right moments when he told her his war stories. She thought he had fought gallantly to preserve and protect the bonnie blue flag. He enjoyed spinning the illusion for her as he enjoyed all the illusions he had built for himself. He did not dare play the hero at work—he too often found himself sitting across the gaming table from a real war hero.

Seeing himself reflected and glowing in her eyes while he told her how he had fought Sherman's army in hand-to-hand combat made those war years seem glorious. Not that he thought the war had been a wasted effort. He had learned a great deal in the war. Neither entering the army nor becoming the general's orderly had been entirely his idea but once there, he had used his time well. For as he polished the general's

199

boots and served the general's meals and held the general's horse, he had observed those affectations of speech, dress, and manners that marked the Southern gentleman. And he had learned one more thing, the most important thing. In the evenings, the general and the other officers amused themselves at cards. Gambling and gaming had never been allowed in his own home, squalid though it was, for his family had religion, but the reality of war soon got him over fears of eternal damnation. There was enough hell on earth. He was fascinated with cards, and he learned everything he could in the officers' tents. When he could slip away from his duties, he practiced his skills on the enlisted men. When the end of the war neared and conditions were difficult, he was able to provide himself with boots and rations and medicine when even some officers were doing without.

Some call gambling a sickness, but Avery knew that with him it was a talent. He had a natural genius for it. Perhaps he would have discovered it without the war, but more than likely he would have ended up as an overseer on some mediocre plantation. So the war had been fortunate indeed. Afterwards, of course, there had been a difficult period until he discovered the Yankees and carpet baggers who had all the money were anxious to increase their unholy gains at someone else's expense, particularly at the expense of someone they thought to be a real Southern gentleman. He enjoyed taking their money. But, as he told Emerald, he would never be able to take another's money if that man had not first tried to get something without working for it. As a professional gambler, he told her, he was more honest and upright than the casual gambler. He was working for what he won.

He successfully made the transition from playing poker or shooting craps on the floor of a ragged army tent to dealing faro in the most splendid gambling parlors of New Orleans. From there, it was a natural step to work the Mississippi river boats. On one of his upriver journeys he had, purely on a whim, left the river and made the dangerous overland journey up the Bozeman trail to Montana and the notorious gold camp of Alder Gulch. The gold camp lacked certain of the Mississippi's conveniences, but having once been there, having once seen thousands of dollars worth of gold dust change hands over the gaming tables as casually as if it was the sawdust on the floors, having seen men made and men broken on the twist of a gold vein or the spin of a roulette wheel, he had to go back. He had to be where the stakes were the highest, where the play went on night and day and at any moment someone might pull a gun and the game would end in death.

There was no old family plantation to win back. There was no other way of life. He could only go on to the next game. And if Emerald didn't like it, well then, he had no doubt he could find some man, respectable or otherwise, in Deadwood to take her off his hands. He might miss her but he was certain he would never let his lust for her grow into a need he could not control.

When he stepped out of the hotel onto Cheyenne's main street, he felt a surge of anticipation. The streets were crowded with men on their way to the Black Hills. Stage coaches left almost daily for Fort Laramie where the passengers joined freight outfits to complete the journey. The route was dangerous, but as more left for the area, the danger was reduced. It was not danger that caused him to linger in Cheyenne. It was, as he told Emerald, that there were easier ways to get gold than to dig for it.

First come the miners to work in the mine
And then come the girls that work on the line

Avery recited to himself the ditty sung in every gold camp since '49. He had made up another line to the verse:

And then comes Austin Avery to make it all mine

He did not let his pleasure show, although his little rhyme pleased him, as did the way the roughly dressed men in the street stepped around him. Not that he was a gun fighter. There were those to whom killing was an addiction and gambling just a way to pass the time until the next draw. But, although he wore saloon pistols in his belt and enjoyed commanding respect, to Austin Avery the guns were only tools of his trade, or his art, for to him gambling was a profession. Not exactly a gentleman's trade, but not a bad ending for a Cracker farm boy.

He stopped at the door to the Inter-Ocean. There was music and bright lights and excitement within. It was time to go to work. It made him happy. He was not a man to whistle or hum aloud. He made an art of keeping his expression impassive, but sometimes on the inside his thoughts ran wild, and he would tell himself little jokes or recite verses. Now he recalled the words of the bonnie blue flag:

> We are a band of brothers,
>   and native to the soil,
> Fighting for the property,
>   ours by honest toil.

Austin Avery had another thought as he pushed open the doors of the hotel and it almost made him smile:

It was time for a little honest toil.

Chapter Fifteen

He had hesitated. For a long time afterwards whenever he would think about what had happened that morning in the camp beyond Custer City, and he would think about it often, Hugh would have to remember that he hesitated.

Later, he tried to tell himself it had been for only an instant and he had, after all, been half asleep when Luther shouted *Indians!* Hugh told himself he had to take time to be certain it wasn't an Indian, even though he knew Jake Lewis had been making trips back and forth to the bushes all night.

But when he got through all that, when he had made every excuse for himself he could, he had to face the fact he had hesitated because through his mind had flashed the thought, *He's going to kill Jake. Luther is going to kill Jake and I can have Molly!*

And so, no matter how many times he told himself he had pushed the thought away the moment it came, that he had replaced it at once with the image of Jake his friend and the man Edwin called father; still he had known that instant of joy at the thought his brother was going to eliminate his rival. He had to face the fact he was not the civilized man he was or thought he was when he left Nebraska.

He hit Luther low, somewhere between his groin and knees, swinging his own body from a sitting position into a quick lunge with his shoulders that knocked his brother off his feet. The shot boomed out almost simultaneously with the moment his body collided with Luther's so that as they landed on the ground together, Hugh was sure he had acted too late.

"What the hell?" Luther said from beneath him.

"Fool!"

Luther tried to break away from him and reach for his rifle again. "It's Indians, Hugh. Quick!"

"It was Jake." Hugh grabbed for his brother, catching him and pulling him back to the ground beside him. "You've shot Jake Lewis."

Luther turned and blinked at Hugh, suddenly sober.

Shouts and footsteps surrounded them as men fell out of their wagons, half-dressed and waving their rifles.

"What the hell's going on?" A familiar voice boomed out.

Still hanging onto Luther, Hugh looked up.

It was Jake. Jake standing there in his long underwear and boots, his beard and gray-flecked hair wild, the look on his face a mixture of fear and anger. "Who's shooting at me?"

Hugh let out his breath in relief and looked at Luther who turned from white to red, blinking rapidly, his jaw hanging slack.

"What's the shooting about?" Emmet Hobart demanded as he joined the group surrounding them.

"Who fired that shot?"

Hugh waited for Luther to speak up but his brother just stared dumbly at Jake, his hands still clutching the needle gun.

Hugh stood up. He felt a little dizzy.

"I thought you were an Indian, Jake," Luther finally said. "I heard something and I woke up and I could see someone in the bushes and I thought it was an Indian."

"I was relieving myself."

"Oh my God," Luther moaned, rocking back and forth. "Oh my sweet Jesus. I thought you were an Indian and I was going to shoot you."

"Holy Mother of God!" a familiar voice roared as another man joined the crowd. It was Donnelly. He was laughing. "What a bunch!"

"I was going to kill you," Luther told Jake again. "I would have killed you but Hugh stopped me." He turned from Jake to Hugh, his face full of anguish. "You ran into me and stopped me."

Hugh wanted to tell Luther it was all right. No damage had been done. But he knew it was not all right. Something had been changed. And that was when it hit him for the first time. He had hesitated. He had almost let Luther kill Jake. He stood there trying to think of something to say.

Jake reached down to offer Luther his hand as if to help him up. "It's okay. Everybody makes mistakes. No harm done."

But Luther turned away from Jake's outstretched hand and remained on the ground, shaking his head and moaning "Oh my God" over and over.

Hugh was embarrassed for Luther. He was lying there crying for everyone to see. By this time the whole camp had gathered around them. Molly broke through the crowd and hugged Jake. She was still wearing her nightdress and had only taken the time to throw a quilt around herself. Her hair was hanging loose around her shoulders. He could see the curve of her hips through the thin gown. Hugh turned away.

The rest of the men began to shift around uncomfortably. Donnelly was still laughing. "Man goes out to the bushes and almost gets shot. That would be a fine way to die, with your pants down!"

"Shut up."

"What?" Donnelly looked surprised. He was a big man, and mostly people took his jokes.

"I said shut up." Hugh made the words cold and hard. "Just let it drop."

Donnelly wiped his nose with the back of his hand, sheepishly, backing off a little from Hugh's anger. He looked around the group grinning, seeking approval of his joke. "No need to get yourself in a tizzy, lad. I was just making a bit of a joke there to take the little lady's mind off it." When his eyes found Molly, she pulled the quilt tighter around her. Donnelly turned to Jake, still grinning. "It wouldn't be the first time some man got himself shot with his pants down. Ain't that right?"

Hugh's fist shot out and he saw Donnelly's look of shock as his face crumpled and he fell back into the crowd. Somebody caught him and he came up fighting, but Hugh was ready for him. Hugh's blood was up. He felt happy. He was going to kick the stuffing out of Donnelly, bloody his whole damn grinning face and knock his teeth down his throat.

Donnelly feinted and when Hugh swung, the Irishman got in a blow to the belly that almost knocked the breath out of Hugh. He realized too late Donnelly must have been a prize fighter but Hugh wasn't afraid. He was conscious of Molly somewhere in the crowd. He would have died to look good for her. He and the Irishman circled each other warily, fists in position. Suddenly Hugh charged in and began raining blows on Donnelly, oblivious to the beating he was himself taking. It felt as good to be hit as to hit.

Then he was aware of other stronger arms around him. He was being pulled off Donnelly.

"Break it up." It was Hobart's voice in his ear. "Break this up. Save it for the Sioux."

"Let me go!" Hugh tried to pull away from Hobart.

"What's with you, Hugh? Everything's okay. No harm done. Donnelly just made a harmless joke."

Hugh managed to jerk away from Hobart. He stood apart from the others a moment, still ready to fight. But Jake stepped between Hugh and Donnelly.

"It's all right, Hugh. He didn't mean anything by it. What's got into you?"

Hugh looked from Jake to where Donnelly stood, nursing his fist and looking as if he didn't understand what had happened. Hugh knew the Irishman had no grudge to pick with him, knew there was no reason to hit the man again; still he had the urge to get in another punch.

"Please, Hugh," Molly spoke and he felt his anger dissolve. He could hardly look at her. He had really made a mess of things now. He was worse than Luther. He'd promised her he could be trusted, but once again he'd been an animal, and now the whole camp was staring at him. The fight drained out of him. The only thing left to do was face up to it like a man.

"I'm sorry, Donnelly. I don't know what got into me."

Donnelly shook hands with him and no one spoke of the incident again, but Hugh could not forget it. He was now aware of his potential for destruction and worse than Molly's tears, the accusing looks of the other men, or Luther's sobbing apologies, was knowing what lurked within him.

It took them nearly two weeks to make the journey to Deadwood, a distance of perhaps fifty miles. Although Donnelly had not been this far into the Hills, they no longer needed a guide, for the trail at first followed the deep wagon ruts left by the Custer Expedition of '74, and even when it left the "Thieves Trail" the country had been forever scarred by the miners as they stampeded to the new diggings.

The road was difficult and slow at best. At its worst, it seemed impossible. Trees had been cut down but the stumps remained. In some places the miners had used blasting powder to blow rocky outcroppings to bits, but in other places, the wagons had to be navigated around huge boulders. Always their desire for speed had to be tempered by the need to preserve the wagons. A broken axle would mean hours of delay. They crossed and recrossed Spring Creek as it wound its way into the Hills. At one crossing, a wagon became mired and they lost hours pulling it from the mud.

Despite their difficulties, the journey lost the tediousness that marked the miles from Sidney to the Black Hills. For now each bend of the constantly winding road held the promise of the unknown. Hugh thought he new how Adam must have felt in Eden, and he suspected some of the other men must have shared his sense of wonder because the grumbling and quarrelling ceased. The country was lush, fresh, and new, a wilderness unmarked by man except for the torn grass and the blasted rocks and the ax-killed trees of the road they followed and widened.

The trail seemed to be always winding upwards. As they moved deeper into the craggy shelter of the inner hills, they were no longer wary of Indian attack, but the trail became increasingly difficult, sometimes so steep Hugh and the other men on foot had to pull on ropes attached to the wagons to aid the exhausted mules. Then upon reaching the summit, Hobart would command them to lean back on the ropes to keep the descending wagons from over-running the mules, a danger despite the fact brakes were used and the wheels were chained together. Hugh marveled again at Jake's skill with his team. In going down the hills, he reined them back until their chins touched the breastplates of their harnesses and they leaned back against the tongue, descending with sure, mincing steps.

Finally they left Spring Creek and crossed several miles of highland which formed the divide between Spring Creek and the next stream. They no longer knew the names that had been given to the streams they crossed. In every meadow they came upon deer so innocent of man they would stand and stare. Hobart rescinded the order against hunting and several men, including Hugh and Luther, brought down deer. Hugh felt a thrill at killing his first buck, but after days of killing and gorging on the fresh meat, throwing away the less-choice cuts because there wasn't time to make jerky, he felt sick at the waste. He realized if the parties ahead and behind them slaughtered as many deer, even this last refuge would soon be as barren of life as the empty plains they had left behind. No one seemed to share his concern. He felt Molly would understand, but he was avoiding any serious conversation with her. He kept to himself.

There was a great deal of excitement early one morning when Morris came upon a bear and killed it. Jake judged it must have weighed six or seven hundred pounds when it was dressed. When the meat was passed around the men said it tasted as good as venison or beef. Morris rolled up the lushly furred bearhide and carried it in his wagon, declaring he would make a robe of it, but after several days it began to smell, so he dumped it over a bluff. Hugh walked by and saw the gleaming fur rotting there and was sorry for the slaughter of the bear.

They crossed the second creek and camped on the north bank beside the blackened coals of previous campfires. Luther found a military collar button and a broken horse shoe from a cavalry pony. Donnelly said General Crook had probably camped there as he sought the Sioux. Everyone felt much better knowing the military had been through the area. They speculated as to where the army was and if they would protect them as they invaded Sioux territory.

As they crossed more small creeks, the road grew so rough they could hardly believe they were on the right path. Stumps crowded the trail which followed yet another meandering creek and had been hacked out just wide enough to allow the wagons to pass single file.

Then once again they began to climb. The road grew worse with each step. It was as if those who had come before them, knowing they were close to their destination, had abandoned all effort to clear a path and clammered over the mountain with no thought to those who would follow. At last, early one morning, they stood on the summit and looked over the edge and knew somewhere in the gulch beneath them, clinging to the banks of Whitewood Creek and hidden in the pines, was Deadwood.

To descend by wagon seemed impossible, yet they knew it had been done, for at the bottom of the divide they could see the twisted and broken skeletons of other wagons. The trees along the trail bore evidence of how the descent had been made. Wide bands of bark had been torn from their trunks as the ropes which had girded them were used to lower the wagons inch by painful inch.

The men sighed and said it was impossible to get the wagons down. And then, since there was nothing else to do, they unhitched the mules and, girding fresh trees, began to do what had to be done.

When at last they had finished, they stood sweaty and exhausted and looked back up the hill. Hobart spat and said now he knew why no one had come back from the new diggings. It was just barely possible to get down to Deadwood, he said, but no one could get back out. They passed the joke around the group, savoring their accomplishment.

Hugh looked around at the whiskery faces of his traveling companions as they sucked at the new blisters on their hands and surveyed with tired and red-rimmed eyes the mountain they had conquered. They all wore the same look of satisfaction, and Hugh felt that for the first and the last time on the journey they had all been truly together. It was late afternoon and within an hour they would re-hitch the mules and be in Deadwood; their adventure together was ending. In Deadwood each man would stand alone. The Hobart Party to the Black Hills would disband without anyone noticing it was happening.

Luther had been subdued since the shooting incident. He seemed anxious to make up for his foolishness and Hugh noticed he pulled more than his share in the back-breaking job of helping the wagons up and down the steep slopes. It was Hobart, however, who took the time to acknowledge Luther's efforts at the end of the trail with a handshake and a word of praise. Luther blinked rapidly and his expression as he received the frontiersman's thanks was almost worshipful.

Once the party had rested from their ordeal with the cliff, the trail to Deadwood beckoned. It was no problem to follow the trail as it moved up the gulch. It could not have been called a valley by any stretch of the imagination, for thickly timbered mountains rose on either side. The summits to the left were capped by towering white rocks, while on the right, the outcroppings were of a less rugged brown stone. The little creek the trail followed, and which they assumed to be the Whitewood, had taken centuries to cut out even this narrow gully between the mountains. It seemed impossible a city could be growing in the cleft between the rugged slopes, yet they knew they were close to their goal.

The wagons traveled single file for the trees were

thick on both sides of the trail. Hugh recognized white birch and quaking aspen as well as pine and spruce. The timber was thick and uncut although as they progressed up the gulch they came upon more and more fallen and rotting logs — the dead wood which gave the area its name. It was impossible to tell whether the trees had fallen to fire or to some sort of disease.

Unlike the sparkling streams they crossed and recrossed during their journey, the creek they followed became increasingly muddy and disturbed. The reason was soon evident as they came across the first drainage ditches and crude sluice boxes; the creek was being diverted all along its course to wash the placer gold from the gravel.

Each set of drainage ditches and sluice boxes was guarded by a cabin of sorts, and as more cabins clustered together along the creek, Hugh wondered where everyone was. The cabins seemed unoccupied and no one was working the placer mines along the creek. Hugh calculated it was Sunday and wondered if the miners were in town, but it seemed unlikely they would be attending services. Surely they would not find that Deadwood, too, had been abandoned.

They heard the town before they saw it. First there was the sound of blasting or perhaps gunfire, distant and sporadic. Then there was the recognizable whine of a sawmill, and finally the rhythmic beat of hammers hitting wood. They smelled it too. The crisp mountain air of the canyon was displaced by pungent odors of chimney and campfires, road dust, manure and outhouses. They came around a bend in the road and suddenly the trail was crowded on either side with cabins. They saw one miner, then two, then a dozen.

As the wagon train rolled on, the road it took became more crowded until there was only room enough for a line of traffic in either direction and the Hobart Party was engulfed in the stream of horsemen and wagons. Men on foot darted between the wagons and crowds lined the road on either side. Hugh realized Sunday must be the day the miners left their diggings to conduct their business in town.

So much humanity was a shock after days in the silent wilderness. The wagon road had become a street lined so closely on both sides by brush shanties, dugouts, cabins, tents, and frame buildings in various stages of construction that they seemed to be touching, even leaning on each other.

Hobart took out his pistol and fired several shots into the air to mark their arrival. Luther added to the confusion by firing a shot, and Hugh would have added his fire to the confusion, but Jake was having a hard time holding in the lathered mules.

Further shots would have been lost in the commotion anyway. Everywhere men were hammering and building, surrounding the log cabins of the previous winter with buildings of green pine, nailed in place as soon as the wood could be hauled from the sawmills. False fronts had been added to the cluster of cabins at the heart of town and even as they passed, a new front labeled Saloon to match its neighbors was being raised. The line of saloons formed Main Street, and those buildings that could not be squeezed in along that narrow street had to cling precariously to the sides of the hills, so closely did the sides of the gulch come together. Deadwood had sprung up in a crevice. There was so little level land for construction that many of the log and frame buildings had already sprouted second stories reached by narrow outside stairways. Here and there a pine tree still stood in the midst of the newly-hewn town, solitary reminders that a forest had almost overnight been hacked down and formed into a mining camp. Everywhere there was evidence of mining: piles of rubble, overturned sluice boxes, prospect holes, even buildings jacked up and set on stilts so the miners could tunnel beneath them to follow the vein.

Hugh marveled at the progress. Deadwood was a beehive of activity. Even the air, smoky and dusty as it was after the clear air of the trail, seemed charged with excitement. Banjo music and laughter escaped from the open doors of the saloons, and once Hugh thought he heard a piano, although it seemed impossible one had been freighted down that terrible hill.

Hugh estimated there were two or three thousand men in Deadwood that day. He tried to take note of everything so he could record it in his journal. He figured the city extended nearly a mile along the creek and contained at least two hundred buildings. The streets seemed littered with miners in various stages of drunkenness. They rubbed elbows with dandies in frock coats. There were Orientals too; men set apart from the crowd by their race and their willingness to do the washing and the cooking, work beneath the dignity of a miner. There were few women. The respectable women wore worried expressions; the others wore painted-on smiles.

Hugh took it all in. He breathed deeply of the new-city smell of the place. He tried to sort out the voices and the banjo music from the pounding of the hammers and the squeaking of the rolling wheels and saddle leathers and the grunts of oxen and men. He wondered what was behind the false fronts of the buildings and he stared at the people, the miners, the gamblers, and the whores.

He loved it all.

He had actually done it. He was in Deadwood and it was both a hundred times better and worse than he had thought it would be. The air was full of hope and promise and adventure. Hugh felt himself charged with excitement. His breathing came fast. For once he was not ashamed. He lusted for his chance to conquer this raw, uncivilized city, to stake his claim and fight to win something from it. It was poor man's gold and painted women and his terrible need for Molly all at once, but it went beyond any of the things he knew or understood. It was like the challenge of the stallion or the bull elk about to claim his territorial privileges. It was a feeling unlike any he had known before. And Deadwood had brought it to him.

It was a wonderful place.

Chapter Sixteen

It was a terrible place. Never in her worst imaginings about Deadwood had Molly dreamed it would be so awful. For years she had looked out the tiny window of the sod house and seen vast, open fields meeting the sky low on the horizon. The openness of Iowa had seemed lonely to her then, but as she rode into Deadwood on the wagon now the mountains on either side and the terrible little shacks along the creek and the swarming hoard of the worst kind of people one could imagine seemed to be closing in on her.

She could not believe they were really in Deadwood. She had pictured a city set in an open parkland like Custer. She had expected to come around a bend in the road and see the mountains drop away and there before her a lovely valley with a city all laid out nice and proper. But it wasn't that way at all. Molly held Edwin close to her on the wagon seat. He was straining his neck to see, looking from one side of the road to the other, but everywhere they looked it was the same, cabins and shacks and buildings framed of green lumber, the purpose of at least half of them even more degenerate than their haphazard construction. It

218

was all so raw. It looked as if the whole city had been thrown up over night. Every other building was a saloon or worse. Wherever a narrow gap existed between buildings, a mountain of refuse filled the empty space. On the whole drive through town, she saw only one other woman who looked respectable, and her face was full of tension as Molly knew her own must be. She tugged at Jake's sleeve to see if he shared her despair.

"Ain't it great?" he said, more to the mules than to her. "Ain't it the finest?"

He looked happier than she had ever seen him. She bit her lip. No use trying to talk to him. It was too noisy anyway. She couldn't imagine people discharging firearms right on the streets just for the fun of it. Fortunately the poor mules were too tired to react, but she held Edwin close. Poor little boy.

"Ain't it great, Ma?" He echoed Jake. "Did you see that lady? Did you see her dress? Don't you wish you had a dress like that? And her face was all white and beautiful—"

"Edwin!" Such women had never walked the streets so brazenly in Pennsylvania or even in Iowa. But it didn't matter because Edwin was already looking in the other direction. "There's a man with a pigtail. Is he a Chinaman too? Pa, why are all those men sleeping on that wagon?"

"They're drunk," Jake answered cheerfully and Molly realized he didn't care.

"How can they sleep with all that shooting going on? Can we shoot your rifle, Pa? How come there aren't any sidewalks and why are all the houses so close together and where are we going to live? I hope we don't have to live in one of those places."

Molly followed Edwin's gaze. The building was long and narrow, the front consisting of a line of doors. The rooms must be like stalls, Molly thought and then gasped as she realized Edwin was pointing to a crib. Half the town was whorehouses and saloons. And everyone seemed delighted about it. Everyone but her. Molly pulled her shawl closer around her. The sun was already low in the sky. They had better hurry and find a place to camp. She was sure they could not afford a hotel, even if there had been a decent one.

The men seemed blind to the squalor. One expected an old reprobate like Caleb Dexter to be in his element, but she had been shocked at the way the others had accepted Dexter's crudeness as they passed through Chinatown. Almost every doorway in that area a bore the legend *Washee House* and Hugh had remarked at the number of laundries. The old man had responded by pointing out that before each of the curtained doorways was a yellow-skinned woman. "A Daughter of Joy," he grinned.

"Daughter of Joy?" Luther asked, staring at the almond-eyed women in the doorways.

"Sure," the old man boomed. "The Chinamen got pretty names for 'em, Daughters of Joy and Celestial Females, but let's face it, Luther, a miner goes to a Chinese laundry to get his wash done and to a washee house when he needs a woman!"

The men all hooted with laughter before Molly grasped the implication of the remark. She knew men had powerful needs but in decent society such things were kept hidden. Now a terrible thought struck her. She had aroused Hugh's passions. What if he visited

220

such a place? The thought made her miserable.

Even as Molly's uneasiness grew, the men seemed to become more jubilant. She wondered why the men seemed unaware of the faces she saw on the street, faces which wore the look she had seen in Frank Pearson's eyes: lust. But this was not lust for women. The faces were like Jake's when he talked about poor man's gold; and so many of them were tinged with worry and fear and discouragement. Molly could see that not everyone in Deadwood was lucky, but she did not want to transmit her fear to her husband. Jake was happy and she would do nothing to discourage him. She told herself that this time they would be among the chosen ones.

The trail continued up the gulch. The ground was pockmarked with exploration holes. Some miners had begun to sink shafts, but most still worked the surface. It was like the scene of some terrible disaster; the trees struck down at random angles as in a tornado; the white splinters of their trunks gleaming in the last of the sunlight.

As they left the clamor of Deadwood behind, it grew quiet around them. The Hobart party had dispersed along the way with no formal leave-taking, until it was only their wagon, Caleb Dexter, Luther and Hugh remaining, the men having agreed earlier to explore Deadwood together. Molly wondered how much longer she would have the reassurance of Hugh's presence now that their journey was ended.

They made camp and Molly was preparing to make biscuits when suddenly she felt chilled and turned to see the sun had suddenly disappeared behind a mountain. There would be no purple twilights and orange sunsets in this canyon. The air was cold and sharp with the pungent scent of pine. She couldn't help shivering.

And then came the cry.

At first it seemed hardly human. The mournful cry echoing up the canyon. Then it came again.

"Oh Joe!"

It sounded like a cry for help. She reached for Jake's arm.

It came again. This time right behind her. She jumped and turned. Caleb Dexter held an open whiskey bottle in his hand, leaned back and wailed again, "Oh Joe!"

"What in heaven's name are you doing?"

The old man's grizzled face broke into a grin and he belched before answering her. "Why that's just Oh Joe, M'am. It's good to hear it again. Sure brings back memories. I figured they'd do it here too."

"Do what?"

"Why holler *Oh Joe* at sunset. They did it in Californy in '49 and in every gold camp since. It's an old miners' custom. Shows who's an insider and who's a greenhorn."

"But can't we do it too?" Luther asked. "We're here now. We're in Deadwood in '76, aren't we? That should count for something!"

"Well," the old man said, scratching his beard, "I guess you could figure it that way." He offered Luther the bottle. "Yep, I reckon' you could figure since you're in Deadwood in '76, you could holler *Oh Joe* just like the old timers."

"But why?" Luther blinked, taking a shot off the bottle.

"The story is some miner came home drunk one night and fell in a prospect hole. He spent the night calling for his partner, a fellow named Joe, to get him out. 'Oh Joe!' Get it?" He made to take the bottle from Luther, but Luther choked down another shot, leaned back and bellowed until the hills rang with it, "Ohhhhhhh Joeeeeeee!"

"Oh Joe! Oh Joe! OH JOE!" It was Edwin. Before Molly could stop him, he climbed up on the wagon seat to screech it out a dozen more times.

At last even Jake and Hugh joined in. And for every time one of them shouted *Oh Joe*! there came a dozen answering cries echoing and re-echoing up the gulch.

Molly sat down on a rotten log and started to laugh. The men laughed with her.

She hoped they didn't notice when her laughter changed to tears.

Molly could tell by the way Jake walked up the hill to the wagon the next afternoon the news was bad. In the years she had been married to him, she had learned to read the signs. He didn't quicken his steps when he saw her waiting, but just kept trudging along, his coat slung over his shoulder and his eyes squinting against the afternoon sun. Edwin squealed, "Daddy's coming" and ran down the hill to meet him. The mules paused in their grazing to watch him approach. Molly busied herself stirring her pot of beans over the fire. *At least I have a good supper for him*, she thought. *I won't ask questions. I'll just let him tell me*. But of course he didn't come right out with it. He killed time hanging up his coat on a wagon wheel, filling his pipe, sending Edwin off to move the mules to a better spot to graze. Finally

223

she could stand it no longer.

"Jake! Tell me what happened. What did you find out?"

"Not much to tell."

"What do you mean? Didn't you get a claim?"

"You think it's so easy. I just walk up to some office and ask for a claim, huh?"

It was obvious he'd had more than a little to drink. Molly sat down on a log, clenching her fists under her apron. She kept silent for a moment. Somewhere back in Deadwood someone was shooting again. She hardly noticed.

"What's wrong?"

"There aren't any claims."

"What do you mean?"

"Every foot of land in this whole gulch belongs to someone. All the good claims around the place they call Discovery were taken up last winter and when the big rush came from Custer, everything else went overnight. Every foot. We're too late." The liquor was making him talkative now.

"But, Jake, all this land. It can't all be claimed. I mean, how much land does it take for a gold mine?"

"The land's gone, Molly. All of it. We'd be lucky if we could buy a spot big enough to put up a cabin. They're throwning up a couple of hotels, but they'll be expensive."

"But I thought you just went down and panned gold out of the creek. Can't we just pick up some nuggets and—"

"You talk like Edwin!"

"I'm sorry," she said stiffly. "I don't know about gold. I thought you knew. I thought you knew what you were doing!" He looked like he had been hit, but she couldn't stop. "What happened to this 'poor man's gold' you're always talking about?"

He put his head down between his hands.

She wished she hadn't said it. She tried to hold back the tears. So poor man's gold was just another dream. They had fooled her too. She could be brave. It wasn't their first disappointment.

She tried to think what to do next though she knew that the decision was Jake's. Jake said he might find work in Deadwood. Miners were being paid up to seven dollars a day, but prices were equally high. The mules were a problem. There was no grazing for them in the narrow gulch and feed was outrageously priced. Molly suggested it was best to sell the mules and wagon as they would still bring a fair price to those wishing to leave the city, but Jake pointed out they might need the outfit if they decided themselves to go home.

"Home!" Molly sputtered. "We haven't any home." Jake looked as if she had struck him and she was sorry for speaking. Then she thought of something that hurt even more than realizing they had nowhere to return to. "What about Hugh and the others? What will they do?"

Jake allowed the boys might still have a chance. They could outfit and go out with Caleb Dexter to prospect in the hills. She asked why Jake could not do that also, knowing the answer even as she asked. He could not leave her and Edwin alone in Deadwood. Jake also reminded her of the danger of prospecting. "You have to go in small parties and there's been a hell of a lot of miners scalped this spring."

"Then I don't want Hugh to go and . . ." her voice trailed off. She had said too much, but Jake didn't appear to notice. "And of course you can't take chances either."

"I guess the only thing to do is go on for wages," Jake concluded. He had accepted failure. He would be content to work for wages, to eke out a living, poorer than in their homesteading days only now not even owing the land on which they slaved. But Molly was not willing to settle for so little. If there was gold in Deadwood, she told herself, there must be a way to share in the wealth, and there must be a way to keep Hugh near her. The only alternative was to swallow her pride and write home for money, hoping her family would send them tickets home to Pennsylvania, and she would not do that even if Jake would. No, she would not accept that. Jake would be a defeated man. He would turn to drink; she sensed that.

She turned back to Jake, hopeful that he had thought of a solution but he was staring into the campfire, his eyes not focused on anything. She saw it would be up to her. She would have to think of something or get Hugh to. She looked anxiously down the road to town. If only Hugh would come back. Surely Hugh would think of something. Surely together they could find a way.

Hugh was, in fact, trying desperately to think of a plan. It seemed impossible that all the joy and excitement he had come to Deadwood with had been snuffed out in just one day, but everywhere they turned, the answer was the same: No. People looked at them as if they were crazy even to ask about how to stake a

226

claim. It seemed impossible, but all the land was claimed, unless you wanted to venture so far you had to prospect with a pick in one hand and a rifle in the other. Hugh was not afraid to do that, but it meant leaving Molly and Edwin. It would be difficult to do that anywhere, anytime, but to leave her in such a precarious place and time was impossible.

Jake was no help. They had gone their separate ways that morning, and when they met for a drink, Hugh could see immediately that Jake had given up. He and Caleb Dexter downed one whiskey after another until Hugh decided he had to get Jake home while he could still walk. Once he had him on the trail toward home, Hugh returned to the saloon to try to reason out a plan. He would have to do it alone. Luther and the old man sat staring into their glasses.

"I guess the best thing to do is try to find jobs," Hugh finally said.

"Shit no," Luther said, pounding the table and hiccoughing. "Thing to do is head for the hills. You and me and old Caleb Dexter out prospecting with our trusty rifles. Just us against the wilderness and the heathen Sioux."

"I think it would be better to try for some sort of job." Hugh said evenly. At least he could be near Molly that way and he wouldn't have to be involved with the old man. Surely we can get some sort of work in one of the mines."

"Being a goddamn grubbing laborer?" Dexter roared. "No, sir! That's no life—grubbin' away in the mud so somebody else can get richer. Only life for a man is out staking your own claim." He drained his whiskey and stared into the empty glass philosophically. "Oh, it's not so bad buying into a claim, cause then you're still working for yourself, but the best way is out following the will-o'-the-wisp, striking out for your own bonanza."

"Thas' right," Luther burped. "Thas' real man stuff. Jus' the three of us against the whole Sioux Nation."

"Always movin' on, knowing that over the next hill, maybe—" Dexter rambled on, but Hugh had stopped listening.

"What did you say about *buying* into a claim?" Hugh asked. "You mean you can *buy* a claim?"

"Sure you can if you got the money." Dexter looked at Hugh sagely. "But I don't suppose you do."

"How much would it take?" Hugh asked, fingering his belt where four twenty dollar gold pieces had been concealed since he left home.

"Oh, I reckon you could find a claim for a couple of hundred if you knew how to spot some outfit that was down on their luck and discouraged."

"But then it wouldn't be worth anything would it?"

"Might or it might not. I reckon as there are lots of greenhorns in this town don't know what they're sitting on. Greenhorns as haven't been around like me and figure if their dirt don't wash out first month or two, they don't have anything worth developing."

"But they might?" Hugh probed. "They might think their mine is no good and it might be worth something?"

"Could be." The old man yawned. He seemed to be feeling the effects of the day's drinking at last. "Could be a regular bonanza or could be worthless. That's the interesting thing about gold mining." He put his head down on the table as if to go to sleep right there.

Luther was watching with fascination at a large painting of a nude being hoisted above the makeshift bar.

Hugh considered the matter. It was an important decision and he needed to use his head this time. The eighty dollars was all they had left in the world. It meant taking a chance on being really down and out in this godforsaken town or having to go back to Carpenter with his tail between his legs and listen to Phineas P. Crandall tell him he had been a fool to join the gold rush. It wasn't the responsible thing to do and he had Luther to think of. Besides eighty dollars wasn't nearly enough. But Jake had the mules and wagon. If he put that up, they would still be partners and he'd have an excuse to be near Molly. The outfit should be worth something, but it still wasn't enough. He nudged the old man awake. "You got any money?"

"Sure," Dexter mumbled without opening his eyes. "Drinks are on me."

"No, I mean real money. Do you have any capital, like fifty or one hundred dollars?"

Dexter opened one eye and looked up at Hugh suspiciously. "Who wants to know?"

"I do. I was wondering if we happened to find a mine to invest in, if you would have enough money to take a share."

"Could if I wanted to."

"You'd have enough cash? I mean you've collected enough dust since you've been in the Hills?"

The old prospector grinned toothlessly and tugged Hugh down so he could whisper in his ear. "I got my lucky nugget and a nice little pouch of dust, boy. But don't you tell anyone. I could buy me a share in any mine I wanted to, but," here his voice became loud.

"But I'd rather be out in the hills prospecting."

"Jus' the three of us against the heathen Sioux," Luther mumbled still staring at the nude and blinking rapidly.

Having made his announcement, the old man slipped back onto the table and began to snore. Hugh sat there and tried to sort it out. He didn't know how much of the old man's company he could stomach. He didn't know if it was even right to get involved in another partnership with the husband of the woman he loved. He was pretty sure it was wrong. The whole scheme was crazy, but he couldn't see any other solution.

Hugh drained the last of his beer, sat back and groaned inwardly. It was either this or let Jake drag Molly and his son back to a life of poverty in a sod hut somewhere. Only now it would be worse for them because they had known hope. He couldn't let it happen to them, and he just could not rely on Jake to take care of them properly. He told himself his motives were pure. To provide for Molly and his son. He thought about it for a long time, and then reached down and grabbed a hank of Caleb Dexter's hair and raised his head off the table.

"Wake up, partner," he said. "We're going out and find us a gold mine!"

Chapter Seventeen

"I'll be an old goat scroat if I didn't get us one hell of a fine gold mine!" Caleb Dexter declared, slapping the thigh of his filthy overalls and taking another shot from his bottle.

If he's said that once, he's said it a hundred times, Hugh thought sourly, staring around the cramped little cabin in which they sat. *He's going to tell the whole damn story of how he got the mine again. Why does he have to do this every single week?* How long had it been going on? A month? Six weeks? Hugh had lost track of time, but it must be near the end of June.

"Yep, I'll be an old goat scroat if I didn't get us one hell of a fine gold mine!" The old man belched.

He'd said it again. He'd actually said it again! Hugh stared at the point where Dexter's rooster-wattle neck wasn't covered by his grizzled gray beard or the top of the long-johns he wore for a shirt and tried to stifle the urge to lunge across the table and choke the old man.

Molly looked strained but she kept smiling as she sat cups around the kitchen table and poured coffee into them. The smell of Caleb Dexter confined in a small room was unbearable. It had not been a part of their partnership agreement for Molly to cook for the whole crew and, knowing what a strain it was on her to have the old prospector in her cabin, Hugh made it a point to discourage any invitations Jake extended for dinner, but it had somehow become a custom after their Saturday night clean up of the sluice boxes to share a plate of beans and bread together before dividing the week's dust.

And somehow it had also become a tradition of these Saturday nights that Caleb Dexter would tell again the story of how he had acquired the mine they had optimistically named The Lucky Six.

Luther and Edwin gave Dexter their rapt attention from where they sat together on a crude log bench, the only furniture in the cabin in addition to the Lewis's double bed, Edwin's pallet, and the table and four chairs. Luther and Edwin never seemed to tire of the story.

"Well," the old man continued, belching again. "I hadn't moseyed around Deadwood for thirty minutes before I knew exactly what was what. You can't fool an old goat like me. No sir, I been to Californy in '49 and I was at Cherry Creek in '58 and to the Comstock in '59, and Alder Gulch in '63 and I could see right away all the placer mines was taken up and they about had the creek cleaned out.

"Now a green hand," he continued, waving a piece of bread dipped in bean juice at Edwin, "A green hand like your papa and you boys here, you would have got discouraged and turned around and gone home or gone out in the hills and got yourselves scalped trying to prospect. But me, old Caleb Dexter, why I wasn't in all those places for nothing. I know my gold, boy. You remember that."

Hugh groaned inwardly. The old man was looking

at him for approval. He certainly wasn't going to encourage the old reprobate. Dexter seemed to forget that buying a mine had been Hugh's idea. Perhaps that was just as well, Hugh declared. It had been an uneasy partnership from the beginning. He'd as soon forget it had been his idea.

"So I says to myself, I says, Caleb Dexter you old fart, there's more to mining gold than most folks know. Folks that wasn't there in '49 thinks you just go down to the creek and pan and that's all. Don't know the finer points. You see, an old goat like me, well, I knows, Edwin boy, I knows."

Edwin nodded.

"So I just mosey around. I just go from one claim to another and I take off my hat and I carry it in front of me like a goddamn preacher, so they'll know I'm not out claim jumpin' and I walk up to every mine I can find and I ask nice and polite how they're doin' and if they got any work for a laborer. Of course, I don't let on I was in Californy in '49, see? I don't let on I know all there is to know about minin' gold, see? I just act dumb and if they got work I ask a few questions and I mosey on."

"Beats all," Jake said, scooping up his plate of beans.

"Cause I ain't lookin' for work, you get that, boy?" Dexter leaned over and pinched Luther's shirt sleeve and winked conspiratorily. "I ain't really lookin' for work. I'm just reconoitering."

He took another swig from his bottle, belched and continued. "So if they looks like they're pretty happy, if it looks like they're cleaning up a lot of dust and if they got work, well I says I'll think it over and maybe come back and I keeps moseying on cause I ain't lookin' for

233

work and I ain't lookin' for happy miners. I'm lookin' for miners that are down and out and discouraged."

"And you found em!" Luther bellowed happily.

"And I found 'em! Sure enough. I found 'em." Again Dexter looked at Hugh for approval. This was supposed to be the best part of the story, but Hugh merely nodded. How could any one man smell that bad? he wondered. And how could it be that only he and Molly seemed to notice? Maybe it had something to do with chewing tobacco. Jake and Luther had both taken up the habit and were lustily chewing away. Hugh had given it a try in self-defense, but he didn't care for the stuff and it was obvious all the spitting annoyed Molly.

"It takes me all day," Dexter continued, "but I finds 'em. One spindly lookin' kid standing there digging out a prospect hole up on the side of the hill. He looks like hell and I know right away this is it, but I just squats down and rolls myself a smoke and makes conversation kind of disinterested and pretty soon the kid's telling me all his troubles. Seems his partner is sick up in the cabin, got a hell of a fever and a bad cough and a case of poison ivy to boot, and the kid says his lungs don't feel too good neither. They been there half the winter and about froze and living for months on meat straight without even salt."

"Ain't that something," said Luther.

"But they found gold. Sure. They had 'em a nice little stake, he lets me know, tucked away in a safe place, he adds, just to let me know he can't be taken advantage of. But it's been damn hard work and now it looks like their luck is petering out. They've worked out all the gravel on the creek and they were only washing out six or seven dollars a day from the hillside and they'll go broke fast that way with the cost of everything and besides he finally got a letter from his sweetheart and she wants him to come home and his mother does too and his partner's sick and it just don't seem worth it any more."

At this point in the story, Hugh leaned forward in spite of himself. Because it was always at this point that Dexter leaned forward conspiratorily, his eyes sparkling wickedly and his voice lowering to a whisper.

"And get this. Get this, folks. The whole time the kid's talking, he's shoveling out these big hunks of cement-looking stuff and wheelbarrowing it over to the tailings pile cause he thinks it's just hunks of conglomerate rock. But me, I'm about to piss my pants, old goat scroat that I am, because I know. I know what he's got there."

"Conglomerate gold!" Edwin piped in.

"That's right!" Dexter slammed his fist down on the table, sending the plates dancing. "The kid knows. See Edwin already knows more than that greenhorn. He had conglomerate gold and he didn't know it." He broke wind as if to emphasize the point.

Hugh groaned. Molly looked faint.

"Conglomerate gold!" Jake pounded his own fist down on the table.

"Yep." Dexter sat back smiling contentedly and lit up a pipe. "He's shoveling out conglomerate gold on his tailing pile and I'm about to piss my pants, I'm so afraid he's going to take a notion to hit one of those hunks of sand with his shovel and it could break open and he'd see the grains of gold because I know what's in there."

"Conglomerate gold!" Luther pounded the table.

"Yep! And he don't know, but I know, old goat scroat that I am."

"Old goat scroat!" Edwin piped in cheerfully.

"Edwin," Molly narrowed her eyes at him from across the table. "What did I tell you about that?"

"I'm sorry, Mamma. I forgot." Edwin lowered his eyes, but a grin played around his mouth.

"Let the boy go, Mother," Jake said. "Can't help get a little bit excited when you get to this part of the story."

"This is the best part," Luther agreed.

"Nope!" Dexter hit the table again. "Nope, the best part is the way I handled it. Somebody that hadn't been in Californy in '49, some old gasser that didn't know his way around would have bit right then, would have pissed right then and given the whole thing away. But not me. Not old Caleb Dexter."

"You old goat!" Jake said.

"Jake!"

"Sorry, Molly."

"Can't help it, Mississ." Dexter winked at her. "Cause this is the best part, the way I just sits there and tells the kid my troubles. How I guided this party all the way into Deadwood and how we had these two young bucks just dying to dig in the mines and how I had this responsible party with this fine wagon and the best set of mules you ever saw and how we were all anxious to have a try in the mines and now we couldn't find an inch of ground to work. How we didn't care so much for getting rich; we was just in it for the adventure since we already had a couple of hundred in gold between us, but we sure hated to go back to Nebrasky without trying our hand at working a mine.

236

How we'd sure like to have just a little dust to show the folks back home to prove we was in the great Black Hills gold rush of '76, seeing as how none of us had been fortunate enough to have been in Californy in '49 and so on. And how this poor fellow with the team and wagon just didn't know what to do cause there wasn't any grazing for the mules and he just hated to buy hay at the price it was and they was such a fine team of mules all trail broke and how the poor man's wife and little boy —"

"That's me!" Edwin piped in.

"That's you, only he don't know that. Well, anyway —"

"To make a long story short," Hugh interrupted.

Dexter frowned. "You got something to do, Hugh? You anxious to get to Deadwood or something?"

"Now see here!" Hugh stood up, but Jake motioned him down. "Don't you two start in again. Finish the story, Caleb."

"Well," the old man frowned at Hugh. "To make a long story short, as Hugh says, pretty soon the kid's asking what I figure you'd need for the team and wagon and I'm asking what they want for the mine, and the next thing you know we have ourselves a deal."

Yes, Hugh thought. *They had themselves quite a deal.* Only when he told his story Dexter never mentioned that digging conglomerate gold was like trying to pickax through cement. Nor that there was no way to get the grains of gold out of the conglomerate without sending it to a mill, and there was not a mill in Deadwood. Nor did he mention the fact that the layer of conglomerate gave out within days and they were now digging through layers of gravel which appeared to be practically worthless.

Nor did Caleb Dexter ever talk about what miserable, back-breaking work mining was. It was shoveling from morning to night. To Hugh, one shovelful of dirt looked like another; he never knew if they were in pay dirt or not. Since Dexter was the expert, he spent his time scampering about the diggings giving orders, while the rest dug until their hands were blistered raw and their back so stiff they could hardly stand erect. Taking a turn at the sluice boxes, hauling water to run through it or shoveling the gravel in it, seemed like a break. Then at the end of the week, they cleaned out the boxes and picked out any tiny nuggets or grains of gold caught in the riffles at the bottom. And every week there was just enough gold there to make their expenses and keep them going.

But the endless, back-breaking, mind-dulling work was not the worst of it. The worst was when Hugh fell into bed at night, exhausted and yet unable to sleep. The cabin he shared with his brother and the old man was only yards from the Lewis's. And that was the worst of it, being in the cabin with the snoring men, or sleeping out under the stars when he had to be alone and always knowing Molly slept in the next cabin, just yards away.

Night after night he lay awake, exhausted, yearning for the oblivion of sleep. Yet his desire gave him no rest. He thought of visiting the cribs of Chinatown or the brothels in the area Deadwood called the Badlands. He suspected Luther would go if he ever got manhood, courage and money at the same time. Hugh understood why men did such things, why they tried to buy love even at the risk of contracting a disease which crippled for life. But he knew that only one woman would satisfy his need, knew, too, if he gave in to his body's demands, he could face neither Molly nor himself. So he suffered and dreamed and tried to make the mine his mistress.

Sometimes when he looked at Molly he would remember dreaming of her the night before in terrible and wonderful ways and it shamed him. He looked at her now, so calmly sipping her coffee as she watched Caleb Dexter divide the week's dust, and he felt his manhood rising. He was a fool not to be in better control of his emotions. Molly looked up and, as if she read his thoughts, she too blushed. Their eyes met and he imagined he could see his own desire mirrored in hers. She fingered her collar button nervously and he wondered. Did she desire him? She had never said so. Sometimes he thought she must be frigid, she seemed so afraid of his touch. Yet he knew how given to touching she was, how much pleasure she seemed to take in cuddling Edwin or in tracing the curve of his cheek as he slept in her lap. Such a woman had to be warm and loving. It was of passion that she seemed innocent, and although Hugh took a morose pleasure in knowing Jake had never known the ripening of first love Hugh had awakened in her that day in the barn, he also felt a sense of loss and guilt. Had he not taken her then, had he been in better control of himself, she might have forgotten him and married some man with whom she could have found joy instead of the dreary existence she shared with Jake. He knew, too, that if he had never made love with Molly, he could now satisfy his lust with a woman of the Badlands, instead of driving himself crazy with yearning for that seemingly holy union of spirit and flesh he had once found with her.

"What're you dreaming of there, Hugh? Poor man's gold?" Jake brought him back to reality with a start.

"Yes," Hugh said quickly. "Poor man's gold."

"Well, pay attention, we're ready to divvy up," Caleb Dexter declared. Hugh was relieved that the ordeal was over for another week. Their shares came to thirty dollars each, before expenses. Jake pronounced it a great week, and Luther and the old man nodded agreement.

"What do you mean?" Hugh demanded. "It's barely day's wages!"

"Well, it's a hell of a lot more cash than I ever saw farming," Jake declared. "I say it's cause for celebration. Molly, hand me that jug."

"I say it's time for a real celebration," Caleb Dexter said reaching for the jug himself. "Let's have a snort here and then head into town for a gold miners' Saturday night. What do you say, men?"

"You can count me in!" Luther boomed.

"Okay with you, Mother?" Jake turned to his wife. Molly disliked his calling her Mother almost as much as she disliked his drinking. She wanted to protest Jake's leaving, though it was not a good wife's place to keep her husband from seeking release, especially when she could no longer offer him the comfort of her body. But as she was about to speak, her eyes met Hugh's and his look seemed to say this opportunity to be alone must be seized. Despite the closeness of their quarters at the mine, they had shared no more than a few moments alone in weeks, moments always tense with the fear that if they dared to touch or to

240

speak of what was in their hearts, someone would come along and discover their secret. She found it hard to believe that anyone with eyes could see them in a room together, could see how they avoided looking at each other or sharing the same bench at table and not know. But Jake and the old man had become so involved with the Lucky Six that they seemed oblivious to everything else. Even when she said Jake should go, and Hugh quietly offered to help her clear up instead, the only one who seemed remotely aware of the look they exchanged or the possibility of something between them was Luther. His eyes ran between them with the same look of fear that Edwin sometimes wore when he sensed something amiss between his parents, something that might disrupt his vision of the world.

"Come on, Hugh," Luther urged. "Molly's used to clearing up alone. You been doing men's work all week; now it's time for some fun."

"I've already had enough 'fun' breaking my back today. I'm going to turn in early," Hugh said firmly, picked up Edwin, who was so tired he cried, and began settling the little boy on his pallet in a quiet corner. Molly sat silent until the men made their noisy exit and then loaded the dishes into a pan on the table, seeming to ignore Hugh. She fetched the kettle from the stove and poured hot water over the dishes while Hugh cradled the already dozing Edwin in his arms. She still did not speak but busied herself at the stove, adding kindling to the embers and refilling the coffee pot. She felt strange and reckless, as if something terrible yet wonderful was about to happen and she was powerless to stop it. It was as if she was moved by a force beyond her control. She felt as if she were

241

sleepwalking.

When she dared look at Hugh again, Edwin was already asleep and Hugh stood looking down at the boy, his back to her. He was such a large man, his presence seemed to fill the tiny cabin. Her vision of him seemed indistinct as if clouded by tears or illusion. She realized that he had changed. He was no longer the boy she had fallen in love with in that faraway time and place. He was not even the lover of her dreams but a stranger, hardened by the trail and the mine, a tall, bearded giant who wanted her and had been denied. She felt threatened by a premonition that Hugh's need for her might one day be expressed in a way that would destroy them all, but even more threatened by the feeling growing within her, which she could not admit, even to herself, was also desire. She only knew that since leaving civilization she'd been increasingly filled with yearnings as confused and primitive as the maze of shacks and mine shafts and lawless humanity which daily destroyed pristine wilderness in the name of the city of Deadwood.

Being alone with Hugh that night both terrified and thrilled her. She knew that as long as she stayed within the cabin she was safe. Edwin's presence kept them from being truly alone. She tried not to think of the temptation of Hugh's cabin only a door away or what it would be like to make love with him again. She wondered about his body, hard, lean and tanned in his workman's clothes. He had been little more than a boy that first time and she a child herself. She sensed this time it would be different. He would still be tender, but he would be truly a man and not old and weary as Jake had been almost since the beginning. This time she might truly know what it was to be a woman. She ached with fear and longing and with determination to remain silent about her own confused emotions.

Hugh turned and looked at her. He seemed to be waiting for her to speak or move toward him. She could do neither. He seemed to want her to tell him she understood something was to happen now that they were alone, to say that she willed it to happen. Did he not understand that she could not say yes to such a thing; that if he was to take her it must be his doing?

She turned away from him and back to her wifely chores, placing the coffee pot where it would heat faster. She tried to concentrate on her task, even as she began to tremble. Through her mind flashed the image of Hugh approaching her and putting his arms around her, caressing her shoulders, then touching his lips to her neck and sliding his hands to her breasts as his manhood pressed against her hips. Yes, that was how it must happen, with her caught in his powerful embrace, too weak and too aware of his terrible need to fight any longer.

Even as the thought came to her, even as she thrilled to the certainty that it was about to happen, she pushed the image away. She slammed the coffee pot down on the stove. How could she imagine such things! She must not let being in this uncivilized place bring ruin on all she held dear. If she gave into temptation she would be no better than the women of the Badland bordellos. She must regain control and never let Hugh suspect her imaginings. She must make polite conversation and not let him think there had been an invitation in that look they had exchanged

243

before her husband left.

"It's been strange, hasn't it, our being so close together here in Deadwood?" She kept her back to him. Her throat felt dry and her words seemed to echo in the small cabin. "I mean seeing each other every day, but not ever being alone." She half turned to look at him.

"It's been hell."

She turned away as if she had been hit. He was not going to make polite conversation.

"It's been hell," he repeated. "It's driving me crazy."

He was moving toward her. It was going to happen. He was going to come up behind he and embrace her just as she had pictured it. She tensed in fear and anticipation, her hand moving instinctively to her breast. She had unbuttoned her collar against the heat of the stove; now she clutched at the front of the dress. Her heart was hammering.

"Look at me, Molly."

He was beside her now, but she could not take her eyes from the stove where the hot flames were licking against the kindling. Her skin felt on fire.

"Turn and look at me."

She obeyed slowly, crossing her arms over her breasts which seemed strangely full.

"I have to touch you, Molly," he whispered taking her by the shoulders, so that his strong, calloused hands covered hers. "I can't keep pretending. I won't keep pretending. I want you. It's been hell, seeing you every day but never daring to touch you, thinking about you every night, wondering what it would be like to have your body against mine—"

"Hugh!" She could only breathe his name in protest

and flash her eyes wildly toward the corner where Edwin slept.

"I'll be quiet," he whispered. "We'll not frighten our son. I'll take you to my cabin; only let me hold you a moment first. I've waited so long."

She let him draw her to him, but could not embrace him even as she thrilled to the wood smoke and earthy smell of him and the roughness of his wool shirt and beard as she allowed herself the glory of one moment against his body. If only it could be like this forever. If only he would hold her and ask no more. But she felt his hardness against her and knew it was impossible.

"Hold me too, Molly," he whispered. "Tell me you want me. Tell me you agree."

He held her away to see her face, and as his hands moved to her arms, his palm brushed her breast and she felt her nipples suddenly ripen.

"Say yes and we'll go to my cabin."

She could not speak. Why was he such a fool? Why did he not just pick her up and carry her to his cabin? Couldn't he see that she could not agree but was powerless to resist? She shook her head but dared not look into his eyes.

"I'll not rape you, Molly. God knows I want you, but I want you to agree. Once I made you mine before you knew the consequences, and I brought ruin on you. This time I want to know it's right. I want to make you my wife."

He was a fool. Couldn't he see that it could only be one way between them? That she lawfully belonged to Jake?

"I'm Jake's wife," she whispered, saying the only words her conscience would allow, while her heart

245

hammered *yes*!

"We've got to change that. I can't go on any longer living this lie. We'll make a plan. We'll find some way to tell him, afterwards."

"Afterwards! How do I know you'll even want me afterwards?"

"Damn it woman!" He spoke through clenched teeth, holding her shoulders so tight her arms ached. "I told you I'd never leave you again. I love you, but I want you so badly now I can't think straight. Touch me, Molly. See how I'm bursting for you."

He took her hand and held it to his groin. Then held her whole body against his. She was weak against the power of his desire. Surely he would take her now. Surely even God could not expect her to resist such desire.

"Tell me," he whispered. "Just tell me you love me. You don't have to tell me you want me. Just say you'll leave Jake." He held her away from him like a rag doll and waited for her answer.

"I can't," she said. "I can't say it and I can't leave Jake. I can't hurt him that way."

"I don't want to hurt him either. He's my partner. But he can't need you like I do. I can't go on like this, wanting you like I do and knowing he has you. I can't go on sleeping just yards from you, knowing he might be having his way with you and I can't even touch you."

"You make it sound as if I'm Jake's property. As if I'd be your property if I ran away with you. But it's not like that. Jake and I are not bound by desire. We are bound by what is right and holy. And if it is any comfort to you," she spoke angrily, "Jake does not have

246

his way with me."

"What do you mean?"

"I mean — I mean Jake and I do not — do not — live as man and wife."

He let go of her and stood back, regarding her with what almost seemed suspicion. "You told me on the trail that you were a true wife to him."

"I was, or I tried to be, until the doctor said we could not have more children, at least for now. The doctor explained it to Jake, and so Jake does not do *that*, anymore, and so you and I, we could not do *that* even if I would."

"The hell we couldn't!"

"What?"

"We would make love, Molly. We would find a way. I'd find a way. Don't tell me Jake hasn't."

"What are you saying?"

"There are ways, aren't there? When there can't be children? Those women in the Badlands have ways of protecting themselves. Maybe Jake wouldn't know about that, but he'd find ways of loving you. He touches you doesn't he? He has you touch him?"

"Jake has been considerate."

"So he pleasures you. He holds you and he kisses you and finds ways, doesn't he?"

"You misunderstand. I mean that Jake has treated me as a lady. He has not . . . touched me . . . in months."

She had begun righteously, thinking that if Hugh knew that Jake no longer touched her, it would make it easier for him to check his own passion. But now she saw that of all the terrible things he had said to her, this was the worst. For Jake had not touched her, he had not found *ways*. They had both accepted the doctor's word as final, and admitting that to Hugh forced her to admit to herself the barrenness of her marriage to Jake. She felt wounded by her admission, but her words seemed to anger Hugh. He looked as if he wanted to break something.

"Then you're lucky, Molly. Maybe he is right for you. Because I couldn't do that. If you were my wife, I'd not let you alone. I'd find a way to love you."

He had taken her by the shoulders again and held her roughly as he spoke. Now he raised a hand to touch her face, but she reacted as if she expected to be struck, and seeing her fear, he stopped and looked at his open hand, stunned by his own passion. He groaned and, filled with rage and frustration, turned and slammed his hand down against the hot stove. He spoke through teeth clenched in pain and anger.

"I'd burn in hell before I'd leave you alone!"

Frantically Molly pulled his hand away from the stove. She kissed his palm and held his hand to her face, her tears soothing the pain. "Oh, Hugh, my dearest Hugh," she murmured, but he jerked his hand away.

"Don't do that, Molly. Don't be kind to me. I won't accept your kindness or your mothering. I want to be your lover. I want all of you. I won't accept less, as Jake has."

She wanted badly to touch him, to hold and be held, but he was making it clear that it was all or nothing. They stood in the little cabin facing each other over what seemed a great distance.

"I'd not get you pregnant, but I want all the rest. I want you to be a true wife, to me. Clearly I can't have

248

you now. Maybe I never will, but I'm giving you notice of how it would be between us. And that I can't go on much longer this way, staying in this crazy mining partnership just to protect you and Edwin and be close to you."

"Are you threatening to leave? You said you'd never leave me."

"Not if staying means going crazy. I'm going to leave you for now, and I'm taking this goddamn jug of Caleb Dexter's with me, because maybe if I drink enough I can get through another night without coming up here after you. But I can't promise you after that. You've got to resolve it with Jake and with yourself. I'll tell him if you can't, but you've got to come to me and be mine or you've got to let me go."

"Tell Jake? Tell my husband?"

"You've got no true marriage with him. I'll give you some time to admit that. When you're ready, Molly, when you can admit you belong to me, then you find some way to signal me, so we can be alone together and make a plan. We'll find a way."

He took her by the shoulders once more and brought her to him and kissed her. It was a kiss full of resolution and power. A kiss she knew she would not forget, but it was his words as he walked out the door which haunted her.

"Remember, Molly. We can't go on like this."

That night and the nights that followed, Molly could not sleep. She tortured herself with fantasies of giving herself to Hugh and with resolutions to tell Jake the truth. In the daytime she told herself she must be possessed by some demon or a cycle of the moon to think such fantasies. She almost hated Hugh for not carrying her away that night but forcing her to take responsibility for what would come to pass. In her anguish she tried to pray for answers, but she did not dare to ask the real questions. She asked how to be faithful to her vow to be one flesh with Jake. She could not yet ask whether their saying the words in a church had, indeed, made them one flesh. She could only wonder if two people are so bound if it is words that makes it so, or if it is something that happens when certain spirits touch.

She thought that she must try harder with Jake. That if she could again be a true wife to him, she would find the courage to let Hugh go. She remembered Hugh's suggestion about there being safe ways to make love, and she thought she must find a way, not for Hugh, nor for herself, but for her husband. And so one night when they were lying in bed, and she was sure Edwin was asleep in his corner, she tried, knowing the time was not right but aware there might never be a better one. She knew the words would not come easily, for in all the years of her marriage, she had never discussed intimacy with her husband.

"Jake," she whispered. "I've been thinking." His response was mumbled and sleepy, but she persisted. "Try to wake up, Jake. This is important."

He struggled to one elbow, "You're not sick, are you?"

"No, Jake. In fact I've felt very well since we've been in Deadwood. That's why I've been thinking that maybe we shouldn't worry anymore about what the doctor said."

"What doctor?"

"Dr. Morgan, back in Iowa. He said we shouldn't have any more babies and so we shouldn't — you know."

"Why're you worrying about that? I been good, haven't I?"

"Oh yes! That's just it. You've been so good, and I've been thinking how difficult it must be for you. Men being made so needful and all, and I've been thinking that maybe the doctor was wrong, and that since I'm well now, maybe we could —"

"God no. Not in Deadwood. I'd not have you risk yourself again in this place."

"Then, maybe . . . maybe there's some way we could you know, without making a baby." Jake was silent. Surely he understood. She stumbled on, her heart pounding, knowing her cheeks must be burning in the dark. "I was thinking about all those bad women in Deadwood. They must have some way of —"

"Molly! What a way to be talking! What those women do has got no place in the joining of man and wife. You got no business even thinking about what such women do."

She closed her eyes against the embarrassment of it all. Jake had shamed her, but she must go on. "I was thinking about you," she said quietly, "how you must be suffering."

He leaned over and patted her shoulder, "Why, that's real sweet of you, Molly. You been a good wife, but you don't need to worry about me. Why I'm so busy with that mine, digging from daybreak to sundown, I don't have time or energy to suffer."

"But you must! You must want me. It's in a man's nature, isn't it?"

"A young man's, maybe. But I haven't got that

251

problem anymore." He yawned and laid back down. "Now you just go to sleep and quit your fretting. There's only one thing I'm needful of now and that's poor man's gold. If the Lucky Six pays off for me, and I've a feeling it will, then it's all I'll ever need."

He reached over and patted her head in the same way he did Edwin's, planted a kiss on her forehead, turned over and went to sleep.

Molly lay there in the dark, knowing she had received the answer to a question she had not dared to ask. It was over. Perhaps it had never been. Hugh was right; she had no true marriage to Jake. But what did she do now? How could she leave a good man who had believed all these years that she had not given herself willingly, but had been wronged? If only he beat her and gave her some reason to turn against him. If the decision would be made for her.

She cried silent tears and touched her own body and knew the warmth and softness of her breasts and thighs. She was filled with yearnings she could not name. She touched herself more deeply and her longing surged, but she did not know how to still it. She thought of Hugh sleeping with his brother and the old man in the next cabin and knew she would find peace only in his arms, but the distance between them seemed impossible.

Something had changed forever, and she sensed that the next step would take them on a journey even more tangled and dangerous than that which had already brought them to the Black Hills. And that step was hers. ●

From Jake's side of the bed came a deep, contented snore.

The step was taken soon after that night. As June ended and the days grew longer and warmer, the men became increasingly discouraged with the Lucky Six. Each day less and less gold remained behind as they washed their surface diggings through their rocker on the creek. Finally when they divided the week's earnings, they had to admit they were making less than day's wages from their mine. Hugh brought them to a confrontation. His words were directed to Caleb Dexter, but she felt they were for her.

"We can't go on like this!"

"Well, I can understand that you're a mite discouraged," the old man said, undaunted. "Some weeks are like this. Now if you had been there in '49—"

"I don't want to hear about '49!"

"Well, if you're that discouraged, I guess it's time to tell you."

"Tell us what?"

"The good news. I think we're about to the bedrock!" He beamed.

"So?" Luther and the others echoed Hugh's question.

"So, if you don't know what that means, it just goes to show you weren't there in—"

"Damn it, old man, tell us!"

"Well, as any experienced miner knows, gold is heavy—even Edwin knows that—so as it sits in the gravel it drifts slowly downward. Then when it gets to bedrock, it stops."

"So?"

"So when you get to bedrock, there's a layer of solid gold!"

"Always?" Edwin asked, his eyes glowing.

"Well, not always. But sometimes. Sometimes there's a sheet of solid gold, and you just shovel it up by the bucketful!"

"Poor man's gold!"

"That's right, Jake! Poor man's gold!"

Only, in their case, it didn't turn out that way. When they finally dug out the gravel from their huge open pit, there was nothing on the bedrock but bedrock. It was called bedrock, Hugh discovered, because the ore was so solid you couldn't crack it with a shovel. Poor man's gold had eluded them again.

This time when they discussed it over Molly's kitchen table, even Caleb Dexter was discouraged.

"What do we do now?" Jake asked trustingly.

"Only one thing to do now," the old man answered.

"What's that?" Hugh asked.

"Quit."

They were all stunned to silence as for once the old man went on without prompting. "Quitting's the smart thing to do. Cash in here. Try to find some greenhorns to buy the mine, dissolve the partnership and head for the hills prospecting for a new strike somewhere else. That's the easiest thing to do in a situation like this. Safest, too."

"And what's the other thing?" Hugh demanded.

Dexter didn't answer right away. He rolled a cigarette and walked to the open door of the cabin to light it. He stood for a moment, puffing and looking at the hill which rose sharply behind their cabins and diggings. Under the old man's directions, they had dug a dozen prospect holes in it. Then he studied the creek a

254

few yards below the cabin where they washed the gold. Finally he came back to the table and spoke.

"Too dangerous. Too dangerous with me the only one to savvy mining. Too dangerous and too costly. It would take equipment. Timbers, a pump probably, lots of blasting powder—"

His voice trailed off and they all sat silent at the table, thinking. For even Edwin knew what he was talking about. Going underground.

They argued about it half the night. It was too expensive, Dexter said. They were talking about capital investment. It would take all the dust they had accumulated so far to finance it. And it was far too dangerous. He suggested they all cash in now while Molly and Jake had enough to get back to Iowa, or even home to Pennsylvania if they didn't mind arriving with nothing to show for their years in the West. The rest of them could head for the hills and prospect. All but Luther. He wanted to join Emmet Hobart in the Spearfish Valley. The wagon master had stopped by the mine the day before and told them of the glories of the valley he had discovered after becoming discouraged with Deadwood. It was broad and lush, the perfect spot for a ranching venture. He would make his fortune supplying the mining towns with beef and produce, but he needed help in holding the land he had claimed against the Sioux, who protested the white settlers' theft of their lands with constant raiding parties. Luther was eager to go, and Molly knew that Hugh, too, would be happier ranching than grubbing away underground. But giving up the mine meant giving up Hugh. The Spearfish Valley was not safe for families and Jake was a farmer, not a rancher. If they

255

separated now, she sensed she would lose Hugh forever.

There were arguments for staying too. Jake loved the mine and had faith in it. They all had a sense that the Lucky Six might yet live up to its name. All around them fortunes were being made. If blasting into the side of the hill should lead them to a rich vein, they might attract capital from one of the investors who were rumored to be coming to the Black Hills on the first stagecoaches. The mine and their partnership was a dream none of them was willing to give up easily, but instead of leading them on with more tales of poor man's gold, Caleb Dexter was brutally honest about the dangers. Undergound mining meant risking lives.

And somehow the decision seemed to become Molly's. Hugh said that if they continued, they all must agree to the risk. And Molly knew that he was asking her to agree to more than the dangers of the mine. His eyes had been on her all evening and she knew that he was telling her this was the time of decision. She must let him go, or she must risk all.

"We can't go on like this," she said finally, looking straight at Hugh and choosing her words carefully, "but I am not willing to give up. We'll find a way. I vote that we retain the partnership and go underground."

"You willingly accept the risk?" Hugh asked.

"I do," she said and knew she had made a vow.

Chapter Eighteen

Deadwood had immeasurably enhanced Emerald O'Brien's image of herself. She was the most beautiful woman in Deadwood. She was easily the most beautiful woman in Deadwood. In fact, Emerald O'Brien decided, walking down Main Street putting her little French kid boots down carefully so as not to step in anything foul while at the same time keeping her chin tilted up proudly, her eyes wide and luminous, she was the only woman in the entire Black Hills who wasn't downright ugly. She figured she had already seen every decent woman in Deadwood. There were so few of them and they were all alike, worried, used-up looking women, bone thin or gone to fat, clutching their shawls around their shoulders, plodding after their miner husbands, some of them even dragging along a crying kid or two. And as for the whores, she had not seen many as they kept to themselves when they were not plying their trade; but she knew whores were a cut below the dance-hall girls who sold their favors only to selected customers, and she had seen plenty of those doing their tired little kicks on improvised stages near the gambling tables, showing gaudy petticoats and plump white thighs. They were certainly not much to look at. Even as they danced and sang or draped themselves over the bar enticing the miners with breasts spilling out of their low-necked dresses, Emerald was certain it was she, Emerald O'Brien, the men of Deadwood were lusting for.

It excited Emerald to think about herself and how she looked as she graced the streets of Deadwood. Her black hair was swept up to reveal her delicate pink earlobes and flashing green earbobs before it curled down in ringlets along her neck. She wore the latest style, her tiny waist set off by the bustle-back of her daytime costume. She had darling little gloves with the fingers cut out and a fussy little beaded handbag dangling from her wrist and a tiny little bonnet perched on her head and high-buttoned shoes on her feet. She felt as if she had just stepped from the pages of *Godey's Lady's Book*. It was hard for her to believe she was real.

She paused in her stroll to look up the street to the second-story window of the hotel room she shared with Austin Avery. She smiled when she thought about the Grand Central Hotel. The name was imposing, but the hotel was merely a huge cabin of green logs with a tacked-on second story of rough green lumber. When she and Avery first registered, none of the partitions between the rooms had reached the ceiling, and the cracks in the walls were wide enough to stick a finger through. Avery raised a terrible fuss about the lack of privacy and advanced a month's rent to properly furnish and complete their room. The next day, a huge brass bed and carved oak washstand were carried in and the walls reinforced and papered with white-washed newspapers. It was far beneath the accommodations to which Emerald had grown accustomed, but she had the finest room in Deadwood. She couldn't tell from studying the hotel window if Avery was awake. He wasn't much good before he breakfasted, which was usually about four in the afternoon. It was not likely this was one of the days he would allow himself to be wakened early. He had gambled until dawn. Watching Avery gamble all night was only slightly less boring than going to bed alone, so Emerald usually went to bed early and rose early to breakfast alone at the I.X.L. Restaurant. She liked to eat before the crowd gathered. She had a good appetite and when she ate in a room full of men, all eyes were upon her and it was difficult to maintain the lady-like posture of picking delicately at her food. When she ate alone, she could chew the meat off the bones and lick her fingers afterwards.

Sometimes maintaining her image was an annoyance, Emerald decided as she stopped before a mud puddle in the street and made a little mincing movement before reaching down and lifting her skirts to reveal her ankles as she stepped around the edge of the puddle. Just as she suspected, when she looked up, she saw three men sitting on empty whiskey barrels before the saloon watching her. She gave them a look of offended modesty and tossed her head so her curls jiggled a little as she walked past them with her chin in the air and her bustle switching. She heard the men groan and could hardly keep from giggling. It was delicious. If only her mother and her hateful sisters could see her now.

The best part was the fact Austin was right. The

men in Deadwood would not molest her. Women were so scarce, even the slightly-tarnished were valued, so even if some drunken miner lost his senses and approached her, a half-dozen others would instantly throttle him to prove their gallantry. Emerald almost anticipated such a situation arising. It would be exciting to see men fighting over her. But it was unlikely, for it was evident she belonged to the gambler whose black frock coat did not quite conceal the pearl-handled pistols tucked into his sash.

Being a rich man's mistress was not a bad life after all, she told herself. Avery bought her everything she wanted. Even among the barrels of flour and whiskey and nails that made up the stock of Deadwood's general stores, occasionally something suitable could be found: a bottle of lavender water, a gilt-edged mirror, a silver dressing-table set. It was as if in far-off Cheyenne and Sidney, as the shipments were being loaded onto freight wagons for the Black Hills, someone knew there would be a woman like Emerald in Deadwood. And Austin Avery was generous. She had to say that for him. Not that she didn't earn everything she got. Well, she would never put it that way. Not that she did not *deserve* everything he gave her. She gave herself freely to Austin because she loved him, and in return because he loved her, he bought her presents. That was the way it was.

She was certain Austin loved her. She hadn't made him say it yet, but if she were clever and subtle enough, he soon would. How could he not love her when any man in Deadwood would give his entire poke of gold nuggets for her? She was sure if she ever tired of Austin Avery, she would find another man in no time at all, one who would make her his wife, too. But for now she was almost content with Austin. He was a challenge to her. For now there were more important things than being a respectable wife. Better to be master of Austin Avery. It would be exciting to feel she had won him and he belonged entirely to her.

She would have been perfectly confident of her ability completely to win Avery's attention had she not been so aware she had a rival for his interest, gambling. Sometimes it was as if gambling was his true mistress, and he turned to Emerald only when he had satisfied his deeper lust. Just the night before she had accused him of being possessed by gambling fever. He laughed at her, his gold tooth gleaming.

"It's my trade, my dear. My profession, like other men doctor or preach or practice law. It's what I do well. I understand gambling. There are odds and you play with them. And if you understand the game and are clever enough, you win more than you lose. You put in a certain amount of effort and risk and you get rewarded. It's only those who try to get something for nothing that lose. Honest toil is what is takes. Why, I don't even believe in luck. It's the amateurs who believe in luck, who think they can get something for nothing. If everyone would be willing to work for a living as hard as I—"

"Avery?" She interrupted. She wanted to tell him to be quiet.

"Yes, my dear."

"Why don't you come to bed?"

It was better than listening to Austin Avery give a sermon. She did not believe for a minute that gambling was merely a line of work with him. It was as if he practiced magic. He had an uncanny ability with cards. Tricks, he told her. Tricks and practice and skill and a face that never betrayed emotion. But sometimes to Emerald, it seemed like magic.

It seemed like a sickness, too, because he could not leave it alone. He drank no more than a shot or two of whiskey in an evening, smoked his cheroots in moderation, and could go days without making love. They had abstained for the week it took them to get to the Hills, first on the stagecoach and then traveling with a wagon train of freight and sleeping outside with a dozen men before the campfire. He had left her alone, keeping just close enough to make sure the other men knew she was his property. But from gambling, he had not abstained. Even on the trail, he was always making a bet or dealing a hand. She noticed he refrained from playing for high stakes with his fellow passengers on the stagecoach. He explained to her it would not do to risk hard feelings with his traveling companions. Yet he managed to win a dollar or two off almost everyone he came in contact with. It irritated Emerald beyond reason.

She remembered the first night out from Fort Laramie with the freighters. After dinner they sat on their blankets before the fire and she, aware of the men's eyes upon her, brushed her hair by firelight, knowing she was beautiful in its reflection and knowing the men speculated about her relationship with Avery. She had turned to see if Avery was watching her, but he was spreading cards out on his blanket for a big slow freighter who squatted across from him with hope in his eyes. It was a simple trick Avery performed for the freighter that night; yet Emerald watched him work it a dozen times before she figured it out. He never repeated a trick on the same man and never took more than a dollar or two from each, so they could only grin foolishly, not out enough money to fuss over. Avery had over a thousand dollars in his money belt at the time, and her handbag was stuffed with jewels. There was no need to add the freighters' hard-earned dollars. That was when Emerald knew gambling was more than Avery's occupation; it was an obsession.

It was not that she had anything against gambling. Every man had his little weakness. She learned that at her mother's knee and supposed if Avery's had not been gambling, he would have drunk too much or lusted after other women. So it was not the gambling itself, but the fact that Avery was not totally involved with her that she could not tolerate. She was the queen of Deadwood and yet, even though Austin made love to her almost every afternoon, he could walk away from her afterwards. He did not worship at her shrine. He merely used her and then went on to his real mistress. Every time it happened, Emerald wished there was some way to get back at him.

That afternoon she had taken her time in strolling up Main Street to think over her life with Avery. It was July and although Deadwood was infinitely cooler than Missouri, she felt a bit mussed. Now that she was before the Grand Central, she must make a decision. It was not quite noon. Austin might not wake for hours. She could slip into their room, undress in the afternoon light, hoping Austin would open one eye and peer at her white and naked body while she pretended not to notice. Then she could slip into bed beside him and if he were still not fully awake, she could grow a bit bold. Sometimes that worked and sometimes it didn't. It drove her crazy when he insisted on sleeping, and today might be one of those days. Besides, whatever time he woke up, he would make love to her. She must not appear eager. He must never suspect how much she enjoyed it. That would give him too much power over her. Besides, he seemed to like to believe he ravished her. She knew only fallen women enjoyed conjugal relations. Passion was not a desirable quality in a wife, and Emerald still planned to get Austin Avery to marry her.

She decided it would be better to make Avery come to her that day. She would return to the I.X.L. Avery would find her there when he went for his breakfast and then she could let him persuade her to return to their hotel room for a nap.

It was better this way, she decided as she sat in the restaurant and sipped her not-quite cold iced tea. But it was boring. Just watching the men watch her drink tea was not an exciting way to spend an afternoon, so she looked up with interest when a man was bold enough to hesitate before her table. She knew instantly something exciting was about to happen. The man was small, nattily dressed and wore his dark hair neatly parted in the middle.

"Allow me to introduce myself," he swept off his hat with a grand gesture. "I am Jack Langrishe, proprietor of the only legitimate theatre in the Black Hills."

She knew him by reputation as did everyone in Deadwood. The whole city had turned out to welcome the coming of his theatrical troupe, for Langrishe's reputation preceded him. He and his wife had operated theatres in most of the mining camps of the West and were known and loved for bringing a brief illusion of beauty and magic to the drab lives of frontier towns. The performances at Langrishe's theatre had just begun, but were infinitely grander than the banjo music and off-color stories of the Melodeon or the vaudeville of the Gem Theatre, a place already more famous for what went on inside the curtained boxes upstairs than for any on-stage entertainment. Avery had taken Emerald to Langrishe's opening night performance, and she had been enthralled despite the fact the performance was given in an unfinished theatre roofed with canvas and when it rained she was thoroughly drenched. She would have been in the audience every night, but a lady did not attend the theatre unescorted even in Deadwood, and Avery would not give up another night's gambling.

Emerald decided to acknowledge Langrishe's introduction, even though it was highly irregular for a gentleman to approach a lady. "Please sit down, Mr. Langrishe. I feel I know you from your performances."

"And I feel I know you, for you drew as much attention in my audience as I did on stage."

Emerald looked down at her tea, allowing herself to blush prettily. It was true, of course, and it had irritated Austin Avery in a most satisfying way.

"Please forgive my boldness," Langrishe continued, "but I couldn't help but wonder. Have you by any chance ever been on the stage yourself?"

Emerald knew what was coming. It was not a proposition; it was something much more exciting. She felt her blush rising beyond the point of attractiveness before she regained her composure. "Why, Mr. Langrishe," she made her eyes wide, "why ever do you ask?"

"Because," the stocky little comedian rolled his large eyes expressively, "if ever I've seen a woman who was meant to be on a stage, it is you!"

"Really, Mr. Langrishe, I hardly know how to respond!" She tried to look affronted.

"You must think I'm being terribly cheeky," Langrishe acknowledged her offended look. "I should have had my wife approach you. When we noticed you in the audience, she agreed you should be on the stage, and I had anticipated having her with me when we called on you, but when I saw you here today without your — er — escort, well, I could wait no longer to beg you to consent to perform at our theatre."

"Why, Mr. Langrishe, I have no acting experience whatsoever. Whatever makes you think I could be an actress?"

She had known, of course, even before he began his speech that she was going to accept, but she wanted to hear what he was going to say. Besides, she had never sung or spoken in public. She was not quite confident she could succeed.

Langrishe made a flowery speech about her attributes and concluded by saying, "Frankly, my dear, you will always attract more attention in the audience than we will on the stage."

It was bit of an exaggeration, Emerald knew. Langrishe was Irish and he was full of blarney, but his speech had convinced her.

Still, she played coy for a while and let him talk on, trying to persuade her. His stage training had reduced the Irish brogue in his voice to a lilt which reminded her pleasantly of her father. It was a delight to hear such an articulate man praise her beauty and charm. She had never been praised before. Her mother had considered her good looks a danger to chastity, perhaps rightly so; and although Avery's actions certainly indicated he found her attractive, he had never told her she was beautiful. Emerald had not realized until she met Jack Langrishe just how hungry for compliments she was.

"Just one song," he said finally. "Just come to the theatre and sing one song and see how it feels, how you go over. Then, if you like it and the audience likes you as I know they will, my wife and I will coach you and you can perform in our regular plays and theatricals."

"I don't know about that, Mr. Langrishe. About joining your troupe, I mean. I am really quite occupied with my fiancé, Mr. Austin Avery. He is acquiring some mining properties, you know. And when he finishes his business, then we expect to return to the South where we shall regain Mr. Avery's plantation lost in the war. We plan to wed there in the old plantation home. Generations of Avery brides have been married on the veranda of the old family mansion and Mr. Avery just would not hear of breaking the old family tradition and that's why—"

"Fascinating," Langrishe said, ducking his bald head around to catch her speaking from various angles. "Utterly charming and fascinating."

"You flatter me." Emerald was glad for the interruption, as her impromptu explanation for the fact that she and Avery were not married, clever though it was, was getting onto delicate ground. "I'm afraid you're full of the blarney, Mr. Langrishe, but you have

267

convinced me to give the theatre a try. Just one song, though."

As they left the restaurant together Emerald tried to look fluttery and shy, but inside her heart was beating wildly. She had the feeling something important was about to happen.

She was not quite so certain of herself later as she stood offstage while Langrishe introduced her. She knew few songs and no dances, but she was going to give it a try.

He played a little introduction to *Weeping, Sad and Lonely*. It was a Civil War song, one that should bring tears to men from both sides. Besides, it was the only song they had been able to agree they both knew. The piano was the first in Deadwood and still a novelty. Emerald hoped no one would notice if her voice wavered.

She stepped very slowly to the center of the stage. It wasn't a real stage, just a large platform hastily constructed of green lumber, framed by a curtain and painted backdrop the Langrishes had packed along from their last mining camp. It wasn't a real theatre, either. The walls were of unpeeled logs and the floor was covered with sawdust. But it was a real audience, a hundred men and every eye was on her!

Langrishe played the introduction and looking at her pointedly. It was now or never. She clasped her hands over her bosom as she had seen a real opera singer do on the river boat. She began to sing in a tremulous voice.

Dearest love, do you remember

268

When we last did meet,
How you told me that you loved me,
    Kneeling at my feet?

There was not a sound in the whole theatre except
the piano and Emerald's voice and her wildly beating
heart. She saw she had them all. All the men in the
audience were with her, their eyes on her. She felt her
voice growing stronger as she began the next verse.

Oh! How proud you stood before me,
    In your suit of blue,
When you vow'd to me and country
    Ever to be true

They were getting tears in their eyes. All those
crusty old miners. They actually were weeping for her.
It was thrilling. As she sang the chorus she began to
relax, to move her arms about, gesturing with her
hands as she had seen real actresses do.

Weeping, sad and lonely,
    Hopes and fears how vain!
Yet praying
    When this cruel war is over,
Praying that we meet again.

It was over much too soon. She folded her hands as
if in prayer and lowered her eyes; there was a tremendous burst of applause, but then it was over. And it
had taken no time at all. Emerald felt bereft.

They were shouting, "More, more!"

Emerald didn't know what to do. She couldn't think

of another song. Her mother had approved of nothing but hymns. She knew a few hymns, but they would hardly be appropriate. Langrishe was looking up at her expectantly. She bit her lip, trying frantically to think of a jolly song. She had brought hardened miners to tears but that hardly seemed the mood in which to leave them. She could think of only one, another Civil War song. She ran over and whispered the title to Langrishe. He nodded and played an introduction. She ran back to center stage, struck a posture, took a deep breath and began, this time making her voice more lusty to match the mood of the song.

Sitting by the roadside on a summer day,
Chatting with my messmates, passing time away,
Lying in the shadow underneath the trees,
Goodness, how delicious, eating goober peas!

She saw the men breaking into smiles as they recognized the song, and it filled her with a heady feeling of excitement and power. As she came to the chorus, she began to dance about the stage, shouting out the words.

Everybody: Peas! Peas! Peas! eating goober peas!
Goodness, how delicious, eating goo-
ber peas!

She paused for just a moment, not quite able to believe she had done it. Not only had she sung a silly song to a whole theatreful of men, she had danced and kicked her legs and showed her petticoats. She felt

270

wonderful and she wasn't about to stop. She repeated the chorus, gesturing for the men to join her in singing.

"Everybody: Peas! Peas! Peas!"

This time she put everything into her dancing, pulling her heavy skirts up and skipping around the stage. She was having fun. The men were applauding and stamping their feet to the music as she skipped and pranced and sang. She felt her carefully arranged hairdo coming down and her cheeks growing red, but she knew she was utterly gorgeous and every man in the room was falling in love with her. And she loved herself. At last she truly loved herself.

Langrishe repeated the chorus again and again and she danced until she was breathless. She signaled to him *one more time* and he slowed the music to signal the audience this was the finale. Emerald knew she had to end her act with something sensational. As she made her last round kicking her legs up over the faces of the men in the front row, she thought of something she had seen dance hall girls do. She didn't know if it would work with her heavy bustled skirt, but it was all she could think of. It was daring and terrible and not the kind of thing a lady would do. But then a lady wouldn't be doing what she was doing.

As the piano trilled its last chord of *Goober Peas*, Emerald turned around quickly, her hands on her hips, then grabbing her skirt on each side, she bent over and threw her skirts over her head. If she had done it right, her drawers would show. Thank heavens they were ruffled.

The audience yelled, stamped their feet and howled for more. She must have done it right!

Slowly, almost haughtily, she turned to survey her audience and saw something she had dreamed of. On the face of every man in the audience was a look of adoration. They loved her.

Then, just as Mr. Langrishe pulled the curtain, Emerald saw a man who was not applauding. He stood in the back of the theatre, his face, ashen white.

It was Austin Avery.

Her first impulse was to tell Austin it was over between them and she was going to stay right where she was, on the stage. The audience was still stamping their feet and yelling for an encore, and Langrishe was looking uncertain, but pleased.

Emerald was out of breath and couldn't for the life of her think of another song. She had worked *Goober Peas* for all it was worth. She was going to have to learn more songs and some real dances, and anyway, she couldn't let Langrishe open the curtain when she was so disheveled. She wasn't about to make a fool of herself. Some instinct told her to quit while she was ahead. The same instinct told her it was not the time to leave Austin. So when he appeared backstage and took her arm, she let herself be dragged away before the startled eyes of Mrs. Langrishe and the other actresses. Emerald was not at all sure that he wasn't going to beat her.

It was exciting to know she had made Austin Avery furious. For once, he had lost his poker face. He looked furious, but he also looked vulnerable. Emerald knew in that moment that she had him. She liked the feel of his hand almost crushing hers as he dragged her out the back door of the theatre, down the street to the hotel and up the stairs to their room. Which was exactly what she felt like doing. Austin Avery thought he was showing his mastery of her, but he was playing out the little drama just as she would have written it.

It had excited her to look down from the stage and see a hundred men wanting her. It had stirred a need in her, and she saw no reason why Austin Avery should not satisfy that need and so, although she pulled back and cried and tried to bite his hand, she went back to the Grand Central hotel with Austin Avery quite willingly.

She needed Austin Avery very much that night.

But it would never do to let him know.

The next morning Austin was contrite. Emerald was tired, satisfied, and slightly bruised. She let Austin see the bruises and kept the satisfaction to herself.

Sometime during the night he had extracted from her the promise she would never again step out on the stage of Langrishe's theatre or any other theatre in Deadwood. It had been an easy promise to give. Emerald decided she could always change her mind, and for the moment, it was not too hard to give up the theatre. For she had succeeded in making Austin Avery angry and that was almost as good as making him love her. She had seen his emotions. His rage and his passion and his need of her had been displayed for all to see. She thought at one point during the night, he had been close to saying he loved her.

Emerald had reached a new height of passion that night. Avery's lovemaking had become more exciting steadily as she learned how to respond to him. Now it was no longer just Avery taking her or even Avery giving her pleasure, it was something she was doing for herself. She was reaching out, wanting and seeking and desiring. It brought them both to ecstacy. It left Avery both delighted and confused. He kept his control by telling himself it was something he had done *to* Emerald.

But Emerald knew she was the one who had changed. It had something to do with what had happened on stage. She had discovered something in herself she had not known she had: a sense of power. The knowledge she could control not only men but her own destiny. She was willing to tell Avery she would give up the theatre for him, because she realized the choice was hers. She didn't have to let things happen to her. She could go after whatever she wanted.

And what she wanted now was to be married to Austin Avery. She was sure he was the right man for her.

If there was a better man in Deadwood, she hadn't met him yet.

Chapter Nineteen

Molly was alone, dozing in a cabin warm from the afternoon sun. She dreamed of a bath, of soaking in a real tub filled with scented water, cool and clean and civilized.

She had only a pitcher and bowl on the table across the room. She stood before it and stripped away her gown, and with a rag and the pitcher of water and began to sponge off her body, letting the water trickle down her skin, then taking soap and lathering her belly. Her body had changed since that night she had willed Hugh to take her. Her breasts seemed fuller, her nipples always erect, her pelvis heavy, almost aching, as if she were ripening for some purpose. She felt almost feverish. The water would cool her. But as she touched her body, she thought of how it would be if Hugh were there. She had the curious sensation of being outside her body, being able to see the two of them together, like statues bathed in the stream of sunlight entering through the window. Dust motes, more golden than any they had found in their mine, danced in the air. He would kneel before her so that she might press his face to her breasts. She would caress his head, touch his golden hair. His hands would hold her waist, her hips. He would kiss her breasts and belly. She soaped her thighs, the mound of golden hair between, and knew his mouth would taste all of her.

And then the dream changed so that it was not a dream of her dreaming of him, but he was somehow there, in the doorway and then moving toward her. And they were miraculously alone in all the world. And she turned and met him without shame or guilt, her body beautiful in the sunlight, her hair a silky spring rain cascading over her shoulders, her arms open to him. He was golden and warm from the sun, shirtless as she had seen him working a hundred times outdoors, the muscles of his chest hard, the hair on his chest transparent with sun, and his body sculpted by light and shadow so he seemed a golden statue before her. Wonderingly, she reached out to him. Only silent understanding between them until his bare chest against her swelling breasts; his rough breeches against her nakedness.

They kissed. Molly willed him to take her. He carried her to her bride's quilt on the bed. He unbuttoned his pants and she saw his manhood, but felt no fear and only gloried in it. Touched it. Touched all of him. He brought his body close to her, and she opened to him willingly, but he did not enter her but offered himself between her legs where she was still slippery and wet from the soap. He had found a way to love her that would not impregnate her, but only unite them and end the torment.

For a moment it seemed as if they were suspended in time. Only their bodies touching, their lips and hands and his throbbing heat thrusting between her legs were real. But it was not enough. She wanted to possess and be possessed. She raised her hips to him, but she could not be joined with him.

And then she woke, alone, her gown drenched in sweat, the empty cabin no longer golden with afternoon sun, but shadowed, dark and empty. And she knew. Knew what it is that truly joins a man and a woman. Knew that she had been fully a woman at last, but only in a dream, and wept with the knowledge that she could not experience such joy with Hugh and remain Jake's wife and a civilized woman.

Then, even as she mourned for her lost innocence, a new thought gave her hope. *Will you take the risk?* Hugh had asked her and she had said *yes*, just as she had already said yes to the dangers of the trail. True, she would be different if she gave herself to Hugh, but was she not already different? She had left behind something of herself in Iowa with civilization and the miserable sod house and sad little graveyard. And whatever it was that had driven her to come to the Black Hills, whether it was fate and her destiny with Hugh or the desperate feeling that she would lose her mind if she tried to endure in the sod house on the prairie, she must trust that the instinct which impelled her forward was that of survival.

Hugh had shared with her his feeling at the burying of the gold camp whore on the trail to Custer that she, Molly Lewis, was destined to be remembered as a pioneer. She had laughed, saying she longed only for home and civilization; now she realized that those who become pioneers do not always choose their destiny; they simply meet the challenges of the journey.

Keeping the vow which she had made to Hugh would endanger everything she believed in and valued, but to retreat now would mean giving up and going home defeated. And she had no home to return to. And no true marriage with Jake. What she had was a challenge and a growing sense of certainty that she could and must seek her destiny.

Molly was not the only one in Deadwood that summer who thought of pioneer destiny. It was the year of the Centennial, and the violators of the Treaty of 1868 now considered themselves rightful citizens of Deadwood and intended to celebrate not just the nation's one hundredth birthday on July Fourth but their own accomplishment in turning the narrow, rocky gulch into a thriving mining town and holding it against the Sioux. An elaborate Independence Day celebration was planned and promoted by the editor of the *The Black Hills Pioneer* to proclaim to Deadwood and to the world at large that the rough and rowdy boom town was now a city, legitimate, respectable, patriotic and, above all, prosperous! The reality that, according to the law of the land, the entire populace consisted of lawbreakers and trespassers did not enter into the editor's decision to declare the good news that civilization had been carried into the wilderness.

Molly looked forward to the celebration in hopes that somehow a fitting Independence Day celebration would mark the beginning of a more orderly and civilized atmosphere in Deadwood. She bore little sense of guilt at having violated treaty rights, for it was obvious the Sioux did not till these lands, and sacred hunting grounds had little meaning to a farmer's wife.

She hoped only that the government would prevail and no more innocent women and children, white or red, would be killed or left fatherless. She did feel uneasy at the knowledge that their illegal status prevented the establishment of any form of law beyond the code of miners' courts which were called only to protect property claims. Her uneasiness in being in a lawless place came not so much from fear for her safety; she rarely went into town alone, but if she did was treated with courtesy as one of the few respectable women in the camp. Her tension came from the incongruity she recognized in demanding civilization of others at the same time she longed to push aside the boundaries of decency to keep her promise to Hugh.

All the partners of the Lucky Six looked forward to the celebration, for they desperately needed a holiday. The men had not taken a day off work since they first drove the mine shaft into the side of the mountain. That meant that Molly, too, labored from sunup to sunset. She could not, of course, work underground, but they were so short handed that, in addition to the cooking and washing, she and Edwin helped with the surface work—the fetching and toting of drinking water, rope, and blasting powder, and the relaying of messages. She found the outdoor work more satisfying than anything she had done in her life and soon became almost as obsessed with the mine as the men. There was always the promise that with the next pickaxe of ore broken away from the mine tunnel, they would see the gleaming vein of the motherlode. The work was backbreaking, endless, and, for the men, dangerous. But all of them were driven on by the hope that finding riches would somehow solve their problems.

The Centennial was to be a once-in-a-lifetime event and Molly intended to enjoy it. The day began when she was awakened just after midnight with a terrible crashing sound, followed by another and another. Her first thought was that the world was ending or at least that the mine had caved in, but Jake calmly explained that it was only the one hundred-anvil salute, a substitute for real fireworks achieved by the miners setting off powder charges packed between blacksmith's anvils stacked and restacked one atop the other. Edwin squealed with delight at the first dozen or so of the explosions; but by dawn when the one hundred blasts were finally completed, he and Molly both slept and so missed the first raising of the American flag over Deadwood. Hugh and Luther were there and later that morning reported it as a thrilling sight, accompanied by singing, shouting and shooting. Luther gleefully conceded that the red portion of Old Glory looked a bit strange, having been made from "an inner garment" donated by a patriotic lady who happened to reside at one of the Badland brothels.

Gunfire celebrations erupted in the smaller mining towns up and down the gulch all morning, so by the time the Lucky Six partners set off for Deadwood, gunsmoke wreathed the gulch like fog. Having initiated the midnight anvil serenade, Caleb Dexter was already somewhat the worse for wear, but still bursting with patriotic furor; so he brought his rifle out of his shack and marked their joining the celebration with an explosion of gunfire. Then all the men had to fire a round; even Edwin, so that he would be certain to remember the Centennial. Caleb was about to put the gun away when Molly announced her intention to shoot. The men had made her a full partner in the mine even before they knew how important her labor would be to them; now she wanted to be a full partner in the celebration.

"I'm a pioneer too!" she declared, hefting the rifle and firing a shot that, despite the pain the recoil brought her shoulder, made her feel joyfully one with the celebrants.

When they reached Deadwood, they found Main Street solidly filled with a happy, noisy, jostling crowd, drinking from bottles and sporadically bursting into patriotic song. The crowd was slow to silence when a dark-coated man mounted the crude stage of green lumber and began to speak, but when the word rippled through the crowd that he was leading a prayer, the crowd hushed; men removed their hats and the painted women who watched from the upper floors of the saloons bowed their heads. Molly was moved by the prayer and by the sight of so many respectable women and families in the crowd. The city grew daily and for once it seemed that decent folk outnumbered the rowdy element.

The prayer was followed by a reading of the Declaration of Independence by the city's new tax collector, who was apparently so uncomfortable at having been sent to the Hills to tax a population the government called trespassers that he immediately read and circulated a petition demanding that the U.S. Congress recognize the rights of its citizens in the Black Hills, numbered now at more than seven thousand "honest, loyal citizens."

Molly thought it a fine petition and wished she

could sign. Being considered a full working partner in the mine had helped her realize how essential women's work was to the settling of the frontier; now she had the radical thought that when Dakota became a state its women might be granted the vote. It was a privilege she thought she had earned.

Isolated by its location and the lack of a telegraph, Deadwood hungered for news. Rumors circulated in the crowd that Generals Terry and Crook were somewhere in Montana seeking to chastise the Sioux and settle the question of the Black Hills. The crowd was especially glad to learn that among the military was the popular and dashing figure of General George Armstrong Custer. The news made them all feel safer. The spirit of the crowd was jubilant, for they expected to receive at any moment word of a victory by Custer and the others. Then they could forget that they were building their hopes on land they did not own and from which they might yet be driven by the Sioux or their own government.

Edwin did not share Molly's new political interest and grew restless with the speechmaking, so Molly took him wandering about the crowd to make the acquaintance of other families. They were both shy, having been so long isolated on the homestead and at the mine. Edwin had been content to "work" with the men at the mine, but Molly decided to seek playmates for him, so that when they got back to a real town he would not have forgotten how to be a child. Although that afternoon she enjoyed Deadwood's bustling crowds and the sounds of the tinny pianos and banjos reaching the streets from behind the swinging doors of the hurdy-gurdy houses and saloons, Deadwood was still to her only a place to be left behind.

The afternoon sun was hot and when the men announced their intention to retire to a saloon called the I.X.L., Molly did not begrudge them their celebration. She had some gold dust of her own to spend, and Hugh made a point of telling her where he would be if she needed him. She thought there was an implication in his manner, some expectation that they might find a way to be alone in the confusion of the celebrating city. In agreeing to the risk of going underground, she had committed herself to him, but she avoided thinking of the reality of what she had promised. She wanted a holiday from all that had tormented her and a lazy summer day to enjoy with her son, who had never known a real celebration. She wanted the day to be for him all the joys of birthday parties, church suppers, sing-alongs, and especially real July Fourth celebrations with fireworks and ice cream socials. Sporadic gunfire continued all day, a mockery of the day in her mind, but the ice cream miraculously was there, even as she tried to describe it to Edwin, and they gorged on huge bowlfuls served in the dining room of the Progressive Hall, one of the city's more reputable establishments which now offered such luxuries. As they ate, Molly promised Edwin that they would often dine as elegantly when they returned to civilization.

"Civilization, Ma?" he asked.

"Yes, Edwin, when we go back to Pennsylvania and meet your grandparents. That's what we'll do if we find gold."

"And leave the Lucky Six? Leave Deadwood?"

"Yes, Edwin. Won't that be wonderful? We can have

a real house with real windows and live in a real city."

"But why would we want to leave Deadwood? Everything's here. The mine and Dad and Hugh and everyone!"

Molly was silent. She should not have mentioned the future. She had always dreamed that everything would be solved when they found gold and could return to civilization; now she saw that her son was already part of the frontier and would never be the perfect, velvet-suited child she had dreamed of presenting to her parents. What was left for her to dream of but union with a man who would take their son away from the only father he knew and build their futures on desire and uncertainty?

She felt heavy with foreboding and could no longer prattle to her son of places and things he neither knew nor cared about. Edwin was also quiet and Molly realized he was exhausted. They went to find Jake, but the crowd at the I.X.L. was so large it spilled into the street. She was afraid Edwin would not be able to find the men, but she had no choice but to send him inside. It rankled her that his maleness made it proper for him to enter a place she would have been mortally embarrassed to enter for any purpose, much less the task of fetching her husband away from his drink. She hoped Jake would not leave her waiting too long.

Edwin returned at last alone.

"Pa isn't ready to go home yet. He says can we wait in the restaurant or go on without him?"

Molly felt herself blush. It was almost dusk. Jake knew she would not want to walk home after dark with the whole town drunk. It was unlike him to be so inconsiderate of his family. She wanted to know if he were intoxicated, but could not ask Edwin.

"Pa's drunk!" he volunteered cheerfully. "Him and Caleb Dexter and Luther! They're drunker 'n I ever seen anybody!"

"Than I ever saw anyone," Molly corrected before she realized the futility of reproaching the boy. He only told the truth. She looked up helplessly and then saw that Hugh was standing in the doorway. She looked away, feeling shamed before him by Jake's indifference. She had seldom faulted Jake for needing his drink, for she knew how life had disappointed him, but he had never before failed in his duty to her or the boy.

"I'll take you home," Hugh said quietly, stepping out into the street with her. "I told Jake I would."

"And did he say that you should?"

"Pa's too drunk to say much of anything!" Edwin reported, taking hold of Hugh's hand.

"Jake thanked me for offering. He's not ready to leave. I expect Luther and I could get him home between us, though Luther's in no mood to end the celebration and Caleb Dexter's passed out underneath the table, but I'll get Jake home for you if that's what you want."

"No, I expect that would be even less dignified than letting them sleep it off in the saloon. But what about you? Do you mind leaving now?"

"I want to be with you."

She saw the possibility of their having a whole evening alone and felt rich. Still, she could not say yes, but only took his arm and let him lead her away from the saloon. Edwin skipped along and chatted amiably until exhaustion overcame him and he accepted the offer of Hugh's back. As they headed up the road to the cabin, Edwin fell asleep with his golden head on his father's shoulder, and Molly was struck by the picture the three of them must make going home together.

They did not talk and Molly did not speculate on how it would happen. She knew it would happen and that was enough. When they reached her cabin, Hugh laid Edwin gently down and spoke at last.

"When you get him settled, will you join me on the hillside? It's a beautiful night and there's enough moonlight to find our way."

She could not speak, but nodded.

"I'll be waiting for you."

She fumbled with Edwin's clothes, removing his belt and shoes so he would sleep more comfortably. When he half-woke, she helped him into his nightshirt and felt the need to reassure him if he should wake and find her gone.

"Edwin, it's still early. I thought I might sit outside where it's cool for a bit."

"With Hugh, so you'll be safe?"

Her heart was hammering as she laid him back down and covered him lightly. "Yes, with Hugh."

"Ma," he gave her what seemed a knowing look through sleepy lashes, "do you love Hugh?"

She could not help gasping, but she made her voice calm before she replied, "Why do you ask that?"

" 'Cause I do. I love Hugh and Luther and Caleb Dexter, and I thought you might, too. Love Hugh, I mean. Not the others, I guess you just like them, but Hugh's special ain't he? I love him best, next to you and Pa."

"Well, I like all of the men. But you're right. Hugh is special."

"I thought so," he seemed to be drifting back to sleep, but then his eyes fluttered open again. He had forgotten his prayers. Molly listened while he said his "God Blesses." He included all the men at the Lucky Six as he had since the beginning of the partnership, but Molly heard only Hugh's name, her heart full of confusion. She could not admit she loved this man, even to her son in the most innocent of declarations, but in a few minutes she was going to him. Now she could not ask God's blessing for herself, but only trust that He would understand and forgive what she must do.

While she waited for Edwin to sleep, she freshened herself with cool water. She wished she had more than the scrap of mirror and a comb to make herself ready for him; then was surprised to see in the clouded mirror that she was already glowing and beautiful. There was no more need to make ready; no more need to hesitate.

He was waiting outside his cabin, holding a lantern and studying the side of the hill. She saw by the sudden delight on his face when he turned to her that he had not been certain she would come.

"I found a place for us weeks ago," he said. "There's a level space on the side of the hill. It's under a tree and cushioned with pine needles. I thought I'd leave the lantern here so we can find our way back to the cabin. We can make our way by moonlight now, but it might be darker when we return."

He was awkward. She saw he carried a blanket and

was both embarrassed and touched by his planning.

She followed him up the hill on a path that continued past the mine shaft to a high place she knew he sometimes used as a retreat from the mine. From this place they could see the cabins and the road, but could not be seen themselves until they returned to the light of the lantern.

He spread the blanket over the pine needles and turned to her. "I hope this is all right. From this place sometimes I can almost forget the mine."

"Yes, it's lovely the way the trees make a shelter. And look how glorious the stars are. The sky looks so much darker from here in the gulch that the stars are incredibly bright and beautiful."

"I know. I've wanted to show you the sky from here." He stood behind her and put his arms gently around her so that she could lean against him while they studied the heavens. "Take a deep breath. You can smell the pine and the mountain air so much better here. And if you listen hard you can still hear the creek and the night sounds of the crickets."

"This must have been a beautiful land before everyone came here to spoil it. This reminds me of that time when we first found ourselves alone on the trail and saw the deer, and I said they were beautiful and you said—"

"I said it was you who was beautiful." His breath was warm against her neck. "Do you want a compliment, Molly?" he teased. "Shall I say it again?"

"You don't need to. Tonight when I was getting ready to meet you, I looked in the mirror and I felt beautiful. Like a young girl whose beau is coming courting. I never felt quite that way before."

"You were never courted, were you? I spoiled that for you."

"Don't," she said, turning toward him. "Don't let's talk about sad times or the past."

"Or the future?" He nuzzled her neck as she buried her face against his chest. "Can we talk of the future, Molly? Can we make a plan?"

"No, Hugh. No, not that."

"I thought you'd not say no to me again."

She kept her eyes closed. His arms were warm and gentle around her, the rough weave of his shirt a blessing against her cheek; but she could feel his tension growing and was aware, too, of an answering softness and yielding in her.

"I can't say yes to anything. I can't speak my feelings, and I can't make plans or promises. But I will not say no to you tonight."

"Oh, Molly, Molly, my love," his arms tightened around her and she raised her face to meet his kiss. Before their lips met, she thought only that she would at last give herself to him. But in the kiss, she not only yielded but took, as hungry for him as he for her. In that moment they were the whole world for each other. There was no mountain upon which they stood, no cabin below, and no Deadwood.

He lifted her then and laid her down on the blanket, smoothing it around her as best he could on the hillside.

"It makes me think of the first time," she said. "Remember us in the barn, arranging the straw and making a home for ourselves in some secret place?"

"We were children and fools then. This is the first time. This is the first time for us both. This is home, at last." He knelt beside her and touched her face tenderly, and as his first gentle kisses found her mouth and neck, she knew he was right.

They had come home and what was happening would change everything. She had come to him that night to fulfill a promise, to do what must be done to keep him at the mine, to hold him against her fear of darkness and loss. But from that first kiss freely given on the hillside, she had become a different woman.

It was indeed, the first lovemaking for them both. With each other, in that time before, they had been children exploring, pretending, caught up in something they neither willed nor understood. With Jake she had been a wife doing her duty, rewarding and comforting him for his protection and support. With others Hugh had been a man taking his pleasure from one who was willing but had no power to hold him or to give him more than physical release.

But now it was all different. And what had been born in them so long before truly began. They made love as if they had eternity instead of a few moments stolen on the side of a Dakota hillside.

Sweet, almost shy kisses. Fingertips caressing her face and neck and then tantalizingly discovering the opening of the dress already made loose and ready for him. He touched with delicate brush strokes which warmed her silken skin and flooded her imagination with glorious color, so that as she sank into the blanket she felt herself a wildflower opening to blossom in this secret place. Blossoming to delight a lover. Only for him. Only for Hugh, at last.

Her dress was entirely open now and her skirts raised, petal-like around her hips. She felt wanton and willing, and his touch and her moans proved her readiness for him.

He stood and unbuttoned his shirt. He seemed like a god as he stood above her half-naked in the moonlight. He seemed to be moving slowly as if to tease. Then he was all naked, proudly erect and unashamed. She did not look away, but held out her arms to him.

He knelt at her side and then seemed to hesitate.

"Molly, my love. I've done something so foolish. I don't know how to speak to you of it. I swore to you that I'd not get you pregnant, and I determined that when the time came, I'd have a sheath to catch my seed and keep you safe, and now—"

"You're not afraid that I would be ashamed because it's not for the joining of husband and wife?"

"No, I'm the one who's ashamed. Ashamed and foolish that I could not do it. Even after you seemed to promise that we might at last be together, I could not think I would really have you at last. It seemed that if I planned for this it would be a jinx. I've wanted you so, my darling, and I made you promise you'd give yourself to me but I never believed it would happen."

"But you said you'd leave me if I did not give myself to you."

"I lied. I could never leave you, even if I never did what I'm burning to do. Even now you could turn away from me."

How her heart leapt then to know that it was not only his desire that bound him to her, but that he would never deny his love for her. She felt infinitely tender and something new. Impatience. "I'll not turn away."

He wanted more. Wanted her to say she wanted

him, but he knew she could not speak her need aloud. As if sensing his thoughts, she reached out and with an instinct she suddenly knew was as old as Eve, found the center of his desire and began to caress him.

"You said there were ways, Hugh. You said there were many ways you'd love me. You said you could never keep your hands off me."

"Oh God, yes. Many ways. A hundred ways that I can love you with my hands and with my mouth and with just the tip of this great need I have for you! I've thought of so many ways, my sweet. And you! Oh, you have found how to pleasure me. Oh, Molly, how you pleasure me. Let me lie here against you, let me just come close to your precious treasure, and oh how we will pleasure each other!"

And so, because the ultimate joining could be theirs for only a moment, that which bound them together was not possession, but the joyous freedom of pleasuring and even squandering their love, one against the other. Their lovemaking was both tender and rough, greedy and giving; a riotous explosion of sensation, motion and mood, kiss and touch, of seed and soul spilled together.

At last they lay in each other's arms in quiet joy. Hugh touched her face and found it wet with tears. To his unspoken question, she said only, "I never knew before. I've lived so long and not known."

"And I thought I knew, and I was a fool."

And if their words made no sense, they both understood and said no more. The night grew cold, and Hugh brought the blanket around them, so they seemed wrapped together in a warm cocoon. He slept, but Molly lay awake watching, her thoughts as crowded and overwhelming as the stars above her. Hugh's head was heavy on her breast and, though it was infinitely sweet to hold him so, his sleeping made her think of Jake and that all men were alike in some things. But even as she thought that, Hugh woke to caress her and whisper, "Stay close, Molly. I love you."

She held him against her as tenderly as if he were Edwin newborn, but she could not answer him. She had thought of Jake. He would be needing porridge and strong coffee in the morning. And she must get it for him. Perhaps the men would not be home until dawn, but she did not dare lie longer with Hugh. What had happened had been a gift. If she never knew a real home with a piano and glass windows, if she had nothing else in her life to treasure, she would always have the memory of this night, but now it must end.

She turned her head so she could see back down the hillside to their cabins. The light of the lantern Hugh had left burning seemed far away and very weak. Even as she watched, it flickered and died.

She looked up at the myriad brilliant stars, heard again the explosion of gunfire echoing in Deadwood, and knew the mine and her cabin, her sleeping son and duty waited; and she wondered how she and Hugh would ever again find their way home.

Chapter Twenty

Once again Emerald O'Brien stood outside the I.X.L. restaurant and tried to decide how to spend the afternoon. She had lingered over her brunch, taken her walk, and now was debating whether it was time to wake Avery. The only problem with being a mistress, she decided, was that the actual time spent in mistressing was so limited. There were long hours of the day and evening to fill.

It was a shame Austin would not hear of her being on the stage. It would give her something to do. Still, her little venture with Langrishe's theatre had been worthwhile. Austin had been especially attentive since the night he dragged her from the stage, carried her to their hotel room, and tore her clothes off. Their lovemaking had taken on a new dimension as she realized her own ability to seek and receive pleasure. She kept her desires hidden from Avery, or so she thought, and instead encouraged him in subtle ways to replay the scene in which he ravished her. The pleasure was always worth the little bruises and the wear and tear on her chemises. Her only disappointment was in realizing there seemed to be definite limits to a man's energy for lovemaking, limits which left her so much empty time. Her boredom made her lonely, sometimes she even experienced little nibbles of guilt. For even as she became her own woman, Emerald could not entirely forget her mother's lectures on sin and whoredom and the folly of loving handsome, dark-haired strangers. She found she missed even the constant squabbling that had been her relationship with her sisters. She could not associate with the other women in Deadwood's Badlands, her "sisters in sin," for being the mistress of a man like Austin Avery was far above being a sporting woman or even a dance hall girl.

Being a mistress, however, was equally far from being a wife. She knew she had left respectability behind in Missouri. No married woman would speak to her, and respectable men would consider her damaged goods, even if they wanted her for themselves. Her whole life was built on one man. She knew this and it made her uneasy, even as she told herself the romance was enough. But for the most part she found she could overcome her loneliness, her boredom and doubts, and even her pangs of guilt with a new hairdo, a leisurely bath in the hotel's copper washtub, or in hatching a new plot to goad Avery into another round of lovemaking.

She was trying to decide which of these amusements she would use to fill her afternoon when she noticed a commotion on the lower end of Main Street. A crowd was gathering. It appeared they were clustered in the disreputable end of the street, but she was delighted at the prospect of diversion and decided the location of the event was not going to stop her from investigating.

A decent woman would never be seen down there, Emerald thought as she hurried down the street, but there were some advantages to being tarnished.

It did not take her long to make her way to the front of the crowd. She found herself standing before one of the town's more notorious saloons. It was called a boarding house, but its rooms were rented by the hour. The crowd was watching a terrific three-way argument between a henna-haired woman in a dressing gown, obviously a tenant of the upstairs establishment, an oily-looking dark-haired man whose gartered rolled-up sleeves and apron marked him as a bartender, and a silk-vested gentleman carrying the black leather bag of a doctor.

"You can't just throw her out into the street," the henna-haired woman screamed, taking a stance before the saloon-keeper.

"Well, I can't keep her upstairs," the saloon-keeper shouted, his fist clenched before him. "She's no use to me now!"

Emerald stood on her tiptoes straining to see who they were talking about. The man in front of her shifted slightly and when Emerald got a clear view, she gasped. Coming slowly down the outside staircase were two men carrying a door fashioned as a stretcher. On the door was a woman. The fact that her face and shoulders had been draped with a fringed shawl could mean only one thing—she was dead.

"You're a cruel heartless man, Al Baines." The henna-haired woman did not back down. "What would it hurt you to let her lie upstairs until we can make arrangements?"

The stretcher bearers reached the street and looked

to Baines for orders.

"It's bad for business, Tiz, you ought to know that. Bad enough she had to do herself in on the premises. How do you think a man feels when he's out to have a good time and hears there's a dead woman upstairs?"

"He has a point," the man with the doctor's bag put in. "Even a vigorous man is apt to lose his libido when confronted with the harsher realities of cohabitating with the weaker sex."

"So what do we do with her, boss?" One of the stretcher bearers whined. "She ain't exactly light, you know."

"Then you take her." Tiz begged, clutching at the doctor's sleeve.

"Please take your hands off me immediately." The doctor pried her loose. "I told you I have no facilities for laying anyone out. It doesn't look right for a doctor to run an undertaking establishment. Conflict of interests, you know."

"But doctor—"

"It's out of the question. You will have to make your own arrangements for your—friend. Now if someone will just take care of my fee, I will be on my way."

"Your fee!" Tiz screamed, making a fist at him. "What did you do to earn a fee? You didn't do a thing except say it was too late. You didn't even say what killed her."

There was a rumble of sympathy from the crowd.

"Good heavens, men," the doctor was answering the crowd and not Tiz. "What difference does it make? She was dead when I got here. Probably an overdose of laudanum. It usually is in these cases. Or else she got herself in a predicament and took some drug to try

297

to remedy her mistake. It hardly matters now." He drew himself up importantly, clutching his bag. "I have done my duty offering medical assistance despite my natural reluctance to render my services in such an establishment and I—"

"Hell, doctor," a voice yelled from the crowd. "Seems I saw you rendering your services at this place before."

"And it wasn't in the afternoon!" Another voice boomed out and the crowd broke into laughter.

The doctor turned white, then quickly regained his composure. "I don't have to be subjected to this." He whirled around on his heel and started to march down the street, but before he had taken two steps, he turned back to Baines. "And you, sir, will be receiving a bill for my services and if you don't pay up, the next time one of your doxies tries to do herself in, I will be unavailable."

As he marched off down the street, a few of the hangers-on started to follow him, imitating his mincing gait. The crowd seemed about to dissipate when Tiz began shouting again.

"Well, what about Marabell?" She confronted the crowd angrily. "How is she to be repaid for her 'services'? You were all of you anxious enough to be her friend when she was alive. Are you going to stand here and let her be thrown out in the street?"

The crowd shifted uncomfortably. There were some murmured conversation and finally someone began to pass a hat.

"Can we set her down, boss?" one of the stretcher bearers asked. "We can't stand here all day." They were leaning toward the entrance to the saloon.

"Not in my place, you don't," Baines said, blocking

the doorway with his hefty body.

"You let her in, Al Baines!" The voice came from an upstairs window, and Emerald looked up to see two women framed in the narrow window, ill-kept hair hanging around their shoulders and their faces smudged as if they had been sleeping or crying. "You take her in or we'll all go over to the Hidden Treasure to work!"

"The girls are right," Tiz had her hands on her hips as she confronted Baines. "You lay Marabell out proper or we'll all go somewhere else to work, or —" Here she cast a meaningful look at the crowd. "Or, we won't work at all."

At this, the hat which had been passed half-heartedly began to fill more quickly as the miners dug deeper in their pockets and pouches. Finally someone handed the hat to Emerald. It was half-full of well-worn bills, coins and grains of gold. Emerald held the hat. She was struck by the incongruity of the picture she must make in such a crowd at such an event dressed like *Godey's Lady's Book*. The whole thing seemed unreal, as if it were happening on a stage.

"Excuse me, Ma'm." The man to her left took the hat. "This ain't no business for a lady."

Emerald stood there numbly as the hat finished its rounds and the men discussed coffins and burial sites and grave diggers. Baines, seeing which way public feeling was going, made a desperate attempt to save the day's business. "All right. We'll lay her out here and drinks are on the house."

It worked. Most of the crowd filtered into the saloon. Marabell was carried back upstairs and Tiz, making no attempt to conceal her triumph, followed the stretcher.

But Emerald, for some reason, could not turn and walk away. And then, as the procession moved unsteadily up the staircase, a breeze caught the shawl and it blew away from Marabell's face.

Emerald gasped. Marabell had been young. She didn't look over sixteen. A round-faced farm girl. A girl like Emerald's little sister. A girl who thought she would find excitement and adventure in the gold camp and had died by her own hand. Laudanum the doctor had said, or something to give her an abortion. That's how whores end up, her mother had always said. They drink themselves to death or they get diseased or take too much laudanum or kill themselves trying to get rid of a baby.

Suddenly Emerald had an awful realization. She turned and fled up the street, her heart pounding. *It could be me*, she thought. *Me, lying there dead for everyone to see. I have laudanum in my reticule. It helps me sleep when Austin has been especially awful or if I have a little pain. That's probably how Marabell started. Taking a little laudanum to dull the pain and the guilt and now she's dead. Or she got in a family way.* That was even worse than suicide. Surely *that* couldn't happen to her. Austin had assured her he knew the secret of preventing it from happening, but he wasn't always careful. And those girls must know all the secrets about not getting caught and it still had happened to Marabell. It could happen to Emerald, too! And she would not even have sisters in sin to bury her.

Austin was arranging the silk cravet he wore at his neck when Emerald burst into the hotel room. He looked up, startled, one hand moving to the pearl-handled revolver in his belt. Emerald thought she saw a look of concern on his face and threw herself into his arms, weeping bitterly.

Austin held her for a moment, then led her to the bed, made her sit down and, taking out his handkerchief, wiped her face. "Get control of yourself and tell me what happened."

Hiccuping back her sobs, Emerald told him about Marabell.

"Probably laudanum," he said. "Most of those girls are addicted to the stuff. Opium and alcohol. It takes the edge off everything. But why are you so upset? You didn't know her."

"But Austin, it could be me! Don't you see, it could be me. She was a bad girl and—"

"Don't be silly, Emerald," he stood up and moved away from her. "That girl was a common whore. Why you have too much pride to ever let yourself—"

"You don't let yourself get *that* way. It just happens. A girl gets . . . gets . . . in trouble and—"

"Gets pregnant, Emerald. Stop being so coy. It doesn't become you. Are you afraid of getting pregnant? Is that it? Didn't I tell you I've been taking care of that?"

"But sometimes you don't. Sometimes you get too anxious and—"

"I'll be more careful. I sincerely don't want to get you in any difficulty."

"But what if you did? What if it happened?"

"Well, then we would try to find a reputable medical man to take care of it, or else . . ." he shrugged.

"Or else you'd marry me? You'd marry me wouldn't you? Isn't that what you were going to say?"

"Don't put words in my mouth." His face was even more impassive than usual. "I was going to say I'd give you enough money to get you back East. You could pretend to be a widow and have the baby somewhere and we'd find a decent family to keep it and—"

"You'd make me give up my baby!"

"Look at me Emerald!" He demanded, taking her face in his hands. "Do you *want* a baby?"

"Of course not," she jerked his hands away angrily. "But you'd make me give it up? You wouldn't even marry me so I could keep my very own baby?"

"I cannot stand it when you persist in being so emotional." He picked up his frock coat and finished dressing while he talked. "You have witnessed an ugly scene and I understand your being upset. I suggest you lie down and compose yourself. I have business to attend to."

"Austin!" she screamed. "You answer my question! Do you mean you *wouldn't* marry me?"

He turned back to her. "I've told you before and I'll tell you once more. People like you and I are not made for marriage and respectability. You can't cage a wildcat. It would kill everything between us."

"But, Austin, I *love*—"

"Don't start that, Emerald." He came to her and put a hand under her chin and forced her to look at him. "Now listen to me. If you decide you are meant to be married, or if you should find yourself with child and you want to play at being a mother, then I will either set you up in some town where you can pretend to be a respectable widow until you tire of the game or else—"

"Or else what?"

"Or else you can find someone else to take a chance

on."

"Take a chance on! Why you make it sound like one of your games. Like gambling!"

"Marriage is the biggest gamble of them all, my dear." He picked up his hat and adjusted it on his head. "And all the cards are stacked against the man." He paused, studying himself in the mirror. "No, I'll take that back. Women lose too. Marriage makes them slaves and shrews. No, marriage is the game where no one wins. Oh, it might be worth it for those who are convinced they'll burn in hell without it. But as for me, I'd as soon take my chances on hell in the hereafter as deal myself in for a sure piece of hell on earth."

"I never heard anyone say anything so awful in my whole life."

"Then it's obvious you've never been around many married people. They say awful things to each other all the time."

"I'd never say anything awful to you, Austin." She sniffed prettily and dabbed at her eyes with his handkerchief, but she knew she had blown it. She should never have let herself get so upset. She should have worked him into marriage more gradually as she had originally planned. Now she had laid all her cards on the table and Austin was going to call her bluff. Somehow she must regain her advantage. The handkerchief was full of black smudges. She had smeared her eye-coloring. She must look a sight. She tried to compose her face into a little-girl pout.

"Of course you'd say awful things to me, Emerald." He moved closer to her. "You'll say awful things to me if we're married or not, but at least this way we can play it honest. This way when one of us wants out, we

303

can just walk away."

"You'd walk away from me, Austin? You'd just leave me here alone without anything?"

"Of course not, dear little girl." He ran the tip of one finger along the side of her neck. "You've a whole bag full of little trophies, don't you? If anything happened to me, you could cash in all those watches and jewels and you'd have more than enough to get you back East in style."

"You think that would be enough?" Emerald pouted. "You think it would make up for losing you?"

"I'm sure it would." Avery laughed. "I'm no prize. I'm sure you'd soon find a man as good for you, or," he turned her face up to him, "or, as *bad* for you."

He gave her a pinch on the cheek and left. Whistling. But his words lingered. She could find another man. She could find one better than Austin Avery. One who would marry her. And she had to be married. She had seen that today. It was the only way a woman could be secure.

If Austin Avery wouldn't marry her, then she would find someone who would.

And that would make Austin sorry.

Chapter Twenty-one

For days after their meeting on the hillside, Hugh and Molly hardly dared look at each other. It was not shame which kept them apart, but the joyful certainty that each had been so changed and marked by what had passed between them that all could see. The physical expression of what had been in their hearts since their first meeting on the trail, indeed, since their first time in that faraway place, changed everything. And yet it changed nothing. Destiny might promise that Molly belong to Hugh, but she was still Jake's wife. It seemed impossible to Molly, but Jake was blind to the change in her. It was as if he had stopped seeing her. Molly tried to decide if it was his obsession with the Lucky Six that made him so unaware of her or if he had always been that way. She wanted to believe that he, too, had once been delighted just to look at her; it seemed too sad to admit that theirs had always been a marriage of convenience.

Jake's failure to notice his wife's distress grated on Hugh, but he had a hard time making himself believe that it excused anything. Molly was still Jake's lawful wife, and Jake was still a good man who did not deserve to be cheated, especially by his own partner.

Hugh did not believe in predestination, that fatalistic theology which seemed to say man was doomed or saved only by the will of God. It was too much like the ancients' belief that man was but the plaything of the gods. It had always seemed to Hugh that man made his own fate, and the world operated on a principle of justice that would reward those who worked hard and did good. He had always believed no problem existed which could not be solved; no moral dilemma that could not be untangled. But since joining in the so-called opening of the Black Hills, the morality of which he himself had questioned in that distant editorial on the sacred hunting ground of Pahasapa, he seemed to have crossed some invisible line which, like the actual crossing of the Platte, marked the point at which civilization was left behind.

And now, finding a way to be joined with Molly and yet remaining a man worthy of respect seemed as impossible a quest as finding riches in the dark and awful tomb they called a mine. And yet, the hope of one more touch, one more kiss, even one more smile was, like poor man's gold, enough to keep him imprisoned in that most torturous of traps: hope.

His inner turmoil was exacerbated as the atmosphere in Deadwood changed from hopeful expectancy and optimism to tension and fear. The city had celebrated its first Fourth of July not knowing that less than two hundred miles away Custer and his entire command had been massacred, a tragedy which those Deadwood "citizens" who were still inclined toward guilt had to admit had been precipitated by their invasion of the Sioux reservation and which now put them all in mortal danger.

Custer's massacre, which would become known as the Battle of the Little Big Horn, occurred on June 25, but word did not reach Deadwood until nearly a month later, on July 20. For years afterward people remembered and talked about what they had been doing and how they felt when they heard the awful news.

That night Hugh had walked into town after supper, wanting to be away from the others. When he saw the crowds gathered, he knew something had happened and hoped it was good news. Deadwood was tired of its common-law status. The only sign from the U.S. government that they existed had been the visit from the tax collector. They could have done without that, but they yearned for the other institutions of civilization: official procedures for dealing with the mountains of garbage that were filling the spaces between the crowded buildings, ways of protecting themselves from fire and, most especially, a legal system. They had created quasi-legal miners' courts to see that mining claims were filed, but without a sheriff or jail, they had only two ways to deal with lawbreakers, banishment or hanging. The value of property and mining claims was growing rapidly, but so was the population of men who obviously had no regard for law and order. The pioneers who braved hardships to come to the Hills in the winter of '75 or the spring of '76 were men willing to break their backs to get their gold. In the summer of '76 came those who knew there were easier ways to get rich. So when Hugh saw the men clustered in groups to talk that July evening, he hoped it meant the Sioux had signed a treaty and civilization could be officially established.

When he heard what had happened, he could not immediately comprehend the magnitude of the disaster. It seemed impossible that Custer, his brother, and his entire command of over two hundred men had been destroyed without a single survivor. Not only had Deadwood, isolated as it was by the lack of a telegraph line, been ignorant of the event which had rocked the nation, but it would have no warnings of future massing of the Indians. Custer's men had encountered five thousand Sioux and Cheyenne. That was why there had been only sporadic raids against isolated settlers that summer. It was not that the Sioux did not intend to fight for their sacred hunting grounds, but that they would not desecrate their holy land by battling *on* them. But what now? With the scalps of Custer and his men, the first invaders of their beloved Pahasapa, waving triumphantly from their scalp poles, would the Sioux not turn their wrath toward Deadwood and those who had followed Custer on his Thieves' Trail?

Throughout July, the situation seemed to be grow more precarious. Travel into and out of the Hills was reduced to parties of well-armed men, and even these were subject to attack. No one knew where the five thousand victorious warriors were, and every issue of the *Pioneer* rumored new massacres; yet the talk in town was that since more copies of the paper were distributed in the East to encourage capital investment and immigration to the gold fields than were sold locally, the paper was actually playing down their danger.

Then on August 2, two events occurred which, had

they happened on different days would have been
disturbing enough but, occurring as they did, within
hours of each other, made Hugh feel the whole town
had gone crazy. *The Black Hills Pioneer*, ever conscious
of the city's image to the outside world, gave only a few
inches to either of the grisly events. The first incident,
the murder of Wild Bill Hickok, would quickly become local folklore to be recounted in years to come as
part of the legend of that summer of '76. The second
happening was one the pioneers would choose to
forget.

It was a Tuesday evening and Hugh, Luther, Molly
and Edwin strolled into town toward sundown. As they
reached the city, once again Hugh noticed, this time
with an uneasy feeling, clusters of men talking and
arguing in the street. They soon learned that James
Butler Hickok, commonly known as Wild Bill, had
been sitting in Saloon No. 10—there were so many
saloons, some were known only by numbers—when a
man who called himself Jack McCall entered and shot
him dead. Hickok was habituously cautious, having
killed many men in his career as a law officer and
perhaps in other pursuits as well. But that day he had
violated his custom of watching the door and was
sitting with his back to it when he was slain. McCall
was chased through the streets by an angry mob and
soon captured. He was tried almost immediately by a
miners' court convened in the Bella Union theatre.
McCall testified Hickok had killed his brother, and for
that or other reasons the jury promptly acquitted
McCall with the provision he leave the Hills, which he
lost no time in doing.

Hugh thought it a terrible miscarriage of justice and

said so. Others in the crowd agreed. One man speculated McCall had been hired as an assassin by those who feared Hickok might bring law and order to Deadwood. Even as he spoke, the man realized the significance of his words and his voice trailed off as he glanced around the crowd.

Hugh was still pondering the remark when he became aware of another disturbance at the upper end of Main Street. As the crowd watched, a horseman charged down the street at a gallop. The rider brandished something in one hand. Hugh assumed it was a dead animal of some sort. Then as the rider reined in, setting his lathered horse back on its heels almost directly before him, Hugh saw with horror that the object held aloft before him was a human head.

The head had been severed at the neck and was even now spattering drops of congealing blood on the crowd. Instinctively Hugh stepped before Molly and Edwin to protect them from the sight. But it was too late. Molly looked as if she were going to faint, then steadied herself and grabbed Edwin who was standing on his tip-toes trying to get a better look.

Hugh picked Edwin up. "Let's get out of here."

"Wow," Luther sputtered. "Would you look at that!"

Hugh couldn't resist taking another look at the grisly trophy. The horseman was now the center of a large crowd.

The head was that of an Indian and the rider held it aloft proudly, swinging it to and fro. Hugh wanted to drag the man from the saddle and put an end to the ghastly display, but Edwin was struggling in his arms, wanting to see.

"Please, Hugh." Molly said, her face deadly white.

"Let's go."

Hugh held on to the protesting Edwin and broke a path through the crowd for Molly. He knew without looking back that Luther would not follow. Luther reported later the head had been auctioned off to the highest bidder. The Deadwood Board of Health paid the bounty on the grounds that killing Indians contributed to the health of the city. It was not the first time Hugh had heard there were those who would pay a bounty for an Indian scalp; yet if he had not seen such a thing with his own eyes, he would not have believed anyone could behave so savagely. Hugh knew that if he had been alone in the crowd, he would have spoken out. He wondered if the crowd would have turned against him. Hugh felt no sense of responsibility, guilt or even horror at Wild Bill's death. He believed that men like Hickok who lived by the gun could be expected to die by the gun. But that people could hold life so cheaply they behaved as did Deadwood over the Indian head made Hugh question what kind of men they had become. Once he had seen the Indian head, Hugh could no longer feel even a vestige of pride in being among the pioneers who had invaded Sioux lands in the guise of spreading civilization.

He tried to explain to Edwin that there was no excuse for men to be so barbaric, even in war, but he doubted that his words could counter what his son had seen, not just the face of the dead Indian, but the faces of the crowd—fascinated, excited, approving.

As for talking to his brother, Hugh knew it would be effort wasted. He had given up trying to set Luther straight about anything. He would wonder later if he should not have tried harder to be a brother to Luther.

He would think often about his brother's last trip to Deadwood and wish that he, Hugh, had done something — anything — different.

It happened on a Sunday afternoon. It was their day of rest, but the cabin was hot and flies buzzed incessantly. They were all irritable and discouraged. Hugh was sitting at their plank table trying to write in the journal while Luther and Caleb Dexter dozed in their bunks. Unable to find the words to express his feelings about the mood in Deadwood, Hugh drummed his fingers on the table nervously.

"Cut out that noise!" Luther suddenly barked. He sat up with a groan and put his head down in his hands. "I can't stand it anymore. Working in that mine all day all week and laying around here all day Sunday. I was having more fun back in Nebraska."

"Yep, it gets to you after a while," Dexter said.

"I know how you feel," Hugh said and closed his journal.

"It was your idea, Hugh! I wanted to be free, out somewhere prospecting or working for Hobart. Somewhere where I'd have a chance for action —"

"For shooting Indians, you mean."

"So? It needs to be done, doesn't it? I thought we came to the Black Hills to have an adventure, not to muck around in the ground like a bunch of moles. Look at my hands. I've got callouses on my callouses."

"You've got man's hands now, Luther. There's nothing wrong with the marks of honest labor."

"I didn't come to be a laborer. Look at my boots. Ruined! And I can't buy new ones. Every speck of gold we get out has to go back into the mine for supplies. When are we going to get anything out of it?"

"We got to hit the right vein," Caleb Dexter interjected. "One of these days—"

"One of these days! I've heard it all before. I'm sick of hearing about it. Poor man's gold and conglomerate gold and bonanzas on the bedrock. I'm sick of you acting like you know everything and I'm sick of Hugh bossing me around and I'm sick of this cabin."

"Well, I reckon it's time then," Dexter said, rolling off his bunk and picking up his boots.

"Time for what?" Luther asked.

"Time for you and me to make a trip to town. Ever' once in a while a man gets cabin fever and there's only one cure."

"What's that?" Hugh asked suspiciously.

"A little trip to the Badlands."

"Luther doesn't need any more drink. He's only sixteen, you know."

"And ain't sixteen almost a man?" Dexter grinned. "Ain't sixteen old enough to know what's what? 'Specially for a kid that's working twelve hours a day in the mines. That grows you up fast, but it makes you tense too and there are certain natural urges that got to be met."

"Hey!" Luther grinned wickedly.

"I hope you're not talking about taking that boy to a bawdyhouse!"

"I *hope* that's what you're talking about," Luther said.

"Well, it all depends," Dexter spoke casually as he drew on his boots. "I figure we'll start with a venison steak and a little drink at the new Gen'l Custer House, just to start the evening with a touch of class. Then we'll work our way down to the hurdy-gurdy houses, see the shows, maybe dance with the girls, maybe stop in and do a little gambling, then . . ." he shrugged, grinned mischievously.

"Then?" Luther urged from the top bunk.

"Then," Caleb Dexter tucked in the red-flannel underwear that served him as a shirt and straightened his suspenders. "Then, we'll just see how we feel. We might take a little walk down to Chinatown and look over the—"

"You're not going to take Luther to one of those whores!"

"Whores? Why, Hugh, I'm surprised at you using such a word. A refined gentleman like yourself! Now the Chinamen they got the right idea. They know how important the girls are to a mining camp and they treat them with respect. They call 'em Daughters of Joy and Celestial Females."

"How can you say they treat those women with respect? The girls in those Chinese cribs are practically prisoners. They're sold as children and brought over here for—"

"Now don't get so excited, Hugh. You may be right. Luther should start with a woman of his own race. No sense getting him off on the exotic stuff when he's at such an impressionable age. I myself started with a Chilean and after that I never could get enough of Spanish whores—dark flashing eyes and lots of spirit. Why if you'd ever known Lola Montez, wouldn't no other woman—"

"You knew Lola Montez?" Luther squirmed on his bunk.

"Why sure I knew Lola Montez," Caleb Dexter said, washing his hands at the basin and slicking back his ragged sideburns with his wet hands. "I was in Californy in '49 wasn't I?" He smiled philosophically, "I reckon I knew 'em all. All the famous sportin' gals of the mining camps, Big Bertha and Ragged Ass Annie, French Emma and Dutch Erma . . ."

"I can't wait," Luther clamoured down from his bunk. "I been thinkin' about it and hopin' you'd take me. I mean it's sort of hard to know what to do ain't it? The first time, I mean."

"Luther! Don't tell me you're really going to—"

"Quit being such a prig, Hugh, and come with us." Dexter said. "Don't you have an itch too? We been here over two months now, don't tell me you haven't been sneaking off to the Badlands yourself."

"Not Hugh," Luther wrinkled his nose. "He's too good for that!"

Hugh stood up, anger surging through him. "Listen, Dexter, I know you don't care about yourself. You're probably syphilitic already, but Luther here is just a kid and I don't want him going down there and getting some old diseased—"

"Don't need to worry about that, son. They got the means to prevent that—course it costs a bit more and ain't quite as much fun, but you're right, a boy like Luther shouldn't take any chances."

"What are you talking about?" Luther asked. "Taking chances on what?"

"Don't you see, Dexter? He's just a kid. You can't take him to a place like that!"

"He's got to grow up sometime." Dexter said, picking up his hat and starting toward the door. "But I don't want to interfere in family business. You two decide. I'll wait outside. If you're coming with me, kid, you better hurry up." He left the cabin, shutting the door behind him with a meaningful look at Luther.

Luther faced Hugh defiantly and started to push past him toward the door, but Hugh caught hold of his shirt collar and held him fast.

"Listen to me," he began angrily and then, seeing the look of frightened determination on his brother's face, he tried to speak more calmly. "Listen, son, I'm supposed to take care of you and I have to tell you this is wrong. I know it's tempting. I know how you feel, but it's wrong to —"

"Wrong?" Luther blinked. "You're a fine one to talk about *wrong*. The way you've been mooning around Mrs. Lewis! You think I'm too stupid to see you're hot for her?"

Instantly Hugh brought up his other hand and hit Luther full in the face.

Luther reeled back, jerking free from Hugh's grip.

"Luther, I'm sorry. I shouldn't have —"

"No, you shouldn't have." Luther said, sniffing back tears. "But don't think I'm going to forget it. You think I'm so dumb, but I'm a lot smarter than you think and I know there's something funny between you and Molly. Jake just mentioned the other day where they came from in Pennsylvania and it's a funny coincidence that we used to live there and —"

"Did you tell him?" Hugh almost shouted.

"You don't have to worry about that. I got that much sense."

"Luther, you've misunderstood. There's nothing between —"

"Then how come you didn't want Jake to know you used to know her?"

"I never said I knew—"

"I know that. I know you never said we lived there. That's what made me start to thinking. Why, if you did know Molly before, you wouldn't have said so right away. And why you always look at her so funny and why she's always blushing and working at her collar button when you're around."

Hugh reached toward his brother, his hand trembling a little. "Come back and sit down. We better talk this over."

"I'm sick of you and your talk. I'm sick of you acting so holy and so smart when you're no better than me. I'm going with Caleb Dexter to have some fun and you're not going to stop me!"

"Luther, damn it, listen to me," Hugh began, but Luther ignored him and stamped out the door. Hugh started to follow as Luther ran down the hill to where Caleb Dexter waited on the path to Deadwood, but he knew it was no use. He went back to the cabin and hit the table with his fist in impotent rage. He stormed about the tiny cabin, trying to dispel his anger. He considered going after them, but knew Luther might make a scene that could fire a rumor about Molly, a rumor that could reach Jake.

The cabin was too small to contain his anger, so he grabbed a pickax and climbed the hill to the mine shaft. Letting himself down by windlass in the iron bucket which raised the ore, he lit a torch and strode down the tunnel to the stope, the room hollowed out by mining. He fixed the torch in a metal spike and drove it into the wall of the stope with the blunt end of his ax, hefted the pickax and attacked the wall with a fury. He knew it was a strange place for a man who

317

hated the mine to be on his day of rest but tearing away at the rock helped to drive away the pictures that were coming unbidden to his mind to taunt him. Women in red silk with full breasts spilling out of transparent garments, rustling skirts raised above black hose and garters and white thighs. Women who could be had for the asking, for a price which did not involve right or wrong, love or the betrayal of a friend.

Chapter Twenty-two

Hugh stayed in the mine until long after dark, but when he returned to the cabin, Luther and Dexter were still gone. He did not wait up for them, but was surprised the next morning to see their beds had not been slept in. So they had done it. Spent the night in a bawdy house. It must have cost a fortune.

He was on his way to the mine, still feeling out of sorts, when he spied Luther and the old man trudging up the hill from Deadwood. They looked exhausted and downcast. Hugh decided they had every reason to look guilty, but who was he to condemn another man for his lust? He would meet them and be tolerant. They approached slowly, exchanging sheepish glances. Hugh was glad to see they were contrite. Perhaps Luther would settle down now. Maybe the experience had even been good for him.

"Well," he asked when they stood before him, "how was it? Did you get lucky?"

Luther didn't say anything. He kicked at the ground with the toe of his ragged boot. He looked as if he had been crying.

"What's the matter, Luther? Didn't it go like you

planned?"

Still Luther said nothing and Hugh began to feel uneasy. He turned to Dexter. "What happened?"

"Well, it's like this," the old prospector began sheepishly. "We had our dinner and a few drinks and was sitting around this hurdy-gurdy house trying to decide if we could get one of the girls to go upstairs with us or if we should just go across the street and take pot luck at one of the regular houses and then we notice there's some gambling going on and Luther never had done any gambling and—"

"And?" Hugh noticed Caleb Dexter was unusually reticent.

"So we started watching the gambling and amongst the pot on the table, they had these brass tokens from the Hidden Treasure."

"The Hidden Treasure's a mine isn't it? What brass tokens? You don't mean they were playing for a mine?"

Dexter and Luther exchanged anxious glances.

"There's a Hidden Treasure mine," Dexter said, "but there's also a Hidden Treasure that's a house. I don't suppose you'd know, being so pure and all, but when you go into a house, you start with a drink at the bar and you make your arrangements with the bartender or with the madam, if they have one, for whatever girl you want."

"I don't need to hear all this."

"I think you better." Dexter said, glancing again at Luther who was busy studying his boots. "Anyway, in a house you can't make your own financial arrangement with the girls, cause they might hold out on the house or you might not pay them beforehand like you're supposed to, so at most houses they sell you a token downstairs good for one . . . one trip upstairs and then when you go up, you—"

"Get to the point!"

"So me and Luther sees they've got some of these tokens on the table. Some guys like to buy a fist-full of tokens when they got the dust. It feels good to have a few jingling in your pockets so you won't have to do without in case you run short of funds. So anyway, along with the dust and the greenbacks in the pot there was a bunch of tokens for the Hidden Treasure and Luther suggests—"

"It wasn't my idea," Luther spoke up. "It was yours."

Hugh was beginning to get the picture. They had spent the night gambling. Well, he supposed not too much harm could have been done. They couldn't have had over ten dollars in dust between them.

"Well, maybe it was my idea," Dexter said. "It don't matter anyway, we decided to sit in on a game or two and see if we could win our tokens to the Hidden Treasure. Seemed like it would be a kind of kick for the kid to get his first that way. Taking a chance on it, you know."

"So get to the point. How much did you lose?"

Again Dexter and Luther exchanged glances.

"Twelve dollars in dust," Dexter said. "And my gold pocket watch."

There was another long silence. Hugh knew there was more coming.

"And the locket with ma's picture." Luther said quietly.

"Ma's locket! You lost our ma's locket!"

"And the mine." Dexter put it in quickly.

Hugh turned slowly from his brother's ashen face to confront the old man. "What?"

"I said we lost the mine."

"What do you mean? How could you lose the mine? You didn't gamble with our mine?"

"Just our shares." Dexter said.

"What?"

"Our shares. Mine and Luther's. We figured our luck was about to change and we put up our shares and then this slick gambler, well, he got 'em."

"The mine. You lost the mine at cards."

"Only our shares." Dexter said brightly. "You and Molly and Jake's shares are just the same. You'll have a new partner, that's all."

"New partner?"

"Austin Avery. That's his name. The gambler. He'll be your new partner in the mine."

"Oh my God."

"Now don't take on so. There's no real harm done. We'll get it back. And Mr. Avery seems real fair. He said since he can't work the mine himself cause of his other interests, he'd going to let Luther and I stay on to work for wages and—"

"You're going to stay on?"

"Just like old times. Since I'm the one with the mining know how, I'll be here advising and overseeing the development of the mine. And Luther here will be working on same as always only instead of having his share of the partnership, he'll be working for wages for Mr. Avery."

"A gambler. You lost our mine to a gambler."

"Austin Avery. You'll be meeting him tomorrow. But don't worry. Everything will go on like always."

"I'll work real hard," Luther said. "I'll work real hard like always and I'll give my wages to you, Hugh, and you can buy back my share."

"No!" Hugh bellowed.

Luther blinked. "I'll make it up to you."

"Get out!" Hugh shouted. "Both of you get out of here."

"I'm sorry," Luther blinked back tears. "I didn't mean to do it."

"I'm sick of you saying you're sorry. You've been nothing but trouble since I brought you along! I should have left you in school in Nebraska. You're nothing but a kid. You never do anything right!"

"Okay," Luther swallowed hard. "I'll get my gear and I'll go. Hobart said I could have a job with him anytime I wanted." He went into the cabin and began to gather up his things slowly, like he was expecting Hugh to stop him. Caleb Dexter had judiciously disappeared. Hugh couldn't stand watching his brother pack. He stormed out of the cabin and started for the mine, passing the startled-looking Jake on his way to work. He didn't explain what had happened, and Jake didn't ask. There was time enough for that later. Jake went underground for his shift, and Hugh took a stance by the tailings pile and began to shovel ore into a wheelbarrow to transport to the sluice box. He took out his anger on the ore.

After a while he began to calm down a little. Luther was still his brother, his responsibility. He wondered if he should go back to the cabin and tell Luther he didn't have to leave. Not that the kid would actually have the nerve to take off by himself.

But Luther knew too much. If he stayed, he was

likely to start blabbing off his mouth to Jake. It would be safer for Molly if Luther were to leave. And, he told himself, probably it would be healthier for Luther too if he was away from the temptation of Deadwood's Badlands.

Hugh was still shoveling ore and trying to make up his mind when he saw Molly walking up the hill toward the mine.

"Hugh?" she said when she reached the tailings pile, a worried look on her face. "What's happened between you and Luther?"

"Didn't he tell you?" Hugh said angrily. "Didn't he tell you he lost his share of the mine?"

"Is that what happened? He wouldn't talk to me. He just said you'd fought and he was leaving."

"He didn't go, did he?"

"That's what I came I tell you. He had his bedroll and everything and he's gone. Caleb Dexter too. I tried to talk to Luther, but he just brushed on past me."

Hugh put down his shovel, uncertain.

"You better go after him," Molly urged. "You can't let him go."

"It might be better. He suspects."

"Suspects?"

"About us."

"Oh." She was not surprised. How could anyone see the two of them together and not know?

"So you see, it's better if we let him go, unless—"

"Unless?"

"Unless you're ready to tell Jake." She looked agonized. As if she had not expected him to say it. As if the Fourth of July had not happened and he had not told her she must make a decision to leave Jake. But of

324

course, she had put it out of her mind. Just as he had let himself forget his threat to tell Jake himself. She was not good at facing up to things. He knew that about her and sometimes it made him angry, even as he loved her for her decency and her wish not to hurt Jake. They were alike in so many ways, but he had to keep trying to make her face the reality of what was between them.

"Will you tell him? Or let me do it?"

"No, I can't tell him." She said it emphatically, and he winced from the force of her words. Then looked down the hill, not wanting to see her, thinking he should throw down his shovel and follow Luther. Walk away from her. He was on the verge of doing it. Then, as if she sensed what he was thinking, she reached out and touched just the tips of her fingers to his shoulder and added a word.

"Yet."

He knew she was trapping him. Holding him to her with that one word of promise. He would insist on more.

"You'll do it then? You'll leave him?"

She would not, or could not answer, yet he sensed a change in her, as if she had begun to realize it was inevitable that they find a way to be together. "You know if we let Luther go, it's on your shoulders too? Sending him away will be your doing too."

She nodded and meant it when she said, "It will be better for him to be away from Deadwood. It's a terrible place. It's uncivilized. He'll grow up faster being away from here and away from you."

"I hope so."

"I'm sure of it. He said something about it. He said

325

to tell you something."

"What was that?"

"He said that he would make you proud of him yet."

They stood for a moment and looked at each other as if aware that their letting Luther go was adding another twist to the invisible cord that seemed to bind them.

She came to him that night. Just as he had dreamed it a hundred times. He was lying on the crude bunk in his cabin, staring up at the log rafters barely visible in the narrow shafts of moonlight admitted by the cabin's single small window and open door but familiar from the sleepless hours he had stared at them when he could think of nothing but Molly. The door was open to clear the cabin of the day's heat, and he was nude, a thin blanket at his feet for later when the night turned cold.

He was alone in the cabin and heavy with anger, guilt and confusion over Luther's leaving. The cabin seemed strangely empty without his brother's familiar snore. Caleb Dexter was gone too; whether escorting Luther to the Spearfish Valley or scheming with the gambler in town, Hugh neither knew nor cared. He knew the old man would be back. He would not let Hugh's running him off the place keep him from returning to entice them with more plots for easy riches. Luther was a different story. The boy was proud and stubborn, and Hugh knew he would not see his brother again until he went after him or sent him word to return to the mine.

And Hugh couldn't ask him back without it seeming like Hugh was the one in the wrong, when it was

Luther who had behaved like a fool and lost his share of everything they'd worked for that summer and even his share of their sad little inheritance. The thought of Luther's gambling away their mother's locket angered Hugh, even as remembering his promise to her to take care of his brother filled him with guilt. For he knew the real reason he had sent his brother away was not to punish him for his foolishness, nor to prevent his revealing his suspicions to Jake — for it would almost be a relief for Jake to know that which neither Hugh nor Molly had the courage to confess — no, the real reason was that he could not bear to face his brother with the truth about himself. Hugh had taken pride in playing the part of the big brother, older, wiser, stronger. He'd always told himself that he was simply setting a good example and that his own successes would make it easier for Luther to achieve; now he had to admit that sometimes his feelings bordered on righteousness. He loved his brother and he wanted his brother's love but, most of all, he needed his respect. How could he look Luther in the eye and admit his own wrong?

It seemed impossible that his loving Molly, an act which time and the night had made almost holy, should have the power to bring ruin on those he cared for most, but he believed it had; yet when he saw her there in the doorway, his resolution to be civilized and decent abandoned him. She wore only a nightgown with a shawl around her shoulders, and her hair was loose and haloed by the moonlight in the doorway. He had seen her like that once before. But she was Jake's wife. Jake was still his partner. And still a good man who had hurt no one and did not deserve to be cheated by those he loved.

She stood there silent a moment and he was aware of his nakedness.

"Are you awake, Hugh?" she asked softly.

"I'm not sure. I've dreamed of you like this a hundred times. Come and touch me to prove you're not a vision." His hand found the blanket, but he did not cover himself. She smiled, he thought, but did not move from the doorway. He was too bold, but after all, it was she who had come to him. "Step inside, Molly, and bar the door behind you."

She obeyed but still did not approach him. He covered his groin with the blanket. "Is something wrong? Where's Jake?"

"He's asleep. Passed out, really. He was very upset about Luther and Caleb Dexter leaving. He drank a great deal."

"He hasn't hurt you, has he? He didn't abuse you in some way?"

"No, of course not," she took a step toward the bed. "Jake has never raised a hand to me. Even if I told him, I wouldn't be afraid of that. No, it's just that I saw how soundly he was sleeping and knew that with Luther and the old man gone, you were alone and—"

"And you wanted me, Molly? You wanted to come to me?"

She was standing at the side of the bed now, looking down at him, and he saw she was trembling. "I thought we should talk. We were both so upset about Luther's running away and the gambler coming and—"

"And what happened between us on the fourth?

You're ready to talk about telling Jake now? About leaving him?"

"Oh, Hugh, be silent. I don't want to talk about any of that. I don't want to talk at all."

And then it was she who acted. She who let her shawl fall away and she who pulled aside the blanket and who knelt beside him and sought his mouth and body. He barely had time or will to find the protective sheath he had bought in Deadwood and explain its use to her. It was she who helped him to contain himself within it, and it was she who raised her gown and mounted him there on the narrow bunk. For a moment he wondered if she had gone mad or if it was he who had lost his senses and confused a dream with reality. But then knew that, whether a dream or a madwoman, she was exquisitely demanding above him, and her body beneath the thin gown which fell from her shoulders as if to conceal their ecstatic joining, was his alone. Then he thought of nothing else until they were released by sweet shuddering explosions of pleasure and could at last lie tenderly embraced and begin their reluctant return to reality.

"I had to come to you," she said at last. "I ached so."

"I know the aching. I've dreamed of you so a hundred times, but never like this. Never did I know it could be as powerful as this."

"Then I must ask you. Am I different from other women? Is there something unnatural about me, about the way I move and feel when we join? It's a trembling I can't stop and then a terrible explosion as if I'm going to die and then a wonderful feeling of peace."

"Sweet Molly, it's a natural thing. It's just your

329

release coming over you."

"But I never had that happen before. It's like what happens to a man. I didn't know that women had such pleasure."

"I don't know about other women, but I'm very glad it happens to you. That I make it happen to you."

"But you've known other women?"

"Molly, what questions you ask!"

"It's all right. I know I can't have been the only one for you, and I've had Jake, but I have so many questions now. So many wonderings I never had before. It's like I thought I knew what a mountain would look like before we reached the Black Hills, and then when I actually saw, why it was so much greater, so much more beautiful than anything I'd imagined. And now I feel all confused as if I've been a child too long and I'm finding the whole world is somehow different than I knew it to be. More terrible and more wonderful."

"And you. You're more terrible and more wonderful."

"Do you mind? Is it all right what I do? Is it all right that I have this aching and I came to you?"

"It's more than all right. It's wonderful. It's more wonderful and, yes, more terrible than anything I ever dreamed of. It joins us together and makes it impossible for there to be any destiny for either of us than to somehow be together. It makes you not just the first, but the last woman in my life. My only love, forever."

They talked of other things then, tried to sort and reason it out, to agree on what must be done about Jake. But all they agreed upon was to hope that somehow their fates would be resolved by the mine.

Jake was sure his luck had changed, and Molly prayed it was true and would do nothing to take away his chances of finding his fortune there. They had all been seduced and made believers by Caleb Dexter's tales of poor man's gold. Molly and Hugh were certain something wonderful was about to happen, and with Jake rewarded for his hard work and his faithfulness, they could use their own share of the riches to buy their freedom.

Later, Molly would not remember that she had promised that when the time was right, she would leave her husband. In the daylight as she saw Jake going about his work so faithfully or saw how Edwin followed after Jake and walked and talked like him, she could not face the reality of what she had said and done. She remembered only that Hugh had told her she was his first and last love. The only woman in the world for him. That seemed promise enough.

Chapter Twenty-three

Hugh was stunned by his first sight of Emerald O'Brien, so beautiful did he find her and so unexpected was the sight of a woman standing at the entrance to the mine when he winched himself up from the shaft. He came out of the mine feeling all knotted with worry over Luther's leaving and the confrontation he expected that day when he met the gambler who was now a partner in the mine. And there she stood and he found himself looking into the most unusual green eyes he'd ever seen. Eyes set in a face that would have been heart-shaped enough without the little curving bonnet that framed it so perfectly. She was a small woman. Smaller than Molly and much more fragile looking, though her body was full and round, revealed as it was by the bustle-back suit she wore. She was, quite simply, the most beautiful woman he had ever seen, and after his months of frustration and loneliness, the white skin, the black hair and the green eyes were enough to make him reel a little. He could not imagine what she was doing there, and he felt his mouth dropping open foolishly as he stared at her.

Then he heard Jake saying his name and realized there were others present. He turned and saw Austin Avery, the gambler. The slick, crooked bastard who had tricked Luther and the old man out of their shares of the mine. He looked just like one would expect a professional gambler to look, handsome, sly, shrewd, dressed in a pin-striped cutaway coat and a ridiculous ruffled shirt and wearing an ascot tie with a diamond stick pin. He made Hugh want to laugh, until with a deliberate gesture the gambler moved so his coat opened just enough for Hugh to see his gold watch and chain, and the pearl-handled pistol tucked in his sash. Hugh got control of himself. He was still full of anger, but he knew he'd have to extend a certain degree of politeness. Avery held the deed to two shares of the Lucky Six.

Caleb Dexter was standing with the gambler and the woman, and Hugh had just time enough to realize that the woman belonged to Austin Avery before the old man stepped forward and began making introductions cheerfully. It was obvious the old man was going to nuzzle up to the gambler for whatever it was worth to him.

"This here's your new partners, Mr. Avery. Jake Lewis and Hugh Everett."

"I don't believe you can consider me your partner, Mr. Avery," Hugh said quietly, noticing the gambler was regarding him cooly and had not extended his hand. "I think I can speak for Jake here too."

Jake gave an affirmative grunt.

Avery was nonplused. "I suggest, Mr. Everett, that we simply regard ourselves as temporary business associates. Believe me, I understand how disconcerting this change of affairs must be to you, but let me assure you, there may come a day when you will look back on this association as the beginning of a streak of good fortune. I do bring a certain expertise in mining affairs to this venture."

"I told you he talks real pretty, didn't I?" Caleb Dexter broke in as if the gambler had totally won him over. "He's a real gentleman."

"I hardly consider a man who makes his living gambling and taking advantage of boys and foolish old men—"

"Who you calling foolish?" Dexter bristled.

"No one forced your brother or Mr. Dexter to sit at my table. They might as easily have been the winners. I trust you are not seeking to impugn my honesty?"

"He means do you think he cheated," Dexter said with a meaningful glance to where the gambler's coat now hid his pistols. "But he didn't. We lost the mine fair and square."

"If there is any doubt in your mind about that, Mr. Everett," Avery said, "then let's call your brother out here and settle this question."

"My brother is gone," Hugh said. "He left yesterday for the Spearfish Valley."

"But I assured him he could stay on and work for wages."

"I didn't think it was your place to assure him of that," Hugh said, noticing that his remark seemed to cause the woman to glance at the gambler uneasily, as if she expected trouble. He wasn't afraid of Avery and he wanted the woman to know that. He certainly wasn't going to have this so-called partner questioning his judgment. "It was a family matter and it has been settled. Luther will no longer be associated with the mine."

"I see. Well then, Mr. Everett, Mr. Lewis," Avery said, removing his hat and holding it before him. "I have no wish to enter into any business venture where there cannot be good will between the members. I can see you harbor some natural feelings of resentment towards my association in this venture. Perhaps the best thing would be for me to buy out your shares of the partnership. Unless, of course, you would prefer to buy my share?"

Hugh and Jake exchanged uneasy looks. It made Hugh feel angry and impotent, but there was no way he and Jake could afford to buy two shares of the mine. He only had a few dollars in dust cached away in a tobacco can buried in his cabin. He was sure Jake couldn't have much more. As if to save them the embarrassment of being unable to make him an offer, Avery stepped smoothly into the awkward silence, "I would, however, prefer to buy your shares."

Hugh didn't speak, but he could see Jake was interested. Throughout the conversation the woman had been pouting prettily, as if annoyed that no one had paid attention to her. Hugh had never lost awareness of her standing there, but he'd kept his attention on his business. Now she broke in with a question.

"Aren't you even going to look at the mine first, Avery?"

Avery acknowledged the remark with only the lifting of one eyebrow, but it seemed clear he was annoyed at her interference. She seemed rather pleased to have annoyed him. There was the trace of a mischievous smile on her mouth. Avery obviously was being forced to acknowledge her in the midst of his business deal.

"Allow me to introduce Miss O'Brien." He said, taking off his broad planter's hat in a courtly gesture. "Miss Emerald O'Brien, meet Mr. Lewis and Mr. Everett. You met Mr. Dexter on the drive out, of course."

Emerald O'Brien. Such a name. It fit her. She smiled graciously to Jake and then offered her hand to Hugh. She was wearing tiny little gloves with the fingers cut out. Hugh had never seen anything like her. He took her hand and held it for longer than was necessary. He hated Austin Avery for having her, for she was quite obviously his mistress.

There was another awkward silence and, once again, Caleb Dexter tried to smooth things over. "Are you sure you don't want to inspect the mine, Mr. Avery? We could lower you in the bucket there."

Avery took a few steps forward and peered past the windlass with its chains and pullies into the darkness of the mine shaft. There was hardly room to stand near the shaft, littered as the area was with piles of rubble and mine tailings. The pump they had rigged spewed spurts of brackish water out its hose and down the hillside. A dank smell rose from the shaft. Hugh could not imagine a man like Avery going down there. Emerald seemed amused by the prospect.

"It won't be necessary," Avery said. "I see you have a water problem. You didn't mention that," he looked at Caleb Dexter pointedly.

"Well, it didn't come up, did it now? I mean it isn't exactly like you bought the mine, is it? Anyway, since you aren't planning on working the mine yourself, a little water ain't going to hurt you."

336

"It certainly isn't going to look good to a prospective buyer, though is it? He'd hardly miss a pump system like that would he? I've never seen one rigged quite that far," Avery's gaze followed the system of aspen poles rigged all the way to the creek and raised and lowered rhythmically by a flume of water flowing upon the water wheel in the stream.

"Well, you got to get your water power where it runs, don't you?" Dexter said. "I'm right proud of it. Designed it myself and had the blacksmith forge the axle-tree and trunnions and then I showed the boys how to rig it. Besides, don't worry about your buyer. Capitalists as would be buying up mines can afford the equipment to work 'em proper."

"You don't intend to work the mine?" Hugh asked.

"No, of course, not. I'd be holding it for speculative purposes." Avery smiled. "But why don't we sit down someplace and talk this over?"

He was entirely gracious. Hugh could hardly refuse to discuss the matter with him, although his impulse was to throw him off the property.

"We can step down to my cabin," Jake offered. "My wife will stir us up a cup of coffee."

Hugh had to nod agreement and Avery took Emerald's arm and followed Jake and Caleb Dexter to the Lewis cabin. Hugh watched Emerald walking away from him, noticing the way her bustle back swung as she walked, showing off her small waist, and the way her hair was fixed in fat little curls that jiggled beneath her bonnet.

He wondered what Molly was going to think of Emerald O'Brien. He was strangely reluctant for them to meet. Then, just as he was thinking about her she

337

turned slightly, her arm still crooked in Austin Avery's and gave him a knowing little smile.

He frowned at her. He would be damned if he would let some fancy piece of baggage take his mind off his business. She was probably in league with Austin Avery to cheat him further.

Besides, she wasn't half the woman Molly was.

Emerald had been as much affected by her first sight of Hugh Everett as he had been by his first glimpse of her, the difference being that Emerald knew the man affected her and was willing to admit it to herself.

Hugh Everett was tall and he was handsome. But so was Austin Avery. Hugh was handsome in a different way. Whereas Austin was elegant and refined, dark and smooth looking, Hugh Everett looked raw and unfinished, but somehow clean as if he belonged outside on a horse instead of down in a mine. His hair was bleached golden by the sun and it seemed to Emerald there was almost a halo-like glow about his head. His beard was magnificent and coarse and his skin tanned. His hands were terribly big and when he'd held hers, she'd felt ever so delicate. She had almost expected him to kiss her hand, for despite his shabby workclothes, he had something of a gentleman about him. She thought he was wonderful; she liked the fact he had the courage to stand up to Austin and when she glanced back over her shoulder to see if he was watching how she walked and saw him staring at her so intensely, she knew she had affected him and she liked that too.

An exciting man, Hugh Everett. Meeting him had made the boring trip to inspect Avery's first mining

338

interest worthwhile.

She was not impressed with Jake Lewis, nor the old man, and she found the cabin dreadful and depressing. She disliked at first sight Molly Lewis. Molly had been stirring something on the stove while her son watched and when they came in, she turned and wiped her hands on her apron and tidied her hair in a wifely gesture that spoke of respectability and annoyed Emerald greatly. She was pretty, Emerald thought. Almost beautiful in a way. The kind of woman who would turn men's heads if she ever got the time and money to get herself together.

Hugh began the introductions. He hesitated as he turned to Emerald, and she knew he must realize she was Avery's mistress and be wondering how to introduce her.

Avery stepped forward to fill the awkward little gap. "Mrs. Lewis, allow me to present my fiancée, Miss Emerald O'Brien."

Fiancée, Emerald thought, stunned. That was a new one! Avery had never before felt the need to sanctify their relationship. What made Mrs. Lewis so special? Why did a man assume a woman was decent just because she was dressed shabbily and had a child hanging onto her apron strings? And did he think making her his fiancée would make her any more respectable to a woman like Mrs. Lewis? For an instant Emerald wished she had stayed in the wagon, but when she noticed Mrs. Lewis' hesitation at speaking to her, she bristled. Why did everyone assume that she was bad, just because she looked so good? She did not intend to let his woman snub her.

"Pleased to make your acquaintance, Mrs. Lewis,"

Emerald said in her best stage voice, thrusting out her gloved hand, pleasantly aware that her elegant outfit and cunning little heart-shaped bonnet made Mrs. Lewis seem even shabbier.

Molly took Emerald's hand and smiled in a way that Emerald had to admit seemed gracious enough. It could have been that her earlier hesitation had been from shyness. She looked to be the kind of woman who blushed easily—her skin was all flushed and rosy now.

And then, almost in that same moment that Molly was shaking her hand, Emerald noticed something. Noticed that Molly turned from her and looked at Hugh and the expression on her face was almost like fear.

Emerald thought about it while they found places to sit and declined Mrs. Lewis's hesitant offer of coffee, it being obvious there weren't enough cups to go around. She had seen that look of fear in the eyes of other women. It meant that she, Emerald O'Brien, was the enemy. But why had Molly turned her look of concern to Hugh and not to her husband? Emerald studied Jake Lewis. He was a weather-beaten man. Decidedly middle-aged and somehow not a match for the blushing Mrs. Lewis. It might be that Molly feared her husband was a philanderer, but it seemed unlikely. He'd hardly noticed Emerald when they met at the mine, and now his full attention was on talking business with the others. Hugh, too, was ignoring her, and yet Emerald felt he was all too aware of her where she sat on the edge of the Lewises' double bed. She felt that Molly was threatened by her looks and by the fact that Hugh seemed so pointedly to be ignoring her. Molly was pretending to be giving all her attention to whatever was boiling on the stove, but she gave away her uneasiness with shy little glances that seemed always to travel between Emerald on the bed and Hugh Everett sitting across from Austin Avery at the table.

So, Emerald decided, *Jake Lewis's wife and Hugh Everett.* It was understandable; them being thrown together in such a place and Mr. Lewis being so much older than his pretty young wife and Hugh being so manly looking. *Were they lovers?* She studied them as they listened to Avery expound on his offer to buy the mine. Unlikely, she decided. There could not be a great deal of privacy about the place and Hugh seemed like too upright a young man to cuckold his partner. And then, noticing Molly's nervous habit of buttoning and unbuttoning her collar button, Emerald was almost certain they were not lovers.

Mrs. Lewis was a respectable woman. That was obvious from the neatness of the cramped little cabin, the worn but clean quilt on the bed, the flour-sack curtains at the window and the well-worn family Bible proudly displayed on a top shelf. There was an attraction between Hugh and his partner's wife, all right, but Molly Lewis had not given Hugh what he wanted. What a man needed. She was not a woman who knew how to please a man, nor how to please herself.

Emerald smiled. The situation seemed full of possibilities. She was making Mrs. Lewis uncomfortable and she was enjoying it. She liked knowing that she was sitting on the bridal quilt of a respectable woman. She liked knowing the woman was really no more respectable than she, Emerald O'Brien. She was just not as brave. Emerald knew how to get what she wanted.

341

And at that moment, she began to think that what she wanted was Hugh Everett. He was a beautiful man. Handsomer even than Austin Avery, at least handsomer in a way. Hugh was a decent respectable man, the kind of man who would feel it his obligation to marry a woman he'd seduced. That made him even more attractive to her. But with the thought of being married to Hugh came the realization that he was poor. Being married would certainly not be worth being poor. Still, it would be thrilling to make him want her. It would be satisfying to see if she could take him away from Molly Lewis, and making Austin Avery jealous always led to sparks between them.

She turned her full attention to Hugh, lowering her chin slightly and making her eyes look wide and luminous. She let her lips part and curve in a smile she hoped was both mysterious and promising.

But Hugh's attention was on Avery. "I don't care how much you offer," he said, slamming his fist on the table. "I'm not interested in selling out."

Jake Lewis looked at Hugh anxiously. "Are you sure? That's a generous offer. You know we can't afford to develop this mine like it needs."

"You take my advice, you sell out," Caleb Dexter put in. "Underground mining's a risky business. We already took too many chances."

Hugh seemed to be considering it. Then, to Emerald's annoyance he turned to Molly. "We've risked so much already. If we stop now, it's been for nothing."

Lewis also turned toward his wife and Emerald wondered if he suspected, but his face was guileless. "What do you think, Molly? It's your decision, too. You own a share. We'd have enough to get back to

Pennsylvania."

"But that's all you'd have," Hugh said. "If we stick it out, we still might make something of it. I hate to give up. I hate to give up if there's still any promise."

Emerald sensed it was like they were talking about something besides the mine and she was jealous of whatever it was the two of them shared.

Molly also seemed aware that something more than the mine was at issue. She seemed to be weighing what she was about to say. When she spoke, she measured her words carefully. She seemed sure, but almost frightened by what she said.

"I think there is promise. I'm not willing to give up now."

"You vote to stay then?" Hugh asked.

She nodded.

"And you, Jake?"

"I vote to stay. This mine's the first thing I ever had there was any hope to. I'll risk it."

"Then it's settled," Hugh faced the gambler. "We won't sell."

Avery was annoyed. Emerald knew that but she admired the way he did not betray his anger. She admired too the way Hugh stood his ground.

The old man, however, was not ready to give up.

"How about if Mr. Avery doubles his price?"

"Really, Mr. Dexter!" This time there was no mistaking the cutting edge to Avery's voice. "I've already made a generous offer. I'm sure it's more than the mine is worth in its present stage of development."

"But you said you could unload it on some eastern capitalist for a tidy profit," the old man declared; and

343

Emerald had to stiffle a giggle at seeing the way Caleb Dexter had revealed Avery's hand.

"You were planning on reselling the mine then?" Hugh asked.

Avery delayed answering a moment by taking out his silver cigar case and lighting a cheroot. "Of course. You can hardly expect me to grub about in a mine. It was my idea to have the Lucky Six developed a bit more and then, when the time came, sell it to someone with the capital to profitably operate a lode mine."

"You know people like that? Capitalists, I mean?" Jake Lewis asked.

"I wasn't aware of any outside money coming into Deadwood," Hugh said.

"There will be, Mr. Everett, you can be sure of that." Avery said. "You see I've had considerable experience in mining affairs and with things continuing as promising in Deadwood as they have these past months, it will be only a matter of weeks before there will be any number of entrepreneurs in here. Men with money for machinery. They'll be buying up whole sections of claims, forming large companies. That's what it takes for quartz mining. These placer operations will be all played out in a matter of months."

"I don't think I like that," Hugh said. "I don't see why easterners have to come in here and take over what we've been building up. I think we can manage it on our own. If there's gold to be mined in Deadwood, the men who came in here first ought to get it."

"Well then, Mr. Everett, I suggest you do just that. You continue to develop your mine and we'll just bide our time. I'll be by every week to go over the books with you, and I'll be keeping my eye out for a

344

prospective buyer. Then when the time comes, we can re-evaluate the situation. Does that seem fair to you?"

Hugh nodded slowly. "I guess that's the best we can do under the circumstances. We'll put your share aside. Jake and I will continue to work the mine."

"With Caleb Dexter's help, of course."

Hugh seemed to rear back. He looked at the old man with disgust. "No, I draw the line there. You've caused nothing but trouble, Dexter. I think it's time we parted company."

"How can you say that when I've been a true partner to you? I know I done wrong with Luther there, but he was your brother and you should have spent more time with him 'stead of leaving it up to me to educate the—"

"Now, listen here—" Hugh sounded angry.

"No, you hear me out. I'm apologizing for losing Luther and my share of the mine, but you wouldn't even have this mine if it wasn't for me. You got to admit that. And you wouldn't have known diddly about developing the mine. You'd have had all your prospect holes in the wrong places, and the mine would have caved in on you the first day if I hadn't been there to show you how to shore up the stopes."

"He's right," Avery said. "I'm afraid his mining expertise is essential to the operation. Although I know a great deal about the business side of mining, I cannot match Mr. Dexter's knowledge of mining methods. It would be absolutely foolhardy for you to attempt to continue working underground without him."

"He's got a point there," Jake said. "We already got a lot of water seeping in the mine; that little vein we been following is about to peter out and I ain't got the

345

faintest notion of where to open another stope."

"It's settled then," Hugh stood up so abruptly he nearly knocked the table over. "It seems like every damn thing is settled before I have a chance to do anything. So we're partners then, Mr. Avery, Dexter. Until we figure out a way to get out of it. Now, if you'll excuse me, I have to get back to work."

He had to walk past Emerald on the bed to get to the door. He stopped and stared at her for just a moment. There was something in his eyes that made her feel he might just pick her up and carry her out the door with him. There was something in her that made her wish he would do just that.

And then he was gone.

That evening as Emerald lay on the bed admiring herself in the red silk wrapper she had purchased in Deadwood's Chinatown and watching Avery dress for the evening, she found herself still thinking of Hugh Everett. She knew she should put him out of her mind. It would be very foolish to become involved with him, though it would be a pleasure to take him away from Molly Lewis. True, he was the kind of man who would marry a woman and she did want to be married, but she was hardly the type to be happy in a miserable little shack built next to a mine shaft.

Avery had been in a jubilant mood since the visit to the mine. Now, studying himself in the mirror, he said aloud. "Well, I've done it. I'm a mining entrepreneur at last!"

Emerald decided to ignore him. He was wearing his ruffled shirt and his white underdrawers and she was amused to note how knobby his knees were. Why, she wondered, had God made women's bodies so beautiful and men's so amusing?

"You don't seem very excited, my dear. I said I'm a mining entrepreneur at last. This is my chance to make a real fortune."

"All you care about is money." Emerald decided to annoy him.

"And I suppose you don't? You only care about spiritual values like truth and beauty and—"

"And love. Yes, that's right. That's the kind of thing I care about."

"And not money. That's strange. It seemed to me you care a great deal about the things money can buy. Like that kimono thing you just bought."

Emerald was tempted to take it off and throw it at him. It would be a grand gesture and it would surely lead to interesting things, but tonight her mind was on Hugh Everett, and a tumble with Avery did not hold its usual appeal. She wanted somehow to turn the talk to the subject of Hugh.

"I don't see why you're so excited about the Lucky Six. It doesn't look to me as if the mine can be worth much. Jake Lewis said their vein was about played out. And they certainly all looked poor enough, even Mr. Everett. What if they don't find another vein?"

"It hardly matters if you know how to play your cards right."

"What do you mean?"

"Just that if one knows what one is doing, if one is clever, and we both know someone who is, well then, one can get quite wealthy on a gold mine—even if it doesn't happen to have any gold."

"I don't get it."

"I don't expect you to, my dear. You shouldn't clutter your pretty little head with business schemes. It isn't womanly. Just trust me. When the capitalists start coming into this town burning to buy up mines, I'll have a mine to sell."

"But, Avery, you haven't even been down in that mine. How do you know anyone is going to buy it? Don't they have to see some gold or something?"

"Certainly, my dear. No one is going to buy a mine without seeing a favorable assay."

"So if there's no gold—"

"Then it's a little more difficult to get a favorable assay. But not impossible."

"Oh." Emerald smiled. So that was how it was. She lay on the bed and traced with one finger the embroidered design of the Chinese wrapper, enjoying the look and the feel of the red silk against the curve of her hip. She thought it over for a while and then she turned back to Avery.

"Tell me more about the mine. If you sell your share, what about the Lewises and Hugh? Won't they get rich too?"

"I suppose so," Avery shrugged. "They don't seem likely to sell out. I'll keep trying to get them to sell to me first, of course, but if they don't, I guess they'll just ride in on my coattails."

"I see." Emerald sat up on the bed and slowly and deliberately removed her hair pins and brushed her glossy black hair until the air was full of electricity. While she brushed, she thought. For once she hardly noticed when Avery left for the gaming tables. If Hugh was going to be rich, then it was a whole different matter, she decided. Of course, Avery would be rich

348

too, but there was no real security for her with Avery no matter how much money he might have. Avery would never make her respectable. But Hugh was different. Such a man could be persuaded into marriage. She could get out of Deadwood and go east on the arm of a respectable man as his wife. She played with the fantasy of walking into her mother's dress shop and introducing Hugh as her husband. Wouldn't that surprise the old lady and her sisters! Yes, she could be a real lady if she played her cards right and she could make Austin Avery sorry. It would be a pleasure to see Avery squirm.

And besides, she thought, her heart beating faster. Hugh was so handsome. There was something so strong and noble about him. He would say pretty things to her. He would appreciate her beauty and call her his beloved and he would carry her to bed in his strong arms. It would be wonderful between them. There would be nothing of the tawdryness she sometimes felt with Avery. He would love her forever and it would be glorious. She wished she could be with him that very moment.

There was just one problem. Emerald realized it a moment later as she stood before the mirror admiring herself.

The problem was Hugh Everett was a young man with ideals. That was obvious from the way he acted toward Avery and the fact he had not consummated his lust for his partner's wife.

Hugh Everett was a man with ideals and Emerald O'Brien was not a respectable woman.

There was no way around it. Hugh had to have realized she was Austin Avery's mistress and while that might make her desirable to him as a man, he certainly would never consider marrying such a woman.

She thought for a moment she would forget about marriage. It would be worth having Hugh Everett under any conditions, but then she remembered the dead woman at the saloon, the laudanum, the botched abortion, the attitude of the men toward the woman they had soiled. No, marriage was the only solution. There was no other way a woman could be safe. Her mother had been right about that much.

Somehow she had to convince Hugh Everett she was not a bad woman. She had to trick him into believing she had changed, had given up Austin Avery and was worthy of marriage.

It seemed an insolvable problem. But there had to be a way.

She sank down on her knees before the bed she shared with Austin Avery. Her mother had always told her prayer was the answer to everything. It might be worth giving it a try.

Seducing Hugh Everett was such a noble cause, surely God would show her the way.

Molly also prayed. She had known the moment she saw Emerald that Hugh would want her and her fears grew in the days that followed. How could any man not want a woman like Emerald O'Brien? Molly had never seen anyone so beautiful, so young and unworn by life, and yet so truly a woman. She had such a knowing look about her, something in those lovely, dark-lashed green eyes and in that smile that made Molly remember a picture she'd seen once of a famous painting called the Mona Lisa. The book said the

Mona Lisa's eyes seemed to follow you everywhere and her smile made men think she knew some secret. It was not just the secret of loving and pleasing a man or of knowing that woman, too, could find exquisite release in lovemaking: it was the secret of daring to do whatever you and your man wished. Emerald had defied society by openly living in sin with a man. If she could do such a thing, Molly reasoned, there must be nothing she was afraid to do, nothing that would make her deny either her love or herself. Emerald would not be afraid to leave one man for another. And Emerald wanted Hugh. She had wanted him the first moment she saw him. Molly knew that, and knew that her every pretty gesture, even her pretended friendship with Molly herself, were only ways to get to Hugh.

She told herself that Hugh was an honorable and civilized man; that he loved her and would not want another woman, even one as beautiful and desirable as Emerald. She told herself a person could not love two people at one time and heard a laughing voice within her that reminded her of her own indecision and taunted her with the dreadful certainty that Hugh, too, could be tempted.

And she prayed against temptation, thinking at first it was Hugh's temptation that must be guarded against. But if she received any answer to her prayer it was only the reminder that the real temptation was hers. And so at last it seemed to be clear that there was only one way she could ensure the safety of them both, and that was to honor her promise to leave Jake for Hugh. They could wait no longer. She would persuade Hugh to secretly sell their shares of the mine to the gambler so that they could get away for a start somewhere else. It would not be enough to get back to civilization with, but she thought they might join Luther and Hobart in the Spearfish Valley. Holding the valley against the Sioux could be no worse danger than they now faced.

She would tell Hugh in the morning as soon as she could find a moment with him alone, perhaps when he took his shift on the surface. Then they would face Jake together.

Tomorrow night when he came out of the mine.

Chapter Twenty-four

Jake walked through the mine tunnel carrying his pick and shovel over his shoulder, holding before him a smoking torch which trailed acrid smoke and cast eerie shadows on the tunnel walls. His footsteps echoed before him. The only other sound was the pump working ahead in the stope. The floor was wet beneath his feet and here and there water trickled down the tunnel walls. He smelled the underground — a damp stagnant smell, sharpened by the smoke from the torch and a lingering odor of blasting powder.

Reaching the stope, Jake threw down his tools and drove his torch into a crevice. The light was feeble but it was all a man needed for pick and shovel work. Jake checked to be sure he had candles and matches should his torch burn out. Satisfied, he exchanged his shovel for the pick and began to work at the face of the ore. Jake was happy. He was always happy these days, but when he took his turn working the stope, he was especially happy.

The work was divided into shifts. One man worked in the stope, breaking out with his pick the ore loosened by the previous day's blasting and shoveling it into a wheelbarrow. Another man worked the tunnel, wheelbarrowing the ore from the stope to the shaft where he would dump it into the huge "bucket" to be hauled to the surface by the man on top who also wheelbarrowed the ore to the sluice box on the creek.

Jake knew Hugh did not like the underground shifts. He'd never said so, but Jake knew, because Hugh only went to work whistling when he had the outside shift. Jake offered to work all the underground shifts, but Hugh said the work must be divided fairly, though they both knew Caleb Dexter used his expertise in mining to shirk the physical work of the operation. He guarded his knowledge, too, refusing to drill the precisely set blasting holes or measure powder into them unless he was alone.

They were terribly short handed. Austin Avery had offered to advance the wages if they'd hire some laborers, but Hugh stubbornly refused, either from his reluctance to be indebted to the gambler, or, Jake speculated, because replacing Luther would acknowledge the fact his brother was not coming back. Jake had urged Hugh to go after him, but Hugh was unwilling in a way that seemed to Jake to be uncharacteristically unforgiving.

At any rate, they were short handed, and with Caleb Dexter so lazy and Hugh just a bit spooky underground, Jake figured he was the best miner. He liked knowing there was something he did best, and he loved the mine. The temperature was always the same, so they could work no matter what the weather. Many an Iowa blizzard had kept Jake cooped up in the sod hut for days, forced to whittle and listen to Molly read from the Bible. And with farming there was always the unexpected. You'd want to plow, but it would be too wet. When the crops needed rain, it was dry. When you needed it dry so as to hay, it would rain. If you once got a good crop, out came the grasshoppers. With farming a man had to always keep one eye on the sky, wondering what God was going to send down on him next.

But in the mine it was always the same. A man had his day's work laid out for him. Today he had to break down this wall of ore and get it into a pile, and beyond that he didn't have to think. Hugh would haul the ore to the entrance; Dexter would hoist it out. Nothing to worry about. You were almost sure of washing out enough dust to feed your family and keep going. And it wasn't boring! With each pick of the ax, you strained forward to see that gleam that meant you had cut into that great golden vein that Caleb Dexter promised lead to the mother lode. Mining was exciting business. He supposed it was something like gambling. Made you understand a man like Austin Avery. Jake had always been unlucky with cards but with mining he knew he had only to keep plugging away and he had as good a chance as anyone of winning.

Jake was happier than he had been in his whole life. He could forget about failure and people like Lizzie Tuttle looking down their noses at him, saying how some folks just had better luck than others, for this time he was going to be lucky. He could feel it in his bones. He was glad he'd let Hugh talk him into staying on and going underground. Hugh had been a real friend, urging him to stick it out, making them partners. Jake valued the partnership and had told Hugh that more than once. He only wished Hugh could be as happy as he was. Hugh was a worrier; that was his problem. He was always thinking too far ahead, worrying about Luther working in the valley, worrying about the Sioux getting closer to town, trying to decide if they should sell out if Avery got an offer for the mine. There was no sense in it. A man couldn't change things by thinking. Custer was dead and all the weeping and wailing and talk of revenge wasn't going to bring him back. Well, he wasn't going to let anything get him down. He kept working, chipping away with his pick with the narrow sideways arch he had developed to adjust to the lowness of the ceiling of the stope only inches above his head. It was a graceful movement. He hardly ever broke the rhythm. Until he heard the sound.

He paused for a moment then. It had been a cracking sound, like something breaking. Jake cocked his head and listened. There was nothing but the steady wheezing suck of the pump and the sputter of the torch. The sound did not come again. If he had been a jumpy fellow like Hugh or Luther or some greenhorn, he would have let his work go and run back up the tunnel to ask Dexter what the noise was. But Jake wasn't that kind of a man. He wasn't going to let anything interfere with his work. He swung his ax into the air again. He was not going to worry.

Hugh had been midway through the tunnel on his way to the stope with an empty wheelbarrow when he heard the noise. He stood still for a moment listening. It had been a curious sound like something breaking somewhere underground. Hugh looked around the tunnel as far as the torch resting in his wheelbarrow would allow. It was not far. He could see only the nearest of the massive timbers which at intervals supported the roof of the mine. He tried to decide if he should go forward to the stope and warn Jake or turn back to the entrance and ask Dexter what the sound could have been. It was probably nothing and Dexter would laugh at him. It wouldn't be the first time. Jake and Dexter probably sensed he was afraid to be underground. He knew it was a groundless fear, that gold mines bored into solid ore. It was coal mines with their soft structure that slipped and sent black death down on miners. Gold mines were really not so dangerous. The whole gulch was now pockmarked with crude mine shafts and as the placer operations were cleaned out and as fall approached more and more men would be going underground. According to Dexter everyone would want to be in deep diggings when cold weather came. Gold mines were fine places. There was no reason to feel you were working in your own tomb. Still, Hugh was afraid. He didn't like that noise, whatever it had been.

He was still standing there, holding on to his wheelbarrow and trying to decide what to do when the roof fell in.

When Jake came to, he was lying belly down in the darkness—the complete and utter darkness of the underground. His torch was gone. It took him a while to think where he was and then to decide what must have happened. There had been a cave-in and he had been knocked unconscious. Now he was awake and lying on his face in the mine, and a terrible weight on his legs kept him there. He reached around behind him as best he could and discovered he was buried from the waist down in loose ore. That bothered him for a while and nearly brought him to panic, but when he brought his arms over his head, he found that as far as he could reach before and above him, he was clear. Part of the roof must have held, he reasoned. He tried shouting, but his yells seemed so soon lost he decided to save his energy. There was plenty of air to breathe even if it was full of dust. He hurt all over but not as bad as if his legs were smashed. He could wiggle his toes so it couldn't be too bad. His shirtfront was wet, but it was a cold kind of wetness, so Jake reasoned it was just water on the floor of the mine and not blood. He could hear the pump still working away somewhere in the stope and its steady sucking at the water reassured him.

A feeling of calm settled over him. He was all right. His luck had not changed. It was a set-back, but he was alive and it was just a matter of time until they dug him out. If he rested his head on his arm, he was fairly comfortable. He worried about Hugh back in the tunnel. There was no way of knowing how much of the mine had caved in. He hoped Hugh was safe. He should have taken warning when he heard the first crack. Hugh was more cautious, so maybe he'd gotten out in time. If he hadn't, Jake hoped he, too, was in an air pocket and not badly hurt.

The thing to do, Jake told himself, was to relax, take it easy and not get into a panic. He would just rest his head on his arms and lie there on his belly and try to keep his mind on other things. He would try to visualize what was going on at the surface. He figured he knew pretty much the steps they would take to rescue him, and if he thought each step out slowly, then he could figure when they were close to him and he should start to yell.

When the mine caved in, Jake reasoned, Dexter would have run for help. Maybe sent Molly and Edwin to do that while he started digging. It wouldn't take long for word to spread, and Jake knew within minutes a hundred men with shovels would be coming to the rescue. Caleb Dexter had told them often that one of the first rules of a mining camp was in case of a cave-in, everyone dropped everything and kept digging until everyone was out. Every miner knew he might someday be trapped underground; so in case of a cave-in, every man was a brother.

With all those men digging in shifts, they could move a lot of rock fast, Jake reasoned. He wondered if the shaft was still open. If the cave-in was only in the stope or the stope and the tunnel and the men could get down into the mine, it might be only a matter of minutes before he was rescued. If they had to re-open the shaft or dig a new one, it would take much longer. Jake tried to calculate how long it had taken the four partners to sink their shaft so he could divide that by a hundred men digging in shifts round the clock, but he found he could not remember even how many days they had worked on the shaft. He wasn't good with calculations at his best; now he suspected he was not thinking clearly. There was no sense worrying about it. He couldn't make them dig any faster. The dust had settled now and the air he breathed seemed good. He was pretty sure there would be enough to last even if it took a day or two to get him out. He'd have quite a story to tell Molly and Edwin. He hoped they were not too worried. He wished there was some way he could tell Molly he was safe. That he had left his curse of bad luck behind in Iowa and everything was going to be all right.

Then the pump stopped.

It had ben churning away steadily for minutes or hours; however long he had been trapped. But now, quite suddenly, it stopped. Jake held his breath and strained to listen, but there was no sound except that of his own heart pounding away in his chest.

Something had happened to the pump.

Jake felt cold sweat breaking out on his forehead. The pump had held all through the cave-in. That was one reason he had figured most of the mine was still intact. But something had happened. It was a long way from the mine to the water wheel on the creek which powered the pump. The connecting rod between the water wheel and the pump was a line of aspen poles nearly two hundred feet long, supported every dozen feet or so upon standards fastened on pivots to firm blocks on the ground. The standards moved backward and forward with the lifting and sinking of the pump. It was a simple system and worked well enough, but with two hundred feet of aspen poles a lot could and did go wrong. It was not unusual to go to work in the morning and discover some animal had knocked down one of the poles during the night and the water had risen to a depth of a foot or more within the mine.

Jake tried to calculate how long it would take the water to rise above his head. He reared up as high as he could and figured he had his nose at least a foot off the ground. But he could not stay that way for long. Fear was making him weak. He lay back on his arm and willed himself to be calm. Surely someone on the surface would notice the pump was broken. It would take only minutes to set it up again. He had nothing to worry about.

But even as he lay there, telling himself his luck was going to hold, he could feel the water rising.

Hugh had stood there clutching the handles of his wheelbarrow and watching in amazement as great chunks of the tunnel caved in around him with a roar, raining blows on his head and shoulders. It seemed to take a long time to happen; yet it was only an instant before the torch was snuffed out and he was left in absolute blackness and silence, still hanging on to his wheelbarrow. There was so much dust in the air, he felt himself strangling. He took deep, frantic breaths until the fact he could still breathe reassured him, and he began cautiously to grope through the darkness, not daring to move his feet as if a great pit might have opened up before him. He felt in the wheelbarrow for his torch, but his fingers met only rock. He dared a step or two and found debris packed all around him as if he were in a giant pocket in the earth. Fighting panic, he leaned on the wheelbarrow to root himself and reached into his pockets with trembling fingers until he located a candle and the matches he kept in a waterproof container. He held a candle and the match safe in one hand and with the other carefully removed a match from the block and struck it against the rough side of the match safe, concentrating on getting the candle lit despite the trembling of his hand. The wick caught sputteringly just as the match burned his fingers. He held his breath until the flame grew and then he dared to raise the candle and look around.

He saw he had been standing directly under one of the heavy support timbers; it had saved his life. He reached up and touched the great pine log. He wondered what would have happened if he had heeded that first warning crack, if he'd have gotten out in time or been caught in that pile of rubble in the tunnel behind him. What if he had gone forward to warn Jake? Had the roof of the stope held? Was Jake dead or was he, like Hugh, buried alive? Hugh stood there, holding the candle in both hands, trembling so the hot wax dripped on his hands. He tried to will himself to be calm, to be strong. Caleb Dexter had told them repeatedly every miner in camp came running if there was a cave-in. With enough men digging, it wasn't impossible they would get him out. Miners never assumed a man was dead, Dexter said. Many men had been brought out of mines alive even after days, so they would not give up until everyone was out. It was just a matter of time, Hugh told himself. The thing to do was not to panic. Not to go crazy at the idea of being buried alive. If only he could do something to help. He noticed the handle of his shovel half-buried in the wheelbarrow. Carefully balancing the candle in a pile of soft dirt, Hugh dug the shovel out with his hands. It felt good to hold it. It gave him a chance. Holding up the candle again, he studied his situation more closely. Although there was debris all around him, it was by no means solid. He could move quite a lot of the loose ore himself, and here and there in the tunnel, there must be other pockets of air where the timbers had held.

Propping the candle between two rocks, he prepared to dig. Then he realized he might have lost his orientation and be digging in the wrong direction. He studied the situation. The wheelbarrow had been in front of him when the roof fell in. Therefore if he dug behind the wheelbarrow, he would be going back through the tunnel toward the shaft and freedom. Possibly the cave-in didn't go all the way. He might meet the rescuers in an hour or two. The shaft might be clear. He tried to think how far into the tunnel he was. Not so far; he could surely get himself out before he used up his air.

And then he thought of Jake. Jake was back there in the stope. It might take the rescuers hours to reach Hugh and then more hours to get to Jake. Maybe too long. If he dug in the other direction, he might be able to find Jake in time.

But Jake could be dead already. It was possible, likely even. But there were strong support timbers in the stope. A hard section of ore formed the roof. It might have held. Jake could be in there with only enough air to last a few hours.

Hugh slumped back against the prison of rock and groaned. So this is what God had sent down upon him! He had coveted Jake's wife, maybe even wished Jake conveniently dead and now God had given him a choice. He could get himself out or turn back and try to save the husband of the woman he loved.

He turned around and began digging toward Jake. He was crying in rage and frustration and fear, but it didn't matter, no one would see. The candle flickered in the narrow passageway, and Hugh realized it was burning up precious oxygen. He would have to snuff it out and work in the dark. He could light a match from time to time to be sure he was moving in the right direction. He almost panicked when he found himself in darkness again. It was so completely black. He made himself go on digging.

He succeeded in making a shallow passageway back toward the stope. A passageway so small he had to lie on his side and use his shovel like a pick to hack the dirt before him and pull it back over his shoulder. There was, of course, no way to shore up his tunnel as he worked, and he realized much of it was falling in behind him as he went. But it didn't seem to matter. He was getting closer to Jake.

Instinct eventually told him something had gone wrong, but he ignored it and kept working. Then finally, lying there on his side in the place he had hollowed out, a place no bigger than a coffin, he realized he was lying in water.

He had forgotten the pump. It was broken and now the mine was filling with water.

For a moment he was too shocked to move. Finally he got his father's pocket watch and checked the time by the light of a match, trying to calculate how much longer he had to live. As he put the watch away, he pictured someone giving it to Luther. Poor Luther; he wished he had done better by him. He hoped he would grow up soon.

So he was going to die. His heart beat faster at the thought and he tried to picture what it would be like. He supposed he should somehow ready himself to meet his maker, but he kept thinking of Molly and Edwin, wondering who would take care of them if neither he nor Jake got out alive. Then he knew he could not just lie there and wait for death. He had to keep trying. There was no longer room to use the shovel. He began digging at the rocks before him with his bare hands.

Chapter Twenty-five

Emerald was weeping in great choking sobs and Avery didn't understand it. He had expected her to cry prettily at the funeral. In fact, he had suspected her insistence on attending the burying had something to do with the fact that she had a new handkerchief of Brussels lace and she fancied the picture she would make dressed in her favorite green velvet traveling costume and drawing attention to her eyes by dabbing at them with the new handkerchief. But instead she had thoroughly soaked the delicate lace handkerchief before the service was half over, and he had been forced to give her his. She had actually blown her nose into it, hardly a pretty gesture. The hot August wind had kicked up dust on the hillside graveyard and soiled her dress and rumpled her hair. The black stuff she used to accentuate her eyes had run down her cheeks and she looked thoroughly disheveled. She was sniffing like a child. It was hardly the performance he had expected of Emerald, and because he couldn't account for her behavior, Austin Avery was annoyed. He liked women to be predictable.

He had gone along with her when she insisted on

coming to the funeral. After all it was proper for a man to attend the burying of a partner. It would build good will and make it easier for him to buy the other partners out when the time was right. He had admired the way Emerald had fluttered into the arms of Mrs. Lewis, hugging and kissing her as if they were true friends. And he had to admire the way she stopped to plant a kiss on the little boy's forehead so gracefully only Avery was aware of the care she took to keep her skirt out of the earth turned up around the open grave. She had managed to come out of the kiss with her hands clasped to her breast and her face tilted toward the child in a perfect picture of tragedy, and yet somehow raise her eyes to meet those of Preacher Smith at exactly the right moment to give him the full effect of her beauty. Yes, Avery had to admire a woman who could look like an angel at the very moment she was enticing a minister of the gospel to let out an involuntary gasp of desire.

But this sniffing and sobbing and hiccuping! This was not in character. He was about to tell her she was overdoing it, when she took his arm and teetered as if she were going to faint. Despite the fact the minister was still sermonizing, the crowd behind them surged forward as if each man wanted to be the one to catch her. Avery put his arm around her protectively and let her lean on him. The feel and scent of her excited him as did the knowledge he alone possessed her. In some ways, he had to admit, it was her unpredictability that made her desirable.

Emerald felt terrible. She looked at Avery's fine cambric handkerchief, all wet and smudged with tears and powders, and she knew her face must be a sight, but she didn't care. All her schemes and plots had come to this bitter end.

It had been going so well. She had accompanied Avery on his visits to inspect the mine and take his share of the profits. Although she had carefully avoided flirting with Hugh, she had made friendly conversation with Molly and Edwin and established a friendship, if not with Molly, at least with her son. She had taken to bringing Edwin small gifts, things Molly could hardly make him refuse without appearing harsh. True, she had not figured out any way to see Hugh away from the watchful eyes of Molly and Avery, but she knew it was just a matter of time before she could contrive some excuse to get Hugh to visit her hotel room while Avery was out gambling. She had hesitated, however, hoping to come up with a more convincing way to make Hugh think she was respectable than simply throwing herself on his mercy, telling him Avery had tricked her into eloping, promising her the ship's captain would marry them, then taken her against her will. She would say she could not leave him now because she could not support herself, and no decent man would have her. She was pretty sure that would work, especially when she nestled in Hugh's comforting arms, nature took its course, and further sobs inspired Hugh to do the gentlemanly thing and marry her. But she had learned from Avery to hedge her bets and she'd had to delay action until Avery went through with whatever devious scheme he had in mind to sell the mine and make Hugh, as well as himself, rich. She certainly didn't want to be married to Hugh badly enough to risk being poor, nor did she wish to give up the attentions of Austin Avery any sooner than was necessary.

Thinking about how close she had been to marrying Hugh sent Emerald into a fresh paroxism of weeping, just as with ropes the coffin was lowered awkwardly into the grave. When it hit bottom with a thump, Molly Lewis stifled a scream. The minister reached the part of the ceremony where the widow of the dead man was to cast the first earth upon his coffin. As Emerald watched Molly release a fistful of soil upon the grave, Emerald dug her fingernails into Avery's sleeve. She was annoyed to see how convincingly Molly winced in shock at the sound of the earth hitting the coffin. But Molly didn't fool Emerald for a moment. As far as Emerald was concerned, Molly had lucked out. Her husband was conveniently in his grave and Hugh was alive. Molly, like Emerald, must have had some bad moments when the mine caved in, especially when the word came that only one of the men was alive. But no matter how sad Molly looked now, no matter how genuine her sobs seemed, Emerald wasn't fooled. Emerald remembered the looks Molly and Hugh had exchanged in the cabin, the something that always seemed to run between them, and she knew they were lovers in spirit if not in body. And now with Jake Lewis dead, it would be only a matter of time before the inevitable happened and they were wed.

And it was so unfair! Just when Emerald had realized her true destiny was to be married to a respectable man like Hugh. Just when she had found a man who was sufficiently handsome and brave and noble to make her forget Austin Avery and his ways, and just when that man was about to become rich, the whole scheme had to come crashing down in a stupid mining accident. Besides, it was unfair that Molly should get another husband so soon, when Emerald hadn't even had one. She could hardly stand to think of losing him before they'd even shared one kiss. She glanced quickly at Hugh from behind her handkerchief. She had not dared look at him since she had ruined her eyes with weeping, now she saw any efforts to attract his attention would be wasted. He looked terrible, and not just from the cuts and bruises he had suffered in the accident, but genuinely anguished, as if he had lost his best friend. Perhaps he really had been trying to dig Jake out as the story went. Hugh's hands were bandaged, so he must have been digging with them, but surely had hadn't been digging *back* toward his partner instead of trying to get himself out. Emerald was sure the story was a rumor. Avery said miners liked a good story as well as anyone and the idea of a man going after his partner instead of saving himself was the heroic thing miners liked to believe happened.

But Emerald was sure Hugh had been thinking only of saving himself. Unless he felt so guilty about wanting his partner's wife. Guilt could do funny things to you. Like sometimes she would realize that her mother would call what she was doing sin, and she would feel strange inside. Sometimes she almost liked the feeling. It made her episodes on the bed with Avery more delicious, made her twist and moan and call out his name.

But in the clear light of day in a cemetery where a person couldn't help but think about death and going to Hell, knowing she was living in sin made Emerald uneasy.

Avery was never going to marry her. He had made that clear, and as long as she lived with Avery, he would have power over her, for even when it was she that enticed him, it was as if he owned her and her passion. With Hugh, she sensed love would have been different, beautiful, like in a love poem.

If only Hugh had gotten Jake out of the mine alive! Then she would have had time to make Hugh forget whatever it was he saw in Molly. But now the two of them surely would be getting married as soon as they could decently arrange it. She studied them, trying to see the situation clearly. They looked terrible. No doubt they felt both grief and guilt. It occurred to her they might not get married right away. Molly was a respectable woman and, even in a place like Deadwood, she wouldn't want people to talk about her. They couldn't leave town until they sold their shares of the mine, and perhaps Emerald could somehow get Avery to delay that, although he was already talking about buying out the widow. Perhaps if she was very clever Emerald still had a chance.

The service ended at last and the crowd began to disperse from the graveyard. Emerald wanted to give Molly another sisterly hug of condolence to show Hugh what a loving, ladylike sort of person she was. But Avery was tugging at her arm, anxious to leave and Emerald didn't want to annoy Avery just then. She intended to hang onto him as long as possible.

She watched Molly and Edwin, uncertain of what to do, and then she saw Hugh step forward and pick up Edwin and hold him close in his bandaged hands even though it must have cost him considerable pain.

She could not see the look Molly and Hugh ex-

371

changed, but she could imagine it. And she knew that Molly had one important advantage. She was respectable. In her washed out gingham and coarse linsey-woolsy she wasn't half as beautiful as Emerald but Hugh's mother had probably worn homespun; and some instinct told Emerald that when it came to taking a wife, men looked for their mothers.

Emerald sighed and let Avery lead her down the hill from the cemetery. She wasn't defeated, but she knew if she was going to get Hugh away from Molly Lewis, she would have to be very clever indeed.

Chapter Twenty-six

Fourteen miles by wagon road northwest of Deadwood lay the broad, fertile, and lovely grassland known as the Spearfish Valley. Surrounded on every side by mountains, it was a land perfect for men who found the rugged interior of the Black Hills confining and were more comfortable where a man could run his horse and swing a lariat or a war lance. White men tried in that summer of 1876 to establish farms and ranches on the fertile grasslands. The price they paid for their homesteads was constant warfare with the Sioux, who sought revenge for the violation of their sacred lands, not against the miners who crowded into the narrow gulches of the interior, but the ranchers of the valley, seeking as their war booty the cattle and horses sheltered in the valley and the scalps of the men who defended them.

On a hot August day Luther Everett tied his horse to a bit of brush halfway up the steep slope of the mountain the ranchers called Lookout Mountain. He climbed on foot to a spot on the rocky face of the slope where he could be out of the sun and still stand guard over the haying operation in the valley.

Luther was unaware of the disaster in the Lucky Six and Jake's death, but he felt confident he had made the right decision in joining Emmet Hobart's ranching operation. Ranching was the life for a man, he thought, not grubbing away underground, never seeing the light of day, chasing some great bonanza which didn't even exist. It wasn't just sour grapes because his brother was mad at him, Luther told himself. He would choose to stay on with Hobart even if Hugh begged him to return to Deadwood.

Not only was ranching healthier work than mining, it was easier, too.

Of course, cutting hay with a hand scythe was no picnic. His shirt seemed always soaked through with sweat, but with the need to post guards over the valley, even in haying season a man was bound to get in a few hours a day on a horse. So it turned out that ranching was mostly riding around on horseback keeping an eye on the livestock and watching out for Indians. Luther liked that. It gave him plenty of time to dream. At first he'd seen an Indian behind every rock or bush and, although it made him jumpy, it was a nice change after the boredom of the mine. Now his imagination had stopped plaguing him and he was beginning to think he'd never have a chance to get an Indian.

He didn't understand his rotten luck. All anyone in the valley ever did was complain about the Indians. How the Sioux had run off half the parties that had been trying since early May to settle the valley and how the settlers would have to build a regular stockade if the new townsite of Spearfish was going to survive. But despite the fact Indian raids, or at least rumors of Indian raids, had been almost daily occurrences since the Custer massacre, Luther always seemed to miss the action.

Still, ranching was a great business, he decided as he sat crosslegged on the mountain, his needle gun balanced across his lap, a sprig of grass held between his teeth, cowboy fashion, and his eyes on the men working in the valley. From where he sat, he couldn't see Hobart's cabin, but he had a good view of the livestock grazing just south of where the men were haying.

Luther was looking forward to fall when Hobart would cull stock from the herd he had been building that summer, and they would drive those not worth wintering into Deadwood for butchering. Then Hobart would give him his pay and he'd buy himself a real outfit—one that even Hugh would envy. He'd have a broad-brimmed Stetson hat and boots with high heels for riding and maybe he'd even get his own saddle. Cowboys always had their own saddles, and he reckoned that was what he was going to be. A cowboy and an Indian fighter, if he ever got the chance. He'd borrow one of Hobart's best horses for the trip, and he'd ride up to the Lucky Six at a gallop. Would Hugh be surprised to see him! He'd grown, he was pretty sure, and besides if he stayed on the horse, he'd be 'way taller than Hugh anyway. He'd sit up there on that horse, holding him in and spurring at the same time, so he'd prance a little. He'd be riding as well as Hobart by then. He'd just be sitting there like he was glued in the saddle and wearing his new boots and a hat. Maybe he'd have enough money to buy a revolver, too. That would be the thing, a six-shooter stuck in his belt; he'd let Edwin shoot it. That would get to Hugh.

He bet Hugh never would have a revolver, even if he did get rich off his old gold mine, which Luther was pretty sure he wouldn't.

Yes, it would be really fine when he rode into Deadwood side by side with Hobart. He'd learned a lot from Hobart about riding and handling horses and livestock; by fall he reckoned he'd know all there was to know about ranching. Emmet Hobart was a real man and ranching was a real business. He should have listened to Hobart and gone over to the valley with him in the first place. He could have saved all that trouble with Hugh over the stupid mistake he'd made in gambling with Austin Avery. But it would be different in the fall. After he saw Hugh, he'd ride on up to the Hidden Treasure and he'd take care of his business there like a man. He wouldn't fool around taking chances on winning his tokens in a card game this time. No sir, he'd pay and he'd get his business over with quickly. Then there'd never be any more question about him being a man.

Luther had been concentrating so hard on watching the men cut hay, he didn't notice the rider at first. It was the cattle moving away from the rider in the tall grass that made him notice someone was coming. For a minute he thought it might be Hugh, and he almost jumped up in his excitement. But then he could tell by the way the man sat in the saddle, it was Emmet Hobart coming to relieve him.

Luther squinted at the sky and tried to judge how long he had been on guard duty. It didn't seem like long, but he supposed an older man like Hobart couldn't stand the haying for too long. Well, he was glad to pull a little extra weight if it would help

Hobart. Hobart had been like a father to him, or maybe even a brother.

Luther was watching Hobart leaving the valley floor for the gentle slope leading up the side of the mountain when a little movement in the periphery of Luther's vision caught his attention. He turned and squinted, then felt his eyes grow wide and his jaw slacken.

Off to the left, moving through a ravine that skirted the edge of the valley was a group of horsemen.

For a moment, Luther couldn't move or think.

He had acted the fool so many times, thinking he was seeing Indians when it had been only a dog moving through tall grass or a cow and her calf wandered away from the herd.

But this was it. A war party.

He couldn't think what to do for a minute. His head was spinning. Hobart was riding slowly up the side of Lookout Mountain toward him, unaware of the Indians approaching through the ravine. It wouldn't be long before they would meet. Hobart had to be warned. The haying crew in the valley had to be warned.

Luther stood up and began waving frantically.

Hobart rode on up the hill. It seemed a long time before he looked up at Luther, and then he merely answered his frantic signals with a cheerful wave.

Get mounted! Luther thought, looking down the hill to where his horse was grazing peacefully. He'd have to ride down and warn Hobart; then together they would meet the Sioux in combat.

He started down the steep hillside, sending the loose gravel clattering down before him and almost falling in his haste. He gripped his needle gun awkwardly in his

377

left hand, using his right to keep his balance.

Hobart reined in suddenly, wondering what had gotten into Luther.

Luther had reached the leveler place where his horse was grazing. He saw Hobart had stopped. Then Luther remembered his rifle. That was it. That was how you were supposed to warn the others. A gunshot would do it. He cocked the hammer, pointed his rifle at the sky and pulled the trigger. The shot boomed out, and the horse let out a startled snort and jumped sideways, tearing the branch she was tethered to from the bush.

Oh my God, Luther thought. *Don't let her get away.* Without stopping to see if Hobart and the others had reacted to his warning, he grabbed for the horse. She rolled wild eyes at him and pulled away frantically, but the branch dragging from the reins caught in something, and Luther was able to grab the cheekstrap of her bridle. He flung the reins still dangling the branch over her head and tried to mount. The horse tried to dance away from him, but he hung on to her, and since she was downhill from him, he managed to scramble into the saddle. He turned the horse and started her down the hill, almost going over her head in the momentum of the downhill run. He leaned back in the saddle as Hobart had showed him, keeping his legs stiff before him and letting the horse have her head until she was on more level ground.

When he got a chance to look up, Hobart had finally seen the Indians. They had kicked their ponies into a run and were charging him, yelling and brandishing their rifles. Hobart wheeled his horse and started to make a run for the valley, but a shot rang out and he fell from the saddle.

They got Hobart. But then Hobart was on his feet clutching his side with one hand and pulling a pistol out of his belt with the other. He looked around as if dazed and made a start for his horse, but she was galloping back to the valley with his rifle still in its scabbard. Hobart spotted an outcropping of rock and ran to it.

We'll have to make a stand, Luther thought. I've got to get to Hobart and make a stand.

Suddenly the Sioux wheeled their ponies and re-grouped, shouting and waving their lances and rifles at Hobart and at him. It was like they wanted to run against them all at once so each would have an equal chance.

It gave Luther time to get to the shelter of the rocks.

"Don't worry," he shouted as he flung himself off his horse and reached Hobart's side. "We'll make a stand of it."

Hobart was slumped against a rock. He looked like he couldn't decide if he should fall down or try to stand up and do some good against the Sioux with his pistol. Blood was seeping between his fingers where he held his other hand against his side.

"Glad you're here, kid," he said. Then, clenched his teeth as if it had hurt him to talk.

Luther made as if to touch the sticky wound.

Hobart shook his head. "Leave it alone. Nothing vital. Just hurts like hell." He strained to raise the pistol while slumping himself over a boulder so it could both prop him up and give him shelter. "See if they're coming."

They were. Eight, maybe ten warriors. There was

379

no time to count. They were riding at Luther, whooping and hollering. There wasn't even time to be afraid.

"Just sight in on one," Hobart gasped, leaning over the rock and using both hands to aim his pistol.

Luther tried to keep one of the braves in his gun sight, but they were coming too fast, bigger and bigger.

The sight started to waver wildly before him. His eyes were watering so he could hardly see.

"Wait till they're closer," Hobart commanded, but Luther had to do something.

He cocked the hammer and pulled the trigger. To his amazement nothing happened. The needle gun was a single shot and he had forgotten to reload. Cursing, he fumbled in his cartridge belt for a fresh cartridge. He nearly dropped the cartridge as he slammed the rifle's hammer to full cock and crammed the breech-lock open. The empty shell ejected just as he heard Hobart take a shot. It seemed like an hour before he had the cartridge seated and the rifle locked again. The Indians were almost upon them when he raised the rifle and without taking time to sight, pulled the trigger.

At the same time a burst of fire came from the Indians, and he saw a red hole open in the belly of one of the warriors as he fell from his pony. There were more shots, but the boulders protected them as chips of rock whanged all around them.

The Sioux were upon them, almost up to the boulders and then they seemed to wheel their horses as one and veer off sharply to Luther's right.

"What the hell?" Luther said, blinking.

Hobart slumped back weakly against the rock, allowing himself to drop to his knees. The shot had cost him. "They're going for the livestock," he said. "They're out to steal horses as much as kill whites. We already warned the herders, so they're going to have to make a fast drive down the valley if they're going to get any stock out of this raid." Hobart sat down and, pulling a handkerchief out of his back pocket, pressed it into his wound. "I think I'll be okay if I sit quiet until help comes."

Luther wasn't listening. He was looking at the Indian he'd shot. The body lay still.

"I got one," he said wonderingly. "I killed me a Sioux."

"Plug him again to make sure," Hobart said. "They'll play possum."

Luther considered it. It didn't seem sportsmanlike, but maybe Hobart was right. Better to make sure. He'd played the fool enough. He reloaded and aimed the needle gun and pulled the trigger. The body of the Indian ripped open again.

"I'm going to scalp him," Luther said.

"What?"

"Sure, what the hell? I'm going to scalp him and wear it on my belt. That'll show Hugh."

Luther started out of the shelter of the rocks, reaching for his knife.

"Be careful!" Hobart yelled. "They'll be coming back for the body."

But Luther already had his knife out and was heading for the body. He'd have to be quick, but it was worth it. He wasn't quite sure how to go about it, but he wasn't going to lose his nerve. It was his trophy and he deserved it. He had held off a Sioux attack! What a story it would make!

He heard the shot at the same time he felt something bite into his shoulder. It knocked him to the ground. He came up on his knees with his needle gun still in his hands. He looked around incredulously, thinking for a moment that Hobart had tried to stop him.

Then he saw the other Indian.

The Indians had posted a lookout too! On the mountain not a hundred yards from where he had been standing guard. He'd been shot in the back by a damn redskin and now the sneaky bastard was getting ready to plug him again.

Frantically, Luther raised his own gun, knowing it was too late.

The damn Indians weren't playing fair!

Chapter Twenty-seven

In her cabin below the shaft of the Lucky Six Mine, Molly sat in her rocking chair, rocking endlessly, her arms folded tightly across her belly, as if to hold in the pain. She had spent most of the three days since Jake's funeral just sitting there rocking, feeling numb and incapable of doing anything more. She vaguely realized her reaction was not healthy, but she felt no desire to do anything more than stare at the wall, rocking and grieving, tormenting herself with both her loss and her guilt. She seemed to have no other purpose in life but to mourn. The people of Deadwood had rallied around her, bringing food, helping to lay Jake out, and minding Edwin. Just that morning a subdued Caleb Dexter had come with his hat in his hand and offered to take Edwin into town. She had let the boy go, although she knew it would be better if she were forced to find the will to get up and do for him. She knew it was not good for Edwin to see her as she was. She had hardly been able to talk to him, to say the necessary things about God's will. All she wanted to do was hold him close to her and rock. He was better off with Caleb Dexter.

She wished she could cry. She hadn't really cried, though she had felt tears burning behind her eyes almost constantly since the moment Caleb Dexter had run into her cabin just as she was punching down her bread dough, and shouted those terrible words, cave-in. Something had knotted up inside her when she knew Hugh and Jake were trapped in the mine, and in the days that had passed, the knot had grown tighter until she felt it would choke off her breath. She felt as if she was going to die herself. Like she just wouldn't be able to catch any more air and she would die. Just like it must have been in the mine. Jake not able to breathe.

She deserved to die. If it weren't for the boy she wouldn't try to go on living at all.

Poor Jake, she thought, poor Jake dying alone down there in the dark. Drowning there in the muck of the mine. She tortured herself with the thought as she had for days. She could not get the picture of Jake dying with his face in the muck out of her mind.

He had been happy in the mine. That was something. But he had been happy with her too and, just like the mine, she had betrayed him. He had never suspected. She was almost sure of that and tried to comfort herself with the thought, but she knew Jake deserved more. He was a good man and should have had some happiness, some success in life. Now it was too late. And she was alone.

She sat there, her arms folded across her middle against the pain and rocked back and forth in the desolate little cabin.

She realized someone was knocking at the door. She sat passively, hoping they would go away. When the knocking continued, she finally said, "Come in," not caring who it was.

Hugh stepped quietly into the room. She was not surprised to see him. He had made several trips to the cabin since the disaster, wanting to help lay Jake out and take care of her, even when he himself needed the services of the doctor.

He looked a little better today. He had taken the bandages off his hands and his cuts and bruises were starting to heal. She didn't look at him for long. She folded her arms tighter and kept rocking. She didn't speak to him.

He pulled a stool over and sat before her.

"Have you eaten, Molly?" he asked.

She nodded but he looked around as if he didn't believe her. There were two plates on the table with last night's food hardening in them. The stove was cold. Hugh got up and took the plates to her washpan on the stove and poured water from the kettle over them.

"I can do that," she said. "I'll get to it later."

Hugh poured a little soft soap into the pan, then wiped his hands on his pants uncertainly. He looked awkward standing there. A big, rugged man who belonged outdoors trying to do women's work. He realized he had forgotten to heat the water and put some kerosene soaked kindling into the stove and lit it.

"I'll make you some coffee," he said.

She watched him do the job awkwardly, thinking she would get up and do it, but feeling unable to move. The odor of the kerosene brought a nostalgic pungency to the air, reminding her of happier mornings.

He finished and returned to the stool and sat facing

her. His eyes were troubled and he didn't seem to know what to do with his hands.

"Molly, I have to talk to you."

She rocked faster.

"Molly, I tried to save him. I really did."

"I know. Everyone said so. Even if they hadn't, I'd have known you'd try to save him."

"He was my partner. And I liked him. I really did. He was a friend to me. If it hadn't been for him, we wouldn't have gotten a place on the wagon train. He was always so steady, so good-natured. He never saw bad in anyone."

"I know. You needn't feel guilty. It isn't your fault he's dead."

"But it is, Molly. That's it. I'm the one that made us go underground. Dexter said it wasn't safe, but I insisted. I didn't want to give up the partnership because—you know."

"I know," she shut her eyes. "That was my doing too. I encouraged you to stay."

"Jake wanted it too. He loved the mine. He voted to go underground."

"I know. I tell myself that, too."

"I feel like everything that's happened is my fault. It's like ever since I made Luther join the expedition, I've been leading us on a path to destruction."

"Don't talk that way, Hugh. It's not your fault."

"I keep wondering what I should have done differently. Maybe I should have stayed in Nebraska. But then I wouldn't have found you again. I wouldn't have known about Edwin and—"

He looked at her as if she should have some answers for him, as if she should not leave it all to him, but she could only keep on rocking. "Molly, look at me. It was right for us to meet again, wasn't it? It *was* meant to happen?"

She turned her face away from him. Why couldn't he understand that she was numb, incapable of feeling or reasoning and could take no part in this? "I don't know, Hugh. I don't know what is meant to be."

"Well, I think it was meant to be," Hugh spoke intently as if trying to project a certainty that would bring her back from the passive shell she had drawn into. "I've been thinking all along what it meant, us meeting again. Edwin is my son and now you can be my wife. Don't you see it's the only way we can make sense out of what's happened? We can still make it our destiny."

Still she was numb. Still she rocked, but a tear fell down her cheek and she could feel it. She wanted desperately to believe.

"Molly, stop that rocking and look at me." He took her hands. "You're cold as ice, Molly. Let me warm your hands."

She was surprised at the touch of his hands. He was so very warm, so very much alive. Something was breaking loose within her, but before the thaw had more than begun, his knees touched hers and she looked up and into his eyes. She told herself it need not be her decision, that fate had settled it for her. Calm replaced her uncertainty. She felt she was dreaming and drifting and all she wanted was to move across the space between them and nestle in his lap. She could lay her head on his shoulder and he would take over the rocking, and she would give it all up to him. It would be such a relief to have someone take over, to have her life settled again.

"Tell me what you're thinking, Molly. I know it's too soon, that we shouldn't be making plans when you're in mourning for Jake, but if you agree, then, then in the fall—" His voice trailed off. The question unasked but understood. She was on the verge, not of answering, but of letting the fact she did not say no speak for her. She wished she could cross that space between them and find herself in the security of his arms. Given time and Hugh's patience and the history of all that had passed between them, she might have found a way. But someone knocked at the door.

She snatched her hands back from his. She felt herself blushing. Jake was hardly cold in his grave. What would people think? What kind of woman was she?

The knock persisted.

"Shall I get it?" Hugh asked.

Molly shook her head and went to the door, wiping her hands on her apron and making the habitual check to be sure her collar was buttoned.

She opened the door.

A stranger stood there. He smelled of horses and sweat and had a day's growth of beard on his tanned face. "Is this the Lewis cabin?" he asked.

She nodded.

"I was looking for Mr. Everett. I understand he lives in the other cabin on the Lucky Six, but nobody's home down there and I got to find him."

"Mr. Everett is here." She stepped aside. "He was my late husband's partner and . . ." her voice trailed off while she wondered why she felt she had to make an explanation. Hugh came to the door and stood beside her.

"Mr. Everett?" The bearded man held out his hand to Hugh. "I'm Pete Simpson. Emmet Hobart sent me."

Molly thought Simpson seemed uncomfortable.

"Come in," Hugh said cheerfully. "How is Emmet?"

"Maybe you better come outside," Simpson said. He took his hat off and held it in front of him. Molly thought he did it awkwardly. If the man hadn't taken his hat off to meet a lady, why was he taking it off now?

Hugh stepped outside and Molly followed him, feeling uneasy.

"I see you have Hobart's wagon," Hugh said.

Simpson seemed to brighten as if the wagon gave him something to talk about. "Hobart asked me to bring . . . this to you. He would have come himself, he said to tell you that, but—"

They had stepped closer to the wagon as they talked. Molly noticed there was something in the back of the wagon covered with a tarp. Simpson was fingering his hat nervously, looking uncomfortable. "I don't know how to go about this," he was saying, but Hugh seemed unaware of his discomfort.

"My brother's working for Hobart," Hugh said cheerfully. "I guess they've got quite a little livestock business going on in the valley. Do you know Luther?"

"Well, we never exactly met," Simpson said. "You see I was just passing through on my way to Deadwood and—"

"I hope Luther thought to send some beef down to us. We could sure use some fresh meat," Hugh said. Just as he reached over to lift the corner of the tarp, Molly knew. "No," she gasped, but it was too late. Hugh lifted the tarp.

389

"Oh my God," he said.

Molly had her hand over her mouth but could not stifle her sob.

"Oh, my God," Hugh said again, still holding the tarp and looking down at the face of his brother.

It was his brother, Luther, in the wagon. Dead.

"Hobart said to tell you he would have come hisself, only he's got a pretty bad side wound. Same outfit as did in your brother."

"Indians?" Hugh said at last.

"Goddamn bloodthirsty Sioux. Probably the same bunch that got Custer. Tried to run off Hobart's horses."

Hugh climbed into the wagon and putting his arm under his brother, raised him up so he could hold him. Luther was cold. Luther was as cold as ice. His body was stiff, yet his head hung back awkwardly. Hugh looked at the body, denying, unbelieving, remembering Luther as a little boy. A little boy tagging after him. A little boy always wanting to impress his older brother. A little boy wanting to be a man.

"You can be proud of him," Simpson was saying. "Hobart said to tell you he saved Hobart's life for sure. He warned the herders and the haying crews in the valley, and he saved Hobart, and he killed one of the goddamn Indians too. Got a clean shot through the breast Hobart said."

I'll make you proud of me. How many times had Luther said that? *I'll make you proud of me yet.* That's what he had said that last day. The day Hugh sent him away.

He tried to hold Luther close. He buried his head on his brother's chest, not caring that sticky clots of blood might touch him.

390

"He done real fine. Mr. Hobart said to be sure to tell you that. To tell you he was really growing up there in the valley and he died like a man."

My fault, Hugh thought. *My fault. Take care of your brother*, his mother had said and Hugh had brought him to this. There was a buzzing in his ears like he was going to pass out and for a time Hugh was conscious of nothing but the terrible pain and guilt that descended on him.

Finally he heard Simpson saying, "So you see, I got to get back, Mr. Everett. I got to pick up supplies tonight so I can get started back first thing in the morning. I don't want to be alone in that valley after dark. So I got to get unloaded now, Mr. Everett." Hugh realized Simpson had said it before. He needed to unload his wagon. Be rid of Luther.

With a great effort, Hugh sat up.

"So if you'll just tell me where you want him, Mr. Everett, I'll help you to get him laid out and then I've got to get going. I'm sorry, but I was just passing through and Hobart gave me this job; him being short handed and wounded and him figuring you rather have your brother buried near."

Hugh lowered his brother into the wagon gently. He reached down to pull the tarp back up over the body and then he noticed Luther's feet. The boots were worn through. The beautiful boots Luther had spent his savings on had worn completely through. Luther had been so proud of them. They were the only fine thing he had ever owned and now they were ruined. Hugh wondered how his brother could have walked in such ragged boots. Luther fighting Indians and dying with ragged boots. It looked as if he had tried to mend the boots with bits of leather and then given up. Luther had never been very skillful at things. There was a great crack in the right boot and Luther's big toe was showing. It was more than Hugh could bear. The naked toe was harder to look at than the wounds. A man could be proud to die fighting but not of dying too poor to cover his nakedness. Hugh wanted to cry like a baby, but he held it back. Simpson was driving the wagon down to the other cabin; he wanted to get unloaded and on his way. Life had to go on.

They had to put Luther in his old bunk. The kitchen table wasn't long enough. Molly offered her cabin — the only words she had spoken, but Hugh said it wouldn't be good for Edwin to see Luther laid out in their cabin so soon after seeing his father that way. They would lay Luther out in his own cabin. It was better that way. Hugh covered him with a blanket. It was good to do this last thing for his brother. There was an undertaker in Deadwood now, but Hugh would lay his brother out himself. It was the least he could do. He'd promised his mother to take care of him.

"Caleb Dexter will be back soon," Molly said after Simpson left, still holding his hat in his hand apologetically as if he knew he had done his job badly. "I have a clean shirt of Jake's," she added. "I'll fetch it."

Hugh nodded. Of course, Luther couldn't be buried in his own shirt. There were two bloody holes in Luther's shirt. Hugh wondered how they would keep the blood from staining the clean shirt. Maybe Caleb Dexter would know. Caleb Dexter knew everything. Hugh knew nothing.

Molly came back with the shirt and set a kettle of

water on the stove. "You better fetch more water. We'll need hot water."

"We don't have to lay him out right away, do we? Can't we just . . . mourn for a while?"

"It's better to keep busy. Keep doing what has to be done, and if you're lucky, you won't run out of chores. Then you don't have to think."

Hugh nodded. He was like a man sleepwalking. Molly was afraid for his sanity. She ached for Hugh. She felt his grief more sharply than her own. She knew the guilt he would feel, that he would remember his promise to his mother to care for Luther. Knew he would remember the way he had sent Luther away to keep him from hinting to Jake that he and Molly were lovers. She had stood numbly by the wagon and witnessed that terrible scene, powerless to make it stop. She had wanted to make it stop happening. She saw now that Hugh was in shock even as she had been that week. But now, faced with the need to act, to care for Luther's body and to comfort Hugh, she found some hidden strength within. Hugh needed her. A moment before she had been unable to bring herself to bridge the space between them and accept his love, but now that his own pain was so terrible, her whole being demanded she let him bury himself and his pain within her. She took off her apron and opened her arms to him.

"Let me hold you."

He came to her and they held onto each other, and, though she had always relied on his strength, now she felt she supported him, as if she were the strong one, the pioneer, and only she had the power to give comfort. And in comforting him, her own pain at

Jake's death receded for an instant, and she knew Hugh had been right to ask her to marry him. Only together would they find peace. She wanted to love and nurture him, to take him away from the horror in this cabin and take him inside her and make him forget for a moment. "Hugh," she whispered, "let's go to my cabin. Let me comfort you. Let me help you forget." She made her body an invitation and offered her lips for his kiss. She felt the anger tense within him even before he pushed her away.

"Make me forget? Make me forget what I've done to Luther? What we've done?"

"Just for a moment," she was stunned by his reaction. "I just wanted to comfort you for a little while."

"With your body? You wanted to trap me again like you did the night you left Jake's bed to beg me with your body not to fetch Luther home!"

"Hugh!"

"You did that. Don't deny it. I wanted to bring him home, but I couldn't because of you. Because of what we were doing to Jake."

His truth crumpled her, even as she determined to deny it. "Luther wanted to go. He knew he had to be away from you and the mine to grow up. And Jake wanted the mine. They made their destiny. Not us."

"No, it was my doing. My lust that brought all this down upon us. Pearson, Jake and now my brother all dead because of me. Because of you."

She saw she could not reason with him, and the same self-doubt that had kept her from speaking her love for him kept her from claiming to understand the meaning of what had happened. Whether the fault was his or hers or a trick of fate was unknown, and would

394

remain unknown. She knew only that she must not let him go, and that they must touch again, lest they lose each other. She could not demand that he listen to her or stay with her, she could only ask. She reached out for him one more time.

"Please, Hugh, please let me—"

His eyes betrayed an instant of longing and uncertainty, but when he spoke his voice was harsh with determination. "Go away, Molly. Leave me alone to bury my brother in peace."

She breathed deeply against the pain and spoke slowly. "I'll come back later. Later we'll—"

"No. No later. You held me with promises too long. Now it must be ended. I want you to leave Deadwood. Take Edwin and go home to your father. I'm sorry I ever laid eyes on you."

He did not know when she left. So great was his own guilt and loss that he was unaware of the pain he had caused her. For a time he did nothing but sit and stare at his brother's corpse. The blanket did not quite cover Luther's feet, and the broken soles of his brother's boots seemed an accusation. He remembered Luther as a little boy. And all the times he'd been impatient with his brother, the boy who had followed him everywhere, even into Sioux lands, and who had left with the promise that he would make them all proud.

Hugh knew he had to do something or he would go crazy. He would tend to the burying. That was the thing that had to be done now. Now was not the time to think of Molly nor of the terrible things he had said to her.

He took the tobacco can with his share of the gold

dust from its hiding place in the dirt of the cabin floor. He would use it all on a proper burial. He'd buy a real coffin and he would buy his brother a new pair of boots to be buried in. Hugh would give his brother the finest boots Deadwood could offer and he would order a real gravestone. His brother would lie beside Jake on Mt. Moriah, and Hugh could visit them both in peace, for he had rid himself of the woman and the promise that had become a curse.

Chapter Twenty-eight

Luther Everett was not the only man to lose his life that day. By sunset of August 20, 1876, five men including Luther and Preacher Smith, the gentle itinerate minister who had set out to walk to Crook City to preach the gospel saying his Bible would protect him, were all victims of a raiding party, or parties, of Sioux.

As if this were not enough for one day, that evening once again a man rode into Deadwood with the head of an Indian dangling from his saddle. And, once again, the trophy was auctioned to the highest bidder. This incident, the second in as many months, inspired the editor of the *Pioneer* to write against the practice of decapitating dead Indians, for "we should always keep in mind that the eye of the world is upon us," and the practice made Deadwood look uncivilized. The editorial concluded, Kill all the Indians that can be killed. Complete extermination is our motto. But when once killed, leave the body intact where it falls."

The editorial stirred controversy in Deadwood, but Hugh did not take his usual interest in local issues. August ended in a blur for him. Only two things were real: his brother was dead, and his relationship with Molly seemed irreparably broken. He knew he'd said something terrible to her after Luther's death, though he could not clearly remember it. He tried to apologize, but her manner was distant when he stopped by to see if she needed anything, and she refused to really talk to him. There seemed an icy wall between them. She had declared her intention to leave Deadwood as soon as stage service was available. Travel was at a stand-still and although the multiple killings had inspired several efforts to organize a local militia, they had all failed, for the city preferred to escape its fears in a frantic search for gold and sin. Millions of dollars in gold were found in the gulch that summer. Sin was even easier to come by.

Molly's being trapped in Deadwood saved Hugh from making any decision in her regard. He suffered from the same shock that had paralyzed Molly after Jake's death. He thought he had said something to her about their love being like a curse; sometimes he believed that. Because he had loved Molly Lewis, three men were dead, one of them his brother.

He continued to work the mine with Caleb Dexter. His heart was not in it, but he knew Molly would need a nest egg to go home with, and work gave him an outlet. He grieved days and dreamed tortured dreams at night. Molly would offer herself to him, Luther would be alive and well and calling to him, and then suddenly he would awake and remember. Emerald O'Brien also appeared in his dreams, but he refused to recognize that fact and never put a name to the dark-haired, green-eyed woman who sometimes took Molly's place in his dreams. When Emerald came by the mine with Austin Avery, he would try to avoid looking at her and when he did, would find her smiling as if she knew what troubled him.

August drifted into September, the weather turned unseasonably cold, and still nothing was resolved.

And then General Crook marched into Deadwood. It was the event the city had waited and prayed for. Crook and the two thousand men in his command announced they had avenged the massacre of Custer by attacking a village at Slim Buttes, capturing two hundred ponies, the winter food supply and blankets, and a Seventh Cavalry guidon flag as proof the Sioux bore the stain of Custer's blood. The troops and Deadwood were triumphant, although history would reveal the battle was a victory over a village of mere women and children. It had been a discouraging campaign. Sitting Bull and his band fled to Canada, and Crook ran so short of supplies the men were resigned to eating their mounts as they dropped from exhaustion. Still, they claimed to have broken the back-bone of the Sioux nation. Indeed, the tribes had scattered to the winds and a massed attack on the Black Hills was no longer a threat. Crook was given a hero's welcome.

Hugh stood in the crowd to hear Crook speak from the balcony of the Grand Central Hotel, but he did not share the crowd's jubilation. To Hugh, the news meant only that the end had come. Molly could leave. Not an hour after the news of Crook's victory reached the city, Austin Avery had called on Molly and offered to buy her shares of the mine. She told him she must consult with Hugh about the price. Hugh had to admit the gambler's offer was generous, so she had just that morning sent Avery a message saying she would sell. As much as he hated to accommodate the gambler, Hugh saw little point in retaining his own share of the mine.

It was, therefore, not from a desire to celebrate that Hugh joined the throngs welcoming Crook. Whether history would regard them as pioneers or trespassers he was not certain, but he had been among those who had defied both the U.S. Cavalry and the Sioux Nation to invade the Black Hills; he would be present for the event he sensed marking a turning point in the city's brief history. The summer of '76 was almost over. Crook's presence amounted to an official government recognition of the white occupation of the Black Hills. Deadwood would become civilized. Carved backbars with brass foot rails, pianos, and gilt-framed portraits of nudes were being hauled in by ox train. They had an assortment of lawyers, a doctor, and a dentist, and although Preacher Smith had been killed, others had come to take his place.

Hugh thought about "progress" and wondered if it was really worth anything. He listened to the sounds of celebration, the cheers and the music of the hurdy-gurdies, the gun powder blasts from anvils and the random shooting and the whistle shrieks from the saw mills. Then he turned his eyes from the bustling, jostling crowd and the painted women who leaned from the upper windows of the brothels waving their handkerchiefs to the troops and looked to the hills. They were glowing with the bonfires lit in honor of Crook. He thought how barren the hills around Deadwood had become as they were stripped of their timber for the cabins and mines and bonfires of the city, and he remembered the promise of the Black Hills and how they had been when they were new.

He did not find civilization beautiful that night.

Hugh followed the crowd from the Grand Central to Langrishe's theatre, which now sported a real roof instead of canvas. Like the hotel, the theatre was jammed and he did not even try to get in although he caught a glimpse of Avery and Emerald entering. Emerald saw him and waved with her fan, but he could not get through the crowd. He supposed Avery had reserved a box. It was like him. Hugh lingered in the street, telling himself it was because he wanted to be a part of this historic event and not because he hoped to see Emerald again. He realized if he sold his share of the mine to Avery, he would have no more reason to see her. There would, in fact, be nothing to hold him in Deadwood. He felt at a loss. His adventure was almost over and what had he proven? He had lost Molly and Edwin and had found neither poor man's gold nor himself.

The crowd inside the theatre passed word outside of the doings inside — handshaking and speech making. When the vaudeville performance finally began, people started drifting out of the theatre. Hugh imagined it was stuffy inside and wondered if Avery would leave early. Pokes of gold dust must be crossing gaming tables elsewhere. Sure enough, Avery and Emerald appeared in the doorway. She scanned the crowd and when she saw him, flashed him a smile which he acknowledged with a tip of his hat. When he saw the gambler was approaching him, he tried to keep his eyes off Emerald, but she seemed to be seeking his attention. Her eyes were wide and sparkly, her color high.

Hugh and Avery exchanged a few words about Crook's victory and when there was a lull in the conversation, Emerald reached over and slipped something in Hugh's pocket.

"I saved this playbill for Edwin. I thought he should have a momento of Crook's coming to Deadwood. It's an important night."

Hugh touched his pocket wonderingly, but kept his attention on Avery, agreeing to meet him at the hotel the next day to talk business. As he turned to leave, Emerald reminded him again to give Edwin the playbill.

Hugh stepped into the nearest saloon and in the dim light opened the folded paper. Across the bottom Emerald had scrawled a message.

Hugh,

Don't sell your share of the mine to Austin. He has a plan to make himself rich reselling the mine and he will make you a lot of money too if you only hold out.

Mrs. Lewis better sell so she can leave town. It's safer for her and the boy to get back to their people, but don't you sell out. I beg you.

Your friend, Em. O'Brien

So he was right. Avery did have a scheme. But why was Emerald telling him about it? He couldn't answer that question, but if there was any possibility of a fortune to be made on the Lucky Six, Molly must have her share.

Only Molly didn't feel that way. She wanted nothing to do with the mine, Austin Avery, or, he suspected, himself, he discovered when he went to her.

Molly didn't understand why Hugh was asking her to stay on. He spoke of her staying only in terms of getting a better price for her shares of the mine later. Did he think money was what she cared about? Had he forgotten his brutal rejection of her after Luther's death, the way he'd accused her of killing Luther and told her to get out of town? True, he had been kind and gentle to her since then, stopping by each day to see if she needed anything, but she could forget neither what he had said nor her own guilt.

"Don't ask me to stay, Hugh. As soon as the route's safe and the stage starts operating, I'm leaving."

"I know you'd be taking a risk to turn down Avery's offer, but if you stay until he locates a buyer, you might still make a fortune on the mine."

"Just yesterday you said his offer was generous. What makes you think that mine is worth anything?" She was angry. Her desire made it painful for her to be near him; and rejecting him, getting angry at him, was safer than admitting her true feelings. She would not risk another cruel rejection or more accusations. "We've never washed out more than day's wages!"

"You don't understand mining. Someone with the capital to invest in proper underground mining machinery could—"

"You're right. I don't understand mining, and I don't understand why you want me to stay now when before you all but ordered me to get out of town, and I don't understand how we find this entrepreneur who's going to make us all rich!"

He was surprised by her anger and not willing to discuss his confused feelings, so he tried to keep the talk on business. "That's why we need Austin Avery. Apparently he's got connections with eastern capitalists and he'll be able to make the kind of deal I can't."

"Do you want the kind of deal Austin Avery can make?"

"What do you mean by that?"

"You know what kind of man he is, a gambler, a man who openly consorts with a woman like Emerald O'Brien!"

"Don't drag Emerald into this! This has nothing to do with Emerald. She's a lovely lady, and she's been nothing but kind to you and Edwin, and she's warned us about

Avery and —"

"I don't trust her. She thinks she can win me over by making up to Edwin, but she doesn't fool me." She was about to go on, but she suddenly realized she could not say aloud what she suspected Emerald of scheming for. Hugh's passionate defense of the woman was sign enough she was winning him over. Molly felt almost sick at the realization.

"You're upsetting yourself. Please let me take care of this for you."

He was treating her like she was a child when he was the one showing poor judgment, but she knew if she said more, she risked sounding like a shrew. Still, she had a very bad feeling about the situation and she could not let Hugh go unwarned.

"Austin Avery is a crook, Hugh."

"I can handle him. Besides, he's got something I don't have — luck! I've heard about him. He almost never holds a losing hand."

"And why do you suppose that is?"

"Maybe he cheats. Maybe he doesn't. But he can't pull the wool over my eyes about the mine."

"So, you'll attach yourself to his coattails?"

"Damn it, I'm sick of losing. Everything I've touched this summer has turned to dust. The man's no Preacher Smith, but Preacher Smith is dead. It's all luck, Molly, and this man has it. Think — if he could get us a thousand dollars a share for the mine, think what a difference it could make to Edwin's future — to *our* future!"

"*Our* future?

He could not admit that he had once again dared to to think of them as together, so he went back to talking business. "There's fortunes to be made in this town and I don't see why we shouldn't have our share."

"Our share? *What of Jake and Luther's shares?* Shall we take theirs too?" She already wished she hadn't said it, but she'd wanted to hurt him as he'd hurt her by hinting again that their futures were one and then talking only of fortunes to be made.

"Must you remind me, Molly?"

"You reminded me. You said that it was my fault."

"No, the responsibility is mine. I take it upon myself. And I take it upon myself to protect your interests and get you the best price for the mine, so that Jake's dying will not be for nothing."

He had spoken of it again. Reminded her of her guilt for trapping them both with her body, for not telling Jake the truth, and worst of all, for only hours before Jake's death actually resolving to leave him.

"Be quiet, Hugh," she spoke sharply in her anger. "Let's not keep talking of this."

"I know. We can't resolve it now. We need time and that's why we have to decide about the mine. Why we must talk business."

"Then talk business. Talk business with Austin Avery. I want to be finished with this mine. I want to be finished with everything. Tell him I accept his offer. The mining shares are mine and I wish to sell and I want you to know: I am not your responsibility."

They faced each other as if across a great distance. They were impossibly asunder, and there seemed nothing he could do but agree to bring the papers.

"It's settled then," he said as he stepped to the door to leave, but she detained him with a touch.

"Just one thing, Hugh."

"Yes?" he asked wanting her to somehow come into his

arms again.

"If you take my advice, if you still care about anything decent, you'll have nothing to do with that man or with his woman."

He pulled away from her and left without an answer and she knew that her words had been wasted.

Avery had three hundred dollars in gold dust in a plump leather pouch ready for Hugh when he came to the hotel dining room that afternoon. Hugh wondered how many turns of the cards it had taken Avery to win that much dust, more than Hugh had earned in a summer of back-breaking labor.

"It's all here," Avery patted the little bundle on the table. "Three hundred in dust. We'll weigh it at the bar after we finish our drinks and our talk. Then you can take it to Mrs. Lewis and tell her I'll be out this evening with the papers for her to sign."

Hugh supposed Avery must be happy that Molly was selling, but the gambler had not betrayed his emotions by so much as the flicker of an eyelid. He offered Hugh a cheroot from a silver case. Hugh declined but could not help but admire the smooth way Avery picked out his own cigar and snapped the case shut with a flourish. He had never seen a man with such graceful hands. Avery held the cheroot until Emerald removed a tiny match safe from her beaded handbag and leaned over to light it for him.

Hugh was fascinated with the idea of a woman doing that for a man. It meant she would do anything for him. He'd tried to avoid looking at her, but now as she held the flame so it seemed to dance within her eyes, he wondered for a flashing moment what it would be like to have her.

There would be no hesitation in her, he knew, no obligation and no reminders of guilt. He felt his manhood respond to her and was glad the table hid the fact. Then a little smile played around her mouth as if she knew.

Hugh forced his attention to the pouch of gold between them. If Avery said there was three hundred dollars in dust in it, he was sure there was, but for Molly's protection he'd have it poured and weighed.

"I suggest you open an account for Mrs. Lewis in the new bank," Avery said, puffing on his cigar. "They can exchange the dust for bills or a bank note if she plans to go East."

"She is going, isn't she?" Emerald suddenly entered the conversation.

"As soon as stage service commences."

"Oh good. I hate to see her go, but it will be better for her and Edwin to be with their people." Emerald wore her knowing smile.

"Now, as to you, Mr. Everett," Avery leaned back to draw on the cigar. "I assume that after the loss of your brother, for which I offer my condolences, you, too, might be ready to return home, so I am prepared to offer you $150 for your single, remaining share in the mine."

"I'm not interested in selling."

"Oh?" Avery said with just the slightest raise of an eyebrow. "Is my offer not generous enough?"

"The price is fair. But I've no interest in going home. I've put a lot into that mine. I'll stick with it."

"You're aware you can't hope to develop it properly without capital?"

"I know that very well," Hugh said quietly. "Jake lost his life and I nearly died myself because we didn't have enough timbers to shore it up properly."

407

"Then why do you think you can continue to mine it yourself?"

"I don't." Hugh saw Emerald was smiling encouragement. "I'm willing to sell to the right party, but I figure if it's going to some eastern capitalist, I'd like to sell directly to him."

"Understandable," Avery smiled, although Hugh had as much as called him a crook. "And you have contact with such men?"

"Of course not. But I figure you do, or you will. Otherwise you wouldn't be so interested in the mine yourself."

"So," Avery drew on the cigar and sent out a screen of smoke. "So, you think I have the contacts and the expertise to make a better deal? You'd ride in on my coattails?"

Hugh winced inside at the reminder of Molly's warning, but he kept his voice even. "If you want to put it that way."

"Well, I admire your honesty. No one appreciates honesty more than I do. You flatter me, of course, but I do have a certain experience and skill in such matters. One would suppose, if one had been to Alder Gulch and had some experience, that one of the first stagecoaches to hit Deadwood will disgorge a real live eastern capitalist."

Hugh suddenly was reminded of Caleb Dexter and wondered if the old man fit into this deal somewhere.

"Winter is coming on," Avery continued, "and the miners will have to decide if they're going underground or getting out. And, as your unfortunate example has proved, underground operations are not for amateurs."

He doesn't mind hurting a man, Hugh thought. He's not the gentleman he pretends to be.

"You are aware," the gambler pressed his advantage,

"that your mine could be worthless? That there's no way of knowing until an accurate assay can be made?"

Hugh nodded. All summer miners had conducted their own primitive tests; now rumor said an assay office would open, staffed by a metalurgist from a foreign university. "I'm willing to take a chance on the assay."

"So you're a gambler too! Well, there's some of that in most men. That's what enables me to make my living. That's what I always say, don't I, Emerald dear?"

"Hugh must have heard of your reputation for holding winning hands," Emerald patted the diamond ring Avery wore. Her hands were small, Hugh noticed, and delicate, compared to the work-worn hands of Molly.

"Some might think it luck," Avery put his hand over Emerald's, "but I work hard for what I get. Emerald and I know it's honest toil."

Hugh looked at the gambler's hands on Emerald. There was something indecent about a man wearing a diamond ring and having hands that white, a man who flaunted his mistress and called gambling honest toil. Impulsively Hugh thrust out his own hands.

"See my hands! Here's how you tell a man who does honest toil! By his hands. See these callouses? These are where I froze my hands panning for gold in the creeks. And these here, these are where I blistered my hands raw opening up that mine. And these fresh scars here, these I earned digging Jake and me out with my bare hands when the mine caved in!"

Avery remained impassive. Hugh knew he was losing his own control, but he could not stop. "It was my idea to buy that mine and my idea to go underground. It was because of me and that mine that Jake is dead. Jake gave his life for that mine. It's all I've got left. All I've gotten out

409

of this crazy, damn trip to the Black Hills, and I'll stick with it to the end!"

"Understandable, Mr. Everett. You're emotionally involved. Not a good idea in business, but understandable. You have an attachment to the Lucky Six, so I won't try to change your mind." He pushed himself away from the table. "Just take this dust to Mrs. Lewis and tell her I'll bring the papers tonight. Then you and Caleb Dexter hire some laborers and keep working that mine. Get a new stope opened somewhere, anywhere, and keep that damn pump working, so when I bring some capitalist to look it over, it looks like a going operation."

"All right," Hugh said, choking down resentment. "I'll do all that."

"Well, then that settles it for now. Agreed?"

"What about the assay? Should I arrange for one?"

"Leave that to me," Avery said sharply. "Tend to the diggings and leave the business end to me." He stood up to signal the meeting was over and offered his hand for Hugh to shake.

Hugh hesitated. He didn't like the way Avery was giving orders and implying he was the brains of the outfit and Hugh was fit only for grubbing in the earth. He felt like he was making a pact with the devil, but when he looked at Emerald, she was smiling and nodding encouragement.

He shook Austin Avery's hand.

The three hundred dollars in gold dust seemed heavy as he walked back to the mine that evening. At eighteen dollars an ounce, it had weighed out at over a pound, but it wasn't just the weight of the gold, it was the knowledge it would enable Molly to leave town and start a new life without him. It spoiled any pleasure he might have felt at withholding his own share from Avery. He did not want her to go, but their relationship seemed doomed.

Molly met him at the cabin door. Her face was white and her eyes were wide and frightened.

"Thank God you're here. I was about to send Edwin to look for you."

"What's wrong?"

"It's Caleb. I think he's dying."

Chapter Twenty-nine

The doctor's face was solemn as he examined the old prospector. It was not the forced solemnity doctors, like preachers, sometimes assume to conceal the fact they are faced with something beyond their understanding, Molly decided, but an expression very close to fear. It frightened her. So did the fact Caleb Dexter slipped between delirium and unconsciousness and had been since he'd stumbled into her cabin late that afternoon burning with fever and complaining of a headache and collapsed as suddenly as if he'd been struck dead.

She'd been afraid to leave him alone and been about to send Edwin to town to try to find Hugh, she explained to Hugh and the doctor she'd fetched, when Hugh had returned. The old man had retched so violently she was afraid he would choke. Even as the doctor examined him, he was overcome by dry, strangling heaves. Then he passed out again, his eyes rolling back in his head, a phenomenon that fascinated Edwin who persisted in staying beside the sick man, despite Molly's efforts to send him outside.

The doctor took his time with the examination, then stood up and grasped his stethescope with both hands before announcing importantly, "he has all the classic symptoms. His skin is burning with heat, but you will notice it is quite dry. His pulse is hard and frequent. He's complained of headache and pain in the epigastrium. He's vomiting and delirious, verging on the point of convulsions. All classic symptoms."

"Of what?"

The doctor took off his stethescope and dropped it into his bag, closing it with an ominous click. He stood for a moment, his bag in his hand, regarding Caleb Dexter with an air of sorrow. He rolled his sleeves down.

"Smallpox."

"Oh, my God," Molly snatched Edwin away from the inert form of Caleb Dexter and held him close to her. "How could you let the boy stand so near if you suspected smallpox?"

"By the time I got here, he was exposed. Smallpox is so virulent just being in the same room with a victim is sufficient exposure. If the boy has not been vaccinated, it is already too late; he will contract the disease, and if he has—"

"Too late?"

"If he has not been vaccinated. Has he?"

Molly finally sorted out what the doctor had said and pulled Edwin's shirt roughly off over his head and jerked up his arm for the doctor to see.

Dr. Gillotz knelt down and examined Edwin's arm carefully. "Very good," he said. "The cicatrix is well-defined. It obviously took well."

"He was quite sick at the time."

"Excellent, then he's in no danger at all." The doctor beamed, but then put on a more solemn expression as he turned to Molly and Hugh. "What about you two? Have you been vaccinated?"

Molly looked at Hugh anxiously, but he was nodding, touching his own arm. She touched hers also. "I have a good scar."

"When were you vaccinated? As children?"

Neither remembered.

"Then I assume neither of you has ever been revaccinated?" When they shook their heads, he continued. "Vaccination is completely effective for only six to ten years. That's why the boy is completely safe. But for adults like you, there is a chance of becoming infected."

"You mean we could get it?" Molly touched her face. Smallpox marked you for life.

"Unlikely, but possible. Seldom fatal in such cases, though you'd still be scarred."

"Let's get him out of here," Hugh said. "I don't want him near Molly."

"It's too late now. You're both exposed. It's better not to move him."

"Is Caleb going to die?" Edwin wailed, returning Molly's attention to the old man.

"That depends."

"On what?" Molly remembered that Jake had been fond of him.

"First of all, on which form of the disease he has, the confluent form or the discrete variety."

"What's the difference?" Hugh asked.

The doctor hooked one thumb in his vest so his gold watch fob showed as he recited: "Variola discreta pustulis paucia, discretis—"

"In English, damn it!" Hugh interrupted.

"If he was variloa discrete he may live; if he has variola confluens, he will most likely die."

"How can you tell which he has?" Molly asked.

"I can't at this point. Although the severity of the pain, vomiting and delirium in the early stages is some indication, we won't know until the pustules form. The eruptions will begin on the third day and must be examined to determine which form he has. If it is confluent, when the secondary fever begins on the eighth day, it will be most severe, most deaths occurring then. So you see," he concluded brightly, "we won't know until the second week."

"You'll be gone by then, Molly," Hugh said.

Molly had almost forgotten. She had plans. She could not be expected to nurse the old man.

"You're leaving town?" the doctor frowned.

"I'm taking my son and going to my people in the East. Unless I can't go? Because of the exposure?"

"No reason you can't. As I said, it's unlikely you'll get it, but if you did, you'd be home where you'd have better care. Better yet, you could stop in Cheyenne and get revaccinated and be completely safe. Yes, my advice would be to leave town as soon as possible. This is the fourth case of suspected smallpox I've seen today. I expect an epidemic."

"That's terrible," Molly said.

"It is," the doctor said calmly. "Especially as most of them will die."

"But you said smallpox isn't always fatal."

"It is when there's no nursing care or hospital. I can prescribe treatment, but with no one to administer constant care, there just isn't hope. The other three men all live together. There's no one to care for them.

I certainly can't act as a nurse, especially if I'm as busy as I'll be once news of this gets out."

"But surely someone will volunteer, to—" Hugh began.

"One can hardly expect volunteers to care for a disease as filthy and disgusting and contagious as smallpox. It's a woman's job, but all the women in Deadwood are otherwise occupied."

"But if that's the case, the whole town could be infected," Hugh said.

"The situation is not entirely hopeless. After I diagnosed the initial cases this morning I informed the sheriff who has already dispatched a rider to the nearest telegraph line. I'm sure there's vaccine at Fort Laramie, so we should soon be able to innoculate anyone who is not completely protected. The situation is only serious for those who already have it. I had hopes for Mr. Dexter here, thinking Mrs. Lewis would be caring for him, but since she's to be leaving, we'd best move him now. We may as well dump him off with the others; at least they'll be together when I make my rounds."

"We can take him to my cabin," Hugh said. "He's my partner. I'll take care of him."

"That's the spirit!"

Molly turned away from the men as they began to take down her cabin door for a stretcher. She had heard about smallpox. It was the most dreaded of all diseases. It made one sick just to look at someone who had it. She had already had enough of the vomiting and delirium. Besides she was going home. She needed someone to take care of her for a change and her parents would do that. She was a widow; surely she deserved some nurturing herself. She'd spent her whole life doing for others. Just because the doctor said it was a woman's job! If only it weren't Caleb Dexter. She had disliked him from the first moment he'd stumbled into their lives, mumbling obscenities. He'd brought them nothing but trouble, luring them on with his talk of poor man's gold.

If it were Hugh who was sick, she would lay down her life for him. If it had been Luther, dear foolish Luther, she would have nursed him night and day, but Luther was dead. Hugh had sent him away to protect her secret and now he was dead. Just as Frank Pearson was killed because of her. And Jake was dead and she was guilty there too. Now if Caleb Dexter died, that would be on her conscience. If only it were someone else. Even those three unnamed miners alone in their cabin. One could suppose they had wives or mothers or sweethearts somewhere who would bless her if she saved their lives, but Caleb Dexter meant nothing to anyone. He had done nothing but cause trouble. Except for the day the mine caved in and he had worked so frantically to get Jake and Hugh out. He had shoveled continually, never letting anyone take a turn for him. Caleb Dexter, who liked to lie in the sun and drink and belch while others were working, had shoveled until he dropped, while she, Molly Lewis, the wife . . .

"Put that man down." She was surprised to hear herself.

"What?" Hugh asked. They had just rolled the old man over onto the door.

"I said, leave him alone. He's not to be moved. I'll nurse him."

"But you're leaving town."

"I can wait. I don't have to go right away."

"Mrs. Lewis," the doctor said. "Smallpox is a very ugly disease. Are you sure you can stand to—"

"I can stand what I have to stand. I can do whatever needs to be done." She held herself proudly and tried not to think of how good it would be to go home and be her father's little girl again.

"I don't want you to do it, Molly," Hugh said. "If you should get it, you could be scarred. You're too young for that."

"I've already been exposed. It can't matter now."

"I'll have to admit, it would give the old man a better chance if he had an experienced nurse," the doctor said. "There's nothing like a woman's touch. Even if he should have the severe form, he'd have a good chance. He looks like a sturdy enough old geezer."

"It's settled then," Molly said, gaining confidence and determination. "Hugh, could you drag the bunks and some bedding from your cabin over here?"

"What for?"

"For the others. We'll set up a hospital and I'll nurse them all."

"It's too much for you, Molly. You're still suffering from your loss. You can't do this."

"I've made up my mind. Someone must care for those men or they'll die."

"Then I'll help you."

Molly hesitated, but the doctor said she'd need help. "There will be a lot of lifting and carrying if the men are to be bathed properly, not to mention the laundry and the cooking. You'll need a fire going and water boiling continually." Molly knew he was right. Hugh

418

would be near her day and night, but with the sick men to care for she'd not have the will to make a fool of herself with him again. She accepted his offer.

Later that afternoon Hugh remembered the gold dust and set it on her table where she was preparing compresses for the sick men. "Here's the money for the mine. Avery's supposed to come out this evening with the papers for you to sign, but now that you're going to be staying for a while, shall I tell him to forget it?"

"For heaven's sake, Hugh! I've made up my mind about that! I told you I'd sell and I will. I never want to hear about that mine again!" It was on the tip of her tongue to add, *and don't think because I'm staying here it means I'm still hoping things can work out between us*. She decided she'd already made that clear. Both to Hugh and to herself.

Emerald looked forward to going with Avery to sign the papers buying Molly's share of the Lucky Six. Not only would it give her the opportunity to see Hugh again, but it would be a great satisfaction to know her rival would be on the first stagecoach out of town. She arranged her face and hair with great care for the occasion, but when the knock on the door of their hotel room came, she was wearing only her chemise and the Chinese silk wrapper.

"Who is it?" Avery asked, and when the answer was *Hugh*, Emerald was delighted to think Hugh would see her in the red silk wrapper, but Avery gave her a warning frown and stepped outside to talk to Hugh in the hall.

Emerald listened at the door but could not make out their words. What was Hugh doing there? She hurried to the mirror and frantically adjusted her hair and powdered her cheeks against the rising blush, planning to slip on her dress and join the men in the hall, but in a few minutes Avery came back into the room.

"You won't need to get dressed. We won't be going out to the mine."

"Is something wrong?"

"It looks like Caleb Dexter has come down with the smallpox."

"Oh. So why can't we go to the Lewis cabin?"

"That's where he is. Molly and Hugh are setting up a smallpox hospital there. Three other men have it and they are afraid of an epidemic."

"Molly and *Hugh* are setting up a *hospital*?"

"Well, that's an exaggeration. A pest house would be more like it."

"Molly and Hugh *together*?" She sat down on the edge of the bed feeling she might faint.

"Don't take it so hard, my dear. Hugh says there's little danger to anyone who's been vaccinated. You have been vaccinated haven't you?"

It was simpler to nod yes than to explain.

"Then there's no skin off our backs. I gave Hugh the papers to have Mrs. Lewis sign so the sale won't be affected. It should be two or three weeks before any capitalists show up anyway, so the quarantine won't affect us."

"Quarantine?"

"Yes, Mrs. Lewis and Hugh will be stuck out there for a couple of weeks at least."

"They're going to be out there for two weeks *together*? How can they do that?"

"Beats me. That Everett has a noble streak a mile

wide. It'll get the best of him one of these days, mark my word. Show me a man with a touch of nobility and I'll show you a fool. But then some people like to be miserable. They'd be unhappy if they ever won anything in life."

Emerald didn't hear the rest of Avery's speech. She sat clutching her stomach as if in pain. Avery bustled about getting ready for his evening of gambling and just before he left, he stopped by the bed and patted her shoulder solicitously.

"Now don't worry your pretty little head my dear. Hugh says its unlikely anyone who has been vaccinated will come down with the disease." He touched her cheek with a tenderness unusual for Austin Avery. "Your skin will always be perfection."

Emerald did not acknowledge the compliment. For once she was glad when Avery left. She had to think about what this sudden change of events was going to mean. Avery was right about one thing, you'd have to be a fool to take on smallpox. She'd seen it and she knew. But Avery was too cynical to see the nobility of the gesture. Molly and Hugh together nursing the sick men! It made her sick. She could just picture Molly Lewis, eyes downcast, offering to delay her trip east and stay with Hugh and nurse his poor sick partner. What a gesture! If only she had thought of it first. Whatever it was that had kept Molly and Hugh apart in the past, two weeks of togetherness while Molly played angel of mercy, and Hugh would be trapped. By the time the disgusting old man was on his feet again, Hugh would have gotten over his guilt about coveting his partner's wife, and he and Molly would be calling for a preacher! And just when all her schemes were working out so beautifully, and she had Hugh set up to make a fortune on the mine and Molly on the first stage out of town! It was so unfair! There was no justice in the world. That Molly Lewis with her gingham dress and her great cow eyes could have come up with such a scheme to snare Hugh, when Emerald had been working so hard on a plan! If only there was some way she could take advantage of the situation.

Emerald caught a glimpse of herself in the mirror across from the bed. Her wrapper had slipped open and her bare white shoulders were showing. She had such lovely arms, she thought, caressing them. She had always been proud of their perfection. The idea came to her slowly, almost reluctantly as she stared at herself in the mirror. She pulled the wrapper down to her elbows to examine herself. She touched the smoothness of her own unblemished skin.

Smallpox was a filthy disease. She shuddered and jerked the wrapper back around her shoulders. She couldn't do it. Even if she were sure it would work but even as she denied the idea, she knew if it would work for Molly Lewis, it would work for her. And she was in no real danger.

But it was no use. She couldn't do it. Wouldn't do it.

Just then the door burst open and Avery came in without knocking.

"Emma dear, I'm afraid I've run short of dust. Would you give me a couple of baubles from your bag?"

Emerald got her beaded bag and handed it to Avery, pretending meekness. She was used to acting as his bank. He'd gambled with her jewels before, and she got them or better jewels back, but she resented handing her trinkets over to him.

Avery poked through the bag and extracted a heavy gold watch and chain and a few stickpins and something else. Her new ear bobs.

"Not the garnet ear bobs! You just bought them for me. You didn't win them. I thought they were for me."

Avery shrugged. "But it doesn't do to lose more than one watch a night. They like to think they're getting your personal property. Let me have the ring then."

"The ring?"

"Yes, that plain gold one. It's not much, but it will do to sweeten the pot."

She hesitated, looking down at the ring. She liked this one because it reminded her of a wedding band. But if it was between the ring and the garnet ear bobs, she'd give him the ring.

When he was gone, she sat studying her left hand and thinking. There was a white mark where she had worn the ring on her third finger. If Hugh put a wedding band on her finger, you could bet he'd never ask for it back. Hugh would cherish her and take care of her. Hugh was a decent man and Austin Avery was a cheat and a crook. That was all there was to it. It didn't matter how she felt about him.

And if a woman wanted to win a respectable man, she had to find some way to win his respect.

She turned back to the mirror and slipped off the wrapper and smiled bravely at her naked reflection.

She would do it.

Chapter Thirty

Of all the plagues God had rained down upon man, Molly decided, smallpox was the worst. The pain was so severe the sick men raved with delirium. Caleb Dexter's convulsions were so violent, Molly and Hugh tied him to his bed in fear he would harm himself. On the third day, the eruptions appeared. Despite their efforts to lessen the outbreak with saline purgatives and tepid sponge baths, the pox spread like wildfire from face to neck, to wrists, spreading and growing until the men's entire bodies and even their tongues were covered with the angry sores.

When the eruptions began, the fever, pain and vomiting stopped, but the agony from the itching began. Molly and Hugh would hardly finish bathing one man with the soothing lotion of olive oil and lime water when the next would begin screaming and clawing at himself. By the eighth day it was necessary to tie all the men's hands to their beds to keep them from scratching. Molly shuddered to think of the scars they would bear for life.

The glands of salivation were somehow affected by the illness so the men sometimes choked and gagged for breath. Their faces swelled so their eyelids were forced almost closed. It became impossible to take their pulses, so swollen were their wrists. The men were so hideous, Molly could hardly bear to look at them. Sometimes the thought she might contract the disease made her tremble.

Molly was relieved when the doctor made his call on the fourth day and confirmed her feeling the disease was the milder, or discrete form. Even so, he cautioned, the men were in danger of death until after the secondary fever appeared on the eighth day of the eruption.

It was the smell of the disease Molly hated most. She thought at first it was just the smell of sick men unused to bathing, but no amount of washing seemed to relieve it, and finally Dr. Gillotz confirmed her suspicion that it was the smell of the disease itself. He seemed to find it rather amusing, saying if he were taken into a sick chamber blindfolded, he could diagnose smallpox by the smell. Molly could only describe it as a greasy odor, but she knew she would not forget it, nor the sweetness of the mountain air when she could steal a moment outside for greedy gulps of air fresh with pine.

Edwin helped by fetching and toting, but she saw he spent most of his days outside or with a neighboring family. It was a terrible time for Molly, a nightmare of washing bursting sores and carrying reeking bedpans and basins. Yet it was also a time of *peace*. She knew God could not send such an awful plague upon them if some good were not to come of it. The illness was so terrible, even the sins of so determined a sinner as Caleb Dexter must be expiated. And so, for hours at a time she was so busy with her work she forgot herself and her own guilt. The glass cage she had erected around herself to shield herself from Jake's death began to melt and she started to feel again. She allowed herself to admire the gentle strength and bravery of Hugh as he helped care for the men. It was not easy for him, she knew, to be confined to the cabin and woman's work, but he did what had to be done, and it was good to be working beside him.

It seemed natural and right for them to be a team. They worked well together, for they were often able to communicate with just a look or gesture, and thus could share their concern over the course of the illness without troubling the men with worried talk.

Yet there was tension between them. Though each longed for the comfort of the other's arms against the ugliness that surrounded them, they avoided touching. There was, of course, no privacy in the cabin with the sick men's eyes always following them. One of them always needed to be on duty, so they had to take turns slipping down to the other cabin for a few hours' sleep, and it seemed that if they so much as stepped outside together for a breath of fresh air while the men were sleeping, Caleb or one of the other miners would sense their absence and cry out for help.

It was more than lack of privacy that kept them from touching, however. They were held apart by the terrible things Hugh had said on the evening of Luther's death. Hugh did not remember that he had accused Molly of causing his brother's death or of saying that their love was like a curse; watching her as she nursed the sick men so patiently, he could think of her only as the most noble and holy of women, but he knew she seemed as forbidden to him now as when she had been Jake's wife. He never doubted that he loved her, but he sensed some nearly insurmountable barrier on the path between them. There seemed no easy way to reach her or to find his own salvation, and so for a time he gave up thinking of himself and his love and concentrated on what had to be done against the smallpox. It had become an enemy he could fight. He put his energy into hating the illness.

Molly knew it was Hugh's own guilt over his brother's death that had made him strike out against her. She understood guilt, and if it would lighten Hugh's burden for her to carry some of his, she was willing, for her own heart was already heavy with remorse, not just for her sin with Hugh, but for secret thoughts she hardly dared admit even to herself.

But Molly understood something else, and that was forgiveness. She had already forgiven Hugh for his terrible words, and as she began to have hope that the men would live, she thought that their act of love in saving the lives of men who were strangers to them must surely count for something against whatever wrong they had done in loving each other.

And that she loved Hugh she was at last able to say aloud, if only to herself. The words came to her a hundred times a day as their eyes met and they seemed to be standing, not in the horror of the sick room, but somewhere on a mountain top, alone with all the fresh and promising world before them. Even if he rejected her again, she knew she must someday tell him the words that her loyalty to Jake had so long imprisoned within her. He deserved to hear from her lips the expressions of love he had so freely given her from the beginning, and she determined she would tell him no matter what, even as she dreaded that moment, for she knew that in telling him she must at last reveal all her guilty secrets.

The eighth day of the outbreak seemed the worst, although the doctor assured them the crisis was passing. Molly and Hugh were exhausted and, as the secondary fever struck, the men became restless to the point of tremors and violent outbursts of temper. The doctor prescribed more purgatives and an opiate solution to keep them under control. By late afternoon the men had finally all descended into a drugged sleep, and Molly found time to start a fresh pot of soup. Hugh was dozing, leaning back in his chair, his feet propped up on the end of a bunk. She turned and studied him, thinking he looked younger since he'd stopped wearing a beard. He needed a shave, she noticed and thought she would heat some water for him. Perhaps she could also find time to wash her hair or slip down to the creek for a bath.

It was nice to have things peaceful again, she decided, the worst was surely over. She hummed as she put the kettle on and got Hugh's shaving things together. It seemed right somehow to be doing a wifely chore for Hugh. Perhaps when her hair was clean and pretty again, they might find time to sit outside the cabin together. She felt light and hopeful inside. And then came a knock at the door.

Hugh woke with a start and got to the door before Molly could maneuver her way around the bunks.

"My God, what are *you* doing here?" She heard him say as she hurried forward to see who he barred from entering the cabin.

It was Emerald O'Brien.

Molly noticed how different she looked. She was wearing a plain blue dress, her hair was tucked back demurely behind her ears, and her face looked as if it had been scrubbed. She could have played the role of Purity in a tableau.

"Stay back," Hugh warned. "Don't you know we've got smallpox in here?"

"I know. I came to help."

Molly gasped.

"That's good of you," Hugh said. "But you can't come in. Even if you've been vaccinated, you could get the disease. I can't let you take the chance."

"Send her away," Molly said sharply. "She shouldn't be here."

"Please, Hugh, Mrs. Lewis," Emerald looked to one and then the other beseechingly. "Please let me help. I've got nowhere else to go and I want to help."

"What do you mean?" Molly asked. "What happened to Mr. Avery?"

"I've left him," Emerald said with a determined narrowing of her green eyes. Then she lowered her lids demurely. "I've been living a life of sin with him, and I just can't go on. You're the only decent people I know and I hoped you'd take me in."

Molly stepped closer to the door. Some instinct warned her she must keep this woman outside. Hugh seemed just as determined not to let her enter the pest house. "I'll give you money for a hotel room," he said. "You can't stay here and expose yourself to smallpox."

"But I have to. Don't you see? It's the only way I can make up for what I've done. I thought he'd marry me. I know it's no excuse, but when he begged me to leave my mother for him, he promised we'd be married by

429

the captain of the ship. But once the ship was under-way, he came into my cabin and—"

"You don't have to tell us this," Hugh said. "Of course I'll help you get away from him. I'll get my pouch." As soon as he stepped away from the door, Emerald stepped inside.

"Don't!" Molly shouted, but it was too late. Once inside, Emerald breathed deeply of the contaminated air.

"There, I've done it," she announced. "Now it's too late to send me away. I've exposed myself and you'll have to let me stay and help nurse these poor men."

The men had been awakened by the commotion, and by the way they were looking at Emerald, Molly knew they too were thinking of how smallpox might ravage her face. A face with skin as white and perfect as alabaster against her jet black hair.

"You'll ruin your face," Molly said. "A woman like you can't afford to take chances." She knew she was speaking too pointedly, but she felt threatened by Emerald's presence in a way she could never admit before Hugh. "If you take the pox, no man will ever look at you again."

"That would be more than I deserve," Emerald said. "I have prayed that someday I will be forgiven for my sin with Austin Avery and might still be a wife and mother, but if God chooses to mark my face so no man will have me, then I guess it's justice."

Molly was appalled by the way the men, even Hugh, seemed to be taken in by what she said. Surely they couldn't believe her. It just didn't ring true to Molly. It was as if Emerald had known the crisis had passed before she came. She was about to step forward and

430

insist Emerald leave, when Emerald turned to her.

"It's you who have inspired me, Mrs. Lewis. You have set such a wonderful example staying here in Deadwood to nurse these poor homeless men. You have exhausted yourself and endangered your health. You look exhausted. Surely you will let me help you."

Molly felt herself wilt. How could she protest without the men and Hugh thinking she was a shrew? Without them knowing why she didn't want another woman around? Besides, she was exhausted. She must look awful. Too confused to argue, she hesitated, and the next thing she knew Emerald was standing at her stove, wearing her apron, and stirring her soup.

As she watched Emerald fluttering around the sick men that afternoon, Molly could not help thinking it was terribly convenient that Emerald O'Brien's conscience hadn't troubled her until the worst of the disease was over. She tried to force such ideas from her head. She knew she was too tired to think sensibly. She told herself she was being unreasonably suspicious of a woman who had never done her any harm. Besides, what motive could Emerald have for exposing herself to such a terrible disease if she were not truly repentant? Surely Molly could understand repentance.

Later that day there was another knock at the door. This time it was bold and insistent. Molly opened the door. There in his topcoat and ruffled shirt, his face more darkly handsome and solemn than she had ever seen it, it was Austin Avery.

"Is Emerald here?"

"She is," Molly said, "but you can't come in. We have smallpox within."

"Then what in God's name is Emerald doing here?

She left me a crazy note saying she was coming here and telling me not to follow her."

"Don't let him in," Emerald shouted from behind Molly.

"Emma O'Brien, get the hell out of there," Avery shouted around Molly who still blocked the doorway. "What do you think you're doing?"

"I told you," Emerald shouted. "I've left you and I've turned over a new leaf!"

"The devil you have!" Molly felt Avery was about to walk right over her as he continued to shout at Emerald. "Get the hell out of there!"

"Really, Mr. Avery," Molly said, "obscenity is not necessary."

"Close the door or he'll come in!" Even as Emerald shouted the warning, Hugh sprang up behind Molly, pulled her inside, and slammed the door in the gambler's face.

"Hugh!" Molly began, "I don't think this is our—"

"Bolt the door, quick," Emerald ran to the door. "He's crazy when he gets like this."

Molly watched as Hugh slammed down the bolt. "Stay out, Avery," he shouted through the door. "She's already exposed herself. It's too late."

There was the sound of fists beating on the door. "Emerald you little fool, don't you know what smallpox could do to your face? Come out of there!"

"Never!" Emerald turned so her back was against the door and stood with her arms outstretched so that, despite herself, Molly thought of Joan of Arc. Emerald's cheeks were flushed and her eyes were sparkling, tendrils of dark curling hair had come loose from her severe hairdo and ringed her face. "Never," she repeated. "I've given up our life of sin!"

"What are you talking about? You didn't mind it last night!"

Emerald blushed but held her head high. "I pretended, just as you deceived me. You promised to marry me and I believed you, but you are nothing but a scoundrel."

"Come back to me, Emerald."

"You don't get something for nothing, Austin Avery. That's what you always say!"

"All right then, damn it. I'll marry you."

When those words came through the door, Molly noticed Emerald seemed surprised. She seemed confused. So that was what she was after, Molly decided. Then, Emerald noticed how Hugh was watching her and, as if she were too caught up in the drama to think about what it meant, she repositioned herself with her back to the door and shouted her reply.

"Never! I'll never marry you. It's too late now. You had your chance. Now I'm going to be a decent woman and no one can stop me!"

Molly had a peculiar feeling she was watching a play. She looked at Hugh. He seemed totally absorbed in the drama. How could he be taken in so easily?

On the other side of the door, Austin Avery's face was contorted as he continued to pound on the door furiously. "You don't know, Em. You don't know what it can do to your face. I saw my sister after the war. The army got to her, gave her the clap. It was awful, just awful. Sores all over her pretty little face. Come out, Em. Don't let them ruin your face. Don't do it, Em."

Avery pounded on the door for some time before he

realized he had lost his control. He stopped then, his hand in mid-air, realizing what she had done to him. He had not bargained for this. He was not a man to be made a fool of by a woman.

"Have it your own way, then," he said quietly and turned and walked down the hill to where his hired rig waited. He hoped the driver wouldn't tell anyone what he had seen and heard. Austin Avery in such a state! He had let his emotions betray him for the first time since the war. It made him feel almost afraid. He had guarded his feeling so closely against just this kind of hurt. He should have known better. What did this woman mean to him after all? What made her so special she could not be replaced? Perhaps there was not another like her in Deadwood, but it did not mean she could not be replaced. He couldn't figure out why she had left him, but he didn't think it had anything to do with decency. He knew Emerald that well. He would have to sort it out later when he was calm. And when he had figured out why she had moved into the quarantined cabin with the sick men, then he would figure out how to get her back. That is, if he still wanted her.

When Austin Avery finally left, Molly somehow felt it was she who had been defeated. Emerald had ignored Avery's proposal of marriage, therefore she had to have some other motive for nursing the sick men. Molly could think of only two. Either Emerald O'Brien was truly repentant or she was after Hugh.

Molly was suddenly aware of how awful she must look. She had hardly combed her hair in a week and it hung in limp tendrils around her face. Her eyes must be circled with dark shadows and she knew her dress was wrinkled and stained. Emerald, in contrast, despite the demureness of her complexion and dress, looked as if she were ready to step out on a stage. How could Hugh not notice the difference between them? It was not just that Emerald was more beautiful, but Emerald was a woman of the world. A soiled dove, a tainted woman, true, but wouldn't a man like Hugh, a man with strong passions, be attracted to such a woman?

In the days that followed, Molly often found herself watching Emerald. Then watching Hugh watch Emerald. Emerald ministered to the sick men with the same gestures Molly had used, yet the men regarded Molly as a mother, while it was obvious, they were all falling in love with Emerald. Emerald obviously knew how to use her body in just the way Hugh had accused Molly of doing, to entice and trap a man. But Molly was certain that Emerald would never be trapped by her body. To a woman like Emerald, desire would be a way of getting what she wanted from a man and for pleasuring herself. It would never be the aching need that made Molly want to cast aside all sense of integrity to beg Hugh's touch. Molly was tempted to try to be like Emerald, to beat the vixen at her own game and win back Hugh's love. But guilt and the memory of Hugh's accusations held her back as did her image of herself as a lady. Being a lady and remembering that she came from decent folk had sustained her during her years on the homestead; it had kept her from Hugh's arms during the weeks they were on the trail, and prevented her running away from him when they reached Deadwood. Now it guarded her from a confrontation with Emerald and from telling Hugh how entirely she still longed for him. She had been taught all her life that a good woman did not take action but only hoped and prayed for what she wanted and, even in her prayers, asked that God's will and not her own be done. Destiny still seemed to promise that she and Hugh belonged together; that they had not come this far for him to be won away by a green-eyed Jezebel, but Molly still believed that behaving as a lady brought rewards, so she took comfort in her work with the sick men and asked nothing for herself; but in the back-breaking and often loathsome labor, she grew curiously stronger. Her sense of guilt and sin was worn away by the good she knew she accomplished. If there was truth in Hugh's accusation that three men were dead because of her, there was greater truth in the certainty that because of her, four men would live.

The smallpox ran its course. Although his delirium had been severe, once it passed, Caleb Dexter's natural vigor asserted itself and the old man made a speedy recovery. Days before the other men were able to venture out of their beds to again breathe fresh mountain air or bathe their weakened bodies in the creek, Caleb Dexter was able to make brief visits to the mine to ensure that the day laborers Austin Avery supplied were keeping the mine operational for the anticipated arrival of the Eastern capitalists. Occasionally Avery drove a buggy out to the mine on his own inspection tour. Molly suspected he and the old man were plotting something in their meetings held within the confines of the shuttered buggy, but when she expressed her suspicions to Hugh, he all but said that since she had sold out to Avery and was so determined to leave

Deadwood she should mind her own business. Living and working together with nothing settled between them and each waiting for the other to somehow bridge the gulf of hurt and misunderstanding made them increasingly terse with each other.

And the presence of Caleb Dexter was more abrasive than ever. He was intensely grateful to Molly for saving his life and followed her with his eyes like some mangey old dog that had outlived its usefulness and which, except for its devotion, one would have taken outside and shot. He seemed to take morose pleasure in lying about Molly's cabin, picking at his scabs and greeting each sick man's return to consciousness with a loud recounting of any gory aspects of the disease the poor man might have managed to forget in his delirium. Finally Hugh persuaded him to move back to their old cabin where he could more closely supervise the mine.

Edwin, however, was delighted that their saving of the old man's life seemed to have burdened them with him forever. He took to "camping out" at the smaller cabin when he was not playing Indians with the neighbor's family. Since he had discovered the companionship of Deadwood's growing gang of children, he had run wild, and Molly was too exhausted to care.

To everyone's great relief the vaccine arrived and most of the city lined up for vaccination. Deadwood also ecstatically greeted the arrival of the first stagecoach September 25, and at the end of the month the *Pioneer* announced the news they had waited for all summer: The Sioux, under protest, had signed a treaty at the Red Cloud Agency to cede the Black Hills for all time. The city erupted into a joyous celebration, but the news was barely mentioned at the Lucky Six. The smallpox sufferers were too weak for celebration, and Hugh was only too aware that with the crisis passed and safe transportation available, Molly and Edwin were free to leave. He was aware, too, that summer was over and his Black Hills adventure coming to an end that seemed to offer no sense of victory but only more questions as to what it all had meant, if, indeed, it meant anything.

The nights turned suddenly cold, reminding them that Deadwood was a city built in the cleft of a mountain and not a place for anyone not already securely established to attempt to winter. Hugh knew decisions must be made, but he felt unable to act. The loss of his brother and his alienation from Molly had robbed him of the certainties that had driven him all summer, and he asked himself if the Black Hills were not to bring them good fortune and if he and Molly did not belong together, what was there left to believe in and to act upon?

As for Molly, her work load lifted as the men grew stronger, but her spirits grew heavier as the time of decision neared. When the doctor vaccinated them, he assured her that the men were nearly well, and that those who were vaccinated were in no further danger of contracting the disease, though they might antici-pate severe reactions to the shot. Molly's arm was soon so tender she could hardly lift it, and the convalescing men, who had weakly discussed returning to their own cabin for several days, persuaded Hugh to let them go so that the women could rest from their own ordeal. Caleb Dexter rented a wagon and he and Hugh helped the men aboard; they departed with great rounds of

438

thanks and promises of undying devotion. Emerald accepted their accolades as if she alone had saved them, and Molly could hardly enjoy her own satisfaction at seeing the men well, so annoyed was she by the pretty pose Emerald assumed as she waved the men out of sight with a lace handkerchief vigorously wielded by the same arm she'd complained all morning she could hardly lift.

When they were finally alone except for Edwin, it occurred to Molly that she might soon be rid of the temptress, but no sooner were the men out of sight than Emerald fluttered about exclaiming that she would just stay another day or two to help Molly return her cabin to order and recover from her reaction to the vaccination. She even offered to help Molly pack.

That suggestion nearly impelled Molly to throw Emerald off the property, but Edwin was as entranced as the other males with Emerald's portrayal of charity, and Molly did not want him to see his own mother as a shrew. Nor did she want Emerald running to Hugh when he returned with tales of Molly's ingratitude. Surely the woman would soon leave of her own accord, and surely once she was gone Hugh would find no excuse to follow her to town.

The sudden realization that Hugh might actually seek Emerald in Deadwood and that the two would surely be together if Molly took the stage east stunned Molly. She did not trust herself to look at Emerald who had prettily arranged herself for a nap in Molly's own bed. Instead she went to the narrow window of the cabin and watched for Hugh to come back, though she knew it was hours too early. She decided she must think of a gentle way to let him know he had no need of Emerald, for Molly was ready to forgive him for what he had said if only he would forgive her for what he thought she had done, but she must accomplish this without making a fool of herself as she once had done by going to Hugh in the night.

While she was thinking she caught sight of movement down at the mine. It was the gambler's familiar rig followed by a buckboard. She knew by the flutter of Emerald's eyelids that she heard when she announced, "Austin Avery's here again."

Emerald always feigned annoyance at the gambler's visits to the mine, but Molly noticed that she always made sure that the man she called a villain would be certain to catch a glimpse of her in a pose calculated to be both demure and seductive.

"He's got someone with him in another wagon," Molly added. "A fat man in a top coat and hat."

"A capitalist!" Emerald shrieked as she shot out of the bed and joined Molly at the window. "Avery's found a genuine capitalist and Hugh's going to be rich at last!"

Molly turned and looked at her curiously and Emerald, sensing that she had said too much, backed away from the window. "I'll need to change into something more presentable; perhaps you had better run see what they want. I'm sure Hugh will want to know."

"Yes, it's curious that they've chosen to arrive when Hugh and Caleb Dexter are gone."

"Well, if it's mining business, I'm sure Austin can handle it." She stripped off the simple cotton gown she had been wearing and began rummaging in her trunk which was crowded under the kitchen table of the little cabin. "Now, I'm sure Austin will beg to see me, hoping that I will come back to him and of course I won't but —"

"But you'll want to look desirable when you tell him that," Molly's voice was sharp.

Emerald looked up at Molly from the trunk, her arms full of silk and lacy things and her plump breasts spilling over the top of her chemise.

"Well, I think perhaps I should talk to him. He does still have my other trunk and my things at the hotel, and I'm dying to know what he's cooked up with the capitalist!"

"And you think he'll tell you more than he'll tell me or Hugh?"

"Well, he did beg me to marry him," Emerald sat back and gave Molly her most innocent look, but the Mona Lisa smile betrayed her. "Besides, Hugh isn't here and you're no longer a partner in the mine and will be leaving town in a day or two, so since I'll be in Deadwood, it seems only right that I try to protect Hugh's interests."

Molly was furious. She wanted to throw herself at the woman, tear up all her lovely clothes, pull the adorable, fat curls away from her perfect face and scratch out those bewitching green eyes. She allowed herself the fantasy, but she knew it would be reducing herself to the woman's level and would make Hugh and Edwin think she was a madwoman. Instead she clasped her fists until her fingernails dug into her palm and strode to the cabin door. Before she left, she turned back to Emerald and said in a tone she intended as a threat. "It's not decided that I'm to leave Deadwood. I belong here more than you."

441

Molly did not so much as get the satisfaction of knowing Emerald had heard the determination in her voice, for Emerald ignored Molly's declaration and instead followed her to the door and called after her, "I'm going to sun myself on the big rock by the watering hole. Tell Austin when he asks for me."

Austin Avery did not use the word when he introduced Molly to the portly man standing outside the mine, but it was evident by the cut of Carson D. McPherson's city clothing and the size of his girth that he was indeed, a capitalist. He might never name the eastern firm he represented, but they all knew that if he was pleased with what he found at the Lucky Six they would be gratefully obliged to sell their dreams to a company with the capital to bring in the machinery and manpower needed for profitable and safe hard-rock mining. Despite the fact that even before Jake's death Molly had hated and feared the mine, she resented the man for the reality that he might so easily acquire that which they had earned with their hopes, their labors and their very lives. His manner was presumptive.

"I'll be gathering the samples myself, of course." He addressed his remarks to Avery as if her presence did not matter. "One wagon load will be sufficient for the mill, so just have your men lower me into the mine and load the samples as I direct."

The gambler was all ingratiatory smiles as he helped the portly capitalist into the set of white workman's coveralls McPherson had brought along to protect his fine clothes and watched the workmen lower him into the shaft, but Molly knew he must be irritated that the man's insistence at gathering the samples himself. She knew there were all sorts of ways of salting ore samples with gold to make it appear that a mine bore high grade ore, and she was convinced that Austin Avery would not be beyond perpetrating some scheme to ensure that the Lucky Six would be one of the mines bought up by McPherson. But the gambler appeared strangely indifferent to the mine once McPherson was out of sight.

"And where might I find Miss O'Brien?" he asked, almost as if he knew she'd be posed waiting somewhere for him. Molly directed him to the secret place on the creek where the men bathed since Hugh had diverted the creek into one of their old prospect holes. She watched him retreat in the buggy, hoping that when he returned he would have Emerald with him. She was sure the unscrupulous pair deserved each other and that Emerald would try mightily to manipulate the gambler to serve her own ends. Protect Hugh's interests, indeed, she thought angrily. She was certain that Emerald cared for no one but herself. Molly would stay at the mine, watching and waiting and doing what she could to be certain that Hugh would not be cheated.

Emerald was actually concerned about Hugh's interests. It was crucial that Austin Avery's scheme to make a fortune on the Lucky Six include Hugh, for it was crucial that Hugh become rich. Emerald had removed herself from much of the suffering and ugliness of the smallpox epidemic by reminding herself that she was only playing a part, and she had been careful not to volunteer her services until the worst of the symptoms had passed. Nevertheless, the horrors of the illness had been much worse than she had expected, and she was determined that the prize for her efforts be worthy of such a fine performance. She had convinced Hugh that she was not only repentant but a veritable angel of mercy worthy of any man's love, and she had convinced herself that not only would marriage to Hugh bring her respectability, it would be a delightful prospect in itself. She was, however, thoroughly disgusted with the squalor and discomfort of her brief return to respectability. She wanted Hugh, but she wanted him rich. And she did not intend to wait much longer. She'd had enough of poverty and dirt-floored cabins.

That Hugh wanted her and was ripe for the picking she was sure. The trick was to reel him in while at the same time eliminating Molly and making certain that Hugh would be able to support Emerald in the style in which Austin Avery had accustomed her. She had been delighted when Molly announced that Avery was back with a capitalist. She had avoided any discussion with the gambler during his previous visits to the mine, though she'd always let him catch a glimpse of herself just to tease him. Now it was essential that she discover just what it was he plotted. Still, she was surprised that seeing him brought not just the satisfaction of knowing she'd soon have some information wheedled from him, but a strange sort of rushing pleasure. Being around Hugh made her feel warm all over, but the sight of Austin Avery made her blush inside.

It would never do to let him know that his presence excited her, so she concentrated on her pose and pretended not to see him. She was wearing a dressing gown of delicate layers of pale green batiste and her hair was down. She sat on the large rock which overlooked the swimming hole, brushing her hair, her gown slightly asunder so the sun could momentarily enjoy her delicate skin.

"You look lovely posed like that, my dear," he said while she pretended surprise at the sound of his voice. "You're a regular Psyche, goddess of nature and love."

"Why, Avery, how gentlemanly a compliment," she purred. What an apt description, she thought. She'd have to find some opportunity for Hugh to see her posed against nature this way.

"And now that the preliminaries are over, come and get into my buggy. I must talk to you."

"How dare you order me about that way! You forget I no longer belong to you. And if you think I would step into that buggy with you so that you might close the curtains about us and do what you would with me—"

"Emerald, I don't have time for your pretty fantasies today, nor for doing what I 'would' with you. I've got to talk to you about selling the mine, and I want to do it before Hugh gets back and sees us together."

Emerald glanced about uneasily. No, it would never do for Hugh to see them together. "Why do you want to tell me about selling the mine? What do your have in mind?"

"Come with me and I'll tell you. If you want your precious Hugh to be a rich man, then I'll need your help."

He had said the magic words and soon she was sitting beside him as he drove the buggy farther up the trail and then off into the woods. He stopped the horse and pulled the curtains around them so that it was deliciously private inside.

"I don't think we need to be this private. Are you sure you don't mean to ravish me again?"

"Ah, Emerald, I'm sure you hope so," he said taking her into his arms and kissing her neck at the open front of her dressing gown. "And I shall if there is time, I promise you, but I've got to ask you to help me tomorrow."

She pushed him just far enough away that she could look into his eyes, yet still feel his hands on her body. How strange that his promise to ravish her should send such delightful shivers through her body! Still, he'd not have her without a fight, though she must be careful not to protest so loudly that someone from the mine would hear and stop him.

"How could I help you and—why *should* I help you?"

"You can help me by keeping Hugh away from town tomorrow morning. And why you should help me is so that Hugh doesn't blunder in and foul up the assay I've arranged for the Lucky Six."

"So you've salted the samples. Hugh will never stand for that. I've heard him telling Caleb Dexter that when the samples are taken from the mine he's not to attempt to high-grade the ore. Hugh wants everything to be done right."

"And Hugh's a fool and you know it. Something as important as selling a mine can't be left to chance."

"But when Hugh comes back and discovers you've already taken the samples, he'll know something's fishy."

"No, he won't. I carefully instructed the laborers to let McPherson select his own ore from anywhere in the stope. Hugh will know there's no way I could have salted the whole stope. He'll believe that I did not salt

446

the mine."

"But of course you did."

"I most certainly did not. McPherson is much too smart to fall for something as obvious as high-grading the samples or shooting gold dust with a shotgun into the stope. I've something much more clever in mind, but I need your help."

"To keep Hugh away from the assay office tomorrow morning."

"Precisely, my dear. I've told the laborers to instruct him that the assay is set for noon if he cares to be present. But by noon the assay will be completed, a very favorable assay, I might add, and I'll be on my way back to the mine with McPherson's generous offer to buy the Lucky Six."

"But why should I help you to deceive Hugh?"

"For his own good, my dear. You know he's much too noble to allow me to help him get rich, and you know you want him to marry you despite the fact he's so obviously destined for Molly Lewis, and you know you'd never be happy with a poor man, so—"

"So you're resigned." Emerald had never felt so hurt. "You'll let Hugh have me?"

"Of course not, my dear. I intend to have you back myself. We both know where you're destined to end, but if you intend to take your chances on playing respectable in the meantime, you may as well do me some good. I'd cut Hugh out of the deal in a minute if I could get him to sell out to me, but he won't, so I've no choice but to bring him on my coattails. And if he gets a taste of you in the meantime, well, I'm sure it will do you no great damage and perhaps only serve to convince you that you're not made for a great lumbering fool like Hugh."

"And I suppose you think I'm made for you?"

"Yes, Emerald, for my hands which even now you let touch your breasts, and for my mouth which will soon be kissing you again, and for the rest of me which has been ready for you since you first stepped inside this carriage, and don't pretend you haven't noticed."

"Oh, Avery, you're a beast," she began to struggle prettily against his hands which were hot and insistent through the foamy green layers of her gown. Her own squirming against the smooth leather seat of the buggy excited her almost as much as his hands until he touched the places only Austin Avery seemed to understand. And then she stopped being afraid that Hugh would discover them together and was only afraid that Austin Avery would heed the protests she must make.

From her vantage point at the mine, Molly was surprised when Austin Avery's buggy returned to the cabin. She thought he must have gone on to town by now. She was even more surprised to see Emerald's figure slipping out of the buggy and into the cabin. She hoped the gambler had persuaded her to return to him, but he didn't linger at the cabin or go in to fetch her trunk; instead he drove back to where Molly stood.

"You've missed McPherson," she told him. "He just left with a wagon load of ore."

"That's quite all right," he said, leaning out of the buggy and removing his hat to her in a sweeping gesture. "I needed the opportunity to try to persuade Miss O'Brien to return to me."

"And did you?" She could not keep the anxiety out

of her voice.

"Not yet. She still has her pretentions of achieving some notion of respectability I can't give her. But I've got faith she'll return. For I have faith in you, Mrs. Lewis."

"In me? What do you mean?"

"Just that my gambler's intuition has told me that it's you Hugh Everett really wants and it's you he belongs with. And I think that if you're pressed hard enough, you'll see that you win him."

"I don't know what you're talking about," Molly was astonished by his boldness and made herself answer with ladylike evasiveness, but she was charged to know he was on her side and thought she still had a chance to win Hugh.

"I think you do, but I must advise you that you must play to win, and you must do it soon or you'll lose him to Emerald and that would be disaster for all of us."

"But how?" she asked, forgetting herself. "How do I play to win?"

"Like a woman. You use the cards and the tricks that fate has dealt you. Haven't you learned anything from watching that little baggage in there?"

"I could never do that. I could never win Hugh through some trick."

"Then be honest. I've always said honesty pays." He picked up the reins and prepared to drive away.

"Just remember, Mrs. Lewis, that if by some stroke of luck Hugh Everett should come into a piece of cash, say enough to set up housekeeping in style, that it's you who deserves to have him. And remember too that you're holding all the cards to win him if you'll just play them. Oh, and when the time is right, don't be afraid to get rid of that little baggage up there in your cabin."

He started to turn the horse to leave, but Molly was moved to reach out and stop him. "You really love her, don't you? You'd take her back despite the awful things between you, wouldn't you? You wouldn't let the past stop you from having the woman you love?"

"That's a bit romantic a view, Mrs. Lewis," he said looking up at the cabin with a speculative smile on his face. "Let's just say two of a kind belong together."

Molly stepped back and he raised the reins again, then turned back to her with another of his secret little smiles. "Do me a favor would you? Ask Miss O'Brien to truly think over what happened this afternoon. Tell her I cherished the time we spent together."

Molly stood in the clearing before the mine and watched him drive away. She turned back and looked at her cabin, knowing Emerald probably watched her from the window. Down the road somewhere Hugh would soon be coming home. She sensed they were nearing a turning point. That fate was about to deal the final hand in their summer of '76. And that whether or not she and Hugh fulfilled any portion of the promise that had brought them to the Black Hills was somehow up to her.

Chapter Thirty-one

Emerald was up and dressed before Molly awoke the next morning, if one could call wearing the delicate wrappings of silk and lace being dressed. Molly opened her eyes just as Emerald slipped into her frothy green batiste dressing gown and so caught a glimpse of her brief chemise and drawers, a matched set of silk embroidered with lace insets and fitted with tiny tucks and gathers to accentutate the curves of her small but perfect body.

Molly closed her eyes against the realization that her jealousy of Emerald extended to envy of the woman's undergarments. Molly's hasty marriage had not merited a bridal trousseau, and the years at the homestead had starved her for the touch of anything pretty. When she had first seen Emerald in the green velvet costume, she had been threatened by the temptation to Hugh; yet had longed to touch once again the softness of garments made not for sturdy duty but for pleasure in themselves. She could not blame Hugh for wanting Emerald when Molly herself ached to see such beauty. Nor could she be comforted in knowing that Emerald had earned her pretty things with sin, for Molly, too, had fallen and had nothing to show for it but the memory of glorious moments that seemed destined never to be repeated.

And now, seeing the confident way Emerald dressed, as if certain of winning what she wanted, Molly wondered if there was any use in fighting. Perhaps she should just give up Hugh and her place in Deadwood and go home to her parents. Emerald seemed to be counting on that. But leaving would be disloyal to all she had struggled for that summer. Even if she could never overcome the terrible rift between them, abandoning Hugh to this woman and the gambler's plots would make a travesty of all their sacrifices and even of the graves on Mt. Moriah.

Edwin stirred beside her in the big double bed they'd shared since Emerald had taken over his pallet on the floor. Molly touched his face as he woke and remembered she had been given one thing which was more beautiful than anything Emerald possessed, and that was her child. Hugh's son. And he was reason enough to continue the struggle.

She turned and faced Emerald. "You're very elegant for morning. Are you planning something?"

"Just to help you get this poor little cabin back to order and pack for your journey," Emerald smiled sweetly as if she had not heard the sharpness in Molly's voice. "But doesn't it cheer you to put on something pretty after such an ordeal as saving the lives of all those poor, dear men? It's just good to be myself again after all that sickness. And I was so exhausted last night I didn't get to talk to Hugh about the sale of the mine."

"Yes, I'm sure your visit with Mr. Avery must have

been quite an ordeal."

Emerald blushed and Molly knew she had hit a nerve. Emerald had taken to bed immediately after the gambler's visit, but to Molly her expression had been strangely serene for a homeless woman recovering from so many catastrophes. When Hugh returned she started to express her suspicions, but Hugh was full of solitious concern for Emerald and implied that Molly should have protected her from Avery's advances. He was also suspicious that Avery had shown up with the long-awaited capitalist and taken ore samples in his absence, but the laborers assured Hugh that the sampling procedure had been honest, and that Hugh was invited to the test at the assay office at noon.

Remembering that it was the day of the test inspired Molly with the thought she might accompany Hugh to the assay office. It seemed her place as one of the original owners to be present for the test which would determine the mine's worth. Surely Edwin could be sent to the neighbors once more, and Emerald could find no excuse to intrude on mine business; so that afterwards, when they were alone and at last knew the value of their labors, she could find the courage to ask Hugh if they still have hope of a future together. If Hugh were rid of the mine and his obsession with it, then she might persuade him to return East with her. There in a civilized place, the calamities of Deadwood and their terrible journey could be forgotten and they could regain the love begun in innocence so long ago.

Feeling she had a plan and hope at last, Molly arose quickly, despite the throbbing pain in her arm and the feverish, unsettled feeling that had plagued her since the vaccination. She dressed in her everyday dress,

453

thinking she would heat an iron and make her better dress more presentable. She realized she might even take a little of her gold dust and buy decent traveling clothes for herself and Edwin. She had more than enough for her stagecoach and rail tickets home, so why not honor Jake's memory by arriving home looking like the widow of a man who had at last succeeded? Hugh would be presented as Jake's former partner and gallant escort to safety, and when, after a decent period of mourning for Jake, she married Hugh, her family would surely sense the rightness of the union and would someday even accept Edwin calling Hugh father. Then she would be happy at last.

"Edwin, please run fetch Hugh. Breakfast will be ready in a few minutes."

It was Emerald who had given the order, usurping Molly's position, and Edwin's hurrying to please her hurt his mother almost as much as the fact he had confided in her he thought Emerald "the prettiest woman in the whole world."

Steady, Molly told herself. Behave decently and in a few more hours she'll surely be gone, and Hugh will know you're a lady and not an impulsive wanton who has no control.

Molly forced herself to remain calm, but inside she was full of swirling energy-draining anger. Hugh arrived for breakfast fresh from a bath at the creek, little drops of water glimmering from his sun-bleached hair and his skin ruddy from the cold and the towel rubbing. It was all she could do not to run to him and throw herself into his arms. Emerald played the part of hostess as she seated them for breakfast, somehow superseding Molly's place at the end of the table across from Hugh, so that Molly was made to feel out of place at her own table. They ate their oatmeal in silence and then when a lunch had been packed for Edwin and he'd been sent off to the neighbor's and the adults lingered over more coffee, Emerald made her move.

"I'll bet the creek was just lovely this morning," Emerald trilled. "As I was sitting beside it yesterday I could not help thinking how lovely it would be to bathe there in the warmth of the sunlight instead of having to sneak down at night and shiver and stumble about."

"The creek is in full view of the road, Emerald. You know why only the men can bathe there in daylight." Molly hoped she didn't sound as shrewish as she felt. She too had longed to enjoy the cold clear water of the creek when the sun warmed and dappled the rocks.

"Goodness, I know it wouldn't be quite proper. But I was thinking if I kept my chemise on and went in mid-morning when there's hardly ever anyone on the road—"

"I hardly think that would be a good idea. You wouldn't want to get your pretty things all wet and muddy, and besides, now that your nursing services are no longer needed, you can move back to the hotel and take your baths in the style to which I'm sure you are accustomed."

"Molly, you don't sound very hospitable," Hugh said. "Emerald came to us for help in leaving Avery; we can hardly expect her to move to a hotel where she'd be at the man's mercy, or at any man's mercy for that matter."

"Oh, Hugh, you are so considerate, but Molly is quite right. I've overstayed my usefulness here. I've no

455

real place here, or anywhere for that matter. I'm sure my mother will never forgive me for running away with Avery, even if I did believe he would marry me. But I've a few jewels I can sell, and I'm sure I'll be quite safe in a hotel, especially if you'd escort me to one, Hugh. I think if the proprietor knew that you were my protector, he'd be sure the men would respect me. Perhaps you could escort me to town when you go in for the assay this afternoon."

"Hugh! I thought *we* would go together," Molly cried.

"Well, there's no reason we can't all go," Hugh said brightly. "If there's something to celebrate, we can make a day of it."

"Yes, and we can stop at the stage depot and make Molly's travel arrangements."

"Travel arrangements?" Hugh looked at Molly strangely. "I'd almost let myself forget. You swore before Caleb Dexter got sick that you'd go home. Are you still determined?"

They both looked at her and Molly felt herself blushing and confused. How could she announce before Emerald that her travel plans, her whole future, in fact depended on Hugh? And how could she now suggest Emerald continue living with her just because she finally realized the little vixen would be a greater threat in a hotel room in Deadwood than sharing her cabin?

"I'm not sure what I'll do," she said quietly but firmly. "I was too busy with the sick men to make any plans. And what of your plans, Hugh? Will you still go East as you planned?"

"Go East? Why? I have no home there. I have no

home anywhere. If Luther were here, I'd probably have taken him back to Nebraska, but I can't go there now," Hugh's voice was full of emotion, but he kept his eyes on his tin mug as he spoke thoughtfully. "It's strange; all our hopes have been based on making our fortunes in that mine, and now when I think it might happen today, that I might be rid of the mine today and have the cash in hand to go anywhere, why I can't think of anywhere I want to go or anything I want, except—"

His voice trailed off but he was looking directly at her, and Molly thrilled to see the old longing there. He had wanted her from the beginning and he had not forgotten how love had bound them together on that glorious night in July. In her joy at seeing the love still in his eyes, Molly pushed away the sinking feeling she'd experienced when he'd said he'd not return East. Surely she could persuade him that only in a civilized place could they overcome the loss and guilt that had come between them.

"Oh, Hugh," Emerald intruded, "I'm sure you'll think of many things you want once you're rich. You've just never had the freedom before to discover what it is you really desire."

She isn't going to give up, Molly realized. She can see that Hugh loves me, but that won't stop her for a minute. Molly realized she must take a stronger stance. She remembered the gambler and what he had said about playing to win.

"By the way, Emerald," Molly said sweetly, "Before he left, Mr. Avery asked me to give you a message. I'm sure it's not important, but he did say to remind you to think about the conversation you had with him. He said it meant a great deal to him."

"Oh the beast!" Emerald blushed furiously. Molly was surprised by her reaction.

"What happened? Did he upset you?" Hugh demanded.

Emerald nodded prettily, as if he relieved Hugh had supplied his own explanation.

"That man's as unscrupulous as they come." Hugh banged his cup down on the table. "I hate having my name associated with his as partners in the mine. I've a good mind to go to town early and warn McPherson about him."

"Oh don't do that," Emerald was again agitated. "You could spoil everything! I mean, it wouldn't do for you to question your partner's honesty before the capitalist. You could make McPherson refuse to even give the mine a fair test. Besides Austin assured me that he'll not try to cheat you out of your share of the mine sale."

"That's because he doesn't dare try anything with me. He knows I'd call his bluff. Still, I might as well go into town early. Neither Caleb Dexter nor the laborers have shown up for work, so I can't get anything done here. I'll go make sure of the time and place for the test, and then I can rent a buggy to fetch you ladies into town later."

"No, Hugh, don't do that," Emerald quickly interjected. "Why there's lots to be done here. All the sick beds to be carried away and I know poor Molly has a ton of washing to boil, and I'd like a bath."

"Well, I'll need to haul water for you. Molly, do you want a fire in the yard for your wash? That would keep the cabin cooler and it wouldn't be much extra to heat some water for Emerald to bathe."

"No, no, I can't make extra work for Molly. I'll just bathe in the creek. It would be so lovely and cool and I feel so hot and sticky since the vaccination, and my poor arm is so sore, and I'm sure I'll be safe there if you'll stay here, Hugh, watching over me while you fetch Molly's wash water."

"Why, of course, Emerald, there's no reason why being a woman should deprive you of a cool bath. I'll fetch along my needle gun and if someone should come along the road, I'll be sure they don't tarry."

While Molly does the wash! Why Hugh was taking her as much for granted as had Jake! Molly burned in shame and anger that he should be taken in so easily. Of course, he would behave as a gentleman, keeping his back turned while Emerald went to the creek, but if the vixen should pretend to slip on a rock or see a snake and make a little shriek, why then of course Hugh would have to investigate, and once she had him alone and he saw her as good as naked with the wet silk clinging to her body. Well, Hugh was no saint. Molly knew that.

But there seemed to be nothing she could do to stop it. Hugh got the water buckets and carried her wash tub out to the yard without even asking her if she meant to do a wash on a day that was supposed to be special and while she herself was aching and feverish from the vaccination.

And Emerald, she was like a cat into the cream as she gathered her scented soap and Molly's last clean towel. They were gone before she could think what to say or do to stop them and she could only sit at her kitchen table and stew.

459

And wait. She thought. Here I am again waiting. Like I waited to see if I could really be pregnant, and I waited for Hugh to come back, and I waited to see if I could not be a good wife to Jake if I but tried harder, and I waited in the wagon while the men fought the Indians and Pearson came to rape me, and I waited and I waited and I waited when Hugh and Jake were lost in the mine and they said only one of them was alive.

And then she knew she would wait no more. And she remembered what Austin Avery had said about beating the little baggage at her own tricks. And she stood up and took off her plain cotton dress and examined herself in her simple muslin chemise. It was not inset with lace and tucks like Emerald's to show the outlines of her body, but when it was wet she, too, would be as good as naked. And hers was the body Hugh had loved and would love again.

He was startled to see her. He was sitting on a stump near the road, not even taking a place on the big rock overlooking the waterhole, but cleaning his rifle and keeping watch over the road.

"Molly, what are you doing out here in your shift?"

"I'm going to take a bath. I'm hot and feverish too, and I've as much right as any man and certainly as much right as that woman to enjoy a bath in broad daylight."

She strode past him and made her way down the steep path to the creekside. Her slippers sent little bits of gravel skittering down the bank before her and Emerald, wading in the creek with the water just reaching the ruffled hems of her underdrawers heard the noise and looked up smiling. When she saw it was

Molly, her expression changed.

"Don't mind me," Molly said sweetly, removing her shoes and stepping into the cold water. Having come this far, she realized she wasn't sure of her next step, but, oh, it felt right to be taking action at last. She sat on the warm surface of a rock in the middle of the creek and began to bathe her arms and legs in the deep water which swirled around it. Getting into the deeper water of the icy mountain stream was always a challenge best begun by cooling one's limbs. Her arm was swollen, hot and sore, from the vaccination; the center already forming the ugly sore that would eventually match the scar from her previous innoculation. She told herself that her body, even with the scars and marks of child-bearing, was as desirable as Emerald's, but she was not certain. Feeling again the foolish jealousy of the morning, Molly studied Emerald. Emerald's body was round and firm, her skin flawless, her hands unmarked from work, her arms and neck as perfect and graceful as a swan's.

Molly stared harder. Something was wrong. Something out of place. Emerald was flawless. Unmarked. Emerald was unmarked.

"Emerald," she said quietly. "Let me see your arm. Where is your scar, Emerald? Where is the awful sore from your new vaccination? You've been complaining all week how sick the shot made you; you almost fainted when it was your turn to be innoculated; now, tell me — why isn't your arm swollen and throbbing like mine?"

Emerald backed away from Molly, stepping deeper into the creek, her pantaloons now wet to the knee. She tried to turn away, to conceal her arm with the other hand, but it was no use, Molly knew and followed her into the creek, oblivious to the soaking of her own chemise.

"All right. It didn't take. So my vaccination didn't take. That's no crime is it?" Emerald stood proudly at the edge of the deeper pool of water, thrusting forward her breasts and flaunting the perfection of her white arms and shoulders. Molly came closer.

"But you don't have any mark at all on your arms. If you were vaccinated before, where is your scar? And you must have been vaccinated before or you'd never have dared nurse those men. The doctor said you were in terrible danger anyway. That you could be scarred for life. All the men feared for you. Hugh feared for you. Even I feared for you!"

"I was vaccinated on my hip. Yes, on my hip where no one can see. My mother made the doctor do it that way because she was so proud of my beauty."

"Show me."

"Molly!" Emerald backed away, slipped on the rocky creek bottom and fell into the water. She came up soaked and shrieking, her hair streaming about her face and her nipples showing hard and pink through the wet silk. As she tried to wipe the streaming curtain of wet hair away from her face, she slipped and went under again, screaming.

Molly waded deep into the water, wetting her own chemise to the shoulders and grabbed Emerald by the hair, pulling her out of the water. "Show me!" she demanded of the sputtering woman, still holding her by the hair. "I'm a woman, there can be no sin in showing me. You've shown yourself to Austin Avery and to half the men in Deadwood on the stage, and you'd show yourself to Hugh, so show me!"

"What's going on here?"

It was Hugh, standing on the bank, clutching his rifle, his face full of alarm.

"Save me, Hugh!" Emerald screamed. "She's trying to drown me!"

For just an instant, the lady in Molly reacted in horror, realizing the picture they made standing now in hip-high water, Emerald's hair soaked and tangled about her face even as Molly let go of her, Molly's streaming wet around her shoulders; both of them covered only by wet and clinging cloth, their breasts high and nipples hard from the icy water. For an instant she was tempted to hide herself with her arms or retreat into the deep water. Instead she held herself proud and faced Hugh squarely as she spoke.

"Nonsense! She slipped in the water and I pulled her out."

"Don't listen to her. She tried to kill me! She's wanted me dead from the first!"

"Emerald, stop being hysterical!" Hugh set the rifle down on the bank and stood with his hands on his hips. "Will one of you please tell me what's happened."

"I confronted her. I asked her to show me the evidence she's been vaccinated. I discovered she's lied to us and let us think she was in danger nursing the sick men, but look, her arm isn't sore and she's got no old scar either. She claims she was vaccinated on her hip, so I asked her to show me."

"Why she's right, Emerald. You haven't a mark on you. I saw the doctor vaccinate you myself. Why aren't you sick like the rest of us?"

"Because she's a witch, that's why!"

"Now who's hysterical?" Emerald shouted. "I told you I was vaccinated on my hip so that I'd not have an ugly scar like you do. You're just jealous because I'm so perfect and all the men want me!"

"I want to see that scar," Molly demanded. "I want to know if you really were in danger of being scarred or you just used us to make everyone think you were noble and good."

Emerald was backing up again, this time toward Hugh on the shore, but she had regained much of her composure. "I won't let myself be questioned by you," she taunted Molly. "Jealousy has driven you crazy!"

"Then answer *me*," Hugh demanded. "I don't believe there's such a thing as a witch, but even if you were vaccinated somewhere we can't see, your arm would be swollen now. How did you escape that? I want to know."

"All right," she posed defiantly, one hand on her hip, the other pulling back her hair, which was already springing back into perfect curls. "If you must know, it happens I'm a natural immune. My mother had the pox when she was carrying me. I've been vaccinated before and I've been through epidemics before. They don't affect me. Nothing will ever mark my perfect skin. It's like a gift from God."

"Gift from God! Why you little tramp!" Molly shouted. "It's the mark of a Jezebel! You used us. You made us think you were risking everything to nurse those men!"

"Why?" Hugh interjected. "Why did you do that?"

"I had to make you think well of me," Emerald hung her head, shifting to the part of the contrite sinner. "I knew you'd never accept me as a decent woman after

464

what Avery had done to me, and I wanted your respect, Hugh. I wanted you to think well of me."

"You wanted him period!" Molly shouted. "You wanted to take him away from me."

"You never had him! He was free for the taking. I had as much right to go after him as you. More right! At least I wasn't married. You wanted him when you were married to Jake. You wanted to commit adultery with him. Would have too, if you weren't such a goody-two-shoes."

Molly started to speak, then bit back her tongue, but Emerald had seen.

"Oh, so you did commit adultery! And then you condemn me! You treat me like a sinner when you slept with your husband's partner."

"Leave Molly out of this!" Hugh commanded. "I want to know about you. About what you wanted from me."

"I wanted you to marry me. I wanted you to make me a respectable woman. And to love me. I wanted you to love me. I still do."

"But that's crazy. I love Molly."

He had said it! He had shouted it to the other woman! Joy soared in Molly's heart. Half naked and dripping wet as she looked and as crazy as she was behaving, he loved her. She had fought for her man and she was winning, but Emerald was not backing down.

"Well 'loving her' doesn't stop you from wanting me," Emerald accused, holding her head high like a queen and flashing her wonderful green eyes so that they touched first her own silken splendor and then Hugh's strong body. "You did want me and you do want me.

465

You want me now! Look at you!"

Molly was still reeling from Hugh's admission of love when she followed Emerald's gesture and blushed to see outlined in his trousers, the evidence of his desire.

Hugh was embarrassed and furious. "Molly's right! You are a witch! Coming here and using those sick men to make us think you'd repented and all the while you were flaunting yourself—flaunting your beauty. Of course, I've wanted you. Any man whose half alive would want you, but that doesn't make it right. It doesn't give you the right to manipulate people!"

"You're such a hypocrite!" Emerald shrieked. "And you're a fool. Austin Avery is right. You're a fool and you don't deserve to have him make you rich. And to think I was going along with it! Keeping you here so you wouldn't be a fool and ruin Avery's scheme—"

"What scheme? What do you mean keep me here so I won't ruin Avery's scheme?"

"To salt the mine. To fix the assay. To make you rich enough to be worthy of me, you fool! He's doing it right this minute. Austin Avery is making you a rich man while you're ashamed to have your precious name associated with his. Well, it's too late now. He's going to pull the mining fraud of the century with your mine, and Deadwood will remember you both as crooks!"

"Damn it! I knew he'd pull something. Where is he? What's he going to do? Get out of that creek, woman, and tell me!"

Emerald climbed out of the creek and stood on the bank, dripping, her proud and naked-looking body just inches from Hugh's as she confronted him

466

defiantly.

"He's got a plan to rig the assay. This morning. Before you get to town. That's all I know. Except that Austin Avery is twice the man you are and I was a fool to leave him. Austin Avery knows how to enjoy life, how to pleasure a woman."

"Then go to him!" Hugh demanded, striding up the hill as Molly joined Emerald on the bank. "But I'm going to find him first and I'm going to do my best to stop him and see he gets what he deserves!"

"He will!" Emerald shouted. "Austin Avery will get what he deserves because he knows how to make things happen. And he knows how to enjoy what he's earned. You and Molly deserve each other. You deserve to be miserable together forever. You two ought to build a damn church!"

Hugh turned and looked down the bank at the two women. He was the picture of frustrated rage. Molly took over. She leaned down quietly and picked up the gun.

"You go on into town and do what you can to stop him, Hugh. I'll put away your rifle for you, and I'll take care of Miss O'Brien. Just stop at the livery stable and have a rig sent back to collect her things. I'm sure she'll be leaving soon."

Hugh gave Molly a trusting wave and was off for Deadwood at a run. Emerald started to call after Hugh, but realized it was no use. She turned and looked at Molly, her eyes wide with disbelief.

"Now then," Molly said, hefting the heavy rifle and slowly swinging it so that it was pointed toward Emerald. "I suggest you get back to the cabin and get into your clothes rather quickly. And then I suggest you get packed and be sitting on your trunk when the rig comes for you."

"You can't tell me—" Emerald tried to sound defiant.

"And then you get out of town. You've been reminding me all week that stage service has commenced. So you find out when the next stage leaves Deadwood, and you be on it."

She stepped toward Emerald, not aiming the rifle, but holding it squarely before her. Emerald backed up the hill, then turned and ran toward the cabin.

Molly climbed up the creek bank and stood in her dripping chemise watching the woman retreating and looking proudly over the scene before her, the cabins and the mineshaft and the rubble of the Lucky Six Mine. What she had said to Emerald sounded melodramatic, she knew, like a line from one of those cheap novels they had begun to write about the west, but it also sounded right.

She felt like a true pioneer.

Chapter Thirty-two

The proprietor of the hotel was delighted at Emerald's return and gave her the key to the room she had shared with Austin Avery without question. The first thing she did upon entering the room was to throw herself across the bed and cry out her rage at the humiliation she had received at the hands of Molly Lewis. Not only had the scene at the creek turned out entirely different from the way she had scripted it in her mind, but all her suffering and sacrifice to save the lives of the miserable, filthy miners had gone for nothing. Of course they would be her devoted slaves, and she was sure the story of how Emerald O'Brien had risked her perfect beauty to save the city from a smallpox epidemic was already becoming a Deadwood legend that would not be tarnished by any spiteful detractions from Molly Lewis, but she would never be Hugh's wife and she had given up Austin Avery for nothing.

Lying on the unmade bed she had once shared with Avery and smelling his bay rum on the sheets sent Emerald into new rounds of sobbing, but these soon stopped when she realized that she might still have Austin Avery. He had, in fact, been most attentive to her in the buggy, ravishing her with a desire made stronger by her absence. Obviously she could get him back, and she certainly would never need to let him know that she had failed with Hugh. It would be much more romantic to let him think she has simply come to her senses and decided that Austin was the better man for her. And indeed he was, she realized, sitting up on the bed and staring at her reflection in the mirror across the room. Hugh Everett might be as handsome and strong as a young lion, but Austin was right. Hugh was too noble for his own good. He would never know how to enjoy life. He would always be struggling for something, and his wife might be respectable but she'd soon be worn out with housekeeping and child bearing. Respectability did not come cheap, and staying in that wretched little cabin with Edwin and the sick men always whining for attention had convinced Emerald that she was not cut out to be a housewife. And, after all, if she really wanted to be a wife, Austin Avery had begged her to marry him.

Thinking about marriage, Emerald got up and went to the larger of her trunks, the one she had left behind. She opened it now and took out a bolt of cloth, one of the purchases she had made in the afternoon of self-gratification with which she had fortified herself before beginning her self-imposed exile in the pest house. The cloth was of deep red embroidered silk and she had pictured herself wearing it on her honeymoon with Hugh, but when she brought it back to the hotel she had been aware of an uneasy feeling and known that somehow her pleasure in her purchase had been spoiled.

Now she remembered that she had felt wonderfully

excited when she found the silk in the shop of Wing Tsue, Deadwood's leading Chinese merchant. The color was perfect to be worn with her latest gift from Avery, a pair of garnet earrings, and it had excited her to think that the silk had come all the way from China to adorn her, once a simple shop girl. But her feeling toward the silk had changed by the time she left the shop, and she realized now, it had something to do with meeting the merchant's wife. For Wing Tsue, believing she was a respectable woman, had invited her to step through the damask wall hangings to the room behind the shop and be presented to his wife, Hal Shek Wong. At the first sight of the tiny little woman dressed in layers of rich embroidered silks and perched on a pile of silk pillows, Emerald had been enchanted, for she was just like the china dolls displayed in glass cases on the other side of the curtains. Her face was chalk white and her expression was painted on, just like the doll's. Her hair was even blacker than Emerald's own and was arranged in an elaborate pyramid laced with carved ivory pins and combs. The merchant's wife spoke no English, but she offered Emerald tea by gesturing with her delicate hands, and Emerald took it from her in tiny cups as delicate as egg shells.

She would have gone away still enchanted had she not seen Hal Shek Wong's feet. She knew that Chinese women bound their feet to make them tiny and pleasing to men, and she, having pretty little feet herself, had thought it a clever idea. But Hal Shek Wong's feet were not pretty at all despite the doll-like slippers she wore. They were grotesquely deformed. A woman could barely walk on such feet, and she certainly could never run away. And that was how it was meant to be, Emerald realized. Wing Tsue kept his wife in a silken prison, just like the dolls in their glass cases.

She had put away her insight about the merchant's marriage with the garnet-colored silk and not let her doubts keep her from proceeding toward her goal of winning Hugh, but now, sitting on the floor and fingering the silk, she realized that her insight about Wing Tsue's wife was true of all marriages. Hugh had been shocked by her independence and her clever deceptions; had she won him as a husband, he surely would have tried to remake her in his own image. Marriage might offer a woman security and respectability, but whether the walls were made of silk or logs, the price was still imprisonment.

Somehow the realization made Emerald stop her weeping and feel stronger. She laid the bolt of silk on the bed and bathed her face with water from the pitcher and then examined herself in the mirror of the mahogany dresser. She was not only more beautiful than most women, she realized, she was smarter, and she was going to win at life just as Austin Avery did.

The window of the hotel room was open and as she arranged her face and hair she heard music drifting up from the hurdy gurdy across the street. She hummed along and remembered her moment of glory on the stage of Langrishe's theater, and then it came to her at last where her destiny lay.

She laughed out loud, looked at her sparkling eyes and pretty white teeth in the mirror and wondered why it had taken her so long to see who she must be. An actress! Of course, that was destiny's promise for Emma O'Brien, now Emerald, the angel of Deadwood's smallpox epidemic! It was a wonder it had taken her so long to realize that she must not depend on Austin Avery, Hugh Everett, or any man to direct her life. She was to be an independent woman in control of her own life, with scores of admirers and the best as her lover!

Emerald ran to the bed and picked up the bolt of silk. The silk shimmered in the sunlight, and as she turned back to the mirror and draped the full length of the fabric around her, she was amazed to see how the deep rich red enhanced her skin and eyes. She was suddenly sparklingly alive and different, a new and exotic woman.

She saw at once what she needed. Not just a new dress and a new career but a whole new personality and a new name.

Garnet, she thought. I've been Emerald O'Brien long enough. I've been Irish long enough. *Garnet* and something Spanish and exotic. She would learn to dance and be the new Lola Montez.

Gabriel! That was it. Gabriel, the angel. How perfect for the legend who had saved Deadwood. She would be Garnet Gabriel. And they would always remember her in Deadwood, but she would move on to new places and new adventures. Molly had ordered her to be out of town on the next stage. Well, she would leave town, all right, but not because Molly had ordered it, but because her disappearance would serve her legend. How the men would yearn for her return when they read of her appearances elsewhere! How those she had saved would struggle to do justice to her beauty and her goodness as they described her!

She stuffed the silk and her toilet articles back into

the trunk and got out her green velvet traveling costume, but as she dressed, she caught a glimpse in the mirror of the unmade bed behind her and she remembered Austin Avery. It was a long way to Cheyenne and a long time before she'd find another man like Austin Avery. She remembered their last encounter in the buggy. They had both known he was not ravishing her but servicing her, and he had serviced her well. He was the one who had awakened such needs in her; how could she be certain another man could satisfy them as completely? Austin was a beast when it came to lovemaking, but he was exciting and he might soon be rich from the sale of the mine, that is if Hugh didn't spoil the assay for everyone. Austin would surely be furious at her for tipping Hugh off. If he caught up with her, he would probably spank her.

She remembered the night he had dragged her off the stage and back to their hotel room. There would certainly need to be some concessions made if Austin Avery were not to be an encumbrance to her stage career, but she had no doubt she could win them if she let him win her first. But she certainly couldn't let him return and find her in the hotel room waiting for him. Getting on the stagecoach was still the best plan, but how to be sure Austin knew about it in time to stop her?

She could leave a note, but he might not find it in time. A messenger would be better. She leaned out of the window to find a likely candidate for the honor of serving as her messenger. To her delight, she saw the familiar figure of Caleb Dexter hurrying along across the street. She hailed him with an unladylike call, and he interrupted his progress to stand underneath the window with his hat in his hand. He clutched a bottle of whiskey to his chest.

A dozen men, alerted by her yell, joined the old man standing underneath her window and gazed up at her adoringly as she gave Caleb Dexter his instructions. She didn't mind the audience.

There was a livery stable at the edge of town, and when Hugh stopped to send a rig back for Emerald, he decided to rent a horse for himself. The assay office wasn't much farther into town, but he had a feeling he might not find the gambler and his unsuspecting capitalist there. He was right. The man at the assay office suggested that if a whole wagonload of ore had been taken from the mine, the first step would be to have it crushed at the new quartz mill which had only recently been freighted in. The quartz mill was located in another of the small mining camps some distance from Deadwood, so Hugh was glad of the horse, even though it was a typical livery hack and needed constant reminders from his heels to make the trip at a gallop.

When he reached the mill, Hugh had to admire Austin Avery. He must have been furious to see Hugh galloping up, but he kept his face expressionless as he stepped down from the load of ore he and McPherson appeared to be guarding and acknowledged Hugh with a theatrical gesture of his broad-brimmed hat.

"Ah, Mr. Everett, you're just in time to witness the first part of the test. I didn't think it was necessary for you to be here for the ore crushing, routine as it is, but you may as well watch, and then go along with us as we take the crushed ore to the assay office."

Hugh swung off the horse, feeling unsure as to how to express his defiance in the face of the gambler's exaggerated politeness and the curious look McPherson gave him and his lathered horse. The gambler turned his attention to McPherson.

"I don't believe you've had the opportunity to meet my partner, Hugh Everett. Hugh, this is John McPherson, who represents a company which is buying mining properties in the area."

"Excuse me for not getting off the wagon," McPherson said, "but my orders are not to let this ore out of my sight until I have the results of the assay. I slept with it last night." He was wearing some sort of white overalls open at the front to reveal an embroidered vest and cravat. "Glad you could make it for the test, Mr. Everett. I understand you've been something of a silent partner in the Lucky Six."

Hugh was startled by the remark. So that was how Avery had presented him. Yes, he thought. I've been a silent partner, all right. Just sweating underground, tearing my hands open on the rocks, struggling and fighting for my life and killing my partner and my brother. He looked at McPherson and the soft, white hand he offered Hugh to shake. He realized McPherson was from another world, a world of security and comfort and high finance. If cheating and fighting went on in McPherson's world, it went on over a board table. Fortunes were made or lives were broken with the stroke of a pen. McPherson was like Phineas P. Crandall, the crusty little newspaper editor who had called him a fool to believe the promises he wrote; they were men who made their fortunes on the struggles of others, and Hugh wanted nothing to do with such men. What he wanted was to beat dickens out of Austin Avery; and yet Hugh knew it wasn't the gambler that made him mad; it was the way men like Crandall and McPherson could turn what he had worked for into dust.

McPherson noticed that Hugh had hesitated before shaking his hand, and his eyebrow raised in question. Hugh made his handshake firm, knowing he'd have to meet these men on their own ground. He spoke with false bravado, "So, we're ready to see what the old Lucky Six is worth, eh?"

"That's right," McPherson said cheerfully. "And from what Mr. Avery has been telling me, you have some promising ore here. If it assays out as high grade as he thinks, I'll be able to offer you a price that will send you home in style."

"I don't have a home."

"Well, then you can buy yourself one, somewhere far away from this miserable place."

"How much of Deadwood do you expect to buy?"

"I personally won't buy anything. The offer will come from my company, the name of which I'm not yet authorized to reveal. You must understand, Mr. Everett, that mining gold is big business. Scientific business. Capital is essential, if not everything. If these Deadwood diggings are as rich as your newspaper has been making the world believe, millions of dollars of capital will be coming in this winter. It takes thousands of dollars to properly develop a quartz mine, you must realize. Geologists and mining engineers, like myself, trained at foreign universities and hydraulic mining equipment, that's what it takes."

"So poor man's gold was just the bait for fools like

me who took all the risks so that—"

"Not all the risks, son. Why, the entrepreneurs will be taking risks also—capital investment involves considerable risk, even for men like George Hearst and J.P. Morgan; men who have already made fortunes in banking, shipping and railroads—"

"While we've been dying in the mines!"

"What's that?" McPherson said. He stopped talking to light a cigar.

"Nothing."

"I was merely trying to explain to you that I am not speaking as an individual, and that is why I'm not authorized to make you an offer until I have an accurate assessment of the potential worth of your holdings. And, of course, you must realize the vast difference between what the mine would be worth to you as an individual who could hope to grub out only a few more months wages with your primitive placer methods, while we can provide the capital to—"

Avery interrupted politely to inform them the mill operator was ready, and the three turned their attention to the mill as the heavy doors were hauled open, revealing the huge machines which would pulverize the ore to a fine powder so the gold could be freed.

"Ah," McPherson said reverently. "The Blake Crusher and Balthoff Ball Pulverizer."

"The first quartz mill in the Black Hills," the operator added.

Hugh stared at it. In a few minutes the ore from the Lucky Six would be dumped into the yawning mouth of the huge cylinder where it would be rolled and tumbled with iron balls until the rock was broken into bits small enough to allow the gold to be freed through

478

one of several mechanical and chemical processes. The gold would normally be extracted from the ore at the quartz mill, but in the case of a mine test, the crushed samples would be taken to the assay office.

The mill operator and a couple of his flunkies produced wheelbarrows and stood ready to transfer the ore from the wagon to the mill. Avery was leaning back against the wagon, seeming to take no interest in the process. It made Hugh wonder. Maybe Molly and even Emerald were wrong about Avery. Hugh had made it clear he wanted the test to be conducted honestly and it looked like Avery was going along with him.

Hugh relaxed a little and entertained the thought the Lucky Six might actually be worth something. It would make a difference, he realized. McPherson was right. With enough money he could buy a house somewhere, maybe even a business. If he gained enough to make it possible for him to take care of Molly and Edwin, then perhaps he could still find some meaning in whatever had brought him to the Black Hills. Money might make it all seem right.

Hugh started to feel almost cheerful. Then, just as McPherson climbed off the wagon and was preparing to supervise the transfer of the ore, they heard a shout.

"Hey, wait for me!"

Hugh turned around. Someone had just come around the corner of the mill. He was staggering and lurching and waving a whiskey bottle as he approached them. It was Caleb Dexter.

"Well, I see Mr. Dexter has decided to show up for the test after all," Avery told McPherson. "He was one of the original partners in the mine with Mr. Everett

479

here and after he stopped being associated in the partnership, he still maintained an active interest in the mine."

"Looks like an old drunk to me," McPherson said.

"Well," Avery whispered to McPherson. "Frankly he is inclined to be intemperate. That's how he lost his partnership, but he does know a great deal about mining. Without him, the boys might have missed all that conglomerate ore I told you about. We sort of humor him along."

"Hugh, old buddy," Dexter stumbled up to the group and threw his arms around Hugh. "Thanks for waiting for me, old buddy. I got detained in town so I'm late. But I wouldn't miss this old test for the world." His speech was slurred and he seemed hardly able to stand up. He straightened up a little and addressed himself to McPherson. "Glad to see you again, sir."

"Can we get on with the test?" The mill operator asked Avery and then, turning to McPherson, spoke more deferentially, "That is if you are ready, sir?"

It's amazing how people can smell capital, Hugh thought. Maybe money couldn't buy happiness, but it sure got you a lot of deferential treatment.

"We sure as hell ought to get on with the test," Caleb Dexter roared waving the whiskey bottle. "That's what we been waitin' for ain't it? To see what the old Lucky Six is worth. I'll be damned if it ain't a hell of a good gold mine. I always said it was, didn't I, Hugh? Right from the start and now here we are getting ready to test our first ore right here at the good old Balthoff Ball Pulverizer."

Funny, Hugh thought. *He can hardly stand up but he can say Balthoff Ball Pulverizer.*

Caleb Dexter climbed up on the wagon and looked down at the ore lovingly. He seemed to sway a little and he kept swinging the bottle to and fro like any minute he might pitch over backward off the wagon. It made Hugh nervous. He wondered if he should make the effort to step forward and catch the old reprobate if he fell off the wagon. The mill workers had put their wheelbarrows in place behind the tail gate of the wagon and were leaning on their shovels waiting for the old man to move away so they could unload the ore.

There was something funny going on, Hugh thought. Something didn't feel right, but he couldn't put his finger on it.

He stared at Caleb Dexter and then realized what was bothering him. As often as Hugh had seen the old man drunk, he had never seen him quite so loose. And it was strange he would choose this morning to get stumbling drunk. Caleb Dexter had put his whole heart into the Lucky Six. Why hadn't he been around when McPherson selected the samples? He had obviously known the test was this morning, so why had he just now shown up and why so drunk? The old man stood on the wagon, brandishing the whiskey bottle, waving it about recklessly. It looked like any minute he might pass out or drop his bottle.

The bottle, Hugh thought. *There's something funny about the bottle*. He realized Caleb Dexter was not drinking from the bottle, nor had he offered a slug off it to everyone in sight as was his custom. And the bottle had a funny, glimmery look about it as if the contents were heavy and slippery, like amalgam. *Amalgam*. That was it. Caleb Dexter had amalgam in the bottle! How many times had Hugh watched the old man use his little bottle of quicksilver to attract the gold particles from the residue caught in the riffles of their sluice box? The mixture of quicksilver, or mercury, and gold was called amalgam. He would put it into a bag and squeeze the quicksilver out to use again, leaving behind the pure gold. While the amalgam was in a bottle, it would be a sort of liquid gold. And if that liquid gold could be dropped into a load of ore awaiting assay, it would make that sample look like it came from a mine full of high-grade ore. If one could risk dropping $100 worth of amalgam into an assay sample, it could mean thousands of dollars more on the sale of a mine!

Even as Hugh formed his theory, the old man staggered forward, just as McPherson signaled the mill workers to unlatch the tailgate of the wagon and prepare to dump the ore into the pulverizer. Hugh saw the old man was going to play his scene for all it was worth, waiting until the last possible moment to drop the bottle. He leaned over the ore as if to give it a final inspection, then raised the bottle as if he were about to drink, but Hugh knew he was keeping his thumb over the neck. He knew, too, what would happen next. When the old man brought the bottle back down, he would stagger back a little as if he were going to pass out and as he caught himself, the bottle would come crashing down in the ore, shattering and spilling its load of pure liquid gold into the ore, just as the tail gate dropped and the ore tumbled into the wheelbarrows.

It was so easy and it would all be over in a second. McPherson would never suspect a thing and would pay a fabulous price for the mine. Hugh looked at Avery. The gambler met his eyes and he was smiling. *He's glad I figured it out*, Hugh thought. He could have found an easier way to salt the mine, bribed the assayer or the mill operator, but he wanted to take a chance on it. Make a game of it. And he's glad I know. He wants me to be a party to it.

And why not? Hugh thought. I've done everything else. I've got murder and lust and the whole damn Sioux nation on my conscience, why not this too?

And then, even though there was no time to articulate the answer in words, Hugh knew.

He stepped forward and with one sweeping motion of his big hands he caught Caleb Dexter by the seat of his pants and hauled him off the wagon.

"Hey, old partner, you were about to fall in there."

"What the hell?" Dexter shouted as he came off the wagon and spun around to face Hugh.

The tailgate was released then the ore began tumbling into the wheelbarrows.

"How about a drink of your whiskey there?" Hugh said, reaching for the bottle.

Dexter hugged the bottle to his chest. For once he was speechless.

Hugh looked at the bottle. Through the amber glass, he could see the glimmering slippery gliding of amalgam.

He had the satisfaction of knowing he was right and the satisfaction of seeing Austin Avery's jaw drop open before the gambler regained control of his expression and regarded Hugh with narrow eyes.

Hugh clenched his fists. He'd have to move fast if Avery went for one of the saloon pistols tucked in his belt.

"That's right, shovel it in, boys!" McPherson directed the mill workers. Avery went white around the lips as if he were keeping control of himself at great cost. Hugh knew he, too, had remembered McPherson. Avery couldn't call him down without showing his hand to McPherson.

The men were already wheeling the ore into the mill.

"I'll be a son of a bitch," Caleb Dexter said to no one in particular. He made as if to take a slug off the bottle, and then at the last minute he remembered and lowered the bottle and stared at it in bewilderment.

Hugh decided there was no point in hanging around any longer. He knew Avery was maintaining his control and not making a scene before McPherson in the hope the mine might by some chance still prove worthy of capital investment.

Hugh had stopped believing in miracles.

He untied the horse and swung into the saddle. He was turning to go, thinking of how to explain his sudden departure to McPherson, when Avery stepped before his horse, blocking his way.

"Not staying for the test?"

"I have business in town," Hugh said more to McPherson than to Avery. McPherson nodded absently, intent on watching his ore samples being loaded into the mill.

Hugh steeled himself for a confrontation with Avery.

"You're a fool, Everett," the gambler whispered.

Hugh said nothing but met the gambler's steely eyes with his own look of determination until Avery's eyes darted back to McPherson and with a look that said a

484

confrontation was still to come let Hugh pass.

You're right, I am a fool, Hugh thought as he rode away, realizing that though he felt little satisfaction at having thwarted the gambler's plan, had he gone along with the fraud, he would have felt guilty forever. *So, I've got my integrity, is that enough to show for my struggles in the Black Hills?* He thought it over, and as the horse picked up speed as they returned to town, he decided that maybe it *was* enough. For he suddenly realized that the heavy load of guilt he'd carried since he first knew he wanted Molly Lewis again, despite the fact she was his partner's wife, was gone. Perhaps it was saving the lives of the miners during the smallpox epidemic that had lifted the burden from him; perhaps it was seeing Molly so confident and free in her anger against Emerald that morning. He only knew that for the first time in months he did not feel guilty and anguished over what he wanted. And what he wanted was to find Molly and settle matters between them.

He kept his mount, forcing it to pass the livery stable and gallop on to the mine. It seemed imperative that he find Molly as soon as possible, but when he reached her cabin she was gone. There was a note on the table telling him that Edwin was still at the neighbor's and that she had gone to Mt. Moriah "to say goodbye."

He crumpled the note into his pocket and climbed back on the horse, suddenly afraid. If she had gone to the cemetery to say her goodbyes, that must mean she still intended to leave Deadwood. He did not want to let her go, but he would not follow her to Pennsylvania. Either she knew by now that they were destined to be together, or she would never know. Whichever it was, it was time to know. He forced the tired nag toward the steep trail leading up to the graves on the hill which overlooked Deadwood. It seemed an appropriate place for them at last to end in understanding what they had begun in innocence so many years and miles distant.

When he saw her at last, she was only a blue speck high on the mountain near the graves. He tied the sweating horse to a small pine tree and, on foot, climbed to meet her.

Caleb Dexter had a hard time keeping up with Austin Avery as he strode purposefully down Deadwood's Main Street. He figured the gambler was in a black mood after what had happened at the quartz mill, and it seemed important to Caleb to make up to him somehow. Dexter felt like hell himself. Hugh had blown not only his own last chance for a bonanza, but Caleb's too. Oh, eventually there would be another new stampede and he'd strike out for the new diggings, but he knew in his heart it was never going to be as it had been in Deadwood the summer of 1876. He wanted to prolong what he had found in this last gold rush, an excitement that was as close to lust as the old man could remember. He felt he could hang on to hope a little longer if he could just stick close to Austin Avery.

"It wouldn't have hurt us to stay with McPherson till the assayer was through," the old man said, trying to walk fast enough to watch Avery's face as he talked. "That smart-assed young fool thinks just cause he's got a university degree he knows everything. We might have been able to give him a wink that we'd made it worth his while if he upgraded the results."

Avery was silent.

"McPherson might have thought it was funny, us not sticking around for the assay."

There was still no response from Avery, so he tried another angle. "Of course, on the other hand, it looks sort of casual. Like we was so confident about the Lucky Six we didn't even have to stick around to see how it panned out."

There was still no sign from Avery that he'd even heard. He wished Avery would slow down, Caleb was getting short of breath walking this fast and trying to keep up both sides of the conversation.

"He still might buy the mine, you know." Caleb wasn't sure Avery had even heard him. The gambler hadn't broken stride since they left McPherson clutching his bags of crushed ore at the Assay Office. Caleb figured Avery was headed for a saloon and he had to admit there was not much else to do at this point but get drunk. He was all for that, but he'd like to know the boss wasn't mad at him. After all, it wasn't his fault. He'd played his part according to the plan. Their scheme would have worked perfectly if Hugh hadn't shown up.

"Yep," he said aloud, trying to sound cheerful. "He might just up and surprise us and buy that mine anyway. I mean even if the assay ain't too good. Of course, it could be better than we think. I mean there was all that conglomerate ore and we have been pulling enough gold for wages out of there all summer and then again, even if the Lucky Six don't pan out too hot, it depends a lot on the kind of properties surrounding us. An outfit like McPherson works for,

487

capitalists like that, they like to buy up a whole series of claims. That way you can follow the vein without any worries about water rights and claim jumping and such. Yep, chances are you're going to get a pretty fair price on that mine any—"

"Caleb Dexter, old man—"

"Yes sir?"

"Shut up."

"Why, Mr. Avery, that's no way to talk to a partner. It ain't my fault Hugh got all righteous and blew—"

Suddenly Avery stopped in mid-stride, turned and grabbed Caleb by the throat of his red-flannel shirt.

"One more word out of you, old man, and I'm going to shoot you dead right here on the street."

Caleb looked into Avery's cold steel eyes and thought of the pistols the gambler wore under his frock coat. He'd do it, all right. The old man let himself go limp and Avery released him as abruptly as he'd grabbed him. They continued to walk up the street in silence.

Caleb Dexter was hurt and he wanted Austin to know it. He sniffed a little, trying to think of the best way to get back into the gambler's good graces. As they passed the hotel, Caleb remembered.

"Well, I guess I can't tell you then."

Avery didn't take the bait.

"Miss Emerald said to be sure and tell you, but if I'm not supposed to say any—"

Suddenly Avery had him by the shirtfront again.

"What? What are you supposed to tell me about Miss Emerald?"

Caleb would have liked to draw it out, make himself more important, but something in the gambler's eyes told him to spill it.

"She said to tell you she was leaving town."

"When? When did she tell you that?"

"This afternoon when I was on my way to the mine test."

"Why didn't you tell me?"

Caleb hesitated. Why hadn't he? He'd forgotten, that was why, but he couldn't say that. Then he remembered. "I was supposed to be drunk. I was supposed to stumble around the corner of the mill at just the minute they were getting ready to dump out the ore. I had to do it just right, act dead drunk, so when I spilled the amalgam in the ore, McPherson wouldn't get suspicious. I couldn't run up to you first and say I had an important message from Miss Emerald, now could I?"

"What did she tell you exactly? Did she tell you to tell me?"

"Well, I don't remember her exact words, but she was leaning out the window of her hotel room right up there," he pointed to the window. "She was attracting quite a crowd, and she says she'd had it with Deadwood and she was going off to become an actress."

"An actress?"

"Yep, and she could do it too. You should have seen all the men gawking at her."

"That little baggage." Avery looked up at the hotel window, his eyes narrowing dangerously.

"That's the way I figured you'd take it, boss. I reckon' you don't care at all that she took off."

"Took off? You mean she's already gone?"

"Well, she said she'd take the first stage out of town and since there ain't no stage parked in front of the freight office over there, I figure it's gone."

"She was bluffing. She was just trying to attract attention. If I know Emerald, she's up in her room right now, pouting and plotting something else."

Avery was staring at the window. He seemed uncertain. Caleb figured he ought to help out. "One way to find out," he said.

Avery looked at him, but didn't speak.

"We could mosey on over to the freight office there and ask."

"Ask?"

"Sure, that would be the way. Just slide in there and ask if there was a Miss Emerald O'Brien on the passenger list."

"No," the clerk said, holding the passenger list at arm's length to peer at it through squinted eyes. "No, no Emerald O'Brien registered."

"I told you," Avery said to the old man. "She was just putting on a show. Wanted to get my attention again."

"Course there was a lady," the clerk volunteered.

"A lady?" Caleb Dexter said. There weren't many ladies in Deadwood.

"And if you don't mind my noticing, Mr. Avery," he offered Avery a diffident smile, "she did appear to be the same lady you have been escorting this summer."

"Emerald?"

"That's what I thought her name was. But that's not how she bought her ticket. She registered under the name of—let me see here." He peered at the passenger list again. Avery snatched it away from him.

"There's only one woman's name here. Garnet something."

"Yes, that's it," the clerk brightened. "I remember

she had to say it for me. Garnet Gab-ri-el. Real Spanish, it sounded."

"Did she actually get on the stage?" Avery demanded.

"Helped her on myself," the clerk beamed, then feeling Avery's gaze on him, he whitened a little. "Of course, I had no idea, that you, I mean —"

"That I what?"

"That you cared if the lady left town. I would have stopped her."

"What makes you think I care?" Avery had straightened himself up and was regarding the clerk coolly. The situation tickled Caleb Dexter.

"The boss don't care." he volunteered. "He could have any one of them saloon girls, just like this." He snapped his fingers.

"Anyone can have one of the saloon girls just like that," the clerk grinned, "provided they got enough gold dust."

"Well, there's nothing we can do about it anyway." Dexter said. "She's gone and it's too late to stop her."

"Oh, I reckon a body could catch the stage, all right." The clerk said. "If you wanted to rent a horse, I mean. The stage took out of here on a gallop, showing off those matching white horses and making a show of it, but just between you and me, they stop at the first camp out of town and switch to a regular team. The whites are just for show. Can't keep up at a gallop all the way to Cheyenne, now can they?"

"You could catch her then," Dexter said, slapping the counter. "I can run over to the livery stable and rent you the fastest horse and —"

"And why would I want to do that?" Avery's voice

was infinitely cool.

"Why, to get her back. To get Miss Emerald back."

"What makes you think I want her back? That I'd take her back?"

"Well, uh," Dexter hesitated, "uh, because she's such a looker, and women are scarce and well, uh," He hated to say anything about love and he figured a word like that wouldn't apply anyway to what was between Mr. Avery and Miss Emerald. "Well," he finished up, "because she wants you to come after her."

"She wants me to?"

"Sure, why else would she have made such a point to tell me to tell you she was leaving on the afternoon stage? If she wanted to get away from you, she'd just have snuck out of town."

"He's got a point there!" The clerk put in cheerfully. "I noticed how she kept lookin' around like she was watching for someone. She acted sort of funny at the last minute like she wasn't going to get on the stage, only by then there was a bunch of miners hanging around waiting for her to climb in the coach so as they could get a gander at her ankles when she stepped up."

"Sure sounds like she was expecting you to stop her," Dexter interrupted, realizing the clerk was on dangerous ground. "We would have too, if the test had gone like we expected and I'd remem — I'd had time to tell you she was leaving."

"Yep, you might say she left a trail a mile wide," the clerk mused. "Garnet Gabriel. It wouldn't be hard to trace a woman with a name like that, especially one with a face and body — ".

"You could catch her," Dexter said.

"I could catch her if I cared to."

"Sure could."

"I could get her back if I cared to."

"Yep, you could catch right up to that coach and—"

"Only I *don't care to.*"

Not hearing him, the old man rattled on, "You could catch up to the coach and stop it and drag her off and sling her across the saddle. Boy, I'd sure like to see that!"

"He said he didn't care to," the clerk pointed out.

"What?" Caleb blinked, pulling his hat back off his head and scratching his bald spot. "You don't care about getting Miss Emerald back?"

"That's what I said. She doesn't mean a thing to me."

"But boss, women are scarce and she's so tasty-looking and so high-spirited and all. You won't find another one like her and it isn't like you couldn't get her back. You could drag her off the coach and make her come back."

"Of course, I could get her back. I'd drag her off that coach and sling her across my horse and gallop back to town with her kicking and squirming and yelling. If I wanted her back. If she mattered to me."

"But she don't."

"She's just a woman. The fellow here is right. A woman like that is . . . Shall I show you how much I care about her? Here, look. I'll show you how much she matters to me."

While Caleb and the clerk watched fascinated, Austin Avery took a $5 gold piece out of his pocket.

"I'll show you how much I care about her. I'll toss a coin, to see if I go after her. Should I do that?"

Caleb Dexter shook his head. "She's quite a woman, Mr. Avery, if I could have her, I'd—hell, I'd go after

493

her even if I didn't care, just for the fun of it."

"That's what I'll do then," Avery said, paying no attention to the old man. "I'll show you how little she means to me. I'll toss this coin. Heads I go after her and tails—"

"Tails?" the clerk and Caleb Dexter asked as one.

"Tails I walk down to the Hidden Treasure and pick out another woman."

By this time a crowd had gathered, and sensing something was going on, moved in closer. Avery came close to grinning. He held the gold piece aloft, twisting it so both the Liberty head and the eagle flashed in the late afternoon sun. Then he lowered his hand, the crowd stepped back to give him room as he repeated the words.

"Heads I go after her. Tails, I forget her."

He threw the coin, and Caleb held his breath as it spun higher and higher, then seemed to hang in mid-air for a moment before it tumbled down and Avery snatched it with a theatrical gesture. He slammed it on the sleeve of his frock coat, then held his hand over the coin and paused a moment, eyeing the crowd. When he saw every eye was upon him, he slowly raised his hand and looked at the coin.

His expression did not change.

Chapter Thirty-three

Like most frontier towns, Deadwood called its cemetery Boot Hill because most of those buried on Mt. Moriah that first summer died, not in sickbeds, but in skirmishes with the Indians or in brawls with their fellow miners. Mt. Moriah was a lonely spot, as visiting the graves of Wild Bill and the other pioneers was not yet a popular pastime. The path to the cemetery was steep, as was the cemetery itself, for with level ground at a premium in Deadwood, none could be yielded to those who had ceased to contribute to the economy.

Molly watched Hugh climbing the hill toward her and waited for him, thinking of all the times she had waited before, and that this must be the last time for waiting.

Seeing Molly standing before the graves with her hair down and haloed in the sunlight, Hugh thought she was like a heavenly apparition, but whether of hope or loss, he did not know. The cemetery itself looked as stark and raw as when they'd buried Jake and Luther. Dug into the side of the mountain, the graves sloped downward, their rough-sawed wood headstones tilting at precarious angles over the barren mounds of fresh earth. The timber grew thinner as the trail climbed, but compared to the barren gulch in which the city crowded, Mt. Moriah seemed lush and Hugh was reminded of his first vision of the Black Hills and their beauty before he and the other "pioneers" spoiled their pristine beauty. The grass was high around his boots as he walked, and he noticed it was yellowing, reminding him again that summer was over.

Hugh sensed even before his eyes met Molly's that whatever happened on Mt. Moriah would either unite them forever or mark their final parting. When he saw the determination in her stance and the tears shining in her eyes, he knew she was also aware of the significance of their meeting. He remembered their joining in love and desire on that other hillside and that it was he who had broken their bond with his unchecked emotions, and realized they could no longer avoid a confrontation.

They stood for a moment, not speaking, but holding each other with their eyes. A breeze played with the hair around her shoulders, and his throat ached with the pain of all that had kept them apart. He was jealous that the breeze could caress her while he dared not. The new spirit he recognized in her excited him, but also made him shy. She had, after all, never even said she loved him.

"I don't know where to begin," he said. "There's so much to be settled between us."

"Then start with what's not between us. What happened with the test? Are you rid of the mine at last?"

"No, I blew it. Avery and the old man had figured

out a way to rig the test so McPerson would pay us a fortune for our shares, but I blew it."

"So Avery was out to cheat you?"

"Not me but McPherson, or his company to be exact. It was a beautiful scheme. Caleb Dexter played drunk, a part he does well, and was going to break a whiskey bottle full of amalgam into the ore just as they were dropping it into the quartz mill. Our ore would have tested out like the mother lode, and it wouldn't have hurt me, except for the truth of what Emerald said. Sooner or later all of Deadwood would know that I was part of the fraud."

"Then you did the right thing to stop it. So why are you sorry?"

"Because I'm such a fool, Molly. Suddenly I saw it all. What a fool I'd been to think joining the trespass to the Black Hills would be an adventure and getting poor Luther to come along, and then not being man enough to tell Jake about you and me, but thinking it would all work out in some honorable way, even after I'd made love to you again. It's like I've been driven by some obsession to win the easy way, to think that fate owed me something. That I was destined to win, or even to be happy."

"You mean you just found out there's no poor man's gold?" There was a trace of mockery in her voice.

"Maybe that's it," he had to laugh at her irony. "I guess I really believed there was such a thing as poor man's gold, and we'd pick it up and all our problems would be solved."

"I didn't," she said softly. "I tried to believe, for Jake's sake and later for yours, but I think I knew all along that it was only an illusion. I think women always

497

know."

"So we're all fools. All of us. Look at this graveyard. Jake and Luther and crazy old Preacher Smith and all the rest. All of them coming here dreaming there was going to be something. Dreaming this was the chance a man works for all his life, and all of them chasing rainbows. Even Wild Bill there thought he'd get himself one last stake so he could give up gunfighting, and instead they got him in the back."

"Hugh, don't—"

"No, let me finish. It's got to be said. They fooled us! They've been using us! We gave up what little we had in the States to rush in here by the thousands, and we scraped our hands bloody panning for gold in the streams, and we got scalped by the Indians and crushed in the mines, and it was all for nothing. There's no poor man's gold. Never was a poor man that got rich off a gold rush. You know who's going to get rich off Deadwood?"

She didn't answer and he kept talking, the words tumbling out, so fast he was really thinking aloud. "Men like McPherson. Men like George Hearst. Capitalists. Entrepreneurs, as Crandall called them. Men with money. Men that don't sweat or need, Molly. That's who will make fortunes here. Not those who risked. It's those who have who get. That's the way of the world."

"But, Hugh—"

"Sure there's gold in this gulch—millions of dollars worth—but it's low grade and it's underground and it's going to take machinery and real mining engineers to get it out."

"What can I say, Hugh? You're right."

"I don't expect you to say anything. I just had to tell you. Maybe I'm just finally admitting it to myself. I didn't want to believe that the world operates that way but it does, and I had to say it to you. This all started with you, and now it's got to—"

"End? Are you saying it's got to end today?"

"It's got to be *resolved*. And yes, today. I've got to have answers about this summer and about you."

"It didn't start with me, Hugh, and I'm not responsible for your disappointment. You didn't know I'd be on that wagon train. You were looking for something when you started, and I don't think it was just gold. Was it adventure or were you out to prove something?"

"Adventure's as good a name for it as any, except maybe destiny. Something vital was happening and I felt driven to be part of it. But if my destiny didn't start with you, it soon became you, and now it seems we'll never get it all untangled."

Still thinking of destiny, he took her hand and started to pull her close to him. She took his hand, but stepped back, indicating he should follow her.

"There's something I want to show you. I don't know if it will help, but I discovered something today that seems important."

She turned and began to climb up a narrow path which rose above the graves. Wondering, Hugh followed her as the path trailed away into the high grass above the cemetery. Above them the white rocks of the summit looked down. Hugh wanted to question her but she did not look back, and he knew she needed her breath for climbing the steep hillside. He saw she was not going to the summit, but toward a point perhaps halfway up the mountain where a rocky outcropping, smaller and less imposing than the summit, but of the same granite, formed a natural overlook. When she was almost there, she turned back to him.

"You've never climbed this high before, have you?"

He shook his head.

"Neither had I until today. I'd visited the graves before, but I never took the time to climb higher. We might even be the first, since there's no path. I don't think most folks in Deadwood have much interest in exploring, but today when I came to the cemetery, I was so full of emotion and I too wanted answers. I said my goodbyes to Jake and Luther, thinking about returning to Pennsylvania, but I only felt more uncertain. And then I looked up and saw these rocks just ahead there at the point all shining in the sun and something seemed to call me. So I climbed up here and saw that from those rocks you can see the whole valley. I stood there looking down at Deadwood with the wind whipping about me and suddenly I felt calm and certain and almost happy."

By the time she finished speaking she had reached the summit and he joined her, wondering what she had discovered there. She turned back to look at him and he saw that there was indeed something new in her eyes. It looked like happiness.

When she turned away to look out over the valley, he followed her gaze. He gasped at the view. The scene was as perfect as if it were a painting of a Swiss village nestled against the Alps. The steep hillsides, which in town were obstacles to orderly building, from a distance provided a magnificent setting for a city that suddenly seemed not a sprawling mass of shacks struggling to climb the hillsides but a jewel in the folds of velvet-blue hills.

Hugh looked out at the city, marveling at the way it nestled into the gulch and then spread its way up the steep sides of the mountain. It was like a toy village, the men swarming through its streets visible, but as tiny as toy soldiers. The mountains, too, were not the brooding slopes that sometimes made him feel claustrophobic, but beautifully serene guardians of the valley. The city grew in the largest gulch where Deadwood Creek flowed into the Whitewood, but there were also dozens of side gulches cut by melting snow into the spring; each bearing the potential of gold-laced gravel. The side gulches deepened in the late-afternoon light as shadows grew. The afternoon sun was hot on his face as it sank behind the mountain he faced, causing the shadows, ever present in the narrowest of the gulches, to lengthen and sweep over the scene.

Hugh was surprised to see the city was so large. He had lived so long within the narrow confines of the gulch that for days at a time he had seen but not thought about the beauty of the mountains which surrounded them, but had focused only on the confusion of the city which seemed to daily grew more crowded and ugly. Cabin crowded upon cabin so that the smoke of one cook fire swirled around its higher neighbor's window, while the seepage from outhouses higher up leaked into the downslope neighbor's yards. In the heart of the city, space was so scarce buildings were almost stacked upon each other. Some were even raised on stilts so that the miners could follow the veins underneath. Rickety outside steps lead to tacked-on second stories, and the narrow spaces between the buildings were filled with rubble from the diggings, discarded whiskey bottles, and worse.

And since that day in June when he first left the serene beauty of the pine-scented mountains to follow the road that became Deadwood's Main Street, an ugly river of humanity fed by muddy tributary streets which traversed the steep gulches or tumbled downward at impossibly steep angles, Hugh had never been completely free of the sights and sounds and smells of the mining camp.

Now it was quiet. He could hear birds and insects and the wind blowing. The blasting and shooting and the hurdy-gurdy music of Deadwood became, like the sound of the creek, only a distant murmur.

The colors surprised him. Deadwood was almost all the same color, that of uncured logs and timber weathered by the sun. But the hills were varied tones of green and yellow, gold and brown. The somber muted tones of timber killed by whatever had laid it waste, giving Deadwood its name, were broken by an occasional tree still standing and patches of the tender, green new grass slowly recarpeting the burned-out areas. In some spots, aspen and birch had already become established and their leaves formed patches of yellow in the distance, while those nearer to them trembled in the breeze and looked like the golden coins of men's dreams.

The lengthening shadows and the occasional pine tree standing alone in a patch of dead wood or clinging precariously to the summit, sentinel-fashion, made Hugh understand why men in the gulch had lost awareness of the beauty of the mountains surrounding them. Shadows reminded one of the cold darkness of the mines and the perpetual darkness of death. A man looking up some morning at a view he hadn't committed to memory might mistake one of those sentinel pines for a Sioux scout seeking vengeance on the trespassers in the gulch.

But the Sioux were gone forever; a treaty forced upon them in retaliation for their victory over Custer. Whatever the right or wrong of it, the white man had won. It was decided. And the gulch was in peace. Smoke from evening cook fires trailed upward. One could make out the figures of men going home from their diggings or making their way down Main Street and disappearing into saloons.

Hugh marveled at how far he could see. The two creeks formed a Y at the heart of the city, the trail following Whitewood creek to his right leading to Crook City and the other mining camps in hidden gulches. If he had known of the view, he would have climbed the mountain before. He could not have imagined Deadwood would look so different from above.

"It's beautiful," he said at last.

"Then you see it too."

He nodded.

"That's what struck me. After all these months of thinking it was the ugliest place in the world, of being so closed in by the mountains and the shacks and the mines and the people, I climbed up here to plan my escape and to think how to persuade you to come with me, and then I looked out and saw that it was beautiful."

"Everything looks better when you get away from it. Every place is beautiful when the sun's about to set.

Everything is more precious when you think you've lost it." He said the last with special significance.

"It's not just that. Not just that it looked beautiful to me. It was the feeling I had. The feeling of being home. I thought I could see our cabin way over there to the left, and suddenly it looked like home. Not just the cabin, but the whole place. The city and the hills all around and the people. I just had this feeling I haven't had since I had to turn my back on Pennsylvania. I never felt I was home in Iowa. We'd get in sight of the soddie after a long trip to town and I'd be glad to be back, to have the trip over and get supper started, but I'd never look down the road and see our place and think *there's home!* I'd forgotten that there was such a feeling, and then today I looked down at Deadwood and I knew it was home. I knew that it is here I belong."

"It's with me that you belong."

"I knew that too. I knew that this morning when I chased Emerald away. I mean I've always thought I belonged to you, but after all that happened there was so much that made me feel it was wrong for me to even think we could be together. But today when I stood here looking out on it all, I knew that it was right. Right that I be in Deadwood and right that I be with you."

He started to reach for her, but she stopped him.

"Let me finish. It's important that I tell you what I've discovered."

"That we've built something here? I see that. Maybe that's why I couldn't go along with the mining fraud. Jake hallowed that ground with his death and I couldn't let it be part of something cheap and dirty.

504

But does it really matter? Are you saying we can't leave this place because we've left Jake and Luther on this hill? Forget the view, Molly, and think about what Deadwood really is. Just another boom town."

"But it's ours, Hugh. It's not much, but it's the city we helped build. And it's up to people like us to make it better. That's pioneering, Hugh. Not pillaging the land and killing the Indians, but building a decent place to live."

He remembered the words Emerald had taunted him with that morning. *You and Molly ought to go build a damn church.* He wanted to laugh, but then it didn't seem so funny. Maybe this is how it was meant to be. They had been tricked into coming. Into thinking they would go away rich, but instead they would stay to build a civilization. To build a city, a life. To make their own destiny. He started to share that idea with her, but he no more than got out the word *Emerald* than her expression told him Molly wanted no reminders of that woman.

"Can you forgive me for her? For that too?"

"There was nothing to forgive, was there? Except temptation and I can't fault you for that."

"There was nothing except my being a man and she being a woman who wasn't afraid to go after what she wanted."

"But that's part of what I've got to tell you. I learned something from Emerald or maybe she just made me realize what I'd learned from becoming a pioneer. Hugh, I'm different. I'm not the girl you fell in love with so many years ago, and I'm not the woman who only waited and didn't dare do anything but try harder to be patient and good. I knew today that I could

505

never go back to Pennsylvania and be my father's daughter and the genteel widow. I don't belong back East anymore. I belong here. I suffered here. I saved all those men from dying and I earned my place in this town. And my son is the son of pioneers and this is his place, too, and if you don't want to stay here, and you don't want the kind of woman I've become, then Edwin and I will stay on alone. And I can do that too because I'm strong!"

"I know you're strong and I know you can survive without me. You've always been strong, Molly, but now you're wonderous and I love you more because of it."

She let him take her hands now, her eyes glowing. "Then it's settled? We will stay here and be married and someday even tell Edwin the truth."

"No, it's not settled. There's something left unsaid. There's still something wrong between us and I won't pretend it doesn't matter. I can't just marry you to make what's happened between us right—to give Edwin a father!"

He dropped her hands and turned away from her, his eyes searching the mountains as he tried to articulate what it was he still wanted from her.

There was a sudden movement beside him and he felt her hit him as if she had stumbled or thrown herself at him. She caught hold of his shirt and held on.

"Don't turn away from me. Don't ever turn away from me again! You want to hear me say it? That's it, isn't it?"

He looked at her. Why was her face so anguished? Why had she never in all these months said she loved him?

"You want to hear me say it. That I wanted you. That I wanted you to make love to me. That I want you now. All right I'll say it. I wanted you from the first moment I saw you again. No, even before that. I wanted you on my wedding night with Jake. I cried for you then. I laid awake after giving myself to my husband and wanted you! Even when I birthed Jake's babies, I wanted to cry out your name. And, then, just when I finally began to forget—just when I thought it hadn't even been real that time with you but only a dream. Then you finally came back. And how I suffered for wanting you and for letting you make love to me again! And how I suffered for wanting you so much that I left my husband's bed to go to you in the night, and then when you accused me of using my body to trap you and—"

"Molly, don't—"

"No, let me finish. I'm going to say it all. I'll keep no more secrets! You shall hear the worst of it. I wanted you when you were down in the mine. Yes! When you and Jake were buried in the mine, it was you I feared for and not my lawful husband, and when they said that only one of you was alive, I prayed that it would be you!"

"I felt so guilty," she began to cry. "I felt so damn guilty. It was like I'd killed Jake. Do you know that the night before he was killed, I'd resolved to leave him? You'd met Emerald and I knew you'd want her and so I was going to leave Jake, and then when you accused me of killing Luther—"

"Hush, Molly, I never—"

He was holding her now, comforting her, but she

507

pulled away once more.

"There I've said it all. All the awful things about wanting you and loving you, all except what I've waited so long to say —"

"Say it now, Molly."

"I love you, Hugh. I've always loved you and I've burned to say it."

"Say it again, Molly."

"I love you. I love you. I love you."

She was laughing now, her eyes sparkling and her whole being transfused with light so that she looked as young as she had been the first time, and yet this time she was infinitely more in every way. He knew there was nothing else to be said. He reached for her and she came to him, in his arms and in his heart and so within him that he did not know where one left off and the other began. He did not need to know anything except that they were together at last. Forever. Kissing, laughing, crying together. He held her away from him so he could look at her again and then they kissed more deeply, this time with passion as well as joy, their mouths almost awkward in their urgency. He desired her and knew he would have her soon and forever. He felt infinitely happy and complete.

He lifted her into his arms as if to carry her someplace. She grabbed hold of his neck and buried her face in his shirt, feeling both child and woman in his strong arms.

"There is no place here for what you have in mind," she whispered.

"What do you mean? We've got a whole mountain top! And why are you whispering when at last we can shout our love to the heavens?"

"But we've a cabin and a bed waiting below."

"And a son who'll be wanting explanations and a preacher who will say tomorrow is time enough. But I want to marry you *now*. Here on this mountain top. I want this to be the sacred place where we at last are one."

And there was a place. A little patch of clover which formed a nest between the white rocks that looked over Deadwood. As he lay her down and busied himself with her buttons, she had to laugh again.

"And someday, husband, when we bring our grandchildren to Mt. Moriah to see where they buried Wild Bill Hickok and Preacher Smith, you'll tell them the pioneers made this into a holy mountain, and I'll have to hold back not to look up to this place and laugh."

And then her eyes met his and she saw that this great young giant of a man, this hero who was hers, was sincere. And he was right. This would be their true marriage ceremony; the preacher would be for their son and the town, but it was the act of love which had bound them together from the beginning, and it was this new act of love that would end the long journey which had kept them apart. They would be trespassers no longer.

He took her hands and for a long time they simply looked at each other, each to the other's soul. The words were unspoken, but each touch, each tender breathing and sharing of the other's essence became their sacred promise. To have and to hold. From that day forth. For time and eternity.

It was the setting sun which finally brought them back to this world. They took a moment to walk back to the look-out point, and stood storing up their memories of what had happened and how beautiful the city was and could be.

At last they remembered their son and the cabin that was home waiting below. As one they turned and began to pick their way across the summit to the path leading back to Deadwood. He took the lead on the narrow path, holding his hand out to her so they moved almost sideways down the mountainside.

They were perhaps halfway down, in sight of the cemetery, when the thought occurred to him.

A complete love — a man and woman destined to be together forever, body and soul. Perhaps this too was like poor man's gold — an illusion, a trick of the gods to taunt men and drive them on. Maybe once again he was being a fool.

He turned and looked back at Molly. She smiled. And he knew that if he was a fool, he no longer cared.

Far below Mt. Moriah, down on Deadwood's Main Street, the street where a man could live for months and never really see the beauty of the mountains all around him, Austin Avery swung into the saddle of the big bay gelding Caleb Dexter had rented for him.

The old man stepped back and studied his boss. He made a fine picture, sitting there on the horse. It was the best mount to be had in Deadwood and it was dancing and champing at the bit. Caleb thought his boss looked like a real Southern planter gentleman, sitting there firm in the saddle in his frock coat and striped pants, his watch fob gleaming across the front of his ruffled shirt and the motion of the horse dancing beneath him causing his jet black hair to blow down a little over his forehead. What a man he was!

Avery wheeled the horse around so as to face Caleb. He leaned down in the saddle to speak to him. "You tell McPherson to write up his best offer on the mine — if he does make an offer — and you leave it for me at the hotel."

"Sure thing, boss. You can count on me."

Avery straightened up and suddenly the old man realized he was about to spur the horse and gallop off. Desperately, Dexter ran forward and grabbed the horse by the bridle.

Avery looked down at him, surprised.

"Boss, wait up. There's just one thing."

"What's that?"

"The coin. You didn't show the coin."

"What are you getting at?" Avery frowned, pulling at the reins so Caleb could hardly hold the horse.

"You said heads you'd go after her and tails you'd forget her."

"So?"

"So you just said it was heads. You didn't show us the coin."

Avery relaxed his grip on the reins. He looked down at the old man with one eyebrow raised.

"Are you implying that I'd cheat? You insist on believing that I care about that woman enough to cheat myself on the toss of a coin?"

"Well, no . . . I mean . . . I don't know, boss. It's just that you didn't show the coin and — "

"And you're wondering if it really was heads?"

"Yep," he grinned. "That's it, boss. Was it heads or tails?"

Avery jerked the reins up and kicked the horse so it danced away from Caleb's grip. Then he wheeled it and turned back to look down at the old prospector.

For the first time since he'd known Austin Avery, Caleb Dexter saw the gambler laugh. His gold tooth gleamed as he leaned down to whisper his answer.

"That will just have to be something for you to wonder about."